PRAISE FOR AMA

the food of love

AMANDA PROWSE

the food of love

LAKE UNION
PUBLISHING

This is a work of fiction. Names, characters, organizations, places, events, and incidents are either products of the author's imagination or are used fictitiously.

Published by Lake Union Publishing, Seattle

www.apub.com

Amazon, the Amazon logo, and Lake Union Publishing are trademarks of Amazon.com, Inc., or its affiliates.

ISBN-13: 9781503940048
ISBN-10: 1503940047

Cover design by Debbie Clement

Printed in the United States of America

For my son Josiah Hartley.
You, Josh, are my finest achievement.
I am proud every time you walk into the room.
And when my time on earth is done I shall sleep
peacefully, knowing that I contributed something
wonderful to the world, and that thing is you.
Follow your dreams, climb high, stay kind, be happy
and know that we are made from the same
batch of stardust . . .

'The main facts in human life are five: birth, food, sleep, love and death.'

E. M. Forster

FROM THE AUTHOR

I started writing at the age of forty, having always been an avid reader. Every book I read I would put into a category of either 'I wish I had written that book' or 'I can do better than that!'

I didn't have the confidence or courage to put pen to paper, fearing my lack of grammar and limited understanding about the world of publishing might hamper my efforts.

It was only after beating cancer that I looked at the world in a different way, figuring that if this was my one time around the block, what did I really want to do? And what I really wanted to do was write stories! I have been writing for four years now and have written seventeen novels and six novellas.

I am pretty much average at everything. I'm a rubbish cook, useless at sport, and can never manage to get the duvet into the duvet cover. They say everyone has one thing that they can do, and I have discovered my one thing: I can write stories very quickly. They play in my head like a movie and all I have to do is write down what I see. I am truly thankful every single day for this gift.

I write about ordinary women, women who find their lives disrupted and need to find strength to overcome the obstacles in their path. I find it amazing when a stranger tells me that they have enjoyed one of my books; that stranger and I are linked by something that germinated in my imagination. If that's not magic, I don't know what is.

PROLOGUE

The sun slowly casting its fire-coloured rays over everything it touched as it sank was one of the most beautiful things Freya had ever seen. She would never forget the sight of pelicans sitting on the Florida shoreline like prehistoric time travellers, masterful and breathtaking, as they balanced on poles rising up from the seabed, stretching their immense wings in the scarlet remains of the day.

Lockie and the girls had earlier fished from the dock – catching nothing but each other's crossed fishing lines. The fun, however, had been in the anticipation, any disappointment now quashed by the sampling of fine gelato as they strolled the streets of old Naples, window-shopping as night turned to day and the sun pulled their tanned skin taut on their weary bones. Charlotte, already becoming a lady at nine, nibbled daintily at her single-scoop cone, while Lexi was fully focused on balancing her towering three scoops, as if unwilling to forfeit a single bite.

Freya laughed at her seven-year-old. 'Goodness me, Lex, carry on at this rate and we'll have to put you in the hold on the flight home; you'll never fit in the seat!'

As they wandered on to the long pier at the end of this golden day, Freya knew this family vacation would be crystallised in memory, there for her to dip into when the cold, grey sky of a British morning threatened to pull the happy from her heart and the spring from her step.

'So can I, Mum? Can I?' Having somehow gobbled all her ice cream, Lexi jumped up and down in front of her, drawing Freya from her musings.

'Can you what, darling?'

'Can I go swimming?' She beat her little fists on the sides of her rounded thighs, irritated by the seconds of delay that this conversation was causing.

'No! Of course not! It's dark! You wouldn't be able to see where you were going, it's dangerous.' Freya shook her head.

'I don't want to swim!' Charlotte got this in quick, in case there was any doubt.

'No one is swimming!' she asserted. 'Goodness knows what sea creatures might be lurking beneath the surface.'

'Please can I?' Lexi whined.

Freya sought out her husband's face, trying to catch his eye. 'Can you believe her?'

Lockie laughed. 'I've already told her that if a shark comes along, she knows what to do. Isn't that right, Lexi?'

Lexi responded by lunging forward and giving her best jab into thin air. 'I have to punch it on the nose!'

Freya looked at Charlotte, who peered cautiously down between the wooden slats into the water.

'Daddy's only joking, Charlotte.' She used her well-practised placatory tone, before turning to bare her teeth at Lockie.

'Of course I was joking!' He winked. 'It would be utterly pointless trying to punch them on the nose.'

Charlotte yelped and pointed. Freya turned her head, as if in slow motion.

While their discussion raged and their attention was diverted, Lexi had slipped away and climbed up on to the side of the pier. Freya's words stuttered in her throat, kept from escaping by a plug of fear. Her arms flapped to no avail as she tried to gain Lockie's attention.

As if time froze, Lexi stood perfectly still, balanced on the narrow ridge of weathered timber; her little toes gripped the surface as she steadied herself with her arms outstretched.

Then, as Freya reached for her, the little girl lifted her chin, her eyes pegged on the horizon, heedless of the long drop into the dark water below, and jumped into the unknown.

ONE

Freya loved the familiar sounds of their home cranking to life: the bur-bling radiators, the creaking floorboards and the rumble of pipes. She found the cacophony predictably reassuring.

Staring out of the sash window of the first-floor kitchen of their redbrick Edwardian villa, with her mug in her palm, she looked over the high-walled garden, abundant with climbing wisteria and flowering jasmine. It was a beautiful morning. The sun rose, dusting all it touched with a peach-tinted blush. Freya savoured this moment of peace on a brand-new day.

They had taken the decision a few years ago to pave the small rect-angle, making a grand courtyard garden rather than a lousy scrap of lawn. The outer edges were adorned with a range of receptacles – old chimney pots, redundant butler sinks, and rusted watering cans; noth-ing was considered too grand or too defunct not to be shoved with soil and a few geraniums or variegated ivy. The effect was stunning. Freya had created a busy, bright private oasis in the middle of the city. And to tend it gave her as much joy as to look at it.

She peered over the wall and down into their neighbours' kitchen, the same space on the ground floor in their house taken up by their TV room, her husband's studio and the now redundant darkroom.

'Good morning!' Lockie bellowed, as he made his presence felt. He always did this: entered the room as though he was coming on from stage left.

She spun around, cheeks flaming, eyes bright and biting her bottom lip.

'What are you looking so guilty about?'

He narrowed his gaze and trod the stripped floorboards, placing his large hands around her narrow waist and pulling her towards him. He looked over her shoulder, his chin trapping her long fair hair against her skin as he tried to see what had caught her eye.

'Nothing.' She blushed.

'Ah, now I *know* you were up to something! "Nothing" is your default when you can't think of a good lie quickly enough.'

'That is so not true!' she protested.

Her husband kissed her on the mouth and she felt the flames of love and longing flicker in her gut, filling her with warmth, even now, after nineteen years of marriage. They were lucky.

'Okay, well, I might have been spying on the Rendletons!' She giggled.

'I knew it!' He slapped his thigh. 'And what salacious titbits did you pick up about their life from your covert operation? Tell me it was something juicy! Was Mr Rendleton having a slug of gin before his cornflakes? Or, worse, was Mrs Rendleton entertaining the postman while her husband was in the shower?' He waggled his bushy eyebrows.

'For goodness sake, Lockie! She's eighty-four!'

'Good point.' He released her. 'Plus I don't think our postman is what the girls might describe as "fit".'

'Poor man!' Freya pictured the chirpy chap that traipsed up the path of their neat front garden in a busy suburb of St Albans.

'I was hoping for sex this morning, but no sooner had I blinked and lifted my head, you'd run away!' he whispered, as she ran her hands through his thick, long dark-grey hair, which he wore slicked back, more often than not secured in place by his reading glasses.

'Not deliberately,' she breathed, 'but I do have a lot on today.'

'You have a lot on every day.'

'True, but today is a deadline day, and there's nothing like the promise of Marcia's dulcet tones on the line to goad me into action.'

She abandoned her husband to the cereal cupboard, where muesli in a multitude of variations sat in expensive, environmentally friendly packaging.

'Can I pencil you in for sex tomorrow morning?' he asked matter-of-factly.

'Yes, I'll put it in my calendar. Remind me to set my alarm a little earlier.'

She nodded, without any sense of irony, as she pulled open the wide drawer underneath the sink and rummaged around for a grocery bag.

'Will do.' He beamed.

'Have you been stealing the plastic bags? I use them for rubbish and all sorts. Now that we have to pay for them, I try to keep a couple in my rucksack for any bits of shopping I pick up, but they seem to disappear.'

'You got me. I do it for the thrill, guv!' he mocked.

'Very funny.' She tutted in his direction.

Lockie reached into the cupboard and studied the cereal box, holding it at arm's length as he lowered his glasses from his head to his nose, reading aloud: 'For a sense of well-being and long-lasting energy, to invigorate, restore and bring out your natural essence.' He sniffed and looked at his wife. 'Lovely. I was hoping to bring out my natural essence. This might just do the trick!' he added sarcastically. 'I remember the days when we bought cereal because it tasted good, not because it was going to change our lives.'

'Yes, but the stuff that tasted good has so much sugar on it, it could rot a tooth at twenty paces.' She laughed.

'But you're missing my point: it *tasted* good!' He emphasised his point with vigour.

Lexi yawned from the doorway, still in her pyjama bottoms, with an oversized sweatshirt slipping from her shoulder, her long hair pulled back into a ponytail, and a crease from the pillowcase still on her cheek.

'Daddy's hankering after sugary cereal.' Freya rolled her eyes at the younger of her two girls.

'It's not the only thing Daddy wants,' he whispered.

'Who's taking me in today?' Lexi asked casually, caring little for her dad's preferred choice of breakfast and even less about the debate that raged across their spacious kitchen. She was far more interested in how much time she had to get ready.

'Dad. He's got a shoot in London and so he can drop you both at school on the way.'

'Can he indeed?' Lockie called from the end of the long refectory table at which he sat, with his bowl of unsatisfying muesli to one side and his laptop open.

'Yes!' Freya called from the sink. 'I've told you, I've got a deadline; my piece on "fuss-free food for fussy toddlers" needs to go off by this afternoon.'

'Ooh, catchy title! Not.' Lexi sniffed, making her way to the sink and running a large glass of water.

'What have you got on today, darling?'

'Nothing.' She sipped.

'Oh, right, well that should be a doddle, then.' She swooped by and kissed her little girl on the head. 'What can I get you for breakfast?'

'Nothing.' Lexi yawned again and continued to drink.

'In that case, go and shower and give Charlotte a shove. Daddy can't hang around.'

'Charlotte doesn't need a shove, thank you very much!' announced Charlotte as she made her way down from her room on the second floor. 'She is up and has been for the last hour!'

'She's only been up for an hour because she's been doing her project that should have been handed in yesterday.'

'Thanks for that, Lexi. Oh, what's that noise?' Charlotte rushed over to the fruit bowl that sat on the end of the counter and picked up a banana from the wooden bowl, holding it to her ear like a telephone. 'Oh hi, Toby . . . Yes, I love you too, more than anything in the world!'

The smile slipped from Lexi's face.

'No, I haven't told my parents that I have a boyfriend who's in the sixth form and two years older than me,' Charlotte continued, 'but it's not because I'm trying to keep you secret, not at all!'

'You're such a bitch!' Lexi shouted, slamming her glass on the countertop before running out of the room. She raced up the stairs.

'Alexia, that language is not okay!' Freya shouted after her daughter. She shook her head. 'That was a bit mean, Charlotte. Is it true? Has she got a boyfriend?'

'Well, I'm not saying now! Don't want to be even meaner!' Charlotte peeled the banana and swept from the room.

'Do you know how much I love living in a house full of women?' Lockie gave a wide false grin.

'A lot.'

'Yes, a lot,' he conceded.

'Surely she hasn't got a proper boyfriend – I mean, she's only four-teen!' Freya folded her arms and considered this. 'Although this would explain the sudden surge in wanting to keep fit.' She had noticed an increase to her daughter's workouts and a more fastidious approach to food.

'And she has always been a little ahead of the pack – it was always her leading Charlotte astray when they were little, never the other way around.'

'True.' She smiled at her husband. 'Our baby might be growing up! Who knows, she might even ditch her baggy sweats and wear something flattering,' she offered with a combination of excitement and regret.

'Yes, hurrah! Just think: only a few more years and we get the house to ourselves. I can walk around in my underpants and we get to touch the remote control.'

'Yes, love. That is certainly something for me to look forward to,' she added drily. 'Don't think I'll ever be ready for them to leave home. I'm not even ready for her to start dating! Not that we know she is, not for sure.'

'I think the best way to find out is to ask her directly,' he offered, while tapping into his laptop. 'You need to communicate with both the girls more openly. They can't always second-guess what you're driving at. Heck, I've been married to you for a hundred years and I still don't know what you are driving at half the time.'

'I can't just blurt things out. I have to tread softly. Teenage girls are delicately packaged. I should know. I used to be one.'

'You are their mum first and their friend second; you can afford to be more direct.'

'I love you, Mr Braithwaite.'

'The feeling, my darling, is entirely mutual.'

Freya trod the stairs with an armful of towels, placing them in the linen press on the landing; she idled outside of Lexi's bedroom, knocking gently as she entered.

'Nearly ready?'

'Yep.'

Lexi was in her school uniform, leaning on her pillows with her phone an inch from her face, paddling her thumbs over the virtual keyboard, sending and receiving messages.

'Have you got your running gear? I left it in the laundry room, all clean.'

'Yep.' Still she stared at the screen.

'Right.' Freya hovered, swallowing the feeling that she was invading her daughter's privacy. She hated the way the girls did this: made her feel awkward and unwanted with just a few well-placed sighs and a lack of eye contact.

'I just wanted to say . . .' She ordered her thoughts.

'What, Mum?' Lexi placed her phone on her leg, still gripping it with both hands, making it clear that this was just a pause; her mother was on a timer.

'You shouldn't swear at your sister. In fact you shouldn't swear at anyone. You don't hear Dad and I doing it and I won't have it.'

'I know, and I don't swear at anyone else, just her. She just makes me so . . .' Lexi bared her teeth and emitted something close to a growl. 'She hates me!'

'What a thing to say! Of course she doesn't hate you. She loves you! You're her little sister.'

'Doesn't mean she likes me,' Lexi pointed out, sounding far older than her years.

'That's true,' Freya conceded, 'but she does love you, even if she doesn't always know how to show it. And showing it gets easier as you get older, you'll see. I promise. When you are in your twenties you'll be best friends.' She smiled.

Lexi shrugged, as if it were easier than disputing her mum's claim.

Freya watched her glance at the screen on her phone. Chat time was clearly over. 'I know you're busy, but you can talk to Dad and me about anything. You know that, right?'

'Yep.'

'Okay.' Freya smiled and made for the door. 'And you can bring anyone home that you want to, anytime. Everyone is always welcome; you know that too.'

Lexi let out a familiar long-drawn-out sigh. Freya couldn't tell if it was in irritation or plain old boredom.

'Anyway, I'll let you get on.'

She backed out of the room, waiting for some further interaction or acknowledgement from her daughter that never came, and swallowing the warnings that hovered in her mouth: *Go slowly with this boy, Lexi, you have all the time in the world.*

She swept into the kitchen, where Lockie was packing his camera bag for the day. The table was, as ever, strewn with contact sheets, lenses, a handheld flashgun, battery packs, and miles and miles of cable. It made her smile, the chaos and the mess he created in any space, as if every day was his first on the job and he was worried about mislaying something vital or of losing the commission. The fact that he had been taking photographs since his teens was neither here nor there.

As freelancers, she a food writer and he a photographer, she likened their careers and financial situation to a poker game; it was all about holding your nerve. The closest they had ever come to folding was a year ago, when a particularly dry spell meant they had reluctantly arranged for an estate agent to come and value their home. It was the house they had always lived in and loved, bought at a time when the area had been a little run down, only to rise over the years in both esteem and value. It was their only asset and their most treasured thing.

This was how they lived, feast or famine, either both in demand, smiling and happy, or sniping at each other, living off their nerves, drinking coffee and hovering near the phone, willing it to ring with a job. Which it always did, eventually.

The estate agent had been due at three o'clock on a rainy Wednesday and at a quarter to, an email arrived, booking Lockie for a fashion shoot in South Africa, all expenses paid. They had celebrated by making love on the floor behind the sofa and ignoring the rapping knuckles and the ringing phone, as the poor estate agent wondered if he had got his dates muddled. On that day, the wolf and the agent were both kept from the door.

Their jobs were how they had met. Freya had been twenty-eight and working as a food stylist for a glossy lifestyle magazine, and he had been the photographer, arriving in the cold, cramped studio in North London with his booming voice, ready smile and floppy hair. She had liked him instantly.

It was as they watched the fake bubbles being applied with a minute spoon to a cup of frothy coffee and an apple tart being painted with olive oil, for extra shine, that they had both collapsed in fits of giggles at the absurdity of the job.

'I'm Matlock.' He beamed, as though this name were in itself some kind of achievement. 'Apparently it is Old English for "meeting place".'

He trotted out the well-rehearsed line, pre-empting the many variants of question that he had no doubt heard a thousand times before.

She had laughed. 'Matlock? Really? I think it should be modern English for "Did your parents hate you?"'

He stared at her, awestruck, he told her later, not only by her high cheekbones and finely arched eyebrows that framed her almond-shaped hazel eyes, but also by her temerity.

'I've always been called Lockie actually.' He blushed.

'Like that's any better!' She giggled.

And just like that, they fell in love.

'Where are you working today?' she asked casually as she reached into the freezer for lumps of frozen spinach, which she lobbed into the blender, followed by half a banana and a whole glug of fresh pineapple juice. Finally, she grabbed an avocado from the salad crisper in the bottom of the fridge and peeled it, using a sharp knife to slice about half, and tossed that too into her breakfast concoction. The remainder was wrapped in a strip of tinfoil and popped back into the crisper.

'Shoreditch. I'm taking headshots for some corporate literature. It's going to be a long day.'

'Poor baby.' She smiled. 'I'll make you a nice supper.'

'By "nice", tell me you mean buttery potatoes or pastry or chips – oh, chips!' He closed his eyes and let his head fall back, as if dreaming.

'I'll make you chips if you want, just not today.'

She smiled at her poor deprived husband who was torn between valuing the healthy lifestyle they lived and missing the taste of the salty chips that he craved.

'Chips would be good, in fact fish-and-chip-shop chips would be better. Let's do that – I'm earning good money today,' he added, knowing the two were directly related.

'We're having pasta – already got the meat out of the freezer. Maybe at the weekend.' She tutted. 'That is, if the girls haven't pocketed your fee by then.'

It seemed they always needed something, and as had always been the case, their needs came first.

'You never did say what the Rendletons were up to,' Lockie said. 'If you don't tell me, it's going to niggle away at me all day, and many of the images I am conjuring are far from pleasant.'

She looked down, as if sharing the admission were a little disloyal. 'They were dancing.'

'Dancing?' He wrinkled his nose; this was apparently not what he had imagined.

'Yes. They were in their bulky dressing gowns, with cord rope belts and old-fashioned slippers. He was holding her tightly, close, and they were dancing in their kitchen. And when they stopped he put his hands either side of her face and he kissed her.' She swallowed, unable to fully express how much this had moved her. 'It was beautiful, romantic and intense.'

'But they're so old!' Lockie pulled a face.

'It was all those things *because* they are old,' she clarified. 'It was very moving.'

'Do you think we'll dance when we are their age?' he asked.

'We hardly dance now. Apart from when you've had one too many glasses of Valpolicella and think you can cut some shapes.'

'We could always start.' He held a flamenco pose with his arm bent over his head.

'We could, that's a great idea. I shall put dancing on the list, next to ride motorbikes along Route 66, swim with dolphins, and streak across the pitch during a cricket match.'

'You forgot about getting matching tattoos.' He pointed at her, clearly loving their virtual bucket list.

'Of course!' She slapped her forehead. 'How could I forget our matching tattoos?'

'Who's getting tattoos?' Lexi queried, as she dumped her school bag on the kitchen table.

'Dad and I, after learning to dance, swimming with dolphins, and eating chip-shop chips!' Freya informed her, as she tipped a spoonful of flaxseeds into the blender.

'Urgh.' Lexi shuddered, her mouth turned down in revulsion.

'What's that face for? You used to love chips. Honestly, Lexi, you can't be that fussy. Especially if, say, someone took you out for supper . . .' She gently dug for information.

'And by "someone" we mean a boy called Toby who is a sixth-former,' Lockie clarified.

'Da-ad!' Lexi shouted, and ran from the kitchen, back up the stairs.

Freya abandoned the blender; her breakfast smoothie would have to wait.

'Oh, that's brilliant, Lockie. Absolutely brilliant.'

She trotted up the stairs after her daughter.

Nine hours to go . . .

'Can I get you anything?'

Freya jumped at the sound of her daughter's voice. Her hand skittered on the page that lay flat on the worn pine desk. She placed the fountain pen on its side and tucked her thin grey dressing gown around her legs, clasping her hands between her thighs as if this might stop their tremor.

'Sorry, Mum.' Charlotte had obviously seen her flinch.

She walked forward, her bare feet making no sound as she trod the carpet. 'I didn't want to disturb you, but obviously I did, because here I am.' Charlotte gave a small nervous, quiet laugh and fidgeted with the multicoloured threads of the friendship bracelets that sat loosely around her slender wrist.

'You're never disturbing me.' Freya smiled at her eldest, tall now and, at seventeen, far closer to the woman she would become than the child she was. Her clear skin, rangy limbs and long tawny hair still took Freya's breath away.

She swallowed, wondering how long it would last: the raw distress, the creeping silence, and this veil of hesitancy that cloaked even the most mundane of actions, making them feel awkward in their own home.

'I . . . I was wondering if you might like a drink? A cup of peppermint tea?' Charlotte asked sweetly, her head bent to hold her mother's eyeline.

Freya smiled at the role reversal: her child showing kindness, worrying and wanting to put things right.

'A cup of tea would be lovely, thank you.'

Tea was in fact the last thing she needed, but she understood that for her daughter, some solace might be found in the ritual.

'What's the time?' Freya had, as was usual of late, lost all track.

'It's still early. Just after five.'

'Have you slept?'

'A little bit.' She bit her lip. 'But I saw the light on across the hall and so . . .'

Freya nodded her understanding.

'Dad's still asleep. He needs it. He was pacing around until all hours.' She smiled.

'I'll try not to wake him,' Charlotte whispered.

'How long do I have?' She licked her dry lips; maybe a cup of peppermint tea was a good idea after all.

'About nine hours.' She took a deep breath.

'Okay.' Freya turned back to the desk and picked up her pen.

'How's it going?' Charlotte whispered.

Freya stared at the blank sheet of paper. 'It's really hard. I don't know where to start.' She reached for a tissue and dabbed at her nose.

Charlotte turned to leave the room, then sighed, her fingers loitering on the door handle. 'I guess . . . at the beginning?'

Freya nodded. This was good advice, providing a moment of clarity in an otherwise cloudy muddle of thoughts. She held the pen and rubbed her tired eyes with her thumb and forefinger.

She remembered walking across town, at the mercy of an autumn day. The pavements were hazardous with fallen, dark leaves that slid under the sole of her boot, and where litter wheeled along the kerb with a mind of its own. It was the day of her twenty-week scan.

The sonographer had smiled. 'You already have a girl, don't you?'

She nodded, picturing Charlotte at home with her dad, no doubt getting up to mischief.

The woman smiled and whispered, 'Do you want to know what this one is?'

Freya beamed and she leant in close, as if they were friends, and the woman whispered, 'It's another little girl!'

She recalled feeling overjoyed, but also a little scared: unable to imagine loving a baby in the same way that she loved Charlotte. She didn't understand how it would work. Thinking it might feel different the second time around. She kept secrets throughout her pregnancy – both the fact that this baby was a girl and all that was worrying her – leaving everyone second-guessing right up until the day Lexi was born.

'Oh, Lexi, that was some day!' Freya spoke aloud. Smiling.

This was always her immediate reaction: to smile. Her new baby was perfect, so perfect. Freya couldn't believe it, couldn't believe that she could be that lucky all over again.

Charlotte had been excited, jumping up and down and fidgeting. She couldn't sit still, and Lockie was joking around, as usual, doing a bad job of keeping her calm. Freya's mum and dad had been in the waiting room, and when they were given the nod they rushed in and just stood there, grinning at her.

Charlotte bent over, stroking her little face with her fingertips, and Freya kept reminding, 'Gently, darling,' as she was too little to understand how fragile a newborn was. Lockie had his arm around his wife's shoulders, like she was a prize.

Granny and Pappy stared, and Freya saw what they saw, a lovely little family, finally complete, and she felt a surge of happiness that she didn't know was possible. Knowing then that her worries, her fears, were unfounded, the love she'd had for Charlotte grew instantly in size and shape and magnitude, until it was big and strong enough to cover them all. It was magic.

She looked at her baby and found it hard to think straight, bowled over, paralysed by the fact that she was so beautiful, and she was hers.

Freya again spoke into the ether. 'I kept repeating in my mind, "I brought this beautiful creature into the world: how is that possible?" Because you are, Lexi, you are beautiful. You are so beautiful.'

Taking a deep breath, she rested her hand on the desk to steady the pen, before writing in her flourishing script:

Miss Alexia Valentine Braithwaite . . .

TWO

'Darling! I love it!' Marcia shouted down the telephone.

As both her good friend and agent, Freya was used to Marcia's rather brash manner, knowing it hid a heart that groaned with kindness.

'Good, and finished just in the nick of time!'

Freya glanced at the clock on the wall above the book alcove. It was a little after two. She had cut it fine, sending the piece only minutes before, jam-packed with ideas on how to make veg and protein look like fun when being served to less than keen recipients. Her particular favourite was how to make fabulous-tasting smoothies that were full of fruit and veg yet to an untrained eye might still look like a treat. She remembered Lockie's desire for the cereal of his childhood and it made her smile.

'Not at all! They said next Monday – but I know how you work best.' She paused, and Freya heard her take a drag on her cigarette.

'Marcia, that was very sneaky!' Freya wanted to respond further, to point out how this was underhand and unethical, and how they should have a working relationship based on trust and honesty, but she knew her agent was right.

'Are you still okay for this piece on PMS and food cravings?'

'Yes, coming along nicely, and eating lots of chocolate – all in the name of research, of course.'

'Good girl, quite right too. Got to dash, Helen's on the other line, speak soon, darling.'

And just like that she was gone.

Freya resumed her position, slumped over her computer, rereading her paragraph about PMS symptoms while tapping her front teeth with the end of her pencil. It was a bad habit, the rhythm of which helped her concentrate. Freya sat at one of the high stools by the side of the breakfast bar in her opulent kitchen space, sipping at the espresso that her funky Italian machine spat out quicker than you could say *Fancy a Starbucks?* Her eyes roved the pale polished granite surfaces and her shiny three-oven stove, with six burners and a detachable griddle. She loved to cook, and to be able to make her living writing and discussing food was an unexpected joy.

She was part of the modern-day 'foodie' revolution, in touch enough to know that the way to get her words out was via regular articles, and attending any and every foodie event this side of Paris and commenting on it. It was a far cry from when she had started out as a keen graduate in the late eighties, typing up and sending out articles in triplicate and waiting days if not weeks for a posted reply.

She realised that she hadn't tweeted for a while and opened up her account, sending out a picture of the wholewheat sourdough loaf she had knocked up on Sunday morning – with the caption 'Bread and butter anyone?' The satisfying little whistles of acknowledgement told her it had been well received.

Brewster, the family cat, sidled up to her and rested against her leg.

The phone rang on the breakfast bar. She expected it to be Marcia again with some new insight into PMS that she would bellow down the line between drags on her cigarette, or Lockie with another unfunny joke. She sometimes wished that she had an office to go to that was outside of the house, a place of work where she could not be reached.

It was a private number that she considered ignoring, without the time or inclination to listen to a sales call for things she didn't want and couldn't afford.

'Mrs Braithwaite?'

'Yes?' She sat up straight, and put the pencil down. The voice sounded officious, instantly setting her pulse racing, but was at the same time vaguely recognisable.

'It's Miss Burke, Lexi's form tutor.'

'Yes, of course. Hello, Miss Burke.' Now she recognised the voice of the woman she had chatted to across a desk on parents' evening. 'Is everything okay?' Freya felt a flicker of nerves. The woman had never called before and these were the calls she dreaded: from school, from the accident and emergency department or the police. Her thoughts tumbled ahead to all the terrible things that might have befallen her children, picturing bumped heads and snapped wrists.

One of her biggest fears was that a car might hit them. She was always nervous of how they pondered their phone screens and stepped so nonchalantly off kerbs with barely a second glance, drilling into them the importance of looking both ways, of staying present and not getting distracted.

There was a second or two of silence, in which her heart beat a little too fast for comfort and her mind whirred with all the dreadful possibilities.

The young woman on the other end of the phone seemed to lose confidence in any of the lines that she may have rehearsed. 'Yes, yes. Everything's okay, I think, it's just . . .' She coughed. 'I was wondering if you might be able to pop into school. I'd like to have a word with you?'

'Is Lexi all right?' She held the phone with both hands now. Despite Miss Burke's words, her tone and request were less than reassuring.

'She is. I just want to make you aware of something. Today is a bit crazy, I have a departmental meeting straight after school, but are you collecting her tomorrow?' The woman added the question quickly, denying her the chance to fire the many responses that danced on her tongue.

'Yes, at four-fifteen. Normal time.'

'Could you possibly come in at three-thirty? I shall be in the school office and we can chat there.'

'Sure.' She nodded, as if the woman could see.

'Great, thank you. I shall look forward to seeing you then, Mrs Braithwaite.'

After hanging up the phone, Freya spoke to the cat as she took a sip of her afternoon pick-me-up.

'What on earth is this all about, eh? Why does Miss Doodah want to see me?' she asked out loud.

Brewster was, as ever, short on a response.

'Toby!' She slapped the cool surface.

The cat ran off.

'Be like that, then,' she called after him. 'Just because you didn't think of it.'

It was simply too much of a coincidence that this boy had appeared on the scene and now Miss Burke had called her in.

Her mind raced. Maybe school disapproved? Or maybe he and Lexi had been caught together? She closed her eyes at the thought.

Surely not!

Freya remembered an article she had read about a school where the head boy had been caught in the IT block with another sixth-former, unaware that their lunchtime dalliance would be beamed via CCTV to any number of computers in the county. She shook her head. 'Don't be ridiculous, Freya! She's a little girl, *your* little girl.'

She gulped her coffee, guilty for harbouring such a thought.

Freya stirred the half-finished ragout that simmered nicely on the stove. Dipping the wooden spoon into the mixture and bringing it to her lips, she tasted the soft tomatoes, with the hint of basil and the overgenerous twist of black pepper. She wondered if she had been right not to mention Miss Burke's call on the way home, figuring it best not to pre-empt any discussion or worry her child unnecessarily.

'Mum?' Lexi loitered at the countertop, tracing invisible lines on the surface with her fingertip, avoiding eye contact. She had changed into her baggy sweatpants and oversized sweatshirt. Both girls, like her, couldn't wait to shrug off any formal or restrictive clothing. She found it interesting that they didn't choose to show off their slender physiques, choosing comfort over style whenever possible, although Lexi's desire to dress down at every and any opportunity was a little frustrating.

'Yes, love?'

Lexi swallowed, keeping her eyes downcast. 'Would it . . . would it be okay if Toby, my friend, came over tonight?'

Freya placed the wooden spoon on the little ceramic rest that sat by the side of the stove. Her instant thought was one of delight: an opportunity to get the measure of Toby before her meeting with Miss Burke.

'Yes, of course, you know you can bring anyone home, anytime, you know that.'

'He's just a friend.'

Freya was amused by the bloom on her daughter's cheeks, which told her that even if this was the case, she might like it not to be.

'Yes, you said. And you know your friends are always welcome. Will he be eating with us? There's plenty.'

'No, but we might get coffee or something.'

Freya nodded at her fourteen-year-old, who hated coffee. The thought of her baby suffering the bitter liquid for the sake of appearing older twisted her heart with love.

'Sure. I know – I'll make some cakes!' She pictured a moist lemon-drizzle and some cherry-and-marzipan buns, eyeing the clock and calculating that if she started now, she would just have time.

Lexi twisted on the spot. 'No, Mum. Don't make cakes, that's so babyish. Just act like normal, don't make a fuss.'

'Okay, but I make cakes for *my* friends, who are nearly all in their forties, and *they* don't think it's babyish.'

'Daddy's home!' Lockie shouted from the hallway downstairs.

'I think you might need to fill him in on the rules for later,' Freya whispered, pulling a face, as her husband bounded up the stairs and grabbed his little girl in his arms, squeezing her tightly, before heading for the fridge and the cold beer that sat in the door.

'I've been thinking about this beauty my whole commute home.' He studied the bottle.

'How was your day?' She smiled at her husband as he filled the space with his reassuring presence.

'Fine, you know, a job, but even *my* smile was slipping after taking fifty pictures of people who all told me how much they hated having their picture taken and had to be goaded into looking natural. And the commute was fun, as ever. But that's done and I'm home. How are my girls?' he asked, twisting the top off his beer with his palm and swigging from the neck.

'All good.' She smiled, glancing at Lexi. She would update him on Miss Burke's request later.

'Ah, that's better.' He closed his eyes briefly, his beer restoring his flagging zest for the day. 'Did you get your article off?'

'Yup. Turns out it didn't need to be with them until Monday, and Marcia was just forcing my hand – said she thought I worked better with a tight deadline!' She curled her top lip.

'Marcia's right. You are a procrastinator.'

'What is this, Pick on Freya Day?'

'Yep, later I'll trap you in the loo and make you give me your lunch money.' He laughed.

'You can cut that out: we are not to be babyish. Lexi has her friend coming over later and we are to be on our very best behaviour.' She winked at her daughter, who made her way to the sink and let the tap run before filling a large glass with water.

'Oh no, not that awful Fennella Fenackerpants – she is scary.' He shuddered. 'She corrected my pronunciation, twice.'

'That wasn't her fault; you kept calling her Nutella instead of Fennella, on purpose.' Lexi gave a big sigh.

'Did I?' Lockie looked perplexed.

'You know you did, and her name is Newbolt not Fenackerpants.' Lexi shook her head at her dad.

'I know, but I just had a bet with myself that I could make you say it and I won.' Lockie jumped up and high-fived his wife.

'This is exactly what I'm talking about!' Lexi shouted. 'Anyway, it's not Fennella who's coming; it's my friend Toby, and you can't muck about or say stupid stuff or make me say "Fenackerpants" or anything else, okay?'

'Okay.' Lockie tried out a serious face, testing it on his wife, who suppressed her laughter.

Lexi let out a noise of utter exasperation. 'I'm going for a run,' she announced, before flouncing down the stairs and shutting the front door a little more aggressively than was necessary.

'Don't be too long!' Freya called, with no idea whether Lexi had heard.

'Toby, eh? Is this the Toby muchly denied this morning?' Lockie asked, as he gathered the newspaper from the table and made his way to the floppy lilac-coloured linen sofa that sat at the end of the room, opposite its twin, where a low coffee table, stacked with books, separated them. The bifold glass doors gave the most beautiful view over not only their courtyard garden, but also their neighbours' gardens as well.

'The very same,' Freya replied, as she tipped diced celery into her ragout and turned her attention to shaping the minced meat, breadcrumbs, onion and beaten egg into meatballs, patting them into golf ball–sized shapes with her cupped palms.

'Intriguing. I shall look forward to having a word with young Toby. Bit odd, though, isn't it? If he's nearer Charlotte's age? I mean, Lexi is only fourteen,' he called from the den.

'Nearer fifteen, though,' Freya pointed out. 'And Lexi was very keen to point out that they are just friends.'

'Sure.' He winked. 'It's strange: I *have* got my head around the idea that Charlotte will no doubt in the near future bring a boy home, especially now that Milly is dating . . .'

'Good for you – keeping your ear to the ground, girlfriend!' She laughed.

Lockie ignored her. 'But Lexi's so little, and our baby. It feels odd.'

'I genuinely think they are just mates. I think that if there was anything more to it than that, she'd probably be sneaking out to see him in private, not bringing him home to meet her odd, embarrassing parents who talk to the cat.'

Charlotte walked in from the hallway. 'Don't worry, Dad. He's not like a regular sixth-form boy. He's a total nerd. Physics club, chess club, debating society . . .' She reeled off his infamous achievements, using her fingers to count.

Freya couldn't admit to feeling a little more comfortable about the boy, now that the image of a young, shirtless Zac Efron had been wiped from her mind.

'Don't be mean, Charlotte. Anyway, I thought geeks were cool?' She recalled a recent backseat discussion concerning smart, bespectacled boys.

Charlotte let out a loud burst of laughter. 'That's only funny because Toby is about as far from cool as . . .' – she rolled her hand in the air, trying to think of a suitable, hilarious comparison – '. . . Dad!'

It was Freya's turn to laugh.

'Thanks a bunch.' Lockie lifted his bottle in salute, while keeping his eyes on the open newspaper. They ignored him.

'Ah, come on, Charlotte, I'm sure he's a very nice boy.' Lockie decided to jump in and defend Lexi's friend. 'It takes all sorts. And you have to remember that just because someone doesn't fit your idea of perfect, they might be just that for someone else.'

'Exactly, or Daddy would still be on the shelf!' Freya quipped.

They both ignored her.

'Cool is when Daniel George puts glasses on and goes totally hipster.' Charlotte stared out of the window, lost in her daydream.

'You okay, Charlotte?'

'Hmm? Oh yes . . . where was I?' She creased her brow.

'You were giving me a definition of cool, saying it was Daniel George and not Toby,' Freya recapped.

'Yes! Exactly. Daniel is gorgeous and cool. Toby is not. He's more weird.' She shivered.

'Weird, as in likes maths? Or weird, as in might strangle us in our beds?' Freya was curious.

'Both.' Charlotte nodded.

'Well that's good to know.' She sighed.

Soon after supper was cleared, Lexi rocketed to answer the front door and the sound of stilted teenage chatter rose up the stairs. Lockie sat at the table editing pictures on his laptop; Freya was on the sofa with Brewster, the chocolate-pointed tabby, pretending to read. Her mind, however, raced behind her tortoiseshell glasses; she was eager to get a look at this boy who had piqued her daughter's interest, making her want to get in shape and start drinking coffee. She sat up straight at the sound of Lexi's laughter and tried to look alert and simultaneously relaxed.

'Hey, Mum, Dad. This is Toby.'

The unlikely duo ventured only a few steps into the kitchen, clearly not intent on staying.

Freya was a little startled. She stared at the diminutive boy with the sheen of grease on his pallid, spotty complexion and the thin, bloodless lips that framed his small teeth. His clothes were old-fashioned: a cream twill shirt, beneath a dark cable-knit jumper and dun-coloured chinos. Despite donning the garb of a middle-aged birdwatcher, he looked a lot younger than his seventeen years.

She and Lockie exchanged a knowing look – part relief, part surprise – as he jumped up and strode forward to shake the boy's hand. 'Hello there, Toby.'

'Hello,' he breathed, without smiling.

'Hi, Toby.' Freya waved from the sofa, not wanting to crowd the boy or make too much of a fuss.

He waved back with a tight-lipped expression, then stood with his arms hanging by his sides and his shoulders sloping downwards. He looked tired and downbeat, one of those people whose very appearance had the ability to leave you feeling a little deflated. Freya tried to erase the mean-spirited thought and smiled broadly, as if her joy might permeate his vanilla-covered crust and give him a jolt.

'Can I get you guys anything to eat?' She couldn't resist. It was almost instinctive, this desire to feed all who crossed over her threshold.

'No, we're fine, we're going to watch *The Walking Dead* on Amazon and do a bit of research,' Lexi answered for them both.

Freya resisted the urge to holler, *Leave the door open, sit on separate chairs! We'll be popping down periodically!* She let her gaze rove over the boy, who looked harmless.

'I had a sandwich and an orange earlier,' Toby offered in a rather nasal tone.

'Right.' Freya noted his rather robotic overshare.

'We might have a coffee later.'

'Okay.' Freya smiled.

With that, Lexi turned and headed back down the stairs to the TV room. Toby smiled briefly and followed suit.

Freya stared at the space they had only recently vacated, and then looked at her husband, who seemed to share her sense of anticlimax.

Freya jumped up from the sofa and cornered Lockie by the table. 'That was all a bit disappointing,' she whispered.

'What were you hoping for?' he whispered back. 'His take on the latest employment figures, fire juggling, a few jokes?'

'I don't know.' She shrugged. 'I guess I thought he might be a bit more of a catch.'

'Poor bloke!'

'No . . .' She squinted. 'I don't mean looks-wise, that's not important. I mean, I don't know . . . I just thought he must be quite dynamic to have made such an impression on Lexi, and yet he seems . . .' She let the thought trail, struggling to find the right word that was a combination of 'dull' and 'pale', without it sounding too much like an insult.

'Bit bland?' Lockie offered.

'Yep. Bit bland.' She pulled a face.

Lockie laughed as he retook his seat at the table.

'I must admit, he looks like a right fun-sucker. That's the trouble with having such a witty, good-looking, accomplished husband: all men are going to appear a little beige by comparison.'

Freya walked over to the fruit bowl and picked up a banana. 'What's that? . . . Yes, I agree. My husband is indeed completely delusional.'

She threw the banana back into the bowl and went to put the washing in the tumble-dryer. Despite their light-hearted exchange, Freya still felt the need to hover outside the TV room, listening for any clues as to what was going on inside. She was relieved to hear their rather dull conversation about zombies. Smiling, she made her way back upstairs, knowing that if they were talking, they weren't kissing.

After Toby had slipped out of the front door without a goodbye, Freya sipped her glass of red and lay with her legs stretched out on the rug, the cat resting on her feet. Lockie took the seat next to her, placing the tray across his lap. On it sat a snack of mammoth proportions: a wheel of Brie, a variety of crackers, a bunch of red grapes and a jar of her leftover home-made apple-and-tomato winter chutney from the larder.

'Ooh, cheese-fest! A great idea!' She beamed.

It felt like a long time since supper. She sat up straight, dislodging Brewster in the process, who rolled on to the floor in a rather ungainly fashion.

'I got a call from school today,' she whispered, twisting her body to face Lockie.

'What did they want?' He too kept his voice low, taking her lead.

'It was Miss Burke, Lexi's tutor. She's asked me to go in.'

'Is she struggling again, the poor love?' He looked worried. 'We can go back to her private tutor sessions if it will help.'

Lexi was severely dyslexic. Her academic life felt like a rollercoaster ride with dips and rises depending on the topic being taught and very often who was teaching her.

Freya squeezed his leg, her kind man, knowing that if that was what it took, they'd find the money somehow. 'She didn't say, but I'm seeing her tomorrow. Do you think it might have something to do with Toby?'

'In what way?' Lockie cut a wedge of cheese and placed the generous chunk on a cracker, before garnishing it with a red grape and passing it to his wife.

'I don't know,' she admitted.

Lexi ran down the stairs, halting their discussion as she scooted across the floor and plucked the grape from her mum's food.

'Oi! We have a grape thief in our midst!' Lockie shouted.

'Ooh, can I have some?' Charlotte arrived, as if lured by the scent of creamy Brie.

The girls hovered on the arms of the sofa. Freya was delighted that there was no ribbing, indeed no mention, of Lexi's visitor, as even the thought of having to referee between the girls at this time of night made her feel tired.

'Funny, isn't it?' Lockie mumbled through a mouthful of crackers and cheese. 'How my offspring only find me remotely interesting when I am in possession of cheese, chocolate or money?'

'That's not true, Dad!' Charlotte chipped in, balancing a dollop of Brie and a grape on her finger. 'We also find you interesting when we need a lift or can't get the top off a jar.'

'Good to know I have my uses.'

'Or when we need something reached from a high shelf,' Lexi added.

'No!' Charlotte scoffed. 'Mum's taller, she's better for that.'

'And just like that I am put back in my place!' Lockie sighed.

'You need to do some practice,' Freya reminded her eldest, aware that she hadn't heard the cello being played for some time.

'I'll do it now.' She sloped off the sofa. 'I've got orchestra tomorrow lunchtime, worst luck.'

Freya winked at her, happy when she didn't have to nag.

'I'll swap,' Lockie moaned. 'I'm seeing the osteopath tomorrow lunchtime.'

'Do you want me to take you in?' Freya asked, as Lexi picked up the cat and snuggled him against her chest.

'Thanks, love, but no. I'm fitting it into an already . . . crackers day.' He held up a piece of cheese. 'No pun intended. I'm working in the morning and then going to the camera exchange when I'm done, to see if I can trade a couple of lenses.'

'Did you have a nice time with Toby?' Freya watched Lexi's expression, seeking out signs of joy or secrecy.

'Yep,' came the rather muted reply.

Freya did, however, note the blush to her daughter's cheek.

'Do you think Brewster ever wishes he could sit with other cats and live with them, instead of being with humans who don't speak his language?' Lexi asked, as she stared at their beloved cat.

'I think he's probably just happy to be in a safe, warm place where he is loved,' Lockie reasoned. 'Plus he could always go out and chat to his cat friends, if he really wanted to.'

'But it's not the same, is it, Dad, when *you* are the only one that's different, the only one who thinks how *you* do?'

Charlotte laughed and Brewster miaowed, as if on cue.

Freya watched as her baby girl closed her eyes and held the cat tight, rocking him gently. She noted her dreamlike aloofness and wondered if she were already lost to this boy, even now feeling the first pull of love.

Eight hours, thirty minutes . . .

Freya narrowed her eyes, as the four words on the sheet blurred beneath her stare.

Miss Alexia Valentine Braithwaite . . .

She put the pen down once again, as if thwarted, and sat back in the chair. Birds had begun to chirp their morning song, the sound itself ordinarily uplifting, sweet and pure, but not this morning. Today it heralded the start of a day that she hoped would not arrive.

She closed her eyes for a second and pictured a particular moment, all those years ago, when they had been staying in Hugh's villa in Florida. It had been the middle of the night. Freya had gone to check on the girls and her heart leapt to find Lexi's bed empty. Frantically she scanned the room and bathroom, before running across the landing and down the elaborate staircase, into the square hallway and through the vast kitchen, past the slumbering appliances. Finally, twisting the black wrought-iron handle, she found herself in the ornate paved courtyard at the centre of the villa.

And there, with a huge sense of relief, she found her daughter, lying on the padded silk counterpane that lived on the chest at the foot of her bed.

'Lexi! There you are!' she whispered, through the half-light.

'I was too hot,' the seven-year-old stated matter-of-factly, as she rubbed her long fringe that was plastered to her sticky forehead. Her cotton nightie clung to her chubby frame.

'Oh, honey . . .' Freya considered the best course of action. 'This is quite an adventure.' She decided against reprimanding her, unwilling to spoil the magical atmosphere.

'I like it out here, Mum,' Lexi whispered.

'You do?' She smiled.

'We're up in the middle of the night!' Lexi looked up. 'I think we can see the whole wide world from here.'

'I think you're right,' Freya agreed as she lay by her side and pulled her child towards her. A gentle breeze flitted over them, lifting the damp hair that hung in tendrils against their clammy faces and sent their skin delightfully goosebumpy.

'That feels lovely.' Lexi sighed.

The sound of a guitar drifted on the breeze, and the two lay in silent reverence.

'I don't think we have ever been outside this late before, do you?' Freya whispered.

Lexi shook her head. They stared up at the vast inky-blue sky, punctuated by a million stars and a big, big moon that hung tantalisingly close.

It was stunning.

'Look at all those stars, Lexi, so far away. And yet so big, so bright, it feels like you can touch them.'

The little girl reached out and closed one eye. 'I'd like to put one in my pocket.'

'That would be amazing, wouldn't it? I think it's incredible that astronauts fly rockets up into space. They launch not too far from here, you know. They just pack a little bag and off they go, to visit the man in the moon and drive around the stars, as if they are on a space motorway.'

'I think I'd like to be an astronaut.' The little girl stared upward, captivated by the moving celestial display.

'You can be anything you want to, Lexi.' Freya took every opportunity to reinforce this, not wanting her recent diagnosis of dyslexia to be a barrier to her dreams.

'I'd like to be an astronaut more than anything in the world!' She paused. 'But I don't know how to do it.'

'Ah, well, that's the lucky thing. I'm your mum and I will help you achieve your goals. I'll help you in any way I can to do whatever you want to do. Always.'

Lexi beamed as if this were good to know. 'I might miss you, though, if I went up into space,' she whispered.

'Well, that's easy.' Freya pulled her close. 'No matter how far away you go from me, no matter how old you are, you have to remember that we are all made of stardust. Mothers and daughters are from the same batch, and when you are sad, I'm sad, and when you are happy, my heart sings! And no matter where you are, this will always, *always* be the case, which means there is never any need to miss me or for me to miss you, not really, because we are part of each other.'

'Is Charlotte made from the same batch too?' She wrinkled her podgy little nose.

'Absolutely!'

'If you went away, Mum, I would write you a note or one of my stories, like I do for Daddy to take with him on his trips, and you could read it and you wouldn't feel so sad. And if I went away, you could write me a note or a story to take with me, and I would read it and I wouldn't feel so sad.'

'That's a brilliant idea.' She bent her head and kissed her little girl's scalp.

'What's on the other side of space, Mummy?'

'Where do you mean?'

Lexi sat up, as if this required greater attention. She turned to her mum, pointing upwards. Freya looked at her little girl, who sat on the floor with the stars and moon looming over her head like a halo.

'I mean that if you drove on the space motorway, and went all the way past the stars, what is on the other side of the black sky that we can see?'

Freya smiled at her clever girl. 'I don't know, my darling. What do you think?'

'I think Heaven.' She smiled at her mum, who couldn't help the stutter of a sob that built in her throat, overcome by the beauty of the moment, as she nodded at her daughter.

'I think you might be right.'

'Mum?' The voice shouted, jolting her from her memories.

'Yes?' Freya jerked her head towards the sound.

'Sorry, were you asleep?' Charlotte whispered.

Freya stared at her daughter. 'I don't know.'

It was a strange thing to confess: that you no longer knew the difference between your sleeping and waking states. It was as odd as it was frightening. Her tears came in great gulping sobs that folded her frame. She could still feel Lexi's chubby, childish shape nestled against her like a warm, comfortable cushion. It was overwhelming.

Charlotte walked closer to the desk and placed her hand on her mum's shoulder, staring at her sister's name, written on the otherwise blank sheet. 'It's not going so well, I see.' Her eyes crinkled into a smile of reassurance.

'Weren't you just here a minute ago?' Freya sniffed, having also lost her ability to judge time.

'About half an hour ago. I delivered your cup of tea.'

She nodded. 'So you did.' She blotted at her face with a tissue.

They both stared at the cup of peppermint tea, now cold and dark with an oily top to it.

Charlotte leant on the desktop. 'Would you like me to have a go?'

'What?' Freya knitted her brows.

'I could try if you like.' She pointed at the sheet of paper.

Tipping her head back, Freya felt the crunch at the top of her spine. She was tired.

'We could both do a bit. You've started, and that's great, but I could have a go, and then you can take over.'

Charlotte was doing it again, using her mothering tone to coax and encourage.

Freya nodded. Bracing herself against the chair to stand, she wrapped her thin cotton dressing gown around her form before walking across her study and sitting again on the ancient plum-coloured velvet sofa that sagged in the middle and lived beneath the window. It was a journey of a few steps, but from the way she sighed, folding her legs slowly on to the cushion and letting her head rest on the sofa arm, any observer would guess that she had crossed oceans.

Charlotte lifted the pale-pink mohair blanket from the hamper and gently tucked it over her mum's legs. Freya's eyelids fluttered in the first throes of sleep.

Charlotte took up the seat at the desk and, leaning forward, lifted her mother's pen. *There are some things that are inseparable,* she began.

> *I can't think of clouds without also picturing the sky, the ocean and fish, and I can't think of me without thinking of you . . .*

THREE

Arriving at the school a little early, Freya sat in the car park, tapping her fingers on the steering wheel of their knackered old Saab estate car. Lockie was convinced that if they kept it for long enough, it would eventually be considered vintage. These days, however, it was more of an embarrassment for her kids; not that she cared.

She looked at her watch: three-fifteen. She couldn't wait any longer.

Freya tousled her hair around her face and applied some lip balm with her little finger before spritzing her perfume around her neck. She was wearing one of Lockie's checked shirts, with most of the buttons undone, over a white T-shirt and her straight-legged jeans. It was the one advantage to being taller than her husband: his jackets and shirts fitted her rather nicely. Freya looked down at her scuffed Timberland boots and wondered if she should have maybe dressed up a little? That was the trouble with freelancing from home: her wardrobe consisted mainly of jeans and borrowed tops or pyjamas.

Slinging her trusty khaki canvas rucksack over her shoulder, she trod the wide steps to the front of the unimpressive seventies building. The orange bricks and large double-glazed windows resembled an office block more than a place of learning. An elaborate, incongruent school crest with scrolls and swirls picked out in gold was fixed to the wall above the entrance. It was a clear attempt that tried and failed to compensate for the municipal look and feel of the place. She spoke through the hatch to the rather scary-looking security guard behind the sliding window of the reception. The very sight of him was enough to send a shiver of fear along her limbs. What dangers were her kids exposed to here that they needed a beefy security guard?

'I've come to meet with Miss Burke, my daughter's tutor,' she gabbled. 'I'm a bit early.'

'Name?'

'Alexia Braithwaite.' She smiled.

'And your child's name?' the burly man asked without looking up.

'Alexia Braithwaite.' She sighed, feeling like she had messed up the system. 'Sorry, mine's Freya.'

'Take a seat.' Unamused or uncaring, he pointed over her shoulder.

She took a seat on the squeaky faux-black-leather sofa in the corner. It was a little before three-thirty that Miss Burke appeared, looking hurried and more than a little flustered.

'Thanks for coming in.' She narrowed her eyes as she turned to walk away, as if time were of the essence. 'This way . . .' She pointed along a corridor, accessed by sweeping her key card along a strip of plastic. 'We can talk in private.'

'Okay.' Freya's voice warbled; she was nervous after her wait.

She tripped behind the short, wide woman, who moved at a surprising pace. It felt churlish to engage in small talk when Miss Burke might be about to reveal all manner of shenanigans or misadventure. The silence, however, in which they walked, with the tutor just slightly ahead, was excruciating.

Freya felt her heart rate increase.

Miss Burke entered a bland square office with closed grey vertical blinds and a large map of the world on one wall. A clock ticked loudly.

The woman took a seat behind the empty desk and opened her palm, indicating a chair on the other side of the varnished blond wood.

Freya sat down and placed her rucksack on her lap: protection, of sorts, from any verbal blows the teacher might deliver.

Miss Burke pushed her flicked-up fringe from her face and knitted her fingers on the desktop. She took a deep breath, as one who was used to giving long speeches might do.

'Do you have any thoughts about why I might want to see you today?' Her tone was soft, her head cocked to one side, as if Freya might need encouragement or coaxing to confess. The woman was clearly not used to addressing grown-ups.

'Is it something to do with Toby?' Freya offered confidently.

Miss Burke's head jerked slightly. 'Toby?'

She instantly regretted the suggestion; judging from the woman's expression, this was wide of the mark.

'Yes, it's probably a stupid idea . . . It's just that Lexi has this new friend, who we met briefly yesterday and, my eldest, Charlotte—'

'Yes, I know Charlotte.'

'Well, she and Lexi were rowing a bit about it in the morning, nothing terrible, you know, just the usual . . . shouting and a bit of door slamming and maybe a swear word . . .' She swallowed, aware that nerves and being in a school situation were making her blab. 'And Charlotte said something unflattering about Toby, and it was all a bit of nonsense really. Anyway, he seemed quite pleasant, bit ordinary, bit odd, but nice and they watched TV and that was that, really.'

She bit the inside of her cheek, as if this might halt further rambling.

Miss Burke looked a little confused; her eyes darted to the map on the wall and back again.

'No, it's not about Toby . . . Do you mean Toby Proudfoot?' It had obviously ignited her interest.

Freya shrugged. 'I don't know. Are there many?'

'A couple, yes.' Miss Burke shook her head, as if to get things back on track. 'The thing is, Mrs Braithwaite, I'm a little worried about Lexi.'

Freya felt her stomach sink.

'Oh? Is she behind in her work? She tries very, very hard and puts the hours in. I mean, I'm sure all parents say that, but she really does, she finds coursework and essays so difficult, because of her dyslexia. I watch her struggle and it's heartbreaking. Mrs White, her special needs coordinator, says she's doing really well. But if she needs extra . . .'

Miss Burke raised her palm. 'No. It's not a work issue, but more of a pastoral concern.'

'Pastoral in what way?' Freya wasn't entirely sure what that meant.

'I'm sure, as you know, it's not always easy being a teenage girl in today's society.'

'It's not always easy being a grown-up one in today's society!' She smiled briefly, trying to lessen the quake of nerves in her stomach.

Miss Burke ignored her. 'Has she ever mentioned her weight to you?'

'Erm . . .' Freya hesitated, wondering how to couch her response. 'She's very into healthy eating, which I think is a good thing. We are quite aware as a household about food and health; it's part of my job.' She smiled, trying to reassure the woman that on this topic she knew her stuff. 'And she loves to keep fit. She runs and swims – we don't live far from Westminster Lodge pool, which makes it easy for her.'

She saw the way Miss Burke looked at her fingers, as if lining up her next phrase and not listening at all.

'Lexi nearly fainted yesterday. She was very wobbly.'

'Oh no! Poor little thing, she never said. I'm glad I'm collecting her, she sometimes gets the bus, but if she's not feeling a hundred per cent . . .'

'She seems fine, but I do have concerns, as I said.'

'What concerns, exactly?' Freya pulled the rucksack closer into her chest.

'Mrs Janosik is head of PE, and also Lexi's academic tutor . . .'

Freya nodded. She had heard the name.

'And she has noticed that Lexi has lost a lot of weight and is more often than not in the gym at lunchtimes or running laps on the field.'

Freya felt the weight of the woman's stare as she struggled to see the issue, considering it a good thing that Lexi had taken control of her health and fitness and had trimmed down her baby fat. Her chubby pre-teen weight had knocked her confidence, but now she was blooming.

'When Lexi nearly fainted, she spoke to Mrs Janosik and told her that she hadn't eaten anything since lunchtime the day before, when she had an apple.'

Freya opened her mouth to speak, but closed it again, trying to picture her daughter's recent mealtimes.

She tried to recall exactly what had happened over the weekend. Last night at supper? Lexi had been out on a run when they ate. And then later? She heard Lockie's shout: *We have a grape thief in our midst!* They'd all laughed. And this morning for breakfast? She hadn't seen her eat anything, but she might have. It had been a rush, as it usually was. She couldn't be sure of the specifics, but knew her daughter had sat at the table over the last week and dined – maybe a little less than usual, but she had eaten something, certainly.

'It's not like I don't offer her food or have food in the house. There's always plenty.'

Aware of her defensive tone, she blushed.

'I'm sure that there is, Mrs Braithwaite, but there's a big difference between having food in the house and Lexi choosing to eat food or choosing not to. There is a pattern that we notice in some pupils who might be struggling with food issues.'

Freya snorted a short burst of laughter through her nose, interrupting the tutor. There was nothing wrong with her child. Yes, she was becoming more body aware, maybe slimming down a little for a boy she clearly liked – who hadn't done that? But 'food issues'? If anything, losing her chubbiness was something to be celebrated; it could only be good for her future health and self-esteem.

'I really appreciate your concern and calling me in, Miss Burke. I think it's great that the school is paying such close attention, vital in fact. But I think you've got the wrong end of the stick where Lexi is concerned. As I have mentioned, I am very food aware and have a great relationship with both of my daughters. I know them better than anyone and I think I might have noticed if one of them wasn't eating enough or, as you are suggesting, had an issue with food.'

Miss Burke sat back in the chair. 'I understand how this must make you feel, and believe me it is in no way a criticism, but Mrs Janosik was concerned enough to take her to see the school nurse, who said that she thought Lexi's situation was one we should keep an eye on. That's all.' She splayed her palms, as if to neutralise the situation, no harm intended. 'No one is bandying around any labels or trying to inflate what might already be a sensitive topic. We are just saying we should all be aware.'

Freya felt a complex range of emotions: concern that Lexi had been earmarked in this way; embarrassed that someone outside of their family might think that things were amiss; and angry that they had put this idea in her little girl's head. She stood.

'Well, as I say, thank you for your concern and please pass that on to the PE teacher, nurse and whoever else has taken time out of their busy schedule today to analyse my daughter's eating habits. I shall have a word with Lexi and take it from there.'

Miss Burke stood too. Her words, when they came, were considered. 'I think *how* you talk to her about this might be very important.'

Freya flashed her a look that made the woman hesitate. She folded her arms across her chest.

'Wh . . . what I am trying to say, is that if you want to talk to me again, or any of the team here that are trained in . . .'

Freya hoisted her rucksack over her shoulder, opened the office door and walked back to the reception.

She had heard quite enough.

She was relieved to place her key in the door, happy to be home, having spent the journey from school stealing glimpses of her younger daughter, who sat on the back seat, engrossed in her phone. She looked at the jut of her jaw, comparing it to Charlotte's, glanced at her willowy legs, and tried to think of her own at a similar age.

'Got any homework, girls?' she asked casually, as she began unstacking the dishwasher.

'An essay.' Lexi pulled a face. Essays were her very worst things.

'Well, if you want to work at the table, I can help you,' she offered, resisting the temptation to grab her child and fire questions at her: *What's going on? They said you weren't eating. Why did you faint? Was it for attention?*

'I'm okay.' Lexi rebuffed the offer and made her way upstairs. Freya watched her go.

Charlotte opened the fridge and selected a yoghurt and three left-over slices of ham that sat in a little bowl; she then reached up to the top shelf of the cupboard above the countertop where multi-packs of crisps lived, before selecting a bag of cheese-and-onion.

'Don't spoil your supper.' Freya's rebuke was almost automatic.

'I won't. I'm starving. What are we having?'

'Erm . . . Spanish omelette, avocado salad, tomato salsa and home-made pitta bread.'

'Lush!' Charlotte rushed to her room with her bag and laptop in one arm and her haul of snacks in the other.

Concentrating on the dicing of tomatoes, the deseeding of fresh chilli and the whisking of eggs helped take her mind from her concerns. She then mixed the dry yeast and sugar with lukewarm water in a large glass bowl, before adding the wholewheat and unbleached flours and placing the mixture on the coffee table in the window, waiting for it to bubble.

When Lockie walked through the door, throwing his keys into the ornate Moroccan pottery dish they had picked up from the souk in Marrakech, she abandoned her preparation and practically ran into his arms.

'Oh, well, I rather like this!' He chuckled. 'Think I should go away for the day more often if this is the reaction I'm going to get. Mind you, I have been gone for a whole eight hours.' He ran his hands over her back as she buried her face in the space beneath his chin and inhaled the scent of him.

'What's up?' He pulled away from her and held the tops of her arms, looking into her eyes.

'I went to see Miss Burke today, at school,' she whispered, before taking his hand and pulling him to the sofa in the den, away from the bottom of the stairs, where sound might travel. Lockie flopped down and she sat next to him, twisting her body to face him.

'Yes? How did it go?' He too kept his voice low, taking her lead.

'She said Lexi was a bit faint yesterday and they were worried that she wasn't eating. They got the school nurse involved and it felt like a really big deal.'

'Are you kidding?'

'No, I am not kidding. I don't know what to do about it or what to say to her.' She bit her lip, waiting for his advice.

Lockie's eyes darted left to right, as if he were considering how best to approach this. 'But she's always eating, isn't she? They both are, and you are always cooking. We are a house of grub!'

'That's more or less what I said. I mean, yes, she's eating less, but I think that's a good thing.'

She sat forward, folding her hair over her shoulder, glad that they were on the same page, reassured by his dismissive tone. There was probably nothing to worry about. No school nurse or PE teacher knew their daughter as well as they did.

'I mean, we do need to talk to her,' he countered. 'If she's nearly fainted we need to find out why.'

'Yes, of course, but I don't want to make it more of an issue than it was, or give her any ideas. She said that Lexi has lost a lot of weight. I can't see it. I mean, she's lost a bit, but she looks great, healthy.'

'Yes, she does,' he agreed. 'I don't know what to suggest.' He looked stumped.

'It's unnerved me a bit, Lockie. I don't know how these things start, and I don't want to paint her into a corner or accuse her of anything. It's hard enough being Lexi as it is. She's up there right now, struggling with an essay.' She pointed to the ceiling.

'Poor love.' He smiled.

They used the silent interlude to process the rush of thoughts.

'How much does she actually weigh?' he eventually asked.

'I don't know. I did when she was little, of course, but I don't know what either of them weighs. I haven't for a while; it's a sensitive topic.'

'But maybe it shouldn't be. Maybe we should just ask, or get them weighed, and then we know what we are dealing with.' He shrugged, as if it were that simple. 'I mean, that's what we need, isn't it? A measurement that we can work from? Without that, it's all guesswork.'

'No, Lockie, this doesn't work like that. It's not something you can apply your bolshie logic to and make about weights and measures. We have to tread carefully.'

'Do you mean because she used to be quite chubby?' He looked at his thighs, picking at a thread on his jeans.

'You see? You've gone coy. Your instinct tells you it's a delicate subject and you're right. It's *partly* because she was carrying a bit of weight, but regardless of that, girls are very fragile when it comes to this kind of thing.'

'How much do you weigh?' he asked.

'How much do *you* weigh?' she countered.

'Two hundred and ten pounds, give or take.' The answer tripped from his tongue, his expression challenging.

Freya swallowed. His instant, honest reply was something she couldn't emulate.

'Maybe it's not only the girls who are a bit sensitive,' he pointed out.

Shooting her husband a withering look, she sat up straight. 'This isn't about me. I've always been tall and slim, it's genetic.'

'Darling, you are indeed tall and slim, but you do work at it.'

'I don't work at it that hard!' She narrowed her eyes.

'But you do, and it's interesting you feel the need to deny it. You only eat healthy and lean, and I'm not knocking you, but it's a fact: you are a bit obsessed with it.' He held her gaze.

'How did this become about me?' She stood.

'It's not!' He took a breath. 'It's about all of us, about our family and food.'

She shook her head. 'I know, you're right. I guess it's just thrown me a little. I worry about her dyslexia, about how she's coping academically and socially, and I don't want to have to worry about her eating as well.'

Lockie smiled. 'I know, but let's bring it out into the open when it feels right and take our steer from her. How does that sound?'

She nodded, reaching for her bowl of fermenting dough. 'Sounds like a plan.'

◆ ◆ ◆

Freya placed the napkin-lined basket full of delicious-smelling, hot, fresh pitta bread in the centre of the table and put the plates in front of everyone, pre-loaded with a folded omelette, heaps of salad, and salsa. She watched as everyone, Lexi included, picked up a fork and dived in.

Catching Lockie's eye, she smiled.

'So . . . Miss Burke asked me to pop into school,' she began, as she helped herself to the pitta. 'She said you nearly fainted yesterday?'

Freya felt comfortable raising the subject in the warm family atmosphere, keeping it casual. She kept her eyes trained on her daughter, watching for any sign of embarrassment or a lie. She saw neither.

'Oh God, Lex! They've found out about your glue sniffing!' Charlotte guffawed, before folding a large lettuce leaf, slathered in dressing, into her mouth.

Lexi ignored her, nodding as she chewed. 'It was horrible; that's never happened to me before. I had gym and forgot I'd skipped breakfast and I came over all whooshy.'

'Whooshy is bad!' Lockie added for dramatic effect.

'I know, Dad.' Lexi rolled her eyes at him. 'I usually get a flapjack or something from the canteen, but I was chatting to Mrs White about the writing assistant for my exams and I ran out of time.'

'How does the writing-assistant thing work?' Charlotte was interested. 'Do they give you hints and clues if you don't know the answer? Like, "Are you *su-u-u-re* you want me to put D? Doesn't C look more tempting?" That'd be so awesome!'

Lexi reached for a slice of bread and shook her head at her sister as she finished her mouthful. 'It's not awesome. You have to sit in a separate room on your own and get your thoughts straight so that you don't write down any old rubbish, and getting my thoughts straight is one of the hardest bits for me.'

'It still sounds like a bit of an advantage.' Charlotte forked a chunk of omelette into her mouth.

'Yes, Charlotte, not being able to read or write as easily as everyone else is really cool, especially when I know what I want to say, but just can't get the words out, or when I look at a page and the words literally jump under my eyes so I can't even focus on one word, let alone a whole string of them, or when I spell my own name wrong, that's always fun and I know it's wrong, but I can't see why, that's a big advantage!'

'She didn't mean it like that.' Freya tried to catch her daughter's eye, offering a smile of reassurance and trying, as ever, to mediate.

'It just makes me mad! Even Mrs White was trying to tell me the other day that dyslexia was a gift.' She placed her fork on the side of her plate. 'I'd like to know who decided it was a present I might enjoy. I'd ask if there was any way I could return it. In fact, I wish I could track them down. I'd suggest they gave it to Charlotte instead – sounds like she'd appreciate it much more, as it's so *awesome*.'

'Like the "Hello Kitty" poster Granny sent you for your birthday!' Lockie chimed in.

It had been the source of much amusement. Lexi was offended by the gift she deemed babyish, whilst Charlotte tried to explain that it was so naff, it was cool.

'Yes, Dad, exactly like that.' Lexi laughed, and Charlotte joined in.

'Honestly, you two . . .' Freya smiled at her girls, happy that they joked with affection, relieved that the topic had been raised and put to bed without drama, but mostly delighted to see her youngest pick up the fork and resume eating her supper.

She pictured Miss Burke, feeling vindicated and secure in the knowledge that she did indeed know her girls better than anyone.

Eight hours . . .

Freya appeared to be sleeping on the sofa.

Charlotte held the pen and wrote:

> *I don't know why this is in my head, but it is! Do you remember when we once went to stay with Granny – I think you were about eight? Mum and Dad had gone to France on a working trip and I don't think I have ever laughed so much in my whole life.*
>
> *Everything was funny, but of course it wasn't. It was us: we were funny, me and you. It felt like we had been let loose and we were giddy with the freedom. We woke up one day and decided to say 'Fanny' instead of 'Granny' to see if she noticed, and you managed it once – you looked at me first to check I was paying attention and then you said, 'Fanny? Can we go and play in the garden?' You pulled it off, spoke so swiftly, not even smiling a little bit and you were so proud of your*

performance, holding it together brilliantly, until you turned around and I was lying on the dining room floor, laughing so hard. I was wheezing and started shouting, 'I'm going to pee!' That was it. You started laughing too and we couldn't stop.

And Granny, wonderful Granny, bent down and said, 'You can of course go and play in the garden. Just give Fanny a shout when you want me to unlock the back door.' She never broke her stride.

I'm smiling now, thinking about that day.

You are brave and brilliant and clever. And even though you are younger than me, you are so much more daring than I ever was.

I envy you that, I always have. Like when we were on the pier in Naples that night and it seemed so high up and Dad told you there were sharks in the water, but it didn't faze you, not even a little. You just climbed up and teetered on the edge and then you leapt in the air.

I watched from the rails, scared on your behalf. You looked so far away, your little arms pulling you through the water, visible only by your splash that was picked out by the moonlight. And Mum, covering her eyes, couldn't bear to watch you jump. I didn't think you would do it, but you did! Graceless and screaming, I'll admit, but you did it, Lexi, you did it all the same.

'Charlotte?' Freya lifted her head from the arm of the sofa and stared at her daughter across the study.

'It's okay. I'm right here.' She twisted in the chair to look behind her. 'Is Lockie still asleep?'

Her tears clogged her nose and throat as she laid her head back down, pulling the soft mohair blanket up to her chin.

'I think so, Mum. Do you want me to go and wake him?' She closed her eyes, unwilling to give in to the emotion that threatened, not while she still had a job to do. Tears would have to wait.

'No. Let him sleep.' Freya's stifled sobs provided the background noise, as Charlotte once again picked up the pen and set the nib on the paper.

FOUR

The radio news programme burbled away, providing the background noise to their morning.

'Shall I ask Toby if he wants to come with us to Charlotte's concert?' Lexi asked as she packed her pencil case and PE kit into her school bag and arranged her folders in a way that made them easier to carry.

'It's up to Charlotte. If she doesn't mind, then yes, of course!'

Freya smiled, unwilling to admit that she would welcome the opportunity to study the boy at closer quarters. The two had been friends for three months, but still Freya's interactions with him were limited to polite, fleeting hellos and goodbyes that did little to reveal his nature. It wasn't that she disliked him, far from it, but there were certain traits that both she and Lockie found a little 'off'. He had a tendency to whisper to Lexi, speaking at a volume that excluded others in the room, and when asked a question would look at Lexi and answer, as if communicating via a ventriloquist's dummy. Both habits verged on infuriating.

'Maybe we could go out for supper afterwards?' Lockie suggested, as he pressed several buttons on their rather complicated coffee machine.

It beeped and gurgled and gave off an unpleasant grinding sound. 'We still owe you a birthday dinner,' he reminded her.

Lexi had eschewed the traditional family meal out and had instead celebrated with Fennella and friends, as was befitting a newly minted fifteen-year-old with the world at her feet.

'Don't press all the buttons, you'll just confuse the machine.' Freya tutted at her husband.

'It's a machine. They don't get confused.' He pressed another button while holding his wife's eye, just to annoy her.

'Stop it, Lockie. I'm not joking. You'll break it. And trust me, that's a situation neither of us wants to find ourselves in. Me without decent coffee is one thing; me without decent coffee because *you* have broken my machine is quite another.'

Lockie pointed his finger and let it drift towards the machine. Freya dashed from the den towards the counter. Reaching up, she grabbed his hand and tried to wrestle him away from the area.

'No bending fingers back!' he shouted as he manhandled his wife towards the table, finally securing her in a bear hug from which she couldn't wriggle free.

'Okay! Okay! I give in, let me go!' she squealed through her laughter, hating to be so confined.

'I will, but only on the condition that you teach me how to use the coffee maker,' he bargained, easing his grip anyway and letting her go. 'And I mean a *proper* lesson, delivered patiently with plenty of time for sample testing and questions.'

'I tell you what.' She placed her hands on her hips. 'Instead of that, I will make you a cup of special coffee whenever you want it. You only have to shout and I will prepare you a flat white or a cheeky espresso, whichever you want, but please stay away from my beautiful machine.'

Lockie kissed her on the cheek. 'You've got yourself a deal.' He winked at his daughter. 'Works every time,' he whispered as he swept past, and down towards his studio.

Charlotte now hammered down the stairs; a segment of wavy hair sat like a genie's ponytail on top of her head and the rest hung limply around her shoulders.

'Have you seen my hair-straighteners, Mum? I can't find them and I *need* them.'

She did that: spoke far too quickly the more urgent a query, or the more stressed she was by the problem at hand.

'Yes, good morning to you too, darling. Try the basket in the bathroom, under the hairdryer.'

'I have. I bet you've taken them.' She gritted her teeth and turned her head, accusing her sister.

'I have not!' Lexi's voice was unnaturally high.

'Please don't get so flustered. It's hair-straighteners, Charlotte,' Freya reminded her. 'Not the Crown Jewels.'

'I know, but she just takes my stuff all the time without asking.'

'I do not, Charlotte. I have my own stuff. You did this last time, going on and on about your fake ID and Tara had it all the time.'

'What fake ID?' Freya's ears pricked up.

'Nice one, dork!' Charlotte stared at her sister, who shrank under her withering retort. 'It's not mine, Mum. It's Milly's. I was just looking after it for her.'

'Oh. Well, I don't think Milly's parents would like her having a fake ID.'

'You're not going to tell them, are you?'

'Of course I won't. I only see them when collecting or dropping off, and only then from the car window. Can you imagine me calling them up, just to drop Milly in it?' Freya rolled her eyes at her daughter's apparent lack of faith, whilst secretly enjoying the fact they shared this minor confidence.

Charlotte looked relieved.

'We were just wondering,' Freya asked nonchalantly, 'whether it might be an idea to ask Toby if he wanted to come to your concert.'

'Oh my God, I can't believe you'd even think about that. He's in my year, don't forget, it's bad enough that she wants to hang around with him, let alone my mates seeing him at my concert. No way!'

'I just thought it might be nice . . .' Freya tried to defend the suggestion, watching as Lexi's face turned puce.

'As if he'd want to go to your stupid concert anyway. I'm not even going – it's going to be crap!' Lexi stormed from the room and up the stairs.

Freya shook her head. 'I honestly don't understand how a basic chat can turn into such a scene. It mystifies me every time. And here I am again, stuck in the middle of you two bickering.' She threw the tea towel on to the table. 'I sound like a broken record.'

'But you're *not* stuck in the middle, are you, Mum? You are very definitely on her side, you always are.' Charlotte sniffed as her lip trembled.

Freya walked forward and took her in her arms.

'I am on no one's side. That's a ridiculous thing to say. I love you both, you are both part of me, and when you try to tear each other apart, it's as if you are hurting me.'

'She gets away with murder, she always has, just because she's the youngest and because of her issues with school and stuff.'

'That's not true, love. I am equally horrible to you both.' She kissed her child and tried to lighten the mood. 'You are both hormonal and a little anxious. You've got your A levels coming up, and Lexi's got her practice tests, and you are both trying to figure out this whole transition from teenager to woman, and it's not easy. I get it. But we can make it easier by talking about it, by talking about everything. I'm here if you need me. Dad too.'

Charlotte shrugged loose, rolled her eyes and left the room.

'Well, that went well.' Freya poked her head around the door. 'We're leaving in twenty minutes!' she called up the stairs.

◆ ◆ ◆

Freya hated to think of Lexi brooding over her sister's comments, and wanted to smooth things before she went to school, knowing that if she didn't, she'd only worry about her all day. She knocked and entered Lexi's bedroom.

'Hey, darling, just to say . . .'

She stopped speaking and watched as her daughter shoved the wide drawer of the divan bed, closing it with a slam. She jumped up from where she knelt as if scalded.

Freya stared, perplexed, as Lexi darted to the other side of the room and back again, as if unsure where to go, hoping for a hiding place, until, realising that she was trapped, she came to a standstill in front of her mother, with her hands on her hips. It was a stance that Freya had rarely seen. Lexi's chest heaved, as if she were breathing too quickly, and her eyes were wide.

'What's going on?' Freya let her eyes focus on the drawer that had been so hastily shut.

'Nothing.' Lexi stared, unblinking. There was an edge of fear to her voice.

'Have you hidden your sister's hair-straighteners?' She felt a flash of irritation.

Lexi licked her dry lips and looked at the drawer, then at her mum. She nodded, quickly, with a small smile playing about her nervous mouth.

'I'm sorry. I'll . . . I'll give them back to her. I'm sorry.'

Freya noticed the sweat that sat in tiny droplets on her top lip.

'Are you feeling okay?' She took a step closer and heard the sharp intake of breath as Lexi took a step further backwards, her calves now resting against the bed, blocking the drawer. Her child looked sickly, afraid.

'What's going on, Lexi?' she asked again, concentrating on keeping her tone level, her voice calm, unwilling to give rise to the concern that was growing at her child's furtive behaviour.

'I didn't want you to shout at me and so I said I hadn't taken them, but I had and I'll give them back to her. Can you just go and let me get ready? Please!' She swallowed again; tears pooled in her eyes.

'I don't shout at you. Not really. I mean, I might raise my voice to get things done, but you seem really scared, and the thought of you being scared of me is horrible.' She gave a short, unnatural laugh.

'Found them!' Charlotte shouted from her bedroom. 'Tara had shoved them in my laundry basket.'

It was as if Charlotte called from the end of a long tunnel: her words had a vague, echoey quality. Freya twisted her head, as if asking the question *Why? Why would you lie about that? Why would you lie at all?*

Lexi sank back on to the mattress, sitting and staring at her mum with her hands in her lap, as both tried to figure out their next move.

'Open the drawer, Lexi,' Freya whispered, as her mind raced, her daughter's lie having sent her imaginings into overdrive.

She thought of the things she hid in *her* room, things she wanted to keep secret: one or two bits of sexy lingerie that Lockie had bought, half in jest, that she wore on occasion; receipts for items she had bought with money they didn't have; and a love letter from a time before Lockie. None of these fitted – certainly not a receipt – and there wouldn't be this much fuss over a love letter. That left underwear: her best bet. She pictured the hapless Toby and felt her jaw tense in anger. *If he has touched her . . .*

'There's nothing in it, Mum. Please just leave me alone!'

'If there is nothing in it, then you won't mind me looking.'

Freya walked forward as Lexi leapt from the bed; she grabbed her mum's wrists, holding them fast as the two were trapped in a bizarre dance, both too frightened by the other's reaction to move. Her husband's footsteps travelled up the stairs.

'Lockie!' she called, her voice shrill.

He pushed open the door and stared at two of the women he loved standing in the middle of the bedroom, his daughter restraining his wife by the wrists.

'What the—'

'Hold her, Lockie,' she snapped.

He stepped forward. 'What's going on?'

'Please, Dad!' Lexi called, her fear finally manifesting as tears that slid down her cheeks.

'Darling! What is it?' He pulled her from her mother, holding her flat against his chest, with one hand on the side of her face, as she shook against him.

'Leave me alone! Both of you, go away!' she shrieked. 'Get out of my room!'

'It's okay. Whatever has upset you, it's all okay.' He tried to calm the child, his expression one of bewilderment.

'Don't open it, Mum! You have to trust me! Please!'

Lexi's pleas fell on deaf ears as Freya dropped to her knees and pulled the drawer that slid open with ease. It made no sense: she came to face to face with an old hoodie from year seven and a random pillowcase that they had taken camping once or twice. She looked at her daughter, as if trying to understand her strange reaction to these innocuous items.

Lexi lifted her head from her dad's chest and looked at her mum, who was crouched on the floor.

Freya stared at her daughter and all three were silent and still, a precursor for what was about to unfold.

Lexi's eye flickered to the drawer and back to her mother's face. Freya noted the way she looked: not at the hoodie, but at the space behind it. She reached her hand in and grabbed the fabric of the pillowcase.

The shout was deafening.

'No! Don't you go through my things! Don't you dare!' Lexi screamed as if her life depended on it. She sank down on to her knees as her dad dropped to the floor with her, trying to cradle her, trying to calm her while she shrieked and railed.

Charlotte appeared in the doorway. 'What the hell . . . ?'

Freya removed the item of clothing and stared at the neat rows of carrier bags, each deliberately packed and knotted about halfway down, then folded in on itself. Some were double-bagged, and all were arranged with precision, covering the base of the drawer.

'What on earth . . . ? Is it drugs?'

Freya asked the questions to both her children and her husband, as if one of them might be able to give her the answer she sought. Lockie shrugged and continued to hold Lexi, who seemed to go floppy in his arms, as if the fight had left her.

Freya selected a plastic bag at random. 'What is this, Lexi?'

'Please, Mum! I am begging you just to put it back and get out of my room!' Lexi tried one final time.

Freya ignored her, feeling the weight of the soft, pouchy contents in her palm. It weighed little more than an orange. Gingerly, she dug her nail into the tight twist of plastic and wriggled her finger into its centre until she was able to loosen the knot.

'No!' Lexi continued to scream.

The smell was instantly overpowering, filling Freya's nose and mouth and causing bile to rise in her throat. It was disgusting, putrid and offensive. It was the smell of her daughter's vomit.

'Good God!' Lockie placed his hand over his nose and mouth and released Lexi as he made for the window and opened it wide, letting the clean air carry away some of the stench.

'Urgh . . . that's disgusting!' Charlotte reeled and walked backwards into the hallway.

'I don't . . .' Freya re-tied the bag and stared at the thirty or forty similar bags, jam-packed into the space under her child's bed.

Miss Burke's words, so easily dismissed, echoed in her mind: *There is a pattern that we notice in some pupils who might be struggling with food issues.* It was as if she had discovered the last piece of a puzzle in a game she didn't know she was playing. The suggestion had been there, and now here was the evidence: how had she missed it? She felt her stomach bunch in fear, her mouth dry.

'Could you leave us for a second, Lockie?' She spoke calmly.

'What do you mean, leave you? I want to know what's going on!'

Freya stood and nodded at him. 'Please, Lockie, just give us a few minutes.' Reluctantly he stepped from the room.

Staring at her daughter, who lay coiled on the floor, she spoke rationally. 'Lexi, I need you to stand up.'

Lexi didn't move.

'Listen to me. I need to understand what is going on here. Today is the day it stops. It's the day we start to get this sorted out. I need to figure out what's been going on and then we work out how to go forward, but I need you to stand up. Right now.' She tried to keep the impatience from her voice.

Her daughter pulled herself into a sitting position, carefully avoiding eye contact.

'Stand up, Lexi,' she repeated.

Eventually she stood, facing her mother, but with her head hanging forward, her hair forming a curtain over her face.

'I need you to take your clothes off for me.' She spoke quietly and slowly.

Lexi shook her head. 'No.'

'Yes! I need you to take your clothes off here so I can see you, so I can understand what's going on.'

'I don't want to!' she cried.

Freya swallowed. 'I know. I know, honey, but right now, this is not about what you want. I am telling you, as your mother, to take off your clothes.'

Lexi lifted her head and, with tears streaming down her face, she gripped the bottom of her sweatshirt and slowly peeled it up over her body. Next she reached for the buttons of her polo shirt and, with trembling fingers, she slipped them through the buttonholes and pulled this too over her head.

There were yet more layers beneath.

Freya stared at the long-sleeved T-shirt with thick vest over the top that gave her daughter a fuller outline. She stepped forward and, reminiscent of the thousand times she had helped this child undress as a toddler, carefully lifted the vest, and then the long-sleeved T-shirt, pulling them over her head to reveal not one, but two sports bras. Deftly she eased Lexi's school trousers over her hips and let them fall to the floor. And there they stood.

Lexi shivered, standing in her underwear, in the cold wind that whipped around the room. Freya shivered too, but not with cold. Her eyes lingered on the large knobbles of spine on her child's back that had once been covered with a comfortable layer of fat. Her ribs were visible from the back and front and her bottom was all but flat, her stomach concave. Her whole body seemed to be covered with a fluffy blond down, particularly visible on her arms and legs.

It was only with her child stripped down, without the artifice of her sweatsuit or the many layers that she had used to deceive, that Freya could see just how thin she had become. Pulling the duvet from the bed, she wrapped it around her little girl and held her close. It was then that her tears came, and her loud sobs, heard outside, brought Lockie's knock on the door.

The family slipped around each other in the kitchen, moving quietly, all trying to reconcile the events of earlier; all sharing a sense of awkwardness and shame, and each in their own way taking responsibility for what was happening. She and Lockie ducked and twisted in silence, making coffee and taking seats at the table, as if engaged in an unfamiliar dance of realisation and denial.

Charlotte hovered in the doorway, holding her files and pencil case. 'I've got to go or I'll be late for school. I'll see you all tonight.'

Freya nodded, barely acknowledging her eldest as she left.

She sat at the table with her husband by her side, opposite Lexi, who held the duvet close about her body.

'We love you,' she began.

'I know,' Lexi managed, her voice small, issued from a slumped posture with shoulders rounded, limbs gathered together and her head bowed.

'And we will do everything we can to understand this, but to do that, you are going to need to help us out a bit, okay?'

''Kay.' Again her voice was nothing more than a warble.

'How long have you been making yourself sick?'

Even saying the words felt like a boulder dropping through the ceiling from the room above, hitting the table and showering them in splinters. *It is a ridiculous thing, making yourself sick! Why would anyone do that? It's disgusting!* Freya quieted her thoughts.

'About nine months.' Her eyes flickered up and then back again.

'Nine *months*?' Lockie asked with emphasis.

Freya placed her hand under the table and laid it on her husband's thigh, reminding him to keep calm. She swallowed; it felt like the three were balanced on a tiny ledge and one wrong move . . .

'Why do you do that?' She asked the simple question hoping there might be a simple answer, because then they could start the process of fixing things. Just like she promised.

Lexi stared beneath the table.

Freya tried again. 'Why did you keep it under your bed?'

Without lifting her eyes, Lexi whispered, 'I knew you'd hear me if I went up to the bathroom, so I did it in the night, under my duvet. And then it was a way to keep a record, kind of.'

Freya dug her fingers into her husband's thigh: the only reaction she allowed herself, a mechanism to stop from yelling, *Sweet Jesus! What madness!*

Lockie pushed her for an answer. 'If you've been doing this for as long as you say, you must have given it a lot of thought. It takes a lot of . . . planning.'

Freya glanced at her husband, sensing how close he had come to using the word 'deceit'. It was a while before her daughter replied.

'I don't want to get fat.'

'But you haven't been fat for ages! Years!' Freya responded quickly and with zeal, trying to reinforce how wonderful she looked and to remind her of her success.

It was only when Lexi lifted her head that Freya saw her expression: wide-eyed, terrified. She had inadvertently confirmed that her child had been fat, and just the use of the word was like poison to Lexi, whose chest heaved and limbs trembled, as rounded tears slipped down her elfin cheeks, and she swallowed, as if gagging on the information.

'Don't cry, please don't cry.' Lockie reached across and held her hand inside his own. 'We will get you better, Lex. We are your mum and dad and we will make this all better.'

Freya looked at her husband, loving the nature of this kind, smart man. There was also a small sense of relief. He was right. They would do what they always did: dissect the problem, understand the issue and find a solution.

The sooner the better.

Freya sat on the same sofa in the reception area where she had sat months ago, the nervous anticipation she had felt before now replaced by the sadness that came with knowledge, and the shame that came with accepting the fact that she hadn't listened.

This time it was Mrs Janosik who met her. The woman was pretty, in her late twenties, comfortable in her tracksuit bottoms and school polo shirt, her long blonde hair sitting at the back of her head in a high plait. She was muscular, tanned and make-up free, boxy and striking, attractive. Freya felt a flicker of guilt at how she judged people in this way, particularly women.

'Mrs Braithwaite?' She smiled and walked forward, hand outstretched.

Freya shook it, happy to feel the force of the teacher's assertive interaction, figuring that if she was this strong, this confident, she just might have solutions, and what she wanted more than anything else in the whole world was for someone to tell her what to do. How to make things right.

'Yes.'

'This way.'

She stepped ahead in her spongy trainers, smiling and nodding at several pupils who shyly caught her eye. They made their way towards the gym, past the girls' changing room, along a corridor where the faint tang of sweat hung in the air, and into a chaotic office. The desk was piled high with books and stacks of paper. The shelves lining the walls bulged with a variety of sporting goods, from a deflated basketball to a plastic tray labelled 'Spare Socks' and yet more books on fitness and physiology.

'Sorry about the mess. I plan every month to devote one day to getting this room straight, but that day never comes.' She sat behind her desk. 'Please sit down, Mrs Braithwaite.'

'Freya.' She smiled.

'Thanks, Freya.' She placed her hand at her breast. 'Marta.' Her accent held only the faintest trace of her Baltic ancestry. 'How's Lexi doing?'

Clearly her message, left on Miss Burke's answerphone in part panic, had filtered through. She bit her lip, wondering how to start.

The words felt surreal, even though she had lived through the previous day, had removed the vile collection of bags, each containing her little girl's stomach contents, and had thrown away the drawers themselves, thinking not only that it was easier than cleaning them, but primarily that if they were gone, then there was nowhere for Lexi to hide things.

'I don't know how she is, really . . .' She coughed. 'Not good.'

'This isn't your fault.'

'I'm sorry?'

'What Lexi is going through – it isn't your fault. I expect that you will be reliving every aspect of her life in recent times and maybe even further back, trying to figure out what you did or said that might make her have an issue like this. But the truth is, disorders like bulimia and anorexia are indiscriminate. You don't choose them; they choose you, and they know no barriers.' She shrugged. 'I have this conversation more often than I care to admit. Boys, girls, all ages. What's key is how we best support your daughter from here on in.'

Freya stared at the stranger who felt comfortable in offering this very personal advice. She opened her mouth, but it was a second or two before she found the words.

'You think she has anorexia or bulimia?'

She noted the almost imperceptible flash of Marta's pupils. 'Don't you?' Her tone verged on condescension.

Freya looked past her, out of the wide picture window that offered a perfect view of the running track. The track where her little girl had run lap after lap, melting the fuel that padded her frame, aiming for thin and then thinner still.

'Those words make it sound . . .' Again she struggled for words. 'Very serious.'

The woman leant forward on the desk. 'It *is* very serious.'

Freya blinked furiously, processing the thoughts and facts that were coming at her thick and fast. 'I was hoping that this might be a blip.'

'I think to assume that Lexi isn't in the grip of something that could alter her life could be dangerous. If it's been going on for as long as you say – nine months?'

Freya nodded. 'That's what she said.'

'It doesn't seem like a blip.'

'I guess I'm having trouble getting my head around it,' she admitted.

'Of course.' Marta smiled. 'I do understand.'

'Who is it best to talk to? My doctor?' This is what she came for: advice.

'Yes. Some are brilliant, sympathetic and aware, others not so much – it's pretty much the luck of the draw. They will be able to suggest a therapist and what you need to be doing at home. I will arrange to have all her lesson plans and notes emailed to her, but we completely understand that schoolwork isn't her priority right now. She can do as much or as little as is right for her. Getting her healthy is obviously the priority, and then she has all the time in the world to catch up.'

'So you think it best we keep her at home?' She was a little shocked, unnerved; staying at home was only for those who were very poorly.

'I think it's up to Lexi and you, but in my experience, getting well might take all of her focus, and that's enough for anyone to cope with.'

'Okay, so we'll keep her home for a bit, while we figure out how to go forward.'

'Of course. You've got my number, Freya. Call me anytime. If I'm in lessons, then I will get back to you as soon as I can, and please give Lexi my very best wishes. She's a lovely girl.'

Freya nodded as she stood. 'Yes. She is.'

She drove home in an agitated state, able to focus only on the mundane: chores that needed doing, tomorrow's weather, anything to divert her brain from her discussion with Marta. She regaled Lockie with the details of her meeting with Mrs Janosik before taking solace in the watering and pruning of her tubs, delighting at the dwarf daffodils that sprang up in clumps here and there. She then swept the courtyard free of leaves before going inside and picking up the phone. She ended the call and trod the stairs, hesitating before she knocked, still wary of what waited for her on the other side of the door.

'Come in!' Lexi called, sounding quite bright.

Freya found her wrapped in her duvet, wearing bed socks, joggers and her favourite baggy sweatshirt. The spring sunshine lit the window and the atmosphere was a little brighter.

'Hey, darling, just got back from school. I had a good chat with Mrs Janosik. She seems really nice.'

'She is.'

'She suggested we go and see Dr Morris and that she will be able to point us in the right direction.'

Lexi gave a single nod.

'I've just got off the phone and made an appointment for Friday. But don't worry about that now, we'll take it slow and we'll get good advice. There is nothing we can say or tell her that she hasn't seen or heard a hundred times before. It'll all be fine.'

She sat on the edge of the bed and patted her child's leg. 'How are you feeling right now?'

Freya couldn't help but view this as a virus, a bug, and just like a bug, she wanted it gone, determined to minister to her little girl until it was behind them and they could all get back on track.

'Okay.'

It was the familiar cure-all word that Lexi cast like a balm wherever it was required.

'What can I get you for lunch?' Freya was determined. 'I've got some nice soup, or just toast? What do you fancy? You name it!' She smiled, in the way she had always done whenever her children were poorly and needed feeding up, trying to make both the food and the medicine sound attractive.

Lexi slumped further down against her pillows, trying to hide. 'I . . . I don't want anything yet, thank you.'

The word 'yet' had given her hope. She hadn't said no.

'Okay,' Freya said, 'but I'll pop back in a bit and see what you might like.' She kissed her forehead before heading back to the kitchen.

Lockie worked at the table.

'How is she?' His fingers paused, hovering over the keyboard.

'She seems a little brighter. Didn't want any lunch just yet, but said later.'

He ran his palm over his stubbly chin. 'Is this what it's going to be like? Waiting on tenterhooks to see if she eats something?'

'Lockie, I don't know. But I do know that it's now not okay for her to jump up and leave the table right after eating or to be really picky. We have to keep an eye on her.' Freya silently reprimanded herself for all the times she had praised Lexi for refusing sweets and second helpings.

'So do we have to spy on her, tempt her?' he offered, half in jest.

'Yes, I think we do, for a while at least. Just until we can break the cycle, get her to relax about food and start eating normally.'

'How long will that take?' He looked at her, confident that she had the answer.

'God, Lockie, it's only been a couple of days, are you fed up with it already?'

'No.' He scooted the chair away from the table a little. 'Not fed up with it, exactly, but my stomach is in knots. I can't concentrate. I keep thinking how horrible it feels when I'm hungry, how greedy I am for food, and I can't bear the idea of her feeling like that for hours on end.'

'I know.' She put the mug down. Coffee could wait. 'The good news is, she seemed quite open to the idea of going to the doctor.'

'When's the appointment?'

'Friday, eight-thirty.'

'Great. I'll come with you. Charlotte won't mind getting the bus to school; she has for the last couple of days anyway.' He tapped into the calendar on his laptop.

Freya drew breath. 'I think it's best if you stay here, love. It might be a bit overwhelming for her and we need to keep things as relaxed as possible. If we all go it just makes it more of a circus.'

'I wasn't going to come into the room. I understand she'll want privacy, of course, but I thought it might be good to come along, to support her.'

'You don't have to, just get the kettle on for when we get back.'

She smiled, hoping that was the end of it. She resumed her coffee making, seeking out the little pod and pressing the button on her coffee machine.

Lockie closed his laptop a little more forcefully than normal. He stood and leant against the table, his arms folded.

'I'm just going to have to come out and say this.' He drew breath, as if nervous.

Freya lifted her little glass coffee cup from the machine and waited for him to speak; it wasn't like him to make such a grand statement or to be so reticent.

'Are you certain that we are doing the right thing, going to the doctor, speaking to her teachers, keeping her off school? I wonder if this is really a thing or are we just making it a thing? Indulging her?'

She thought how best to answer. 'The truth is, Lockie, I don't know what the right thing to do is. Her teacher said she was anorexic or bulimic.'

It was the first time she used the words to Lockie that they had been very careful to avoid.

'What's the difference?' he asked.

'I'm not entirely sure, but I think one you overeat and then make yourself sick and the other you don't eat, but I don't really know.' She hated how little she did really know.

He stared at her. 'I think everyone needs to slow down. There's a million miles between not wanting to eat, having a mini meltdown for a bit of attention, and a diagnosis like anorexia. I'm just worried that we are jumping the gun by labelling her, or worse, putting her into a system that will label her for us, and then what? It might be hard to retreat when it all blows over.'

'I did think that the first time, when I went to speak to Miss Burke. I thought I knew best, and I put any doubts out of my head because we sat down that night and had dinner. I'd made omelettes, and I watched as she reached for the bread and told us that there was nothing to worry about. I believed her.' She faced her husband. 'But then I found the bags full of sick under her bed. You saw them too! She was tricking us. Why would she do that? And she is so very skinny.'

She pictured Lexi in her underwear, the sharp bite of her collar-bones and hip-bones, stripped of the layers she used to deceive.

'I hear you. I just think we need to be very careful of going down a route from which it is impossible to do a U-turn. That's all.' He spoke reasonably.

Freya nodded. 'And I agree with you. I told Mrs Janosik that I thought it was a blip and I *do* think that. We are not the kind of family who will sit back and hope for the best. We are good parents; we know our kids and we will work with Lexi to get her back on track, I'm absolutely confident of that. And when she's feeling better, we can move on – it doesn't have to be mentioned; we can't let this define her. We will beat it. I know we will.'

Lockie nodded at her and smiled. 'I hope so.'

'I know so.' She countered. This, she had to believe.

Seven hours, thirty minutes . . .

Freya sat up and stretched her arms above her head. It was still strange to her that she could sleep and wake feeling physically refreshed, but with her mind so very weary.

Charlotte was slumped over the desk, her head rested on her arms. The creak of the floorboards under her mother's foot drew her from her repose.

'I needed that. Thank you, darling.'

She felt a little more with it, but only a little. She didn't want her daughter to think that her efforts and kindly gestures had been in vain.

Charlotte sat up straight and ran her hand over the page. 'Do you want to take over?' she asked.

Freya nodded and hugged her girl, as she vacated the chair. 'Thank you.'

'I think I might go and have my shower,' Charlotte whispered into her mum's hair that covered her face.

'Good idea. How long have I got now?'

Charlotte pulled away and looked at the clock, doing the mental calculation that on any ordinary day would be easy, but this was not an ordinary day.

'Erm, we are being collected at two and it's now six-thirty. So, seven and a half hours.'

As Charlotte closed the study door behind her, Freya sat and took the pen in her hand.

Brewster gingerly crept into the room. With his back arched, legs stretched and tail up, he looked as elegant as ever. He glanced at her quite dismissively and hopped up on to the sofa, curling into a soft circle, with his pretty head resting on his tail and paws. He blinked once, twice, and sighed in the way that cats sometimes do.

Freya envied the deep and restful sleep that engulfed him, pulling her long hair into a ponytail and folding it over, securing it high in a messy knot. Tendrils escaped instantly, falling over her blotchy skin and red-rimmed eyes. She plucked a tissue and blew her nose before beginning to write.

> *Brewster has just arrived. You know how he pulls that snooty face, as if we all need reminding that he's the boss, we work for him and have disappointed him in some way? He did that and is now curled up on the sofa, sleeping. Do you remember when we first got him? He was so tiny and you just couldn't leave him alone. He was your baby, wasn't he? Daddy said he had to be shut in the kitchen at night so he could go out hunting if the fancy took him, but he loved nothing more than to be on your bed, curled up in the warmth, next to you.*

> *I used to listen to you sometimes. I'd stand outside the door and hear you chatting to him.*

Freya stopped writing and looked out of the window, thinking of the day she was called in to school, the first time she had heard the word 'dyslexia' bandied about, 'dyspraxia' too, a difficulty with fine and gross motor skills; Lexi's teachers had used the terms so comfortably, saying them every day, writing them on various tick sheets and reports, as a catch-all for all sorts. But for her, it had felt like a physical blow.

The thin man with the double-breasted suit, close-cropped beard and yellowing teeth, who came quarterly to assess any stragglers, kids who lurked at the back of the pack, was keen to talk about percentiles and to show her Venn diagrams that might in some way help her understand. And they did to a point. He played back a recording of her sweet girl burbling with excitement about her day spent on a boat.

Freya smiled, picturing that very day in Florida, when they had all trundled back to her brother's with sea salt–scorched skin, wobbly sea legs and faces that ached from laughing. Hugh had let Lexi skipper, revving the engine and cutting through the water in wide arcs that gave her mastery over the wind and sea, while she shouted at any other vessels, 'We are on a boat!' lest anyone should be in any doubt.

The tape was hypnotic, Lexi's babyish seven-year-old voice babbling with such energy about the whirr of the engine, the seagulls that had cried over her head circling the boat, and how the land had got further and further away until they were floating in the middle of the world like an island, and how it had made her feel a bit worried, as there were no other people around and she didn't know their destination, but she didn't tell anyone this, and she was mainly excited, as she got to steer the boat and then jump into the sea.

Freya had smiled at him, proud; Lexi had used the word 'destination' and hadn't taken a breath, desperate to tell him more. The thin man had then asked her to write down what she had said, to tell her story on the paper. 'No need to change a thing, it's a good story,' he encouraged.

He had then stopped the tape and handed Freya a notebook. She flicked open the blank pages and there in the middle two, where the staples lurked, Lexi had written three words that filled the space. Each letter was approximately three inches in height and spidered over the lines.

'It took her an hour,' he added, as if to emphasise the disconnect between her verbal and written acuity.

Me teh boot.

Freya continued to write.

Me teh boot.

That's what you'd put, Lex. Do you remember? He asked you what it said and he told me you blushed and kicked at the desk, angry and embarrassed at the same time.

'Me on the boat,' you replied, 'with my family, in the sea, and it was a really lovely day.'

I knew then that life would throw up challenges for you. I also knew that you were incredible, and I couldn't begin to imagine what it must feel like, having all those words and ideas fizzing in your mind and not being able to get them down on paper. You described it once as like being the only person in a very busy, noisy place who doesn't speak the language. That stuck with me, and all I ever wanted to do was be your translator, help you find your way.

And you were right, darling: it was a really lovely day.

FIVE

The room was bright, austere, functional and a little on the chilly side. A child's photograph sat on the desk, a little boy in denim dungarees with a pudding bowl haircut. He beamed at the lens, his snub nose wrinkled. He was cute as a button.

'I'm going to need to measure and weigh you today, Lexi.' Dr Morris spoke with authority, tapping into her keyboard as she did so. She was smartly dressed in a navy wool frock beneath her white medic's coat. 'I know that the idea of that might be scary.'

Freya turned to look at her daughter, who had shrunk back in the plastic chair. Her chest heaved and her eyes were wide. She looked terrified.

'It's okay, darling.' She tried to calm her, alarmed by her child's reaction to the seemingly innocuous request.

Lexi shook her head.

'I . . . I can't.' Her eyes darted towards her mum.

Dr Morris tucked her short, neat geometric haircut behind her ear. Leaning forward in her chair, she spoke directly to the scared teenager. 'How often do you weigh yourself, Lexi?'

'She doesn't, really; we don't have scales in the house. I've never seen the need,' Freya interjected. She was not a vain woman, typical of those who are blessed with good genes and an easy grace. Far more important to her than her weight was that she felt good, and she usually did.

The doctor nodded, ignoring her in part. 'Is it because you don't want your mum to know what you weigh, or because you don't want to know?'

'Both.' The one-word response was barely audible.

'I understand that. And I also understand how much courage it took for you to come here today and to open up to your parents. It's brilliant, Lexi, it really is, but it's only the first step. I give you my word that I will always be open with you and we shall go at your pace. I am going to ask you to trust me. How does that sound? Do you think you can trust me?' She was firm, yet friendly.

Lexi nodded.

'That's great.' She smiled her encouragement. 'The starting point to manage your situation is for me to know your weight. It's a marker, the foundation, and I can't go very far without it because we'd have nothing to build on. I need you to get on the scales.'

Dr Morris stood and walked over to the scales in the corner. They were high-tech: a tall white column, a weighing scale with a black rubberised non-slip footplate and a long T-shaped bar with a double LCD display on top, one for weight and one for BMI. There was a smaller keypad for personal data to be entered.

'Take off your shoes and your hoodie, please, Lexi, and any other bulky items, and remove any objects that might be in your pockets or anywhere else.'

Freya looked at the doctor. It was a very strange thing to say. What did she think Lexi had secreted about her person? She gave a small cough, keeping her word to intervene in proceedings as little as possible and to stay calm.

She watched as her little girl pulled off her trainers; there was the unmistakable clink of coins. Lexi blushed and hurriedly pushed them under the chair; ironically, from where Freya sat, this gave her a clearer view inside. She stared at the glint of metal, quite thrown by the sight of the two-pound coins that sat side by side, lining the inside of her shoes. Lexi glanced at her mum, aware that she had seen and grateful that she chose not to comment.

Slowly she slipped her arms from her hoodie and pulled it over her head; the front pocket sagged with her phone, iPod and purse. Freya considered that the items were too obviously placed to have been hidden. But maybe Lexi thought no one would notice? Freya dismissed the thought.

With one arm anchored to her side by the other, Lexi walked slowly across the shiny linoleum floor as if she were walking to the gallows. Her hesitant steps were painful to watch.

'Come and stand against the wall, here.' The doctor spoke in a matter-of-fact tone as she pointed to a metal-bar height chart fixed to the wall, with a sliding metal triangle that sat on top of the head to give the most accurate measurement, making swift work of bouffant hairdos. Lexi did as she was told. Her expression was excruciating.

Freya could hardly bear to watch. She distracted herself by thinking of what to make for lunch. Something she could tempt Lexi with. She pictured fish tacos, one of Lexi's favourites. Deciding on seared, blackened tuna fillets, with a sour-cream-and-chive dressing, served on deep-fried tacos with crispy shredded lettuce and grated beetroot – maybe she'd add a dash of wasabi in the dressing – and of course a quarter of lime left on the side. In her mind, the end result looked fresh, bright and Instagram-worthy; surely her daughter wouldn't be able to resist?

The sudden jolt of fear at the prospect of preparing food and then sitting at the table with Lexi sent guilt swimming into her veins. Instead, she turned her attention back to her child, who raised one foot and then the other, wobbling slightly on the platform that was no higher than three inches from the floor.

'Nearly done. You are doing great.'

Dr Morris punched a few of the buttons and they beeped accordingly. A single long beep signalled the end to her child's immediate discomfort. The doctor made a note with a ballpoint on to a Post-it note, squinting and double-checking both digital readings.

'You can pop your clothes back on, Lexi. That was really well done.' She screwed up her face in a genuine smile of warmth. Freya liked her even more.

'Okay!' the doctor announced, with such energy that it sounded like a beginning, and that was all Freya wanted, the beginning of the end of this situation.

She transferred the numbers from her Post-it note into her computer and sat back, waiting for Lexi to pop her hoodie back on and to slip her slender feet into her coin-filled shoes. The chink of coin against coin was evident, but Dr Morris didn't mention it. She did, however, momentarily catch Freya's eye. There was a split second of understanding, woman to woman, mother to mother.

Lexi, now with her clothes and shoes, fully restored, sat back in the chair next to her mother.

'Right, can you see this, Lexi? Come closer if you can't.'

She pointed to an image on her computer screen of a chart. It was a mass of tiny squares, filled with numbers, sitting on a vertical and horizontal axis. The whole chart was then shaded in four colours sitting inside of four arcs: green, yellow, amber and red. Lexi shifted forward in her chair and nodded. She could see it perfectly.

'This is a chart to show BMI, or body mass index. I'm not going to confuzzle you with numbers or the science behind it right now, but by weighing and measuring you today, I can tell you that you are sitting here on the chart.'

Freya concentrated as the doctor placed the tip of her pencil in the bottom left-hand corner.

'You are five foot six and weigh a shade under six stone, three pounds, or eighty-seven pounds. Your BMI is fourteen point two and that puts you in the danger zone, Lexi. That's why it's red. Red for danger.'

Freya was aware that she had gasped. *Eighty-seven pounds . . .* she repeated the figure in her head.

The doctor continued, her voice a little echoey. 'There can be certain health issues associated with such a low BMI. I saw on your notes that you have started your periods; are you still menstruating?'

Lexi shook her head and again glanced at her mum.

'I didn't know that,' Freya whispered.

Again she remembered her confident tone when addressing Miss Burke: *I have a great relationship with both of my daughters. I know them better than anyone and I think I might have noticed . . . Noticed what, Freya?* She silently asked the question. *You didn't notice anything!*

She was only vaguely aware of the conversation between the kindly doctor and her child.

'So, we will put your care plan in place, Lexi. I will give Mum some nutrition information, advice on protein shakes and some food-log sheets and we need to get your calorie intake up, to get you from here' – again she pointed at the red – 'and into here!' She tapped the amber. 'Just baby steps that are manageable. How does that sound?'

Lexi nodded, which was good enough for Dr Morris.

'Great!' The doctor spoke with more enthusiasm than Freya felt.

'When is a good time for me to call you, Mrs Braithwaite, so we can organise our next appointments? Is this afternoon okay, about half-two?' Again, she held her gaze a fraction longer than was necessary.

It was Freya's turn to nod.

◆ ◆ ◆

Lockie was pacing the kitchen by the time they trod the stairs; her guess was that he had abandoned his laptop when he heard the key in the front door.

'How did you get on?' He rubbed his palms together, wasting no time on preliminaries.

'She did really well.' Freya nodded towards their daughter, who hovered by the table.

'That's great, Lex! Well done. So what's the plan?' he continued eagerly.

'The plan is to take it slowly, to go through these nutrition sheets and to keep a food log and to get her daily calorie intake up.'

Lockie gave her a knowing look; she knew that he, like her, would be thinking that it sounded great, but in practice however . . .

She gave her false smile that was becoming so convincing, she could only just remember what her real one felt like.

'What can I get you now, darling? A slice of toast?' Lockie tilted his head and held Lexi's eye.

'Sure. No butter.' She looked from one parent to the other. The relief in the room was palpable.

'Would you like a cup of tea?' He pushed his luck.

'Sure. Can I have it upstairs?'

'Yes! Yes, of course!' Lockie grinned.

Freya understood; such was her joy, she would have agreed to her eating it on the roof, anywhere. Anything! Just as long as she started eating and they could start to put this whole horrible business behind them.

Lexi went up to her room and Freya pictured the coin-filled trainers, deciding not to confide this to Lockie. It was hard to explain just how her stomach had caved at the sight of the coins that would add a few measly ounces.

'What did the doctor say?' He was keen to be updated.

Freya rubbed her eyes and exhaled. 'It was painful to watch. The way she walked to the scales, it was torture for her. Her weight is low, eighty-seven pounds, with a very low BMI, and the goal is to get her BMI up. I only took in about half of it. Dr Morris is calling me at two-thirty and I can ask more then. Oh, Lockie!' She watched as he popped the bread in the toaster. 'I feel sick.'

'I know, love. Try not to worry. I'll take it up to her and watch her eat it, not in a pressuring way, but just so we can have a chat, and I'll sit with her for a wee while afterwards, to make sure it stays down.' He was clearly happy to be part of the plan, his tone and actions telling her that he was now far less dismissive of his daughter's illness.

True to his words, Lockie had sat and watched as his daughter slowly, slowly, ate a slice of toast, following each mouthful with a gulp of tea, washing the offensive substance down her throat. He described the feat to Freya, detailing how he had sat on the end of her bed, chatting about his work, an upcoming photo shoot, Brewster's antics, anything to fill the silent void and provide a smokescreen to the real purpose of his presence.

It was a little after two-thirty that the phone in her study rang. Freya was already at the desk, waiting impatiently. She grabbed the phone in anticipation. It was Dr Morris.

'I wanted to chat to you in private.'

'Yes.' Freya held her breath.

'I expect you have lots of questions?'

'I do, but I don't really know where to start.'

She tried to put her thoughts in order; closing her eyes, she let the words escape that had been battering her mouth for days. 'I guess the main thing I want to know is how Lexi got like this, and more important, exactly how do we fix it? I know it's just a blip, but to find those bags and to see her shoes this morning with coins in them—'

'I noticed that too,' Dr Morris interrupted, 'and frankly, it doesn't surprise me, not at all, but it's a case of picking your battles. People with eating disorders are often deceitful; there are a dozen tricks they employ to hide weight loss and non-eating. It can feel a bit like a war, each side making moves and countermoves. And while we are on the subject, you do have scales in your house; you just might not know about them.'

'My daughter is not a liar.' Her tone was a little more assertive than she would have chosen were she not panicking inside.

There was a beat of silence before the doctor continued.

'I don't know Lexi like you do, but I do deal with eating disorders every day of the week, and I find that the person you know and love can be altered, consumed by the disorder. Because of that, they may act in ways that you don't recognise, and deceit is a big part of it. They are ashamed, and very often the last thing they want is intervention, and that means they have to lie.'

Freya chose not to reply. She thought this was a bit extreme; they were, after all, talking about a fifteen-year-old girl.

Dr Morris continued. 'Her weight and her habits are of concern, but she is borderline right now for intervention. We need to see how it goes over the next few weeks.'

'Are you saying she has to get worse before we can get help?'

'Effectively yes, but the ideal is that she doesn't get worse and that we can get her weight up and support her and this is, just as you say, a blip. I would advise that we get Lexi on the waiting list to see a therapist.'

'What kind of therapist?' She was aware she sounded dismissive and tried to counter it.

'There are some very good ones locally. And her home feeding plan, combined with cognitive behavioural therapy, will hopefully get Lexi back to health.'

'I'm not sure what cognitive . . .' Her mind went blank.

'CBT? It's based on the theory that how we think about a situation affects how we act, and, in turn, our actions can affect how we think and feel. The therapist will try to show Lexi how her thoughts might be unhealthy, that she might have unrealistic beliefs about food and diet, to highlight them and break the cycle.'

'Okay.'

Freya didn't like the idea of Lexi going to talk to a complete stranger, and at some level agreed with Lockie that she didn't want her to get entangled in a system that might make it worse. She hoped that the whole thing might be cleared up before it got to that stage. She smiled now at the thought of her eating a slice of toast earlier. It was a start and felt like a win.

'There is always the option of private therapy,' Dr Morris continued. 'Same deal, just without the waiting list. It can be pricey; I just wanted to point that option out to you. But right now the best thing you can concentrate on is getting Lexi to eat. That's the only goal, because when her weight is up and the ship is a little more steady, we can then start to look at the reasons behind her issues and we can think about the future, but right now, as I say, it's all about getting her to put on those pounds. The protein shakes I suggested might help.'

'I don't know why she is doing this.'

She hadn't intended to verbalise the thought.

'She's doing it because she is ill.' The doctor spoke definitively.

'But it doesn't make much sense to me. I work with food and have always tried to set the right example by eating right and staying fit. I cook for them too; healthy food. And I've taught them how to watch their weight, keep strong. It feels like an odd thing to choose. She always loved eating and mealtimes.'

'That's the thing, Mrs Braithwaite: anorexia is not about food; it's about control.'

And just like that, there it was, that word again: 'anorexia'.

It seemed that the more she tried to run away from it, the closer it crept, placing its cold hands on her shoulders until she had no choice but to acknowledge its presence.

The next day, the three books Freya had ordered online were delivered by an indifferent deliveryman who had no idea of just how much the words he handed her in their corrugated cardboard wrapping were anticipated.

Shutting her study door, she ripped the packaging, flopped down on the old sofa and read the titles: *My Journey In and Out of Love with Food*; *Starvation and Me: A Tale of Anorexia*; *Ten Steps to Recovery from Self-Loathing to Self-Love*. She let the books fall open at various pages and let her eyes rove over the painful accounts. She felt a spike of sadness pierce her core at the photographs of emaciated bodies and words that leapt from the page: 'disgust', 'purge' and 'decay'.

Closing the pages, she quietly put the books in the bottom drawer of her desk, deciding it might be a mistake to read these very graphic accounts, written by women who seemed to be suffering to a far greater degree than Lexi. They were scary to look at, and more fear was the last thing she needed.

Lockie knocked and entered.

'Hey, you.' He smiled and put a large mug of peppermint tea on the coaster on her desk.

'Thank you.' She closed her eyes.

'Books any good?' He turned the redundant desk chair to face his wife and sat down.

'I've had a quick scan. They're quite graphic, so I've put them in a drawer. Denial, I know, but it just feels easier to shut it all away and get through today.'

Lockie nodded; this he understood.

'I'm going to cancel my shoot for the end of the week. I think I should be here, even if it's only to bring you tea.' He reached for and handed her the mug, which had cooled a little.

'There's no need to do that, love. Firstly, I don't think one or both of us being here will make any difference, and secondly, we need the money.' She sipped her tea, hoping to dilute the bitter taste of the unpalatable truth.

'Fine.'

'Dr Morris said that Lexi is probably weighing herself, and that we probably have scales in the house we don't know about.'

Lockie knitted his brows. 'Well, there aren't any in the bathrooms or the loo. I haven't seen any.'

'Me neither, but she suggested that Lexi would hide some and lie.' She watched his jaw tense, mirroring the anger she had felt at the suggestion that in any other circumstance would have sent them raging to her defence.

'I clearly don't know enough about this bloody eating disorder, but I do know a bit about human nature, and I believe that trust breeds trust. We know our daughter and we trust her and we should continue to do so. We need to encourage her to be truthful. So let's just ask her about the scales.'

'If you think we should.' She blinked.

'I do.'

Lockie heaped brown rice on to his plate and a good helping of spicy roasted vegetables, including butternut squash, onions and carrots, along with a mint and yoghurt raita on the side. Charlotte followed suit, taking the serving spoon from her dad and dipping it into the steaming fare before positioning it on her plate, just so.

Freya stood and reached for Lexi's plate. She felt hopeful, supremely confident that this was all that it would take, a few healthy meals to ease her back into eating.

'What can I get you, darling?'

She avoided looking at her daughter, concentrating instead on the bowls of food, faking that this was simply any other evening with any other meal waiting to be served. Ignoring the quake in her stomach and the tremor to her hand, and with a quick shake of her head, the image of the knotted carrier bags secreted under the bed were wiped from her mind.

'Erm . . .' Lexi stared at the food on the table as if the decision were too great, her complexion wan. She looked a little clammy. Her deterioration had been steady; smaller portions and a certain awkwardness at eating in front of others now manifested itself as this total dislike of having to eat at all.

'How about a little of each?'

Freya didn't wait for a reply, but instead scooped no more than a tablespoon of rice and the same of vegetable tagine on to her daughter's plate. It looked appetising, bright and not over-plentiful.

'Ooh, this looks lovely.' Freya smacked her lips together in the way she used to when the kids were little and she could encourage them to eat by expressing desire or envy for whatever she was trying to get them to munch: *Oooh, mashed potato, my favourite! Quick! You'd better eat it all up or Mummy will!*

'How are rehearsals coming along, Charlotte?' she asked, consciously trying to switch focus and involve her other child as she set the plate in front of Lexi and proceeded to serve her own food.

'It's going okay.' Charlotte spoke between mouthfuls. 'Except Mr Gordon's being a right pain. He reckons we need another three or four full rehearsals and we're running out of time. Some people have exams, practicals and things, and so we can't all get together that often.

I think he's just panicking.' Her eyes darted to her sister, who had yet to start eating.

'The performances are always polished and perfect and I'm sure this will be no different. How is it, Lockie?' she asked her husband with a false brightness that seemed to stun him slightly.

'It's good.' He nodded, reloading his fork.

The sound of Lexi picking up her cutlery was a sweet note that rang out around the room.

Charlotte glanced at her little sister. 'I was thinking, Lex, if you want to bring Toby along then of course ask him. I shouldn't have gone off at you like I did. I was feeling nervous about the concert and was stressed because I couldn't find my straighteners and took it out on you. I'm sorry.'

'It's okay.' Lexi smiled.

Freya exchanged a look with her husband, both lit from within by pride at their eldest girl's lovely, conciliatory gesture at a time when it was needed, and the sweet interaction between the two people they loved the most. It was a moment that brought a lump to her throat in her heightened emotional state; she coughed and heaped her supper on to her fork.

Lexi swallowed her mouthful and then another, smaller bite. She then toyed with the food on her plate.

'Keep going, darling, you are doing really well!' Freya offered the words of encouragement.

It was the sound that first alerted her. Freya was savouring her mouthful when Lexi's head fell forward and a revolting gagging sound came from her mouth. Charlotte, sitting opposite, scooted her chair back from the table, just as Lockie jumped up and put his arm around his daughter, who instantly pushed him away.

'Is she choking?' she screamed.

'No!' Lexi managed, with her arm outstretched.

Her body seemed to convulse as she gagged and retched, her head bent over, her hair falling over her face and her feet planted firmly on the floor.

'What is it, Lexi? What's wrong?' Freya fired off, as she stood behind her. She caught Lockie's eye and looked away. 'Can I get you a glass of water?'

It was a pathetic offering in lieu of a more constructive thought; as ever, her instinct was to do something.

Lexi sat with her shoulders rounded. Every heave left her body like a ripple of revulsion that started in her gut and continued until it found her mouth, coming to the surface and ending with the translucent, grey-green goo that she spat on to the floor. It was only as the gagging stopped that she found her strength and left the table, running up the stairs as if desperate to escape.

The three remaining family members looked from one to the other, hoping that one of them might provide insight. Lexi had left the room, but the shadow of her actions cloaked them, burying joy and normality under a dark cloud of tension and confusion.

The food cooled on the table, but no one had the confidence or inclination to resume eating. This horrible disruption and fear of food was grabbing territory; not satisfied with getting its claws into Lexi, the consequences were now affecting them all.

Freya pictured anorexia as a giant bird that had her child in its talons and whilst the rest of them were free of its grasp, they were still exhausted and fearful, jumping high to hold on to her and shielding themselves from the beat and brush of its giant wings.

Lockie grabbed his waxed jacket from the back of the chair.

'Where are you going?' Her tone, a little accusatory, betrayed her irritation that he was leaving.

'Out.'

'Do you think we should check on her or give her some space? I don't know what to do!'

He opened his mouth to speak as he zipped up his jacket, but closed it again, as if changing his mind.

'I need some fresh air.'

'What do you mean, you need fresh air?' Freya stared at him.

'I mean I can't cope right now with the crushing disappointment. We think we are making progress and then, bang, back to this!' He indicated the mess on the floor. 'And to watch you pandering to her, offering to get a drink of water . . .' He sighed.

'What am I supposed to do? Yell? That's about as useful as running out,' she retorted.

'I just need a bit of space.'

And with that he was gone.

'I'd let her calm down, Mum, and go up in a bit,' Charlotte offered, before padding up to her room, where Freya knew she would call Tara and Milly and they would throw a virtual arm around her and wrap her in their love and understanding, making her feel special, taking the sting out of the event, analysing and rationalising, which strangely would provide comfort when the time came for lights out and sleep.

She looked at the serving bowl of food, spoiling in the middle of the table, the abandoned plates and the shiny pool on the floor in front of the chair that Lexi had recently vacated. And she wished, just for a second, that she too could run out, leave the house or, at the very least, go and lie on her bed and harvest the sympathy of her friends, who would tell her that it was all going to be okay.

Instead, she cleared the table, stacked the dishwasher, mopped the wooden floor and headed upstairs to talk to Lexi.

Her daughter was shivering under the duvet.

'Let's see if your radiator's on,' she said as she bent down, peering at the metal knuckle on the end of the pipe, trying to figure out which way was off and which on; it was tricky to see clearly without her glasses. 'I'll get Dad to check it's on when he gets back.'

'Where's he gone?' Lexi peered out from the edge of the cream-and-blue tartan duvet cover.

'Just for a walk.'

'Is he angry with me?'

'No, Lexi. We are not angry with you, just very worried about you. And I'm nervous of doing the wrong thing and worried about not doing the best thing to help you, because I don't know what those things are. It feels like a very tricky puzzle.'

'I'm sorry.' Pulling her knees up under the cover, Lexi laid her head on her folded arms and cried.

'I don't want you to be sorry; I just want you to tell me how to get you to eat. Because you have to eat, Lexi; that is non-negotiable.' Freya sat on the edge of the bed. 'Don't cry, darling, please don't cry.'

She rubbed her child's thin back and ran her fingers through her hair. As she removed her hand, she was horrified to see several strands entwined about her fingers. Surreptitiously she curled her fingers and ran them over her palm, twisting the long hair into a knot and placing it in the pocket of her jeans.

'What happened at the dinner table? You seemed to be doing well.'

'I could only manage a little bit.' Lexi lifted her head, her voice warbling as if they were in the middle of winter.

'What changed?'

She swallowed and tucked her hair behind her ears. 'It was the thought of it being in my stomach.'

In an almost involuntary motion, Lexi bared her teeth and her skin seemed to jump. She shook her head as she continued. It was a strange animal reaction that sent a bolt of fear through Freya.

'I don't want anything in my stomach, Mum. Even the thought of it makes me sick. I can't help it.' Lexi rubbed the tops of her arms.

Freya jumped up and left the room, returning swiftly with the pale-pink mohair blanket that lived on the arm of her floppy old sofa in the study. She shook it out, ignoring the dust and loose fluff that rose into the air and fell like soft drops of rain. Folding it in half, she placed it over her child's shoulders like a shawl.

Lexi gripped the sides together under her chin, rubbing her face against the soft fabric.

'You look like Brewster when he snuggles up to something soft.' She smiled, stroking her daughter's leg over the duvet. 'So it was just the thought of eating that food that made you retch?'

It wasn't easy to resume the topic, but she knew that if she was ever going to understand this situation, it was vital that she did just that.

Lexi nodded.

'But you ate the toast Dad made you yesterday afternoon,' she thought aloud, trying to figure what had worked about that food, but not hers. Her eyes were drawn to the mug, still sitting on the windowsill.

Call it instinct, but Freya walked over and lifted the mug. It was half full of tea, but that wasn't what caused her stomach to shrink around her bowel. Sitting on top was a mass of bread, chewed toast, expertly spat into the liquid. Dr Morris's words rang loudly in her ears, *People with eating disorders are often deceitful; there are a dozen tricks they employ to hide weight loss and non-eating.*

'You didn't eat it?' She stared at her child, who shrank back against the headboard.

'I did, I . . .' Lexi stared at the mug in her mum's hand.

'Do you have any scales, Lexi? Do you have scales hidden somewhere that you use to weigh yourself?'

The girl shook her head, as her tears fell. 'No!'

'And you did eat the toast?' she pushed.

'Yes! I told you!' Lexi beat the duvet with her fist.

'This munched-up toast that I am looking at with my own eyes, you did eat it?' She held the mug out towards her child, daring her to dispute the evidence.

'Yes! I did!' she shouted. 'I just . . .'

'No, you didn't! It's here, in this mug, you spat it out!' Freya again tipped the mug to show her little girl the contents.

'Mum, please, I . . .' Her mouth flapped, as she looked from side to side. Her thoughts and lies couldn't come fast enough.

'Do you have weighing scales hidden, Lexi?' She kept her tone firm.

'No! I don't, I don't have any scales!'

'And you did eat the toast?'

'Yes! I did!' she shouted again.

'But you didn't, Lex, it's here. And I think you have scales hidden. Where are they?' It was Freya's turn to shout.

'In my wardrobe!' Lexi yelled, immediately crawling forward until she was kneeling on top of the duvet. The blanket lay across her back like a cape. 'But please, please don't take them, Mum! Please don't. I need them.' Lexi sobbed.

'Why do you need them?' Freya struggled to keep her own tears in check.

'To check my fat! To check I'm not getting fatter. I need to keep checking. I don't want to be fat! I don't want to be disgusting!'

Freya put the mug back on the windowsill and fell forward on to the bed, taking her little girl in her arms, rocking her gently, until her body stopped trembling and her tears subsided.

'Don't cry, Lexi,' she whispered.

'Please don't take them, Mum.'

She sounded petrified at the prospect. Freya looked towards the wardrobe door where the object of obsession was secreted.

'I won't.'

Lexi's body seemed to melt against hers in complete relief. With her arms curled in against her chest, she snuggled against her mother, as her breathing slowed and her tears dried. It was in this calmer environment that Lexi whispered, 'Thank you, Mummy.'

Freya kissed her scalp and held her tightly, hating how much her child relished the stay of execution.

Lockie's key in the front door roused her. Curled on the sofa in the den overlooking the garden, she had been lost in a daydream, staring at the Rendletons' kitchen window, lit by lamplight. She wondered how they both were, picturing Mrs Rendleton's gloved hand gripping her husband's arm, seeking solace, trusting the man to keep her afloat in a choppy, hostile sea of confusion.

'People are so fragile,' she spoke aloud.

'Who are you talking to?' Lockie threw his keys into the bowl and slipped his arms from his jacket, shrugging it off and laying it on the nearest chair.

'Myself.' She smiled.

'I went to the pub,' he announced, as if quickly confessing helped lessen any guilt associated with the event.

'Good for you. See anyone interesting?'

He shook his head. 'Couple of the dads from swimming were at the bar, but I just waved and found a quiet spot with my pint. I'm not really in the mood for small talk. I can only think about Lex, and there's a danger of pinning down a complete stranger and telling them every last detail of what's going on.'

'Like you used to when they were little,' she reminded him. 'I'd catch you in shops or in the street saying, "And then she took three steps and is already saying 'mumma', 'dadda', 'cat' . . ." They'd stare at you, bored stupid, but you carried on regardless, giving them all the details, as if no one had ever owned a toddler before.' She smiled at the memory of that simpler time.

Lockie sat next to her and twisted until his head lay on her lap and his feet hung over the arm of the chair. She ran her hand through his thick shoulder-length hair.

'I think Lexi's losing hair.' She pictured the little clump nestling in her jeans pocket.

Lockie closed his eyes, as if to spare himself the image.

'I've decided to take control, Lockie,' she continued. 'I need to get a grip, get over the shock of what's happening and put a plan in place. I agree with Dr Morris that the most important thing is getting her weight up, but I think it's also good for Lexi and us if we understand it a little more. I want to pay for her to see a therapist. If we have to wait it might be an age and I think we need help sooner rather than later.'

'How much will it cost?'

She knew that it was a worry about affordability and not a lack of concern that prompted his first question.

'I'm not sure. Dr Morris said it was pricey.'

'I'll ask Mum. I know she won't mind, and if you think it will help.'

'I don't know anything, but I think we have to try, don't we? Tomorrow we shall start with the protein shakes and I've decided to take her shopping with me, let her pick out things she might want to eat. Help us to help her.'

Lockie eased himself up and swung his legs around until he was sitting next to her. 'I've got to be honest, Freya. This is exactly what I was afraid of.' He ran his fingers through his hair. She smelled the beer fumes.

'What?'

'This whole pandering to her every wish when it comes to food. You taking her shopping, instead of saying "Just bloody eat this!"'

'I wish it were that simple.'

'Maybe it is!' He raised his palms. 'Maybe that's just the point. We have to stand up to her and tell her no, we are not going to let this spiral out of control. Like I did yesterday. I'm not saying I have all the answers, but I sat on that bed and she knew I wasn't going anywhere until she'd eaten that toast and she did. She ate every bit because I didn't let her get away with it.'

Freya stood.

'You think you know what's best, Lockie, but you don't – neither of us do, because this is all new. But at least I realise we are walking a tightrope across a ravine and I will do all I can to keep things steady.' Walking forward, she grabbed the mug from the draining board, tipping the contents into a shallow pasta bowl before slamming it down on the table.

'Come and look at this.' She stood with her arms folded.

'What is it?' He was reluctant to leave the comfy spot.

'Just come and look!'

He walked slowly from the den.

'What's that?' He wrinkled his nose at the dark, oily tea with the tiny sludge mountain that sat in its midst.

'That, Lockie, is the toast that you confidently watched your daughter eat, washing each mouthful down with a sip of tea. Only she wasn't; she was spitting it back into the cup.'

'That's revolting.' He stared at his wife, his tone incredulous. 'I can't believe she lied to me!'

Freya gripped the back of the chair. 'Yes she did and you are right, it's revolting and upsetting and deceitful, which is why we have to take extra care that she doesn't jump. We have to do whatever it takes!'

Her tears coursed down her cheeks unbidden.

Lockie walked forward and took her in his arms. 'I'm sorry I went out. I felt like I was suffocating.'

She nodded against him. 'I know that feeling.'

'Did you ask her about the scales?'

'Not at first, it felt like another pressure. I was afraid to. But eventually yes, and she went nuts! She was shouting at me, but confessed that she has some hidden in her wardrobe. I told her she could keep them because I was too scared to take them away. She was so relieved; I honestly don't know what she would have done if I'd taken them.'

Lockie held her at arm's length. 'Could you ever have imagined a situation where you were afraid to have a conversation with our little Lexi?'

Freya hung her head forward, until her chin was on her chest, as her tears fell again.

Seven hours . . .

'I've just thought of something I'd like to put.' Charlotte poked her head around the door.

'Oh.' Freya laid the pen down. 'I guess I could go and have my bath; how long have I got?' She stood, twisting her aching neck to the left and right.

'Seven hours, Mum,' came the whispered reply.

Both were thinking that time was going far too fast for comfort. Freya felt a jolt of fear as she thought ahead.

'Oh God, Charlotte!' She placed her hand over her face and tried to breathe, tried to stay upright.

Her daughter held her. 'Shh. It's okay. Keep breathing and go and have your bath. And I'll be right here.'

She nodded, as the cat jumped up and left the room, a little perturbed that his sleep had been disturbed. Freya followed him, closing the study door behind her.

Charlotte sat at the chair that was still warm with the memory of her mother and smiled at the idea that people no longer present could leave such an imprint, a shadow, a reminder. It was a good thing.

She picked up the pen.

I don't know why I am thinking about this, but do you remember that weekend when you were about ten and we decided it would be a fun thing to tie our socks together and walk everywhere joined at the toes? We put on our longest socks, pulled them down and knotted them together. We got Dad to pull the fabric doubly tight and off we set! Circumnavigating the kitchen table, holding on to each other's forearms, like very stiff dancers, and then going up and down the stairs. We even climbed in and out of the bathtub. How we roared!

One of us walking backwards, or scooting together, side by side, usually out of time so we both stumbled, falling headlong into doors and bed frames. It didn't stop us, did it? It was the best game ever. And at suppertime, we couldn't figure out how to sit opposite each other without undoing our socks, which would have meant, as we agreed, the end of the game. Dad came to the rescue. He moved the chairs out from the table and got us to sit underneath it facing each other and then wriggle backwards, until our bums were on the seats and our legs and feet were suspended beneath, like a sock bridge. It wasn't comfortable, but did we care? Not a jot. I could hardly eat for laughing and Mum and Dad were laughing too at how bonkers we must have seemed. That was one of my very best days, Lexi, just you and me and a pair of long socks. Brilliant. I'd like that day again.

I'm not sure how I'm going to get through the day. Perhaps I should be like Granny at Christmas and hit the booze. (And now I'm smiling again, picturing you judging me. Little Lexi Goody-two-shoes.) You know, when she keeps topping up her glass of Baileys until the bottle is empty (don't worry, I won't be doing that!) and then sits snoring in the corner. It's one of Dad's favourite things, isn't it? I can picture him chuckling and winking at us the next morning when she claims to have no clue as to why she's got a headache and hunts around for the bottle of Baileys that has miraculously disappeared!

Happy times.

I used to get really annoyed when we were little and everyone bought us the same presents, even Uncle Hugh and Granny and Pappy, as if it were too much effort to think of two gifts for two girls of different ages. The only person who went to real effort to buy us cool and unusual things was Marcia; she once got me a make-up palette, I thought it was ace! And for birthdays, she picked out books for us that we actually liked. Yours were always audiobooks, remember? Good old Marcia.

If I look back at the photos of when we're small, we're in the same pyjamas with the same dressing gowns, holding the same toys. It drove me crackers, until a few years ago, when I thought it would be nice to have the same as you, be the same as you, but I guess that would have been a bit odd. We'd look like those one-hundred-year-old twins you see in National Geographic who still sleep in bunk beds and plan their identical outfits the night before, creepy!

I'm a mess, Lex. I'm a total mess . . .

SIX

The upbeat pop song, as selected by Charlotte, provided the background music to their journey. The traffic lights turned green. Not that it mattered. Sitting bumper to bumper along the London Road, they weren't going anywhere. An impatient finger, too far back in the traffic to see the gridlock, pressed the horn anyway, as if this irritating noise might somehow have the power to make the cars, lorries and buses disappear and propel her forward.

Freya felt her stomach clench and her jaw tighten at the sound.

'Think I might be late at this rate.' Charlotte pulled out her phone and started texting. 'I'll get Mills to say I'm on my way. That should buy me a few minutes.'

'I'm sure they'll understand. You can't help the traffic, love,' Freya soothed.

'True, but I can help leaving fifteen minutes later than usual.' She kept her eyes on her phone screen.

'I'm sorry. I just wanted to check on Lexi and make sure Dad was going to wait with her until I got back.' She looked to the left at her beautiful girl.

''S'okay. I know it's all a bit difficult at the moment.'

Freya gave a small laugh at the understatement. There was a second or two of silence, while both contemplated the day ahead.

'Do you think it's my fault?' The question came out of the blue.

'What?' She twisted to face her daughter.

'Lexi. And not eating and stuff?' Charlotte kept her eyes averted, staring at the parade of shops outside of the passenger window, where a man with a shaved head and a large hoop earring bent low and lifted the graffitied metal shutter, rolling it away and preparing to start his day.

'No! Of course not, Charlotte! No, you must never think that.' She placed her hand on her child's shoulder.

'I feel really guilty.'

'Why do you?' Freya was keen to understand.

'Because . . . because I've been mean to her about Toby and I've been mean to her about other stuff, but I kind of thought it was a joke, Mum, just how we were, taking the mick out of each other; we've always done it.'

Charlotte shrugged and flipped the phone in her palm, glad of the distraction.

'You two love each other; don't ever doubt that. And being sisters is sometimes tricky, especially when you are quite close in age. Being the oldest means you break boundaries she is yet to experience and she gets away with things because she's the youngest. It's not always easy, darling, but you mustn't feel guilty or let what's happening to her shade *your* life. Does that make sense?'

'Kind of.'

Freya took a deep breath. 'I can't fully explain what Lexi is going through because I don't really understand it myself. I think it's *partly* to do with what goes on around her, but mainly it's because of what is going on inside her head.'

Charlotte's body shook as she cried.

'Don't cry, darling! Please don't cry.'

Freya leant in and held her in her arms, struggling to reach her, as she negotiated their seat belts.

The lights had completed a cycle and were now back to green. The car behind beeped and this time she had no recourse other than to disentangle herself from the embrace and shove the car into gear.

Freya pulled up outside school, as other late arrivals in various states of dress made their way hurriedly across the concourse.

'I'd better go, Mum.' Charlotte grabbed her bag from the footwell and reached for the door handle.

'It'll all be okay, you know.' Freya smiled at her daughter, hoping she was telling her the truth.

Charlotte looked at her earnestly. 'I know, but the trouble is, I think what's happening to Lexi is already shading my life, shading all of our lives, and I don't know what to do about that.'

Freya watched her pick up speed and jog into the building, feeling nothing but guilt at her daughter's words which she knew to be the truth.

By the time she got home, Lockie had his camera bag packed and was ready to leave for work. He was pacing the kitchen impatiently.

'I'm so sorry. The traffic was a nightmare! Charlotte was a bit upset as well. Oh God, Lockie, I didn't know worry could be this exhausting.'

He looked at her and sighed, as if he really couldn't take one more bit of negativity. She decided not to expand on the subject.

'I hope you haven't missed your train?' she offered.

He looked at his watch, as if he hadn't been doing so every few seconds for the last ten minutes. 'I should be fine if I leave right now.' He slung the strap of his bulky bag over his shoulder and kissed her on the cheek. 'I'll see you tonight.'

'Lockie?' she called, as he made it into the hallway.

He gripped the frame and popped his head back through the door. 'What?' His impatient tone verged on aggressive. 'I cannot miss this train!'

'What's that?'

She pointed to a flat, square glass object on the table, questioning him calmly, as if unaware of his urgency.

'That, Freya, is Lexi's scale. I have been reading up about this bloody situation, and the very worst thing is for her to have access to a scale, where she can obsess about every ounce lost and gained and use it as a stick to beat herself with or beat us with. I can't talk about it now; I have to go.'

'But I promised her!' She was aware of the nasal tone to her retort.

'Well, I didn't, and in case you hadn't noticed, she has two parents, and what I think counts just as much.' He tapped on the door frame with his wedding ring, like a bell signalling the end of the round, and dashed down the stairs.

Freya scanned the bedroom, unsure whether Lexi was in it, until a slight movement of the duvet revealed where her daughter was hiding. Gently, she peeled back the cover to reveal her tear-stained face, staring vacantly ahead.

'Dad took my scales,' she offered calmly.

'I know.' Freya considered how to proceed without showing dis-loyalty to either of them. It wasn't easy. 'He thinks it might be better for you not to have access to them all the time or to have to hide them away, and he might be right.'

'I want them back,' she croaked.

'What about if we agree that you can weigh yourself with me pres-ent at a certain time each week? We need to do that anyway, to check on your progress and see that you're heading in the right direction.'

'What if I just keep them in this room and promise not to look at them so much?' She leant up on her elbows, trying to bargain, negotiate through her tears.

Freya felt torn. It was hard to resist not only her daughter's pleading expression, but also the idea that Freya didn't want to go back on her word.

'Let me think about it, Lexi. I don't know what the right answer is.' She pulled the duvet over her daughter's shoulders. 'But I do know that today is a brand-new day and we are getting into action. We are going to start your food log and go over the nutrition sheets and we are going to the supermarket together. You can help me, advise me on what you might like to eat, and we can write your eating plan together. And I shall make a few phone calls and see about finding you someone to talk to. Someone who knows how to help.'

Lexi lay back on the pillows and nodded.

'I'll leave you to get ready.'

Freya smiled brightly, the grin slipping the moment she left the room. She decided to look for the positive: Lexi hadn't exactly enthused, but at least she hadn't refused altogether.

'Is it nice to be out in the fresh air?'

Freya smiled as they abandoned the car and went in search of a cart in the supermarket lot. She watched as Lexi unfolded her limbs from the passenger seat, wanting to stare at her large knees in her skinny jeans and the narrow width between the sharp triangle of her shoulder blades or her very strong, square jaw.

She was certain that Lexi had lost weight in the last couple of days, although she was not about to raise that with her child or, God forbid, Lockie.

Earlier, while Freya had written up her shopping list, Lexi had drunk a banana-flavoured protein shake, puncturing the little foil strip on the coated cardboard box and sipping it endlessly through the narrow straw.

It took all of Freya's reserves not to urge her daughter to drink quicker; the time it took was excruciating, but at least her daughter had managed to finish it and had kept it down. Guilt swam in her veins at the irritation she had felt, reminding herself to be patient, just as she would with any other ailment.

Freya had only given the carton one surreptitious shake before popping it into the bin and was delighted to find it was empty. *Two hundred calories: yes!* She saw this and every mouthful consumed as a small win.

'Okay.' She'd straightened the list on the table. 'So you tell me what you might be able to eat and I'll pop it on the list.'

She had almost sung, trying to keep things positive and matter-of-fact.

Her daughter had swallowed, pulled her sleeves over her hands and bitten her bottom lip, as if she found saying the names of foods a challenge, let alone putting them past her lips.

'Maybe yoghurt, but only plain yoghurt.'

Her fingers poked from her sleeve as she toyed with the straw, twisting it between her thumb and forefinger.

Freya had nodded encouragingly as she added the item on to her shopper's jotter.

Lexi continued, her voice quiet. 'And plain, hard crackers, like cream crackers or water biscuits. Clear soup, but not with too much meat in, like maybe chicken-and-corn soup, but not ham and pea or anything like that. And corn not in soup, frozen and not in a tin, and broccoli stalks, but not the flower bits . . .'

The specifics, the finicky requests, were as infuriating as they were ridiculous, but she didn't care. Whatever it took, whatever Lexi wanted, she was determined to get the girl to eat.

If it had been for any other reason that she had ushered her from the table and immediately down the stairs into the car, preventing her from going into the loo, it might have been amusing.

'Right, let's go!'

She pulled the shallow cart from the row in which it sat and, with her head held high, entered the store. Lexi placed her hand on the metal side, whether helping with the navigation or holding on for support, Freya wasn't sure.

Meandering through the fruit and veg displays, tossing lettuce, tomatoes, carrots, broccoli and onions into the trolley, she tried to look indifferent, aloof, like every other shopper, and not reveal the sense of panic that swirled in her gut.

'Are you okay?'

Lexi nodded. 'Shall I go ahead and look at the soup?'

'Yes! That's a great idea!' she enthused, massively encouraged by this sign of commitment.

Striding purposefully up and down the aisles, Freya completed her list and went in search of soup. Lexi was taking an age.

She halted her trolley at the end of the row; unseen, she hovered, blocking the corner and making it harder for people to get around. Not that she noticed; her attention was entirely taken up studying her little girl. She stood back a little so she could watch without being seen.

Lexi stood in front of a large fridge, her legs firmly planted, her hips forward and her posture rigid. In each hand she held a carton of fresh soup towards her face. With a contorted expression, she first studied one label, her eyes roving over the details, her mouth moving, reciting the information. She then switched cartons, staring at the other, trying to compare, mumbling to herself and looking at the picture and then the contents and nutrition information again. Remembering lists and retaining the similar, minute details was very difficult for Lexi.

But that wasn't what upset Freya the most.

She would have found it hard to explain to others just how much her daughter's actions distressed her. It was the intensity: oblivious of anyone else, she agonised and repeated, evaluating to see which might be the best to eat, when her true choice would be neither. Her task was all-consuming, and unlike most health-conscious teens, this was not a choice about whether to eat a doughnut or stick to fruit; she was comparing two remarkably similar cartons of chicken-and-corn soup.

Removing her hand from the cart, Freya placed her flattened palm on her chest, trying to stop the sob that built there and to slow her heart that flipped.

'How are you getting on?'

She walked forward, whispering, trying for nonchalant, as if she had happened upon her child by accident.

'I . . . I don't know if it's better to get one that's lower in sodium or one that has less carbohydrates per hundred grams. I don't know.' Lexi furrowed her brow and looked towards her mum.

'Which do you think you might prefer to eat?' Freya coaxed, applying some simple logic to the situation, despite barking at Lockie for doing the same.

Lexi put both cartons back on the shelf and tucked her palms under her armpits. 'I don't want either. Can we go now?' Lexi almost shouted with a sense of panic.

'Sure. I'll just pay, nearly done.'

'I want to go! Now!' She raised her voice.

'I know and we are leaving soon. I just need to pay,' she soothed.

'Please hurry!' Lexi spoke with urgency.

Freya watched as the girl's eyes darted from person to person, hugging her form and keen to get outside. She loaded the car in silence as quickly as she could. By the time she put the key in the ignition, Lexi was highly agitated.

'I think it's disgusting, all those really fat people buying fatty food, like cheese and cake. They make me feel ill. Choosing to put fat food into their fat mouths. I hate to think about it and I hate to see it. I don't know how they can do it!'

She chewed her nail, biting and spitting out the tiny fragments as she ripped them with her teeth.

'How can they stand to look like that? And they are choosing it. It makes me feel sick!' She placed her hand on her stomach, her breath coming in short bursts.

'Nearly home, Lex.'

In the face of her daughter's odd, angry outburst, it was all she could think to say, while swallowing her own guilt, remembering the time she had pointed out girls at the mall who were wearing shorts that were two sizes too small or raised her eyebrows as a heavy woman asked for a second serving in a restaurant. She recalled how she had commented that rather than eat more, she might instead be better off running around the block. *I didn't mean it!* But the fact was she had meant it, and it was only now in the face of Lexi's illness that she questioned the phrases and observations that tripped from her tongue with ease.

Freya was delighted that Lockie came home late. She had fed Charlotte, Lexi had managed another shake and an apple, and Freya had managed to wolf a couple of slices of toast between chores. A dish of braised pork and pak choi awaited her husband.

'I spoke to Mum. She said she was more than happy to help out with Lexi's therapy bill. Said she'd pay it direct or write us a cheque, whatever was easiest.'

'That's so kind of her. I think I've found a lady. She works out in Harpenden. Her name is Hilary Wainwright. I spoke to her earlier, she sounds great.'

Lockie nodded, still looking less than comfortable with the idea. He sat at the head of the table and lifted his fork. 'Thank you. This looks delicious. Everyone else eaten?'

It saddened her that the common phrase was now so heavy with connotation. She nodded.

'Yes. Just shakes for Lexi, but she's kept them down. Oh, and an apple, I forgot.'

It felt strange that something as ordinary as eating an apple was now the cause for mini celebration.

He ignored her and ladled the tender meat into his mouth.

'I took her shopping with me. It wasn't pleasant. Like torture for her really,' she began.

'Don't you see?' he interrupted her, placing the deep spoon in the bowl. 'We are falling into that trap of pandering to her. It's what I dreaded most, what I tried to guard against.' He sighed.

'No, actually, I don't see. We are *in* this situation. It's not like it *might* happen and we have a window to figure out how to avoid it. It's happening! And if you could have seen her today, studying packets and labels, literally agonising over every choice . . .' She took a second to calm herself. 'It was horrible to watch.'

Neither had heard Lexi tread the stairs, only aware of her presence when she was a few feet from them.

Lockie looked up at his little girl who stood in the doorway, clutching her laptop. She was wearing leggings and a long-sleeved T-shirt and she looked very, very skinny.

'Hi, Dad.' She lifted her hand in a wave.

Freya caught his eye, unaware of how much Lexi had heard.

'How's my girl?' he asked, pushing the bowl away into the middle of the table, as if he'd been discovered.

Freya watched him, wanting to show him that whilst he was quick to point the finger at her, he too acted instinctively to lessen Lexi's discomfort.

'I need to do an assignment for Mrs White. She's sent my work through and I'm a bit stuck.'

'Oh, well, can I help?' He smiled.

Lexi nodded and walked forward. She took the empty chair next to her dad.

'What is it we have to do?' Lockie pulled his glasses from the top of his head and popped them on.

'I have to make out I'm starting a restaurant and think of a name and prepare a menu. It can be any type of restaurant, but we have to think about the balance of the food and stick to a theme.'

Lockie looked first at his wife and then back at his daughter. 'Is this a joke? Is that Mrs White positively bonkers?'

'What do you mean?' Lexi twisted her head to one side to look at her dad quizzically.

Lockie sat back in his chair. 'Here's the thing, Lex. The kind of restaurant you want to eat at would serve fresh air for a starter, or maybe a single kiwi-fruit pip, followed by a light foam of nothingness with half a strawberry for sweet! We'd all have to go to the fish and chip shop on the way home! That is if your mother wasn't with us. She'd much prefer that we picked up sushi and quinoa!'

'That's true, I would actually.' Freya giggled, happy for the change of atmosphere.

Lexi's smile turned to a laugh. 'You're right, Dad, my restaurant would be rubbish!'

'But there would be plenty of water right to wash everything down with,' he carried on.

Lexi giggled and nodded with the beginning of tears in her eyes. 'I know it's weird what I do. But I can't help it.'

The admission caused Freya's tears to pool. *Oh, my little girl . . .*

'Weird? It's not weird! It's positively preposterous, little Lex!' He placed his hand over hers on the tabletop.

'What are you all laughing at?' Charlotte asked, as she entered the kitchen.

'Lexi is thinking of opening a restaurant!' Lockie announced, banging the tabletop loudly.

'Good luck with that!' Charlotte laughed with something close to relief and smiled at her mum.

'And on top of everything else, we need to give it a name!' he roared. 'I'm torn between "Go Eat Somewhere Else" and "Don't Bother!"'

The girls laughed at their dad.

'What about "Seconds? Not Likely!"' Charlotte joined in, tucking her long hair behind her ears as she went to the fridge for juice.

'I know! We can go through some of my recipe books and see if anything jumps out at you, Lex, and we can steal the descriptions for your menu!' Without waiting for a response, Freya jumped up and began poring through her bookshelf, selecting books at random, any with bright covers and appealing dishes of beautifully photographed, appealing food made the cut. And just like that, the Braithwaite family sat around the table, as Lockie reached for the spoon and dipped into his supper bowl and the girls flicked through the glossy pages, talking about and getting lost in descriptions of food.

'Are you okay with this, Lex?' she asked, wary of her previous reactions to food.

'Yes!' Her daughter smiled, as if this was a revelation for her too.

The optimism Freya felt at this interaction was quite overwhelming. It filled her up.

The evening had felt like a reprieve.

As Freya switched off the landing light and closed their bedroom door, Lockie was sitting up in bed, resting against the headboard.

'I'm sorry, Frey.'

'What are you sorry for?' she asked, as she massaged cold cream into her neck and face.

'For thinking I always know best, for not wanting to acknowledge what's going on, for being so shit scared that I want to run away.' He held her gaze. 'I can't stand it. She's my little girl and the thought of her . . .'

Freya pulled the curtains closed and flicked off her bedside lamp. Hopping under the duvet, she shuffled over to his side of the bed and laid her head on his broad chest.

'I understand. I do. And you were amazing with her tonight. She was laughing and that whole discussion was around food! I can't believe it.' She lifted her head and kissed his chin. 'It's made me feel quite hopeful, happy.'

'I know what might make you feel happier,' he growled. 'In fact I think it would make us both feel happier.'

Reaching out, he turned off his bedside lamp before taking his wife in his arms and pulling her down under the duvet.

For the last few weeks, things had been on an even keel. Lexi had put on six pounds, and with this gain Freya and Lockie had lost most of their initial panic. This had a ripple effect; with their lack of tension Charlotte had relaxed, and as the atmosphere of the whole house lifted, Lexi seemed to have more life in her, gravitating towards any hubbub, joining in. Even mealtimes seemed more jovial. Freya no longer approached the twice-daily event with a twist in her gut or the need to scrutinise every morsel that made its way into her daughter's mouth. She did as Lexi had asked, trusted her, and that trust was rewarded with the consumption of food.

They were winning.

For Freya, Lexi's returning to school had been a landmark day, with her restaurant project under her arm and a desire to catch up with Fennella proof of her return to normality. She had watched as her little girl bit her lip and blinked away her fears, treading the steps slowly, without looking back. It took guts.

She was a little concerned about Lexi's return to exercise, running when the fancy took her, but remembered what the doctor had said:

that allowing Lexi to feel comfortable and lead a healthy life was also important. It was yet another delicate balance to be negotiated.

As Freya had driven back to an empty house she had cried tears of relief, finally believing that they were nearly over the blip and overjoyed that Lockie had been right: there were indeed a million miles between not wanting to eat, having a mini meltdown, and a life-changing diagnosis like anorexia.

It was four in the afternoon when Marcia boomed down the phone.

'Darling! I need to run this by you. You've been asked to write an exposé piece on the hidden additives and high salt levels in baby food. What do you think?'

'I think it sounds interesting, scary but interesting.' She decided not to admit to Marcia that at the present time, she wished she had any other job. Having to write about, analyse and compare food for work when her every waking moment was filled with doing just that in regard to Lexi was torturous.

'You're a doll. It doesn't have to be in for a few weeks, so I know you'll leave it till the last minute!' Marcia assumed gleefully. 'How's the family? Lockie still snapping away instead of getting a proper job?' She snorted.

'I'm telling him you said that! You're too funny. He's great, working lots, so happy.' Freya smiled at the thought.

'And the Gorgeous Twins?' Marcia had no children and Freya knew that she genuinely couldn't see what all the fuss was about.

When Charlotte had been tiny, Marcia stared at her, asleep on the sofa, and asked 'What is it she does?' Her expression was one of pure disappointment, as if she'd been given a gift without the batteries, or one which promised so much more in the advert. Freya, whilst understandably miffed by the slight towards her newborn, had laughed. 'She doesn't *do* anything!' This had only served to baffle her agent more.

Marcia was no more enamoured by the baby than she would have been with any other small offspring, like ducklings or guinea pigs.

For all her initial indifference, however, as the girls had grown, so had her love and generosity towards them. Marcia adored her girls; of this Freya was in little doubt.

'They're great!' She smiled across the table at her daughter. It wasn't that she was deliberately trying to deceive Marcia, but rather that she chose not to divulge Lexi's issues, unable to face the hours of dissection and advice offered good-naturedly. If she was being truthful, it felt good that for the seconds she spoke to Marcia, her life felt like it used to, when everything was good.

'So glad to hear it. Give them my love. So this piece . . .' Marcia was keen to get back to business. 'Look at the organic brands too; we need a good cross-section sample. I'm going to whizz you some stats and quotes over, they make for an interesting read. It's a fine line. We don't want to scare parents, but at the same time I think it's only right we debunk the myth that just because something says "organic" or "additive free", we can't instantly assume it's bursting with goodness. How does that sound?'

'Sounds good. I'll get straight on it.'

'We both know that's a lie!' Marcia laughed.

Six hours, thirty minutes . . .

Charlotte sat at the kitchen table and took a deep breath. Her writing meandered across the page at an angle; not that it mattered.

> *I wonder what kind of granny Mum will be? Not that I can think that far ahead at the moment. I can't think about tomorrow. I keep looking at the clock, counting down the hours . . .*

> *But that's not what I want to write! No!*

> *I want to share stories with you. That's the idea.*

> *I'm trying to think of something you don't you know about me? Okay, here it is, the big one.*

> *I'm not a virgin.*

I know — big news, right? I used to think that when I had lost my virginity everyone would be able to tell, that maybe I'd be marked in some way that only other non-virgins could recognise, like we had been initiated into a secret club. But no. I didn't learn a secret signal or sport an identifying stain on my body like a birthmark, nothing like that.

In fact, the whole episode was nothing like anything. Let me explain.

In my head I had always thought it was the biggest deal. I remember Mum saying once that she could tell which of her friends had had sex when she was younger, as they were the ones that stopped talking about it. I get that. But I don't think they stopped talking about it because they were ashamed or because they knew secrets. I think it was because it would have been hard to describe the lack of drama, the let-down. Or maybe that was just what it was like for me.

I know you will want to know who and where.

It was Daniel George, at Tara's house party. I've liked him for ages, obsessed about going out with him — and there we were, in Tara's room, with the chest of drawers pushed across the door. It was what I had dreamed of. We took off our clothes and I realised at that moment that even though I had thought about him for a long time, I didn't know him at all. I wouldn't have recognised his scent or his touch, I knew nothing about him, and that made me feel quite sad.

I loved the idea of him, the stranger. The reality was very different. I didn't like the way he kissed me, didn't like the silence that the whole event was wrapped in.

When I had imagined it, we had laughed and chatted, like they do in a movie, where they bump noses and it's sweet and lovely and he only thinks about me, only focuses on me, only wants me. But this wasn't a movie. It was me and a boy with whom I had nothing in common and who I had never really chatted to and with whom I had sex.

He didn't mention my sheer floral shirt that I agonised over. He didn't care about much. And it wasn't sweet and it wasn't lovely. I did it because I was drunk, or rather the booze fuelled my confidence, allowing me to do what I had thought about on so many nights.

He left the room afterwards and I knew that I wasn't going to dream of him again. He wasn't the person I thought he was and I wasn't the person I thought I was. I was changed.

He gave me a lift home, just as the sun came up, and we didn't speak, not one word on the whole journey.

It made me feel like nothing.

I guess I did have a secret revealed to me and that was this: first-time sex ain't all it's cracked up to be.

I'm hoping the second time might be better. I'm going to wait and do it with someone who will make me laugh and who I can chat to, who will say 'Hey, nice floral shirt, you smell gorgeous!' and who won't leave me shivering in a room, alone and crying.

And I am crying now, as I think about that night all over again.

SEVEN

Lexi visited Hilary twice. Each time, the woman greeted them warmly, initially explaining her modus operandi before ushering Freya to a comfortable sofa with a stack of magazines and a coffee machine that wasn't a patch on her own. The room was a waiting room disguised as a lounge, and it was where she was encouraged to wait while her child sat behind a closed door and spoke to a stranger.

The first time, she had sat with clammy palms and palpitations, wondering what deep, dark secrets Hilary might prise from her daughter's mind, nervous that she was being judged. Had she inadvertently done something wrong? It was with huge relief that she'd seen Hilary smile as they left, telling her that Lexi had done really well.

Lexi herself had offered a beautiful insight: 'I'm a bit like a computer that needs reprogramming; the way I think about food is muddled, and when we have sorted that muddle out, the clearer I will be about it all.'

Freya wanted to turn the car around and go back and kiss Ms Hilary Wainwright. Lexi had not only understood that her thoughts were not the norm, but also that it could and would be fixed! It was a good day.

◆ ◆ ◆

Lexi was hunched over a cookbook, scribbling on to a notepad in her messy handwriting, her tongue poking from the side of her mouth; this task took all of her concentration. With one finger following the lines on the page, she read out loud, struggling with some of the words while making a shopping list of all the ingredients she would need. This was her new thing, a diversion that neither of her parents would have guessed at: cooking.

'Why doesn't cooking food make you feel sick, but the thought of eating it does?' Charlotte asked with refreshing candour.

Lexi had shrugged. 'Don't know. But it's like I can deal with my obsession with food knowing I don't have to eat it, and that makes me feel comfortable.'

Freya was delighted, as not only did it demonstrate a healthy interest in food, but it was also something they could do together.

Over the past few weeks, she had watched her daughter patiently churn out batches of soft-baked chocolate-chip cookies, crumbly frangipane tarts, deep-fried arancini and fancily piped cupcakes, taking her time with each creation, as if only perfection would do. Lexi didn't eat the food she produced, that would be a step too far. But the way she beamed at the praise given freely and sincerely by her dad and sister told Freya that this hobby was nothing but a good thing.

'What's this word, Mum?' She held the book up.

'Spell it for me.' Freya lifted her head from her laptop, where she was starting to explore the world of baby food.

Lexi held the page close to her face. 'P-a-n-k-e-t . . .' She paused. *Panket? Panket?*

Freya was trying to guess ahead; she still found it unsettling that her smart girl chose the almost babyish, soft-letter sounds of *puh* and *tuh* and not the more adult *pee* and *tee*. It was another little reminder of her daily struggle.

'Panket?' she spoke aloud, wondering at the unfamiliar ingredient.

'Hang on, there's more!' Lexi smiled at her mum's confused expression. Again, placing her finger on the word: '. . . t-a. That's it.'

'Sorry, Lex' – she shook her head – 'I'm going to have to read it myself.' Leaning over her child, she squinted at the word 'pancetta'.

'Ah, that's a tricky one: pancetta! The *cuh* is a *ch* sound.'

'Oh, pancetta, of course!' Lexi tapped her own forehead.

They both laughed.

'Can we go shopping to get my ingredients?' she asked brightly.

'What, right now?' Freya looked at the clock, torn between not wanting to dampen her daughter's enthusiasm for the task in hand, but also not that keen on sitting in the traffic as rush hour approached.

'I'm making a Spanishy dish, chicken and spicy sausage, and it's thickened with paella rice and cream.'

'Wow, sounds delicious and expensive!' She sucked air through her teeth.

'I'll cook it tonight and it will be better tomorrow night. We can have it for supper. It feeds six, it says.'

Again she turned her attention to the glossy text.

'Ah, I'm afraid that's written by someone who hasn't met your dad. Come on then, let's go shopping!'

Freya shut down her laptop, reached for her rucksack and car keys and closed the front door behind her.

As she buckled up her seatbelt and prepared to drive off, Mr and Mrs Rendleton sauntered along the street, arm in arm, out strolling around the block in the late-afternoon sunshine. He looked wonderful, as ever; his Crombie coat was buttoned up, his thinning grey hair combed to one side and held in place with shiny pomade.

His wife was similarly well turned out, in black patent shoes and olive-green leather gloves to set off her black coat with its shawl collar. Her usually understated make-up was, however, a little garish, reminiscent of when the girls used to delve into her make-up bag as kids. The hot-pink lipstick had gone a little astray from her lip line, and a ring of kohl, usually subtle, had been drawn with a distracted hand and sat like comic glasses around her eye sockets.

'Hello there, Freya!' Mr Rendleton inclined his head, as was his habit, his mouth hidden behind his bushy grey moustache.

Freya wound down the window and smiled out at him. 'Good afternoon!'

'Only just.' He checked his watch. 'Nearly evening. How are you all?'

'We're good, just off to the supermarket, can I get you anything?'

She didn't make a habit of offering, but when they were in front of her and she was making the journey anyway . . .

'That's very kind, dear, but we are fine, aren't we, Miriam?'

Miriam. She repeated the name in her mind. They had been neighbours for nearly two decades, but Freya had not known her Christian name until now. It was pretty.

The image of them waltzing in their dressing gowns sat behind her eyelids. She smiled at them fondly, as if they now shared a secret.

He nodded, patting his wife's knobbly hand. Just thought we'd get a drop of fresh air, blow the cobwebs out – didn't we, darling?'

He spoke to his wife, who gave an almost imperceptible nod and looked past him, concentrating on something on the opposite side of the street. Mrs Rendleton was unusually silent.

'I . . . I need to get back.' Mrs Rendleton ran her fingers over the brooch at the neck of her blouse. 'I need to get back now. They're delivering my pram; I should be there.' She turned to Freya, her thin lips parted to reveal caramel-coloured teeth. 'It's a Silver Cross. It's navy blue.' She nodded proudly at Freya.

Mr Rendleton patted her hand. 'We'd best be getting back.' He smiled, as if his wife had not made the statement.

Freya watched them trundle down the street.

'Is she a bit loopy, Mum?' Lexi placed her finger in her mouth, chewing on her fingernail.

'That's not a nice word, Lex. I think she's struggling, yes, poor old thing. It might be dementia, I don't know them well enough to get involved, but she seems happy and he clearly adores her. Still sad, though.'

She pulled the car into the traffic.

'Do you think it's easier to go through things if you have someone to look after you like that?' Lexi glanced at the elderly couple as they passed.

'Yes. I do, actually. I think everything is easier if there's someone to share the burden.' She thought of Lockie and how he had cheered her spirits over the last few weeks.

'I don't.' Her voice was barely more than a whisper.

'You don't?'

'No.' Lexi shook her head. 'When things aren't going right for me, I'd like to shut myself away and not have to talk to anyone or see anyone. I'd like to disappear.'

'Oh, Lex! Even me?' She pushed her bottom lip out.

Her daughter held her eye. 'Even you.' Her voice was cool.

The magnitude of Lexi's words and the tone in which they were delivered stabbed her to the core. Freya always assumed that no matter what was going on in her kids' lives or how desperate things became, she would always have a part in it, rationalising that they would need her.

They drove to the supermarket in silence, their bubble of joy quite burst.

The supermarket was busy; queues of shoppers stood in impatient lines that snaked back from the tills down the aisles.

Lexi had posed her question to the grocery assistant with a sense of urgency.

'I'll go look out the back if you like?'

The boy stared at Lexi, his expression hopeful that she'd smile, shake her head with embarrassment and say 'Oh no, not to worry, I don't want to be any bother . . .' – but she didn't. She stood still, seemingly unaware of the chaos all around, the gridlock of carts and baskets full of produce, as rowdy customers shoved and elbowed their way towards the organic avocados and fabulous dining offers. Freya watched as she nodded serenely and murmured, 'Thanks, yes,' with relief, as if the sourcing of fresh tarragon was the most important thing in the world.

Freya had to admit it was a little awkward, but compared to the nervous antics of her child that last fretful time she had been in a supermarket with her, this was entirely preferable.

Lockie and Freya lounged on the sofa in the den as Lexi tightened her apron, stirred the sauce, splashed cream, boned chicken thighs and sliced chorizo. The smell of pancetta crisping with onions in the pan filled the space.

'Someone's busy.' He kissed his wife's head, which lay against his shoulder. 'Smells delicious, Lex!' he called across the open-plan space to the stove.

She ignored him, entirely engrossed with the preparing and cooking of the food. Referring frequently to the recipe, she checked and rechecked the measurements, whizzing around the kitchen like a thing possessed.

The front doorbell rang.

'No rest for the wicked.' Freya swung her legs from her seat.

'It'll be for you, then.' He winked at her.

Freya flicked on the hallway light and trod the stairs to the front door. A cool chill whipped up from the street and she regretted not grabbing her cardigan. She didn't recognise the outline of the stout figure on the other side of the glass until she was upon it.

'Mr Rendleton! Come in, come in!'

She opened the door and stood back. She realised that it had been at least six years since he had last crossed her threshold, in response to a note Lockie had pushed through all the neighbours' doors, apologising in advance for any mess, dust and upheaval during the conversion work on their house. She recalled he had been gracious, grateful for the forewarning, and assuaged their concern, saying that a little dust and noise was no trouble at all.

'I won't, but thank you.' He hesitated.

'Is everything okay?' Freya stepped forward and pulled the door to behind her, to keep the heat in and their conversation out.

'Well, yes . . .' He paused. 'I wanted to explain about Mrs Rendleton.'

'Oh!'

She wanted to assure him it was none of her business, but didn't want to sound disinterested, unsure how to preserve his privacy whilst being neighbourly.

'She's going downhill, I'm afraid. Getting very forgetful and a little confused.'

Freya nodded. 'I could see earlier that she was preoccupied.'

'Yes, preoccupied.' He nodded. 'We lost a baby, a little boy, stillborn.'

'Oh, goodness! I'm—' she began.

Mr Rendleton held up a palm, as if to silence her.

'No, please, it was over sixty years ago, but it seems to be playing on her mind more and more recently. I suppose I wanted to warn you that if she seems distant, not quite herself . . .' he floundered.

'I completely understand. And if there is anything I can do . . . ?'

He smiled at her, flattening the front of his coat with his palm. 'Nothing any of us can do, I'm afraid.'

'We're always here, Mr Rendleton, just the other side of the back wall, if you need anything, day or night.'

'Thank you, dear. I'd better get back.' He pointed along the street. 'I've left her alone and she'll start to fret. We shall see you soon.'

He smiled and made his way back down the path.

'Who was it?' Lockie laid his open book face down on his chest as Freya came back into the living room.

'Mr Rendleton. I think he just wanted to tell someone he's worried about his wife. She's getting very forgetful and obviously deteriorating. Sad, really.' Freya took her place once again by his side. 'To look at them through the window, you would never guess what they are going through.'

There was a beat of silence, when both recognised but declined to comment on the parallel.

'Nothing sad about reaching a ripe old age and being warm and loved with a roof over your head,' Lockie said finally.

'I guess. But it still feels cruel, unfair.'

'Taste this, Dad!' Lexi ran over with a wooden spoon held flat over the outstretched palm of her other hand. She stepped over her mum's legs and pushed the spoon towards his face.

He sat up straight and touched the sauce to his lips before finishing it all with one swallow. 'Wow!'

Lexi beamed at his response.

'That is so good!' He licked his lips. 'I tell you what, I've changed my mind, I think I will come and eat at your restaurant after all!'

'Can't wait for tomorrow night,' Freya added, truthfully.

'Is it okay if I invite Toby?' Lexi bobbed on the spot, still enlivened by the compliments.

'Of course!' She smiled, happy that her girl wanted to mix, and reminding herself to warn Charlotte to make him feel welcome.

Lockie waited until his daughter turned her back before curling back his top lip in dread for his wife's benefit.

◆ ◆ ◆

The next day, with the house tidied, the loo bleached and fresh flowers sitting on the table in a vase, it was suppertime.

Lexi had been nervously flitting from stove to fridge and back again for a good hour.

'Come on in, Toby!' Lockie boomed, as he uncorked a chilled bottle of white.

'Thanks.' The pale, greasy boy standing in his chinos and navy-and-grey-striped jumper nodded at his hosts for the evening.

Lexi stirred the pot on the hob. 'I made this yesterday; it's a Spanish recipe. I hope you like it!'

The pink blush to her cheek spoke volumes.

'I can confirm that having been chief taster last night, you are in for a real treat.' Lockie rocked on his heels.

'Hi, Toby.' Charlotte, as per her earlier instructions, sidled into the room and took a chair in readiness for supper.

'Hi.' He stared at her. 'Are your applications in?' His robotic monotone was less than endearing, any question sounding more like an instruction.

Charlotte visibly bristled. 'Yes.'

'Where have you applied?'

'Er . . . Durham, Bath and Nottingham.' She toyed with the edge of the place mat.

'To read what?' he pushed.

'History of art.'

'That should be easy,' he replied, seemingly with no idea of how insulting or demeaning his response might be.

'For you maybe.' She gave a small giggle. 'But not for me.'

'I think it's an easier degree than maths or one of the sciences.'

Charlotte stared at her mum in pure frustration, her anger welling. Freya could almost see the steam coming out of her ears; she tried to intervene in order to steer the conversation.

'Oh.' Freya was a little lost for words. 'Where are you applying, Toby?'

'Imperial.'

'Just the one?' She was curious, knowing that school had advised applying to at least three universities.

Toby gave a burst of derisory laughter. 'My dad read maths at Imperial, my grandfather read maths at Imperial, my great-grandfather—'

'Let me guess,' Lockie interrupted, 'read maths at Imperial?'

Toby stared at him. 'No. He was killed in the war.'

'Well, I'm sorry to hear that.' He sipped his wine.

Freya exchanged a glance with her husband, to which he raised his eyebrows and widened his eyes.

'Do you have air conditioning?' the boy asked suddenly, as he took a seat at the table.

'Air conditioning?' Lockie repeated. 'No, we prefer the old open-the-windows-and-let-the-fresh-air-cool-your-bones approach.'

'I'm allergic to air conditioning, or more specifically, the change in temperature. It irritates my chest. I have asthma.' He made the announcement with his index finger raised.

'Oh.' Lockie reached for the wine and topped up his large glass. 'Sorry to hear that too, but you are quite safe.' He winked.

'I'm also allergic to paracetamol, bees and cats.'

Freya opened her mouth to respond when Brewster tiptoed into the room.

'I'll shut him upstairs.' Charlotte jumped up, seeming glad of the chance to leave the table, even if it was only for a few minutes.

'I am fairly certain that there are no bees or paracetamol in tonight's supper, and with Brewster incarcerated, you should be fine!' Lockie raised his glass.

'My father works for the government,' Toby announced, as he rearranged his cutlery until it was perfectly symmetrical with the edge of the place mat.

'So did mine!' Lockie boomed. 'He was an army man.'

Toby stared at him. 'I'm a pacifist.'

'Amen to that! Although, I think it's fair to say that most people are until the marauding masses are battering down the door with a burning torch in one hand and a big swag bag, waiting to be filled, in the other.' Lockie raised his glass again.

Freya could see that this was her husband's intention, to get through the evening with the aid of wine. She pushed her empty glass towards him. It sounded like a fine plan.

'Ta-dah!' Lexi lifted the big casserole pot and placed it in the middle of the table, just as Charlotte reappeared.

'Smells delicious, Lex!' her sister enthused, as she retook her seat.

Lexi beamed as she spooned a large portion on to Toby's plate.

'Does this have tarragon in it?' He lowered his nose towards the dish, inhaling the pungent scent of liquorice.

'Yes.' Lexi beamed.

'I don't like tarragon,' Toby stated.

All eyes turned to Freya, who sprayed wine as she laughed, the sound erupting suddenly at the boy's revelation.

'I'm so sorry!'

She hid her mouth with her cupped palm and laughed some more, aware the sound was a little close to hysteria.

The adults were keen to claim washing-up duties and sent their off-spring and rather awkward guest off to chill out after supper. Lockie held an earthenware platter in his palm and dried it with a tea towel.

'Do you think it's safe to let him go up to Lexi's room?' he whispered to his wife.

Freya, with her hands in the sink, submerged under the bubbles, gave him a sideways look.

'I think with any other seventeen-year-old boy I would be most agitated, but with Toby . . .' She took a deep breath. 'I feel that she is entirely safe. He's a funny old fish,' she whispered back.

'Funny? Charlotte is right! He's a proper weirdo!' He laughed quietly, shoulders hunched.

'Don't be so mean!' She flicked bubbles at him.

'You started it!'

'Sssshh!' She flapped her hand. The wine they had consumed over supper now provided a gloss of hilarity over all they did and said.

'I'm worrying now, though. Perhaps we should be more concerned, perhaps he is actually a red-hot sex god and his nerdiness is his disguise to lull parents into a false sense of security.'

'Well, now *I'm* worried!' She paused from her pan scrubbing.

'Go up and check.' Lockie nudged her.

'Why me?' She laughed. 'Why don't you go?'

'Because if there are any shenanigans going on, you will politely ask him to leave, whereas I would break his neck.'

'Good point.' She giggled. 'But I thought our policy was you have to give trust to get trust, remember?'

'Your parents trusted me, *remember*?' He grinned, reminding her of the weekend he had first been introduced to her family and their desperate, hurried trysts in her childhood bedroom, conducted against the door to block the path of any potential intruders.

'Right. I'm going up.' She threw the sponge into the sink. 'Shall I take biscuits?'

'Depends.' Lockie placed his hand on his chin, as if in deep contemplation. 'Do the biscuits contain any cat, paracetamol or bees? Or have they been exposed to any air conditioning? And more crucially did they read maths at Imperial?'

'You are not remotely funny.'

She tried to contain her amusement as she wiped her hands dry and made for the stairs.

Hovering on the square landing outside Lexi's room, she listened at the door. It was hard to hear anything distinct. There was possibly the low whisper of voices, but that might have been coming from Charlotte's room, where she chatted endlessly to her friends.

Pulling her shoulders back, she took an age to turn the handle, giving it a little rattle and twisting it both ways before pushing open the door, giving the occupants a few precious seconds in which to . . . Actually she didn't want to think about the possibilities that Lockie had placed in her brain.

'Hey, Mum.'

Freya smiled at the two who sat on the bed with their backs against the wall and their legs dangling over the edge. They neither jumped nor seemed surprised, and there was certainly no indication of alarm.

'Can I get you guys anything? Biscuits? A drink?'

'No, I'm fine.' Lexi smiled.

'No, thank you.' Toby was cool and polite, as ever.

She took a step closer to the bed and Lexi shut the lid of her laptop. There was something in her gesture that caused Freya's pulse to quicken.

'What are you looking at?' she asked casually.

'Nothing.' Lexi wriggled backwards until she was even more upright, as if poised to flee or fight.

'Well if it's nothing, you can show me?' she asked with a slight smile, trying to keep things friendly and calm.

'It's nothing.' Lexi repeated the unsatisfying explanation.

'You should tell your mother. There's no shame in it.' Toby stared at Lexi, addressing her as if they were alone.

Freya swallowed, her mind raced. *What on earth . . . ?*

'No shame in what? What exactly are you looking at?' Her friendly note had all but disappeared.

'Nothing, Mum! Can you just leave us alone?' Lexi slapped the duvet in frustration.

'Saying "nothing" when you are clearly looking at something is not going to reassure me in any way, so I suggest you either show me what is on your laptop or I shall take it from you!' She hated how quickly the situation had deteriorated; this was the last thing she had wanted, especially in front of her daughter's guest.

'You'll take it from me? You can't! It's my laptop!' Lexi shouted.

As she might have predicted, Lockie bounded up the stairs and into the bedroom.

'What's going on here?' His expression was no longer amused.

'Lexi won't show me what they've been looking at and Toby says he thinks she should confide in us, as it's nothing to be *ashamed* of,' she quoted for full effect.

'Is that right?'

She watched the twist of Lockie's jaw.

Lexi grabbed the laptop and held it against her chest. Her tears fell as she lowered her head, holding the machine under her chin.

'Please don't cry, darling, we are just trying to keep you safe!' The sight of her tears melted Freya's resolve. She was aware of her flip, but was equally as aware of her daughter's fragility, and to see her tears, shed in front of the boy she liked, was heart-wrenching. Freya eyed Toby, who sat rigidly on her daughter's bed. She wanted him to leave.

'It's something that we have in common,' he began.

'Shut up, Toby!' Lexi screamed at him.

He stood, his face pale, his expression one of utter confusion. 'I believe you can be just as dishonest through omission as you can from lying, and I am not a liar. You should show your parents.'

'What exactly are you talking about?' Lockie placed his hands on his hips and stood in front of Toby.

'We met in a Pro Ana chat room.' Toby stared at him, as though his words would be enough.

'A what?' Freya leant forward, trying to recall the word he had used. 'Pranna'? She hadn't heard it before.

'And actually it wasn't just Pro Ana, it was for safe self-harming in a supportive community. And despite what people think, it's not a disease. It's a lifestyle choice.' He jutted his chin.

Lockie grabbed Toby by the arm. Hearing the word 'self-harming' was all it took to tip the balance.

'I don't know what you are talking about and I don't know what game you are playing, but you get out of my house right now and you don't ever come back, and you stay the hell away from my daughter. Do you understand me?'

Toby looked at him. 'I help her, I—'

'Get out!' It was Freya's turn to shout.

Charlotte came out of her room. 'What the hell's going on?'

Toby hesitated on the top stair.

'I was just trying to explain to your parents about Pro Ana and our choices, how it's better to conduct yourself and live your life in a controlled way, a safe way, with support.'

He walked calmly down the stairs. Freya noted Charlotte's expression of disgust.

She listened until she heard the faint slam of the front door before sitting on her daughter's bed.

'What is he talking about, Lexi? I'm quite scared,' she admitted.

Lockie paced the room, as Charlotte stood at the foot of her sister's bed calmly, her arms folded across her chest. Freya saw in her daughter's expression that she knew more than she was letting on.

'Do you know what this is all about?'

Charlotte nodded and paused.

'Seriously, love, I am this close to exploding!' She held her thumb and forefinger close together, warning her daughter that she could only take so much more of this subterfuge. It was rare for her to raise her voice and react in this way.

The two sisters exchanged a look, one trying to decide whether to spill the beans and the other silently imploring her not to.

Charlotte closed her eyes, as if this made the betrayal easier. 'They've been looking at websites that talk about anorexia and eating disorders.'

Freya let out a sigh of relief as she swept her palm over Lexi's flustered brow. 'Well, that's nothing to hide or feel worried about and there's certainly no need to be so secretive. I think it's good that you look to resources for help and advice, you silly thing, no need for tears!'

'It's more than that, Mum,' Charlotte continued.

'In what way?'

'It's a community called Pro Ana, or just Ana – they are often pro anorexia; they support an anorexic lifestyle.'

'Lifestyle?' Lockie balked. 'It's not a bloody lifestyle; it's an illness!'

'You don't understand!' Lexi shrieked. 'They help me! I thought I was the only one who felt like this, I thought I was a freak, but I'm not. There are lots of people like me, and knowing that helps, and being able to talk to them helps even more. No one understands what this is like for me unless you have lived it, and the people I meet on here do. They get it.' She clutched the computer even tighter.

Lockie stared at his wife. 'No, she's right, I don't understand! Am I supposed to accept that she wants to talk to some strangers that she has never met on these unfathomable sites, but not us? I wish someone would explain to me what the hell is going on here.'

'I think we all just need to calm down!' Freya patted the air. 'Lockie, let's you and I go downstairs and let everyone just catch their breath. Lexi, we don't want to make you anxious, we are just trying to understand.' She nodded at her youngest, who visibly cowered on the bed. 'And Charlotte, any insight you can offer would be a good thing.'

Charlotte nodded and left, as if keen to escape and avoid her sister's scowl.

Freya crept from the room and down the stairs. Taking her seat at the table, she flipped open her laptop. Lockie sat next to her, having gone via the fridge for another bottle of white, the veneer of happiness provided by the previous bottle now well and truly gone. He poured two glasses and sat back.

Freya typed 'Pro Ana websites' into the search engine and watched as a list of sites popped up in front of her. "Thinspiration", "Thin secrets",' she read aloud, "'Ana diets", "Ana tips", "Hiding Ana" . . .' She clicked on a site, a blog.

Lockie put his glasses on and leant forward, resting his chin on his fist, his elbow propped on the table.

They both read in silence.

Freya reached for the glass of wine and drank quickly.

'"How to manage on one hundred and sixty calories a day",' she quoted. '"Sip water frequently, drink a pint before each meal, cut your food into tiny pieces."' She looked at her husband, who was reading by her side. 'This is advice on how to eat less, how to stay thin.'

'One hundred and sixty calories *a day*? Surely these sites must be illegal?' Lockie looked as stunned as he did saddened. 'I mean, these girls are already vulnerable, and you are telling me this is available at the touch of a button?' He shook his head.

She was equally shocked.

'They are probably not committing any crime, and if they are, there are so many of them, I don't know how you'd keep on top of them. Look: pages and pages.'

'I told you he was a weirdo.' Charlotte's voice drew them as she sloped in in her pyjamas.

'If you had been a bit more specific and not simply generalising over his weirdness, we might have paid a bit more attention!' Lockie growled.

'I didn't know any specifics!' she barked in defence. 'All I heard is what Tara told me – that they started talking in some chat room about self-harming and eating disorders and stuff and that's how they met. I don't know how true it is.'

'Self-harming? When did you hear this?' Freya turned to her.

'After they were already mates, after he'd been here a couple of times.'

'I can't believe you didn't tell us about this, give us a pointer.' She turned back to the harrowing phrases that leapt from the screen.

'I didn't want you to worry any more than you already are, I didn't know how much of it was true.' Charlotte raised her voice. 'This is not my fault!'

'We are not saying it's your fault,' Lockie began.

'That's what it feels like,' she interrupted. 'I'm sick of it! Everyone rushes around doing what's best for Lexi, but try being me. Everyone at school wants to talk about it and if they don't ask outright, they stare at me. And it's nothing to do with me! And now you're having a go at me!'

'We are not having a go at you,' he continued. 'We are trying to figure out what to do for the best and it's like walking barefoot, surrounded by broken glass, one false move and . . .' Removing his glasses, he rubbed his eyes. 'We are not saying spy on your sister, of course not. Lexi is not your responsibility. But if you do hear or see anything, I would ask that you tell us, so we can' – he swallowed the catch in his voice – 'we can help her.'

'I thought things were so much better.' Freya stared at the screen.

'They are better, she's put on weight,' her husband reminded her.

Freya nodded. 'I thought we were out of the woods; now I'm not so sure.'

'That boy is not coming back in this house,' he announced.

'You can't stop them being friends, you can't be at school with her or monitor how she chats online,' Charlotte reminded him.

'No, you're right, I can't stop them, but I can assure you he will not be setting foot in my house again, and I will do everything in my power to keep him away from my daughter. My instinct is screaming that the doctor, the literature, these websites, even the way you indulge her, Freya – it is all pushing her into a corner, giving her this banner, this movement to hide behind, when all she probably needs is a bit of TLC and time to grow up.'

'You think I don't give her TLC?' Freya asked, stung.

'No, of course not, I know you do! I'm simply suggesting that everyone has to stop taking this so personally!' He drained his wine glass.

'I'm her mother. How exactly do you suggest I do that?' She watched him look towards the ceiling, struggling for a reply.

The whole house was in darkness when Freya crept from her bed and across the landing; she wanted to look in on Lexi. The bedroom door creaked and her daughter roused, throwing her arm over her head and letting out a small moan in the disturbed air of her room.

'Shh. It's only me, darling, I'm just checking on you.'

'Mum?' Lexi propped herself up on her elbow.

As their eyes adjusted to the darkness, they blinked. Freya knelt on the rug by her daughter's bedside.

'I am sorry the evening ended how it did, darling. Your food was really delicious.'

'Thanks.' Lexi paused. 'It's not your fault. I didn't tell you about the sites because I knew you wouldn't understand,' she whispered.

'That's true, I don't understand, but that will only change if you talk to me, explain it to me,' she countered.

'They help me, Mum.'

Freya was silent, suppressing the desire to shout that that was a crazy idea. They could only harm her, either by giving her ideas or by normalising her skewed views; instead, she chose her question wisely.

'Some of those sites talk about self-harming. Is that something you have ever done or thought about doing?' Holding her breath, she waited for the response.

'No.'

'Are you certain?'

'Yes, Mum. Positive.'

Freya exhaled.

'I'm glad about that, darling, and you know if thoughts like that ever cross your mind, you have to talk to me first, whenever or wherever. You tell me and we can get through it together. Remember?'

Lexi nodded. 'Some of those blogs, Mum, I like reading them.' She paused. 'It makes me feel better to know that I'm not the only one who feels like this.'

'Like what?'

Lexi sighed, twisting her body into an upright position and lifting her knees under the duvet. 'Like . . . like I'm pointless. Like I'm rubbish.'

The rush of tears was unexpected, arriving with such speed Freya had no time to blot her eyes or nose or disguise her wave of distress.

'Don't cry.' Lexi placed her hand on her mum's cheek.

'I'm crying because that is one of the saddest things I have heard. And it's not true! You are not pointless and you are not rubbish, you are my amazing girl and I love you so much.'

'I knew you'd say that, but no matter what you think, if it feels true to me, then it is, isn't it?'

Freya opened her mouth, but no words came. Instead, she laid her head on her daughter's duvet and cried some more, wishing that she knew when these feelings had started and what, if anything, had been the catalyst. Her tears flowed, a visual display of the guilt she felt and the overwhelming feeling that she had failed her child.

Six hours . . .

Freya walked into the study; her wet hair lay in tangles on her shoulders. She had got back into her pyjamas and dressing gown. Clothes, make-up: today everything felt like a chore.

'Do you feel better?' Charlotte turned to face her mum.

Freya shrugged. 'Better? No, but cleaner and slightly more awake, I guess.'

'I just told Lexi that I lost my virginity.'

Freya took a couple of steps backwards and sat down hard on the sofa. 'Well I never.'

'I wanted to tell her something that she didn't know.'

'Something that none of us knew, Charlotte.' She placed her hand over her mouth. 'Do you have a boyfriend?' she asked.

Charlotte shook her head. 'No.'

'Do you want to talk about it?' she offered with more of a sigh than she had intended.

'Not really.'

Freya nodded, slightly relieved. 'Are you . . .' She wiggled her fingers in the air, as if the words she searched for might be lurking in the ether for her to grasp.

'I'm not pregnant or harmed or distressed or overly keen to repeat the experience.'

'Well, I think that answers all my questions.' She smiled briefly at her daughter.

'All seems like a bit of fuss over nothing.' Charlotte twiddled the pen in her fingers.

Freya closed her eyes and leant back on the sofa. 'When it's right it can feel like everything, about as far from nothing as it's possible to be.'

'So I guess I've got that to look forward to.'

Opening her eyes, she looked at her daughter. 'You have *everything* to look forward to, Charlotte. Everything.' She closed her eyes again.

Neither chose to comment on the sour note of resignation that seemed to lace these words, the message loud and clear: *Be thankful for what lies ahead of you. Be thankful that you managed to dodge the bullet that caught Lexi.*

The front doorbell rang.

They both looked towards the door.

'Do you want me to go?' Charlotte sat up straight.

'No. I'll go.' Freya nodded. Placing her fingers in her hair, she twisted it to remove some of the excess water.

'We could ignore it?' Charlotte suggested, seemingly not noticing the tears that slipped silently down her cheeks.

'Not today.' Freya took a deep breath and headed down the stairs.

EIGHT

Freya came in from the courtyard, where she had removed some dead tendrils that had snaked over the wall from next door, and had spoken kindly to her lavender, of which she expected great things this summer.

She wished she could eradicate the mental remnants of the previous night as easily as she had the dirty dishes and leftover food. The words written by girls just like Lexi had haunted her thoughts until the early hours. Painful, self-indulgent missives, littered with offensive words like 'fat bitch', 'ugly pig', 'greedy whore', terrible, horrible nouns and adjectives, italicised, highlighted and spat with venom. She shuddered, overwhelmed with sadness at their very existence, and again thinking of the phrases she had uttered without thought: *I'm the size of a house!* when the waistband of her jeans felt a little snug; *Roll me off of the couch!* when she had sampled a morsel of pudding.

Opening up the article she was writing for Marcia, she read the last paragraph, written before she had served supper:

> . . . if a label has a leaf on it, parents automatically think of nature, a piece of fresh fruit and the mind jumps

to 'goodness'. Sunshine equates to vitamins – the tricks deployed are multiple.

She paused to consider the parents just like her all over the country who would read her words, each making a judgement call whilst navigating the minefield that was child nutrition, and her heart sank. She didn't want to make it any harder for them than it already was.

Charlotte interrupted her, bumping her cello case down the stairs.

'All set?' Freya painted on a smile, not wanting to spoil the day of her concert.

'Yep.' Resting her cello case against the wall, she headed for the cereal cupboard. 'Make sure you don't sit where I can see you tonight. If I catch your eye it will only put me off. You can tell me afterwards where you sat, but not in my eyeline, deal?'

'Deal. But I can stand and clap and shout "bravo" and "encore" and all that stuff?'

'Well, yes, but only at the end. And only if everyone else does,' Charlotte clarified.

'Well of course at the end! What did you think? That I'd jump up when the fancy took me? Give me some credit, Charlotte.' Freya laughed at the thought.

'Actually it's not you I'm worried about, but I wouldn't put anything past Dad.'

'Good point. I shall brief him thoroughly on concert etiquette.' She smiled, turning her attention back to her computer screen.

'You're not still looking at those blogs, are you, Mum?'

Her accusatory tone made her sound so much older than her years, reminding Freya so painfully of her own mum that it took her breath away. She wished she were still around, certain that she would shoulder some of her worries and make things better; that's what mums did.

She cleared her throat. 'Not still looking at them, no, but certainly still thinking about them,' she admitted.

'I'd say don't worry about them too much. It might even be that Lexi gets some practical help from them in some way.'

'That's what she said.'

'Well there you go.' She poured a healthy pile of cereal into the bowl.

'When did you get so smart?' Freya smiled at her girl.

'I wish.' Charlotte splashed on the milk and filled her cheeks with cereal, crunching loudly. 'If I was, I wouldn't be so worried about my uni applications; as Toby says, I'd think it was easy!' Speaking with her mouth full, she sprayed the area with cereal.

'I think you can safely ignore what young Toby says. He strikes me as quite troubled.' She spoke quickly, wanting to change the topic. 'You're going to be great tonight. I'm so proud of you.'

'Imperial great? Or just Nottingham great?' She laughed.

'Very funny, Charlotte.'

Lexi arrived and went to the sink to fill her water bottle.

'She's only teasing.' Freya stood and hugged her little girl, placing her hands across her back; she felt the ribs at the back of her nightie.

Don't be stupid, she's doing great. She tried to ignore the leap of fear in her stomach.

'Are you not coming to school today?' Charlotte queried, now quite used to her sister's erratic attendance.

Lexi shook her head, avoiding eye contact as she trod the stairs, heading back to the comfort of her room.

'Yep, well, good luck, Charlotte! Have a good one! See you soon!' Charlotte mockingly spoke the words that her sister had omitted.

Freya opened her mouth to make an excuse on Lexi's behalf, but thought better of it.

It was mid-afternoon when Lockie's mother, Diana, floated into the house in the brightest of moods, looking nautically chic in her navy blazer with a red-and-white scarf knotted at her neck. Her grey hair had been cut into a blunt bob that naturally curled up at the ends.

'The house looks lovely, Freya! This large window at the back of the den lets in so much light. It's quite beautiful.'

Freya smiled; she had to admit that on a bright, sunny day like this, with a simple green jug of daffodils gracing the long table, she felt enormous pride in their family home.

'I'm so excited about this concert.' Diana clapped her hands. 'It will be wonderful. Can I take photographs? I've been practising with my phone.'

She held up her new phone, as if proof were needed.

'I should think so. That is if we get a clear enough view and aren't stuck behind any hat-wearing, bushy-haired giants. Plus I have promised Charlotte that we won't sit anywhere that might distract her; apparently the sight of me is enough to put her off.'

'How charming.' Diana giggled. 'Such a clever girl, being able to play the cello. It's quite something, isn't it?'

'They're both clever, must take after their dad.' She smiled.

'Hi, Gran!' Lexi rushed across the room and welcomed her granny with a hug.

'Goodness me, hello, Lexi! It's lovely to see you. How are you, darling? You have always given the best hugs.'

Lexi beamed. 'I'm good, thanks.' She tucked her long hair behind her ear.

'Well, I am jolly glad to hear it. I hope this therapist lady is helping you. Daddy said you'd been having a bit of a problem with eating; I was very sorry to hear that.'

Freya froze. They made it a rule not to discuss her therapy, let alone the specifics of her illness.

'Thank you.' Lexi glanced at her mum, unsure of the expected response. 'And yes, Hilary is really good.'

'What can I do to help?' Diana was determined. 'Is there anything you fancy to eat? How about a nice piece of steak or a baked potato with cheese? I'm sure Mum would rustle you up whatever you liked, wouldn't you, Freya? Or we could go and get you some noodles or fish and chips, whatever you wanted!'

She nodded at her mother-in-law in response, wishing that it were that gloriously simple, and similarly trying to work out how to change the subject.

But Diana wasn't done.

'I bought you some chocolate, that's always a favourite.' Diana reached into her Birkin-style bag and pulled out a family-sized bar of Galaxy. 'Shall I leave it on the table or do you fancy a couple of squares now?' She waved it at her granddaughter, as if this might be enough to tempt her.

Lexi folded her arms across her chest. Freya noted that she had gone a little ashen. She felt the tension rise in the room. Nerves fluttered in her stomach, tinged with a little anger, as if she hadn't already offered to make her daughter any type of food, day or night; she would do anything! Diana's suggestion that this might be the solution sent ripples into the room. And still she had more to say.

'I can't understand it at all, Lexi. You were always such a little greedy guts. Pappy or I would be feeding you in your high chair and you would bash the plastic tray with your little spoon if we didn't go fast enough! And you were always bonny, rounded. You loved your puddings; we could encourage you to behave with the promise of sweeties. You were an adorable, chubby little thing! Everyone said how gorgeous you were and you still are . . .'

Freya zoned out from Diana's rambling. Watching, as if in slow motion, as Lexi's chest heaved and her stomach seemed to cave. She held the back of the nearest chair, almost like the strength had left her legs. She looked . . .

Freya struggled to find the word.

She pictured Lockie feeding her as a baby, sitting in her high chair. Remembered the sense of pride she felt when her baby ate what was offered to her, confident that she was going to grow big and strong. Lockie had loved to feed her, a chance to spend time with his youngest.

'Here comes the choo-choo! Come on! Open up! That's my girl! Ooh, she loves this mashed carrot and lamb, or whatever the hell this is.' He pulled a disgusted face at his wife and looked at the grey goop in the bowl.

'Ah, don't look like that, you'll put her off!'

'I doubt it!' Lockie laughed, as Lexi leant forward with her mouth open, ready for the next spoonful, like a little bird.

Freya laughed. 'She certainly loves her grub, don't you, don't you, my beautiful baby?'

Freya left her daydream and stared at that baby, now a grown fifteen-year-old who found life hard and was cowering in the wake of her gran's good intentions. She recognised in the woman's words the lack of awareness that had snuck up on her and grabbed her without warning; she herself had uttered so many pointless, damaging words to soothe and distract, all doing more harm than good. This realisation was almost more than she could bear.

'For God's sake be quiet, Diana! Just be quiet!'

She hadn't meant to shout.

Lexi appeared not to have noticed her mother's outburst. Freya watched as her daughter's mouth moved silently, as if recounting her gran's words. Diana, on the other hand, looked mortified. She swallowed, playing with the scarf at her neck as if it might choke her. All stood in silence for a couple of seconds before Diana grabbed her large handbag and swept from the room and out of the house.

The word that had eluded her earlier came to her then, suddenly and unbidden.

Lexi looked *terrified*. Utterly terrified.

◆　◆　◆

It was nearly midnight when she heard the key in the door. Freya looked up and realised that she had been sitting in the darkness for some time, hardly noticing when the sun had finished its shift, handing over to the moon. The only light came from the Rendletons' upstairs window that cast long shadows over the wall and on to the courtyard.

Lockie walked in and flicked on the light. She squinted at the bright intrusion and could see instantly by his set expression that he was less than impressed. He threw his keys into the bowl and slipped his arms from his corduroy jacket.

'Where's Charlotte?' She looked past him towards the hallway, expecting her to appear, fixing her smile.

'I said she could stay at Milly's. They finished late and were on quite a high, as you can imagine. The concert was first class. It felt wrong to drag her away. Milly's parents were keen; they seem like nice people. They said they'd get the girls tucked up with hot chocolate and then drop them both into school in the morning. I didn't see the harm.'

'Of course.' She nodded, wishing that Charlotte were here, firstly so she could apologise for missing her concert, but also, at some level, knowing that someone else's presence might help prevent the row that she knew was brewing.

Don't be such a coward, she silently reprimanded herself.

Lockie leant on the semi-industrial console that lined the wall, rescued from a locker room in the old sports centre; its grey metal was battered, aged, but still functional, and now a statement piece and talking point. He rested on it, placing his hands in his jeans pockets.

'Okay, Freya, let's have it, what happened today?' He wasted no more time on small talk. 'I have never heard my mother so distressed, never.'

She shook her head. 'I never wanted to upset your mum. I love her; you know that. I don't really know what happened. It just—'

'Don't tell me it "just happened". Anything but that. You have known her for nigh on twenty years, never a cross word, and then this, snapping at her out of the blue? I can't fathom it.'

He stood with every muscle coiled, his eyes blazing.

'She . . . she was chatting to Lexi, going on and on about how she used to be bonny, rounded – that was the word she used. "Rounded"!' She blinked rapidly at the uncomfortable recollection.

'My mother adores Lexi, adores both the girls, adores us all, you know that! She would have only meant it as a compliment,' he spat.

'I know she loves the girls, but the fact is I don't actually care how she meant it.' She sat up straight and knitted her hands at the knuckles to stop them shaking. 'Lexi has a very real fear of fat and of being fat. It's that simple. You should have seen her face. It was like she had been struck!'

'Jesus Christ, have you heard yourself? A "fear of fat"? Where has that come from?' He paced, snorting his derision through his nose.

'Well, what did you think, Lockie? What did you think this was all about? Getting a week off school? You just don't get it!' She stood now, matching his stance.

'I tell you what I don't get' – he pointed at her – 'is just how willing you are to roll over and give in to this very destructive behaviour, or how you could just drop Charlotte, miss her concert. You *know* how hard she has worked, all those hours practising, rehearsing, with you pushing her. She was so proud, excited, and then you flaked on the day and didn't turn up. It's mind-boggling!' He placed his hands at his temples for added effect.

'Don't be so dramatic. I haven't *dropped* Charlotte. It was one night. She'll understand that I couldn't leave Lexi, I just couldn't. It's been the worst day imaginable; your mum didn't exactly hold back.'

'Yes, I think you are right, this whole nightmare is my mother's fault because she has very kindly dipped into her pocket so that Lexi can spend hours chatting to a stranger in Harpenden and had the audacity to buy her grandchild a bar of bloody chocolate. The woman should be whipped!'

'Don't be clever, Lockie. You are oversimplifying things to win the argument and make me sound at fault and I am not. I couldn't just up sticks and go and clap politely in the interval. Lexi needed me!'

'Well, here's a news flash: Charlotte needed you too.'

'She will understand.' Of this she was certain.

'Yes I'm sure, she was after all so *very* keen to rush home and tell you all about her evening. Oh, wait a minute, no she wasn't!' He gave a fake laugh.

'You can be such a shit, Lockie.' She grabbed her laptop and her glasses.

'Don't worry about being disturbed; I shall sleep on the top floor,' he called after her, like a boxer with plenty of fight left in him, wanting to get in one final jab.

'Do what you like.' Freya swept from the room, keen to make it to the stairs before her tears started to fall.

She slept fitfully, turning a couple of times, noting the absence of her husband in their bed and remembering all over again why he wasn't there. She could count on one hand the times he had decamped to the spare room during their marriage, and on nearly every other occasion it was when one of them was ill and the other one was avoiding the unpleasantness that went with a sickness bug or the flu. This felt different, and she didn't like it one bit.

Waking before her alarm, Freya grabbed her notepad and pen and wrote Charlotte a note. Having texted her last night, she wanted her to find this lasting message, a reminder. Six words that she hoped would convey all she needed them to: *I'm sorry, Charlotte. I love you.* She placed it on her daughter's cool pillow before showering and pulling on her jeans and a shirt. She then knocked on Lexi's door.

'Morning, sweetheart.' She opened the curtains to let the day in and gently nudged her daughter's sleeping form. 'You have to get up and get showered, darling, we've got your doctor's appointment first thing.'

Lexi turned over and stretched her arms over her head. Her breath, as ever, was putrid. Freya tried not to breathe in through her nose, tried not to react to the noxious, sweet, yet foul smell that dogged her child. She knew this was the result of ketosis and an almost zero-carb diet that often caused chemicals to be released in the breath as the body burned fat.

'Five more minutes.' Lexi turned her face towards her pillow and closed her eyes.

Making her way to the kitchen, she trod the last stair with trepidation, feeling an unfamiliar nervousness in her own home. Lockie was already at the kitchen table. It felt odd to her that she didn't know what to say to the man with whom she shared everything, carrying an awkwardness that was as unfamiliar as it was uncomfortable.

'Can I get you a coffee?' She figured this was a safe place to start.

He lifted a mug. 'Way ahead of you on that one. And don't worry, I didn't touch your machine.' He gave a small smile.

Freya braced her arms on the countertop, all her resolve disappeared, and she cried, huge gulping sobs.

'I never wanted to upset Diana. She's my family! I love her and I know I let Charlotte down! I honestly thought that because you were there it made sense for me to sit with Lexi, I couldn't leave her and I didn't know what else to do!' Her nose and mouth both clogged with tears.

She heard the scrape of Lockie's chair on the wooden floor and within seconds his arms were around her. He held her tightly and kissed her scalp.

'I shouldn't have been so angry and taken it out on you the way I did. I'm sorry too. It was the worst thing hearing my mum upset like that and not knowing how to fix it. I don't know how to fix anything.' He sighed.

She twisted inside his grip until her face was flat against his denim shirtfront. 'I hated not sleeping with you,' she whispered.

'Me too.' He sighed. 'There was no one warming their cold feet on my legs or stealing the duvet or shouting out random facts and ideas in the dead of night.'

Freya smiled, knowing she did all three. 'I love you, Lockie.'

'And I love you, and that is why we will get through this and why we can get through anything.' He tilted her chin with his finger until she was facing him and kissed her gently on the mouth.

'What's your plan for today?' He released her and made his way back to his coffee and the morning's headlines.

'Lexi has a doctor's appointment first thing, then I'm going to work on my article and that's that.'

'I'm in the studio, editing all day, but obviously here if you need me.' He was being overly attentive, trying, as was she, to make amends.

She sniffed away the last of her tears and nodded at the man she loved.

She tried not to let her own nerves jump across to her daughter as they parked outside the doctor's surgery, humming, rummaging in her bag, anything other than pay heed to the rising tide of anxiety that sat somewhere beneath her throat. Dr Morris smiled her welcome.

'Hey, Lexi, how are you? Come and sit down.'

Freya took a seat next to her daughter as the doctor ran her eyes over the notes on the screen. 'So it's been nine weeks since I saw you. How have you been getting on?'

'Bit better, I think.' Lexi spoke to her lap.

'Would you agree with that, Mum?' the doctor asked brightly.

She swallowed, wary of saying the wrong thing. 'Lexi certainly started out eating more, which I know was the goal. She's done amazingly well. We have had a few wobbles.'

'In what way?' The doctor sat forward.

'I . . . I don't know.'

Freya was ashamed of her lack of specifics. It was hard to explain that they walked on eggshells one minute and seemed to be back to normal the next, difficult to put into words just how it felt to watch her child deliberate over two brands of soup, trying to identify which would be less harmful and choosing neither, or the sheer joy she felt when Lexi managed to consume a measly protein shake.

'And you are still seeing Hilary Wainwright?' she addressed Lexi.

'Yes.'

'And that helps?'

'Yes.' Of this she sounded certain.

'Okay.' The doctor drew a deep breath. 'Well, let's get you weighed, Lexi, and we can go from there.'

Lexi stood and slowly, reluctantly removed her trainers, her hoodie, and placed her phone with her folded clothing on the seat of the chair.

'You did brilliantly before, I just need you to do the same again.'

Dr Morris stood by the scales and waited for Lexi to step forward. Which she did, treading gingerly, as if the machine itself might cause her pain. Slowly, hesitantly, she placed one foot on the black rubberised pad and then the other. Freya tried not to stare at the curve of her daughter's spine as she leant forward.

The doctor once again punched the keypad and made notes on her little pad of Post-it notes.

'Thank you, Lexi, you can pop your clothes back on. Okay, well, the good news is you have gained four pounds.' The doctor turned to Lexi and smiled before returning her attention to the screen; again she pointed with her pencil. 'This puts your BMI at fourteen point eight five. You have crept just from the red to the amber. You have done so well. Still a long way to go, but this is a brilliant achievement!'

Freya smiled. *Thank God!* They could now, finally, start to put this behind them. The attention at mealtimes and Hilary's sessions were working. She felt her spirits lift.

'I would suggest carrying on with the therapist, and then I'll see you again in a few weeks, when hopefully those pounds will have crept up. How does that sound?'

Lexi nodded. 'Sounds good.'

She turned her head to look at Freya, meeting her eye for just a second, before looking away, as if embarrassed or as if she were lying. In fact, exactly like she was lying. Freya could see that the idea of more weight creeping on or in fact visiting the doctor again sounded far from good.

Freya sat at the desk in her study, drumming her fingers, trying to write, reading the papers online and waiting for the call that she knew would be coming through. Sure enough, a little after half past two, the phone rang.

'Mrs Braithwaite?'

'Yes. Hello, Doctor.'

'It was great to see Lexi sounding more positive, and I'm glad that the therapy is popular, that's half the battle, but I am still a little worried about her weight; she needs to gain more if she is to get out of this danger zone.'

'She is taking the shakes.' Freya knew she sounded defensive.

'I know, but we need to up her daily calories. Her BMI of fourteen point eight five needs to reach sixteen point three: a weight of about one hundred pounds.'

'What do you suggest? Sneaking butter into her soda? Shoving doughnuts in her mouth while she sleeps?'

There was a slight pause.

'I'm sorry, Doctor; I shouldn't lose my temper with you. I just find the whole thing so frustrating. I'm her mum. I should be able to feed her, make her better, that's my job.'

'No need to apologise. I understand and, for the record, your butter in the soda means you are thinking along the right lines.'

The woman's words did nothing to ease her apprehension. She still, even after this time and much advice from the experts, felt ill-equipped to handle Lexi and her illness, and that realisation was hard to swallow.

Five hours, thirty minutes . . .

Freya crept back into the study.

'Who was it?' Charlotte asked.

'Mr Rendleton. He gave me this.'

She held up a jam jar full of freshly cut lilac that drooped around the glass. Sitting against the green leaves, it looked beautiful. Placing her fingers under the bloom, she lifted them towards her nose; the scent filled her head.

'That was so kind!' Charlotte's tears pooled.

'Yes, it was. Why don't you go and get some coffee?'

As her daughter left the room, Freya smiled softly at the jar now sitting on her desk.

Lockie poked his head around the door, he looked dishevelled. His pyjama top was misbuttoned. 'You should have woken me earlier.'

'I wanted you to try and get some rest.'

'Thank you for that.' He nodded. 'Where's Charlotte?'

'Gone to make coffee.'

'I'll go and have my shower.' He retreated to the landing.
Freya picked up her pen.

*Being Mum to you and Charlotte has always been my
very best thing. You are my proudest achievements. I know
it's my job to look after you both. My job to make sure you
are protected, safe, happy and fulfilling your potential, and I
take that job very seriously. I used to think this was easy and
that we would figure it out as we went along. I watched you
bump along from baby to child to teenager; of course none of
these stages was without tears, yours or mine! But when you
felt a little adrift at school, worrying about a boy or deliberat-
ing about what the future might hold, it all felt manageable.
Maybe I was complacent, took my eye off the ball? I don't know.*

*I think a lot, Lexi, about why you feel about your body
the way that you do, wondering if it is because of one thing or
several, if it was something I said or did or didn't say or didn't
do. I often lie awake into the early hours, recounting phrases
I uttered without thought.*

*Did they stick in your mind like those tiny seeds that get
carried along on the wind? The ones that travel along until
they find a home in the crevice of a brick, taking hold and
growing against all the odds, carving through the structure,
destabilising it, until the wall simply crumbles around the
uninvited resident? Is that what it was like? A single word
or idea cast indifferently in your direction that grew into the
illness that it became?*

What should I have done differently, Lexi?

Daddy once suggested that I didn't set the best example, fretting over a tightened waistband and priding myself on my flat tum. I didn't mean to. I really didn't. My obsession with food and cooking . . . I thought it was healthy, I only ever wanted to nourish you all. I had no idea that it might be doing the opposite.

I wish I had told you that a little bit of spare weight was not the end of the world, and that the most beautiful part of any human is their soul. Beauty is on the inside, beauty is goodness and it is nothing to do with a number or a dress size or a shape.

I have looked back a lot over the last few weeks and I know that I have let you down, haven't been the best example of myself that I could or should have been. I think the truth is that I am a good mum when things go right, but when they started to go wrong . . . I failed, I dissolved in ways I never thought I would. And I know that was when you needed me the most. I'm sorry, Lexi.

I love you and I am sorry.

NINE

'You're very quiet, Lexi,' Freya said across the car as they drove to her session.

Lexi shrugged in response.

'You should be feeling very pleased with yourself. Dr Morris is proud of you. We all are!' she enthused.

'I know I *should* feel happy, Mum, I want to and I'm trying, but I can't really.' She spoke in a whisper, her voice faltering.

'Why can't you? Tell me,' she urged.

Lexi's fingers fidgeted as she tried to find the words and the courage.

'I'm only eating because I have to, not because I want to, and I know I have to, so I will, but I still feel really bad about it. Every mouthful makes me feel so horrible, like I'm making myself ill, like it's poison.' Her bottom lip trembled and her tears fell. Freya's gut twisted with a feeling of utter helplessness.

'Oh, darling, I know, and the fact that you have gained, feeling as you do, is such a sign of strength. It's incredible, and Hilary will help you turn that corner; she will help flip that switch so that you do want to eat and that will start the whole cycle of you feeling properly better.

You have to believe that. You'll get there, Lex, and I will be with you every step of the way.'

Pulling her long sleeves over her hands, Lexi wrapped her arms around her trunk, self-soothing. 'I think that if I eat bad food I will be a bad person.' Her distress flowed at the admission.

'But, Lex, you have only eaten healthy food!' She tried to rationalise, stopping herself from saying, *You haven't eaten anything bad,* trying to change her own as well as Lexi's habits – the idea that some foods were good and others bad.

'It's not so much whether it's healthy food or not. It's more about too much food. I can't be fat, Mum.' She shook her head, the gesture reminding Freya of Charlotte when she was small, fearful that she might be asked to go swimming with her sister. It was the same head shake at the perceived horror of the consequences.

'You're not overweight, Lexi, and everyone needs some fat on them; it keeps us healthy! Alive!' She tapped the steering wheel, as if this enforced her point.

'But I will be' – she shook her head and screwed her face up, as if something had offended her senses – 'if everyone keeps making me eat. I will be fat inside and out. How can you not see that?' Her tone now was quite agitated. 'And that would make me a bad person and a pig! A fat pig!' she barked, twisting her hands inside her sleeves. The snap was out of character; she sounded like a stranger.

Freya concentrated on the traffic ahead, glancing to her left when she could afford to take her eyes off the road. *Did you see Diana with the eclairs? She was pigging them down!* Freya recalled using the phrase in the car, talking to Lockie while the girls played in the backseat.

'But that's not true, darling! The food you eat and the person you are are completely separate!'

'For you maybe.' Her daughter stared at her, as if it was she who didn't get it.

'Are you going to talk to Hilary about this?'

Please talk to Hilary. Let her help you because I don't know how to right now, Lexi. I don't know what to do for the best and it's killing me . . .

Again she shrugged. Not for the first time, Freya felt glad not only that Lexi had someone to talk to, but also that the professional Ms Wainwright might, unlike her, know the right thing to say.

It was three days after Lexi's visit to Hilary when Freya opened the door to Diana. There was the briefest moment of hesitation until she stepped forward and placed her arms around her mother-in-law.

'I should never have snapped at you like that, Diana, the last time you came.'

'Darling, you've already apologised on the phone! No need to mention it, none at all.'

She patted her back and released her. The two stood facing each other, making no attempt to go upstairs, happy to snatch this time alone on the doorstep. And happy to be at ease in each other's company.

'I know, but it's not the same as saying it in person. I felt, in fact I *feel*, like everything is imploding, but that's still no excuse and I'm sorry.'

'I understand, I do. I was trying to help, but I should have asked you *how* to help instead of wading in without knowledge. I must admit I find it jolly hard to understand, Freya, how this disease works – is it a disease, even? I don't even know if that's the right term!' She blinked.

'It's an illness, yes.' She tried to reassure her, not wanting Diana to feel this unconfident in her choice of words or actions.

Diana shook her head. 'I don't think we had eating disorders in my day. Goodness, we were living in the shining glory of the post-war years and the variety of food was such a treat. Everyone seemed to work hard physically and people had got into the habit of growing food. There was just about enough, but I don't recall seeing people who were horribly overweight – or under. There didn't seem to be the extremes or the obsession. Maybe I just didn't notice it, but nowadays it's everywhere. Why do you think that is?'

Freya beckoned her mother-in-law in as she spoke. 'I don't really know. I wish I did. It might have helped me keep Lexi safe. But I know you are right, it is everywhere, along with this horrible pressure that kids feel. I hate it and I hate that I feel it myself to a lesser degree. That pressure, a kind of fear, I suppose, of not being slim.'

'Be that as it may, right now we only really care about little Lexi, don't we? And the question is, what do we do to make her better? Lockie seems to think it's a case of least said soonest mended.'

Freya followed Diana up the stairs. 'I know he does, but I'm not sure if that's what he really believes or whether he is too scared to face what's really going on.'

Diana reached the top of the staircase and turned back to face her. 'He's lucky to have you.' She leant forward and kissed Freya on the cheek.

Freya smiled, knowing that this simple gesture meant any rift between her and this kindly lady who loved them all was most definitely healed. 'We're lucky to have each other.'

'Hi, Gran!' Lexi greeted her from the kitchen.

'Hello, darling! How are you doing?'

Freya noted the twitch to Diana's eyelid; she was still nervous of saying the wrong thing.

Lexi cut to the chase, giving the answer she knew was the salve for all their worries: 'I put on four pounds.' She bit her lip.

Freya saw for the first time how the collective hope of the whole family rested on this girl's narrow shoulders. It was certainly a pressure she could do without.

'I'm very proud of you.' Her gran winked.

Lexi nodded and tried to swallow the words of disgust and recrimination that Freya knew bubbled on her tongue.

'Hello! Hello!' Lockie called, arriving home from the school pickup with Charlotte in tow.

Charlotte ran up the stairs and burst into the room, dumping her bag on the floor. She gripped the back of the chair at the head of the table and proceeded to jump up and down, like an ungainly ballet dancer.

'Guess what?' she squealed, hardly able to contain the excitement that fizzed from her.

'What?' Freya abandoned the vegetable peeler and the fat carrot in her palm. It was a huge relief to hear her eldest child so animated; gone was the brooding silence that had followed her like a cloud since Freya had missed her concert. The snaking looks of reproach were more punishment than she could handle. This bright, lively entrance suggested that Freya might have been forgiven.

'I've got offers!'

'Oh, darling, that's wonderful! What did you get?' Freya rushed towards her from behind the counter, smiling at her clever girl.

'Nottingham want three Cs, which is easy; my predictions are much higher than that. Bath, B, B, C. And Durham – unconditional!' she screamed, as she resumed her bounding. 'I'm going to university!'

Diana clapped and beamed. 'Well done, Charlotte, that is such great news!' Her face split with pride.

'We'd better get saving, eh?' Lockie jokingly grimaced at his wife while placing a large open box of baklava on the table and making his way to the fridge for a bottle of Prosecco; both would do the job by way of celebration. She smiled at Charlotte, happy for her achievement and what this represented: a bright future, a plan. Her child looked elated, exactly as she should.

'I didn't think anyone would want me. I'm so relieved!' Charlotte was unable to wipe the grin from her face.

'Of course people want you. You're amazing! Well done, darling! You've worked so hard for this, you really deserve it. We are so proud of you.'

Freya's smile, however, faded when her eyes shifted to Lexi. Her younger daughter's expression was one of pure anguish. Her eyes were wide and haunted, her body rigid with fear, but whether at the prospect of her sister leaving home, or whether this achievement felt like holding a mirror up to her own life – or whether it was simply the idea of having to refuse to eat the rich, sweet honey- and nut-laden cakes that were a family favourite – she wasn't sure. Either way, her little girl looked utterly crushed.

Lexi's expression at that single moment in time was one that Freya would never forget. Call it a mother's instinct, but while Diana cheered, Charlotte bounced and Lockie fetched glasses and popped the cork, Freya watched in slow motion as Lexi shrank, withdrew.

It was as if something clicked in her brain, a sixth sense that told her that this was not the start of her child's recovery, as they had hoped; it was in fact the true start of her anorexia.

It was the first time she was able to say the phrase in her head: *My daughter has anorexia. Lexi, my little girl: she is anorexic.*

Freya looked up and saw that Charlotte was staring at her, her expression one of sorrow. She forced a smile of apology and beamed at her daughter on this momentous day. Charlotte blinked and looked away.

'Come on up!' Hilary buzzed her in.

It felt strange to be treading the steps without Lexi; illicit, almost.

'Hey, Freya, how are you?'

She nodded, making her way into the cosy, busy room. 'Thank you for seeing me. I know you're busy.'

'Not at all. I assume you are here to talk about Lexi?' she offered in her no-nonsense tone, pushing her glasses up on to her nose as she took her seat, extending her palm towards the empty chair.

Freya sat. 'Yes. She's . . .' Her tears fell unbidden.

Hilary swiped a tissue from a man-sized box sitting on the little table between them and flicked it at her, holding it between her thumb and index finger, a practised motion that she had perfected. Freya wiped her eyes and blew her nose. 'Sorry, I can't seem to stop crying.'

'So, Lexi?' the woman prompted, kindly, yet aware of time.

'She . . . she seems to have taken a dive, mentally and physically.' It felt like failure to admit.

'In what way?'

Freya swallowed. 'She seems listless, like she's given up. She looks sad, not even pretending anymore.'

'Was there something that prompted the change?' Hilary jotted something down in her notebook.

'It started a couple of weeks ago. Charlotte, her sister . . .'

'Yes.' Hilary nodded. She of course knew all about Charlotte. She continued writing.

'She got her offers for university, we were all delighted, but as we celebrated I watched Lexi: she seemed to crumble before my eyes. It's hard to describe, but her face . . .' She paused. 'It was as if Charlotte's success confronted her with a picture of her own life. She looked beaten. I knew something had changed, and since then she's become more withdrawn and a little hostile. She's hardly eaten. She manages a mouthful here and there, and the odd slice of carrot, or a cracker, but little else.'

She swallowed, ashamed of the admission, and continued.

'It's a battle to get her to take her protein drinks, let alone anything more substantial. I had started to mix double cream into the shakes, told her it was just a thicker shake, any trick I could to get her to take on calories. Mashed potato packed with butter and pepper and wasabi to disguise the taste. She was doing so well, as you know, and this feels like a real setback. She says she isn't purging and I haven't seen any evidence of it, but' – she wiped her eyes once more – 'I can't be sure and I really don't know what to do.'

Hilary nodded sagely. 'I know that Lexi wants to please you all and I would suggest that she might have been a bit sunnier on the outside about her gain than she was letting on.'

Freya nodded. She knew this was true.

'I also wouldn't be too certain that she isn't purging; just because you haven't witnessed it or found evidence doesn't mean it's not happening. As we discussed before when I first met you, people with this condition are almost programmed to deceive; it's part of it, secretive behaviour, lying to achieve their goals and evade capture, if you like. It's quite strategic; for every part of a regimen that you put in place, she has to find a way to evade it.'

Freya pictured the bags of sick hidden in the drawer under her child's bed, the layers of clothing, the secret scales, the two bras, the coins in her shoes . . .

'It's also not uncommon for there to be this rise and fall.' She made loop shapes with her finger in the air. 'It's a complicated illness and there is no quick fix. And as hard as this sounds, sometimes sufferers have to fall further, hit the bottom, before they can start to climb back up again. I know that doesn't offer much that is pleasant, but it *is* hopeful. Because when she *has* hit the bottom, there really is only one way to go.'

'I'm worried for her physical health more than I ever have been. She looks terrible. Weak. It's unbearable . . . I alternate between wanting to wrap her in cotton wool and hold her tight, and wanting to shake her and shout her into submission, and if I thought either would work, I'd do it.'

'Have you taken her back to your GP?'

'She doesn't want to go. She went hysterical when I mentioned it. And I'm so tired of fighting with her, it felt easier to give in and stop the tears.'

'Well . . .' Hilary folded her hands in her lap. 'That's where the job of mum comes in. She's a child and you need to tell her what's going to happen, not negotiate. She needs to see someone, and it's not fair on her or you that she is allowed to control the situation. Different phases in this illness require different approaches. Sometimes I recommend "softly, softly", but when weight is dropping there needs to be an intervention.'

'I worry that if I come down hard on her she will clam up even more. I feel like I'm the one person she can talk to without fear of reprisal, and if I have to get tough, then it's like I'm removing her safety blanket, and that scares me.'

'I think' – Hilary seemed to be choosing her words carefully – 'that sometimes those closest to the source find it the hardest to act objectively . . .'

Freya heard Lockie's words: *I'm simply suggesting that everyone has to stop taking this so personally . . .*

'. . . And that actually by removing her safety blanket, you might force her to act, force her to face her illness. It could be the very best thing for her.'

Freya nodded, both women silently acknowledging that she knew what had to be done, but the simple fact was she was dreading it. It didn't matter how much sense Hilary's words made in the cold light of day, even the thought of Lexi's tear-stained face threatened to melt her resolve.

Arriving home, armed with the shot of confidence that Hilary's words had given her, Freya was resolved to take control, deciding to strike while her will was strongest. She quietly opened Lexi's bedroom door and stared at her daughter's frail back, watching her unseen as she did numerous sit-ups. Her skinny arms were locked behind her head, her long, bony feet hooked under her bed and her narrow thighs in black leggings set apart. She exhaled, pumping up and down, breathing, counting and lifting her weary body again and again to work off the invisible fat that she admitted picturing on the inside and outside of her body.

It was horrible to watch.

'Lexi?' She spoke softly.

Her daughter spun round and moved quickly to a sitting position, her breath coming fast through her pale lips. Her skin was mostly grey, with two high spots of colour on each cheek. Freya decided to pick her battle and chose not to mention the exercising; her single goal was to get Lexi to see the doctor.

'I've been to see Hilary.'

Lexi stared at her; her chest jumped.

'The simple truth is, I need to know what to do for the best and I am struggling. She said it was very important that we get you to see Dr Morris to work out how we go forward, and I agree with her, I'm not going to take no for an . . .' She paused.

Lexi placed her palms flat on the floor either side of her legs and opened her mouth, as if struggling for breath.

'What's the matter?' She leant forward.

Lexi's head slumped forward a little and her shoulders sagged.

'Lexi? What's wrong?' She was unable to disguise the urgent tone to her question.

'My heart feels funny, Mum.' Lexi stared unblinking at her mother. Her expression was one of abject fear.

'Lockie!' Freya screamed as she fell to the floor, cradling her daughter to her chest. 'Lockie!'

She desperately hoped her shout would travel down the stairs and into the studio, to be heard above the burble of the radio.

'How do you feel now, darling?' She hoped for improvement, trying to keep the edge of panic from her voice.

'Same . . . and like I might faint,' she managed.

'Lockie!' Freya screamed again. 'Hang on, my love; it'll all be okay. I promise.' She kissed her.

'What's wrong?'

Freya felt a wave of relief at the sight of her husband, knowing her tone and volume would have left him in no doubt that this was anything other than an emergency. He leant on the door frame, panting after his dash up two flights of stairs.

'She says her heart feels funny! And she's dizzy, faint.' Freya wished she had medical knowledge, wished she knew what to do. 'Call an ambulance!'

Lockie stared at the ashen face of his little girl, who was slumped forward in her mother's arms. He stood frozen to the spot.

'Now, Lockie!' she screamed. 'Call an ambulance now!' Lexi started shaking and Lockie sprang into action, running from the room.

Freya remembered little about the dash to the hospital; could hardly recall the way her daughter's limp frame had been strapped in for the journey, the way her lank hair fell towards the floor or the kindly words of the paramedic, informing and reassuring with well-rehearsed phrases, issued from lips immune to the deep panic she felt. The only thing she could recall were Lexi's eyes, fear etched across the pupils, as she held her mother's gaze.

'Sorry, Mummy,' she muttered listlessly, while Freya shook her head and ran her fingers over her child's translucent skin, taut across the meandering veins on the back of her hand.

The young male doctor in the emergency room was aloof, cool with flashes of irritation. He seemed to prefer looking at his clipboard and notes than at his patient. Freya took an instant dislike to him.

She, however, was too busy processing the images of her daughter's naked body, seen for the first time in an age, when they had removed her clothes and placed her in a hospital gown. It had taken all of her strength not to howl.

Lexi's thin skin was pulled tightly over her breastbone. It looked so fragile; she feared it might tear at the slightest movement. The buds of her chest, where a bust had been promised, were now flattened, and the curve of her ribs stood proud over a concave stomach. The mere sight of her caused both her and Lockie to weep. The collarbone looming large beneath her jutting jaw, and her arms, pale bones where the elbows looked disproportionately large: these were the images that would haunt her dreams.

Freya wanted to take the young doctor outside the ward and shake him, make him aware that, yes, this was self-inflicted, but that a mental illness with physical effects was just as worthy of treatment as any that was purely physical. She doubted he would have felt the same way had he lived long enough to become a parent and love a child unconditionally. He was, however, the conduit between her sick child and the treatment she needed, and for that reason she smiled and nodded in all the right places, keeping her opinions to herself.

'What's the matter with my daughter?' Lockie stood, meeting the young man eye to eye.

The doctor took a deep breath and began, speaking freely in front of their child in a way that did even less to endear him to her. 'Early indications suggest that as well as bone loss, she has a heart issue that's fairly typical with prolonged anorexic behaviour.'

'So it *is* her heart?' Freya needed it confirming.

'Yes.' He nodded. 'She's at the age where—'

'*Lexi,*' Lockie interrupted him. Freya could see from the set of her husband's jaw that he too took offence at the man's manner. '*She* has a name and that name is *Lexi.*'

The doctor was silent for a beat, and then continued. '*Lexi,*' he stressed, in a way that was more placatory than sincere, 'is at an age where she should be accruing bone, but due to her severely restricted calorie intake, in particular a lack of calcium and fats, she has in fact lost bone, and that, I'm afraid, is irreversible.'

Freya squeezed her daughter's hand, feeling the frail bones beneath the palm of her hand. 'It's okay,' she murmured, for whose benefit, hers or her daughter's, she wasn't sure.

'So why does her heart feel funny?' Lockie pushed, wanting to understand.

The doctor tilted his head to one side, as if he was getting to that. 'A side effect of starvation is that it causes devastation to the heart. As well as losing bone mass, you lose muscle as well, and the heart muscle in particular. Lexi's heart is getting smaller and weaker. I see she was exercising just prior: a weakened heart is not as good at circulating the blood needed for exercise, and therefore blood pressure can drop dangerously low.'

Freya felt the strength leave her knees as she swayed on the spot. The doctor's words played inside her mind on a loop: 'devastation to the heart' . . . *No! No! No! We can do this. We can fight it! Please fight this with me!*

'We are going to move her to the critical care unit and start treatment.' He tapped the clipboard with the end of his pen and gave a forced smile, indicating the end of their discussion.

'What is the treatment, exactly?' Lockie spoke for them both.

'We will give her – *Lexi*,' he corrected, 'nutrition via a feeding tube.' He nodded matter-of-factly.

'What do you mean by a feeding tube?' Freya found her voice, wanting to understand. 'Is it the same as drinking through a straw?' She knew this had helped Lexi get her shakes down before.

The doctor gave a slight, almost imperceptible snort. 'Not quite. It's where we insert a tube through the nasal passage, down the oesophagus, and into the stomach. We then deliver nutrition directly to the stomach over a specified period of time via a pump.'

Lexi lifted her heavy head from the pillow. 'No!' she shouted with as much energy as she could muster, her body arching from the mattress, her distress causing her to writhe.

Freya placed her hand on her chest. 'Calm down, Lex! You need to keep calm!'

'Don't . . . don't let them, Mum! Please! Please! No!' She fought for breath.

'What are the alternatives?' Freya looked from her child to the young doctor, silently pleading.

'She *has* to take on nutrition, there's no discussion to be had.' He stood firm.

'I can make her eat! I can! Just give me a bit of time, and if it doesn't work then we can try your way, but please just give me a bit of time. Please.' She looked at her daughter, who loosened her grip on the bed-sheet, and saw her shoulders relax against the mattress.

'What's going to make her better the quickest?' Lockie asked. 'That's what we need to understand.'

Freya shot him a look.

The doctor sighed. 'I have to weigh the distress and reluctance factor against the benefits of a feeding tube. The goal is to get her to eat, and if her mother feels she can achieve that, then I'm happy to let her try, but if your daughter hasn't taken on food within the next hour we'll do it my way.' He swept from the room.

Freya leant close to her daughter's head. 'Did you hear that, Lexi? You have one chance! You have to eat or they are going to make you, with a tube down your throat.' Her own throat seemed to close at the thought.

Lexi nodded.

'I can't believe you almost pushed him to do that, Lockie. I can feed her!' She raised her voice.

'I wasn't pushing for anything. I just want the best and quickest way to make her better. Can't you see that? You are so desperate to avoid discomfort for her, upsetting her, that you are in danger of not seeing what will help her!'

She ignored him, unable to explain that every time she looked at her little girl, she saw her as a toddler who needed her protection. Two nurses arrived to wheel the bed to the critical care unit.

Freya's telephone rang.

'Mum?'

'Yes, darling?'

'I've just finished school. You said you'd pick me up. Where are you?'

Her tears fell as she realised that yet again she had quite forgotten about Charlotte.

'Charlotte, I am so sorry! Jump in a cab; there's money in the jar on the sideboard in the kitchen. We will be home as soon as we can. Lexi isn't well. I'm—'

'Yeah, I know, Mum. You're sorry. So you've said.' She hung up the call.

'Is she okay?' Lockie looked angry.

She could only nod, unwilling to discuss another of her failures.

The smiling nurse delivered a banana-flavoured protein shake, a different make to the ones Lexi had been taking at home. Freya watched, amazed and horrified that even here, even now, Lexi propped herself up on her elbows and tried to read the nutrition label.

Freya turned it round, wary not only of her daughter's reaction, but also of Lockie's. She knew him well enough to see that his patience was being stretched.

'Here we go, Lex. Let's sit you up, darling.' She reached behind and repositioned the pillows, before holding her daughter under the arm and lifting her light frame upwards. Placing the straw at Lexi's mouth, she nodded and smiled, as if this might be enough to get her to drink.

'I can't, Mum!' Lexi cried, fat tears rolling down her emaciated cheeks.

'Yes, you can.' She kept her tone level. 'You can and you must. Let's try again.' She held the straw to her bottom lip, willing her to suck.

Please, Lexi! Please do this! Do it! I need you to; I don't know how much longer I can keep things at bay. Please . . .

Lexi's flow of tears made it almost impossible to draw breath, let alone take on food.

'I don't want that inside me. I don't,' Lexi mumbled, as if she were alone, caring little who heard or what the consequences might be.

Lockie stepped forward and sat by the side of the bed. 'Enough, Lexi. Enough! You drink this shake and you keep it down. Because if you don't they will put a tube down your throat and force you. What bit of that don't you understand? They will put a tube down your throat!' The hardened edge to his voice sprang from frustration, but did little to encourage his daughter.

'Don't get angry with her, Lockie!' she barked. 'It's not helping!'

'Angry?' He bowed his head. It was only when he lifted his face that she saw it was streaked with tears, as he too cried.

'Look at her!' He let his eyes rove over her ravaged form, as he shook his head in desperation. 'Look at my little girl! I just . . . I just want her to drink this. She has to. She has to, Freya, or they'll hurt her! I can't stand it.'

With his elbows resting on the mattress, he placed his face in his hands and sobbed.

Five hours . . .

Freya stared out of the window. She heard Lockie tread the stairs to the kitchen as she carefully chose her next piece to write.

> *I've been thinking about that day, Lex, that terrible day when you were taken to hospital. I shan't ever forget it. I think that was the day I realised two things.*

> *First, just how dangerous your illness was, that it could kill you, a thought I had managed to bury until that point.*

> *Second, I understood that it didn't matter how much Daddy, Charlotte and I loved you, how hard we tried to be a supportive family and make everything better: at best we could only offer a sticking plaster, and it was going to take a lot more outside intervention to make you better.*

> *That was a tough one for me.*

Up until that point, I believed that by giving you the odd protein shake and sneaking other food to you when we could, and the comforting chats with Hilary, it would all be okay. I knew it would take time, but I believed we could get there. This was the first time I questioned our approach.

I wasn't banking on your determination. Crazy, really. You have always been very tenacious in your approach to just about everything.

When you were about four, you asked me if you could cut your hair; you were desperate to get hold of scissors. I told you that your hair was pretty and didn't need cutting and I said it was dangerous, which only seemed to intrigue you more.

I should have suspected you were up to something when you went quiet on the topic, only to emerge from my bedroom with the front of your hair hacked off and big chunks missing from the back where your scalp was visible. I asked you if you'd cut your hair, and you shook your head and said, 'No, Mummy,' staring at me, as if this couldn't have been further from your mind; and I would have fallen for the sweet, sincere denial had I not been staring at the evidence.

TEN

Freya had sat in the ward and listened to Dr Roberts, the psychiatrist who had been assigned to Lexi. He was an older man, kindly and unflustered, with little round metal-rimmed glasses that were too small for his large bearded face. No matter how well delivered, his words made her feel hopeless, picturing their life on this merry-go-round of destruction.

She spent hours lying awake at night, trying to fathom the dilemma. They had been told that anorexia was not about food, and the advice was not to make an issue out of Lexi's eating and purging. But then the medical team hourly reminded her of the importance of getting her child to take on calories, reinforcing the message that, above all, Lexi had to consume food. Freya felt pulled in every direction, overwhelmed by doubt, and could only imagine what it felt like for Lexi, who was also battling her fear of eating.

Dr Roberts explained that, in his experience, people with eating disorders were usually experiencing underlying emotional distress, and were dealing with difficult life changes or past trauma. This sent Freya into a spin, analysing every month of Lexi's fifteen years on the planet, trying desperately to spot the point when things had started to fall apart. What had they missed? She had even gripped Lexi's hand: 'Is there anything you want to tell me, darling? Any reason you can think of as to why you might have these feelings?'

Bracing herself for the answer, Freya hoped there was a reason, something she might be able to understand, while praying that there wasn't, that nothing had hurt or damaged her little girl and that she hadn't inadvertently committed a dreadful error. She wanted, above all else, to be a good mum.

Lexi had looked her in the eyes. 'There's nothing, Mum,' came her heartbreaking reply. 'I wish there was, in a way. I don't know what it's like for other people, I only know what it's like for me, and I can't help it.'

Freya couldn't wait to see Dr Roberts again, telling him that she was unaware of any past trauma or difficult life changes, as if this might exonerate her parenting, absolve her of at least one layer of guilt.

Freya closed the curtains in Lexi's bedroom and smiled at her daughter, who lay in her bed. Finally she was back home; this in itself was a huge achievement. In the nine weeks she had been in hospital, her weight had plateaued, and her resistance during hospital mealtimes had lessened, as if she'd accepted, begrudgingly, that this was the only way she would ever get home. It had been a stressful time. Freya had felt pulled: whether at home with Charlotte or sitting with Lexi, she always felt guilty that she was not with the other. It was a horrible no-win situation. She crawled into bed each night, weary from the travel, the lack of routine, and the gut-twisting worry about her children.

Much to Marcia's annoyance, Freya had hardly worked, and left the daily running of the house and the ferrying of Charlotte back and forth from school to Lockie. She had eventually confided in Marcia, without giving too much detail, simply giving her enough information to let her know that they had hit a bump, crying as she outlined Lexi's struggle, and crying some more with every word of sympathy her friend muttered.

Lockie and Charlotte took their meals on the fly or sourced them from the fish and chip shop; this was yet another avenue of food for her to feel guilty about.

'Happy to be back?'

It was the first day out of hospital.

Lexi nodded as she shivered, her teeth rattling as she sank down lower on the bed.

'Are you still cold?'

She nodded. This too was now familiar: Lexi's lack of body fat meant she was invariably freezing.

Freya unfurled the patchwork quilt that had graced her parents' bed and laid it over the two duvets that already held Lexi fast. Still she shivered.

She and Lockie had, after consultation with the specialist team, decided against referring Lexi to an in-patient facility, and the look of total relief on her daughter's face told her this was the right choice. Instead, they were adopting an approach that meant she could stay in the family home.

The specialist explained it was a way of treating anorexia in a familiar environment, with treatment by the family, whilst still under the out-patient care of the hospital. A specially trained therapist would visit them, fully explain the plan to them and, most importantly, maintain the stance to Lexi that starvation was not an option. To them it made immediate sense to keep Lexi in her home environment, where phase one was for her to gain more weight. Freya felt anything was better than sending her to an in-patient facility. Lockie, however, had taken a little persuading; his resistance only provided more fuel to Freya's fire. She was determined to make it work.

Their therapist was of Chinese heritage. She was a sober, efficient graduate called Iris, who had a strange sense of fashion but a wide smile and a calm manner that gave them confidence. She arrived one evening bringing bright-green tights, yellow shoes, a pink shirt and buckets of hope into their family home.

'I shall merely observe tonight.' She smiled. 'Please go about your family meal as if I weren't here and then we can chat afterwards. How does that sound?' she asked as she took a seat at the countertop, pulled out her laptop and popped on her square-framed glasses.

Freya swallowed as she reached into the crisper for the veg. Her hand shook. 'I feel like I'm taking a test that I don't want to fail.'

Iris laughed. 'I know, everyone says that. It takes a bit of getting used to. It's not like I'll be here for every meal, just a couple, to observe and help if I can, and more if you need me. But try not to think of it negatively. Just ignore me; we are on the same side and there is no right or wrong. You can't fail: we can only learn what Lexi needs right now to thrive, and help put it in place.'

Her words were gratefully received, but in truth did little to calm Freya's nerves.

Lockie looked sheepish as he came up from his studio and headed towards the fridge. 'Hello, I'm Lockie. And you must be Iris?'

'I am. Hello, Lockie, how are you?'

'Nervous.' He exhaled. 'I want a beer with my supper, but fear that might earn me minus points.'

'Not at all, you have to relax. Have your beer.' She smiled.

'Ah, "relax" . . . Yep, well, that's certainly a lot easier to do when we are not being observed. There's a knot in my gut when I think about what Lexi might do next. I'm also afraid of her slipping up again and ending up in hospital.'

Iris and Freya stared at him. It was rare for him to be so forthcoming with his emotions.

Iris pushed her glasses up on to her nose. 'I know this is a difficult time, but as I was just saying to Freya, we are on the same side, presenting a unified front. This isn't about scrutiny or blame; it's about helping Lexi gain. That's it, right now. That's the goal.'

'Okay.' He nodded and pulled the dark-green bottle from the fridge door, flipping the lid with the bottle-opener end of the corkscrew.

'How you doing, Lexi?' Iris smiled and crossed her legs on the stool as Lexi skulked in. Her flared pyjama bottoms dragged on the floor and the hood on her grey Jack Wills sweatshirt was pulled up, hiding her hair and half her face.

Lexi stared at her with a look of naked aggression that Freya hadn't seen before, and her heart sank. She swallowed the desire to tell her to be nice, to make Iris welcome; this was, after all, a therapist, here to observe, and not simply an extra guest for dinner.

'Ooh, lovely,' Charlotte sang as she sat down. 'What are we having? I'm starving.' She had been briefed on Iris's visit.

'I hate you, Charlotte!' Lexi yelled. Her anger, volume and choice of words were so entirely out of character that the whole room went quiet, as each looked from one to the other, trying to figure out what might come next.

It was Lockie who found his voice. 'Ignore her, Charlotte. That is a horrible thing to say, and I feel sad, Lexi, that this is how you choose to talk to your sister.'

Freya kept her eyes downcast as she served the chicken breast, steamed vegetables and spicy rice on to the plates and set them down with a trembling hand. Charlotte began eating straight away, carefully avoiding eye contact with her little sister, a stranger to them all.

Freya didn't know whether to comment on the fact that Lexi placed her hands in the front pocket of her hoodie, determined not to eat. She sat next to Lockie, knowing the only way to get through this family therapy session was with their thighs touching under the table, providing not only comforting contact, but also a steady anchor when it felt as if everything was in free fall.

It took all her strength to smile and make small talk, bracing herself, waiting for the next heavy, blunted act of aggression to hit her on the side of the head.

'Eat up, Lexi,' Lockie commanded.

'I don't want it,' she snapped petulantly, pushing her plate a little further on to the table.

'I understand, but it's not about what you want anymore, it's about what you need. Do you want me to feed you?' His offer was sincere, as if the issue might lie in the actual cutting and lifting of the food.

Lexi snorted her reply. 'No!' She looked and sounded like a frightened toddler.

'Okay, then cut the food into pieces and make a start. You are not leaving the table until that plate is clear, and it will be more palatable when it's warm.' He remained articulate and cool, whilst cutting into his own food.

Lexi's anger then turned to distress; her tears seemed to make further protest hard. Freya noted the way her eyes strayed to Iris, confirming not only her embarrassment at the display in front of their visitor, but also that she was still a little girl, just a confused one.

It was heartbreaking.

Freya caught Iris's eye. The therapist gave her a small nod of approval. They were all doing fine.

It was a little after ten that evening. Iris had been waved off an hour or so before, and Freya finally finished up the dishes and was clearing the kitchen. Lockie completed the picture edit he was working on. The two slumped wearily on the sofa in the den. Lockie ran his hand over his face and hooked his hands behind his head with his eyes closed and his glasses on the table.

'An hour and a half we sat at that table,' he lamented. 'I wanted so badly to say, "Okay, just leave it!" but I knew that if we gave in this time, we'd give in every time.'

Freya nodded as he continued.

'I've got to be honest, I was so stressed by the end of the meal, and I know that if Iris hadn't been there, I'd have caved in.'

She sat back, resting her head on his chest. Lockie brushed her hair with his palm.

'It's hard, Lockie,' she confessed.

'It is.' He sighed. 'But the point is, she ate and she kept it down. Charlotte sat with her and has made sure she didn't visit the bathroom. They watched TV in her room, and that seems to have put things right between them.'

'Poor Charlotte – the way Lexi spoke to her was awful. It's not her, it's like the other Lexi that pops up from time to time, but that aggression, the meanness . . . I don't even recognise it!'

'Me neither,' he confirmed. 'And I feel so pulled. I want to reprimand her more, not least of all for Charlotte's sake, but I'm also very wary of not adding an ounce of stress to her. She looks so fragile, I don't know how much more she can withstand.'

Freya stroked the back of his palm. Both sat in comfortable silence, weary.

Charlotte walked into the kitchen.

'There she is! All okay, darling?' Freya called out.

Charlotte nodded. 'Yep, Lexi's nodded off. I'm going to have a bath, then read a bit before I go to sleep.'

'Not too late, love,' Lockie added.

'I know.' She nodded.

'Dad and I were just saying. She didn't mean it, you know.' Freya felt the need to point this out. No one asked her to be more specific: Lexi's words and actions still loomed in their minds.

'I know,' she uttered again. 'It's still shit, though.'

Freya looked at Lockie, both wary of chastising her curse. She had had quite enough to deal with for one night.

There was the delicate sound of pitter-patter on the open window.

'Be a darling and call Brewster in, would you? He hates being out in the rain.'

'Sure. That's me: a darling,' Charlotte sniped. 'Just give me an instruction and I'll run off to do it!'

'Well, don't then. I'll do it.' Freya sighed.

'I said I'd do it! God, Mum!' Charlotte slunk from the room.

Freya rubbed her eyes, hating the way everyone was so angry, so emotionally taut.

Lockie sighed. 'I miss you.'

'I'm right here.' She smiled.

'I guess what I mean is, I miss *us*, the way we used to laugh all the time, our chat, our sex.'

'I know.' She closed her eyes.

'I am tired, Freya, and Friday night was always a good night for going to bed, with no alarm set for Saturday, but the truth is I'm nervous right now, because the sooner I go to sleep, the sooner I have to wake up and face another day of conflict when we get to go through the whole thing again.'

Freya nuzzled against his chest, knowing there were no words of solace. They had a feeding routine to maintain, living under the shadow of this horrible disease; still clinging to the legs of their child while the giant bird flapped its wings and cawed in response.

The next morning, the Braithwaite family sat in silence. No one had mentioned the fear-laden warble with which Freya had called her family to the table for brunch or the tense atmosphere that prevailed. Gone was the familiar banter and noisy exchange over the table. Instead, every stilted communal mealtime brought with it an awkwardness and a tension that was a sadness to them all.

Freya felt her pulse race in anticipation as Lexi came into the room, again with her hood pulled up and her sleeves over her hands, as if she were trying to hide.

Freya had cooked the scrambled egg, crispy bacon, avocado, mozzarella-and-tomato salad and wholewheat toast with a feeling of dread, underlined with sadness, remembering when food was such a lovely part of their life. Now it felt like a taboo topic and a challenge for them all.

Freya knew she had to ask what Lexi wanted on her plate; her palms were clammy and mouth dry in advance. The way her stomach jumped meant that food was the last thing she wanted too, but she was ever conscious of setting a good example.

'What would you like, darling? I've got fluffy scrambled egg, a nice salad, home-made bread, honey or jam, bacon?' Her fake tone of joviality was as irritating as it was obvious.

Lexi shook her head, vigorously, as if all on offer was abhorrent.

'Okay, then.'

Freya took a deep breath and spooned the scrambled egg on to a slice of toast; she would yet again have to make the decision for her.

Lockie quietly took his seat at the table.

This became their life; they were, as a family, utterly consumed, living in a bubble that kept them isolated from the real world. Lockie had refused several jobs, as he was needed at home, and any friends who suggested getting together were given a polite refusal. Carefully monitoring every morsel Lexi ate, counting every calorie she managed and preparing for her next feed was like having a small baby, but one that glared at you from the other side of the room and begrudged every mouthful.

The hospital had blind-weighed her, a neat trick of getting her to walk backwards on to the scales so as not to alarm her about her gain or her actual weight, whilst monitoring her gradual improvements. Her periodic blind-weighing saw them hold their breath, waiting to see if the number crept in the right direction, whilst trying not to let Lexi know, as any hint that she had gained would send her into a blind panic, a torrent of abuse directed at whoever happened to be closest.

Four weeks after Lexi had returned home, Freya called Iris and gave her the good news of Lexi's current weight gain, informing her that it appeared to be stable. Their persistence was paying off: this alone made the mealtime struggles seem worth it.

'In that case . . .' Iris paused, as if knowing that the next instruction was tough. 'We need to carry on with the regimen, but up her intake, increase it to around two thousand calories a day. That would be perfect.'

'Gosh! That's a lot. Compared to what she's been taking.' Freya spoke aloud her immediate thought, knowing that this might be the average for a normal functioning woman, but for someone like Lexi . . . ? It felt like a huge challenge.

'It is, but it's what she needs, Freya. Trust me.'

'I do.' Her brain whirred, trying to think of how she could further supplement the foods Lexi ate with extra calories.

So began a new phase of Freya's subterfuge, stuffing butter into sponge cakes and dousing muesli with sugar-coated nuts and frosted fruits, encouraging Lexi to nibble soft cookies between meals, while serving ice cream—laden milkshakes in opaque drinking glasses so that the contents were harder to see.

Even though Lexi only managed a mouthful before her brain rejected the offering, every bite, every sip, caused Freya's heart to leap with joy and her gut to twist with guilt. It was the right thing to do, but she was still deceiving her child. It was one stressful way to live.

'Can you call Brewster in?' Freya called from the sink. 'It's spitting again.'

Lockie looked up from the table. 'No, it's not!' He looked towards the garden, now bathed in the half-light of dusk, and back to his wife.

'It is, I heard it!' She laughed, removing her hands from the sink and looking at him, as though at least one of them might be losing their reason. Wiping her hands on the dishcloth, she made her way to the back window and felt the quake that started in her knees travel up her spine. She teetered backwards, fearing she might lose her balance altogether.

'Are you okay?'

Lockie scraped the chair along the floor and went to assist his wife.

Her eyes were fixed on the tall window of the bifold floor-to-ceiling windows at the back of the den.

'What is it?' he repeated his concern, his tone a little more urgent.

'You were right,' she whispered, pointing her finger towards the garden. 'It wasn't rain.'

Lockie took a step closer and peered at the glass, now covered in a fine sticky spray. He walked forward and opened the window, examining the glass before looking back at his wife, confirming her fears.

She hadn't been mistaken: she had indeed on more than one occasion heard the soft pitter-patter, but not of rain. Focusing on the window, she was now able to recognise the cubes of tomato, the specks of egg and fine shreds of carrot; she realised what it was that had splashed the window in the dark of night. Peering down on to the courtyard below confirmed that it had been her daughter's vomit, launched from the window on the floor above.

They thought they had been smart, asking Charlotte to sit with her directly after supper, even covertly timing her visits to the loo. All of their efforts were to no avail, pointless in the face of this new development.

'She's been throwing up out of the window,' she confirmed. 'She knew we'd be listening out for the bathroom, checking the loo.'

'Sweet Jesus.' Lockie stared at her, seemingly at a loss for what to say next.

Freya felt her shoulders curve in distress as her tears fell. 'I'm so tired of it, Lockie.'

With his fists clenched, he fled the room.

'Lockie!' she called after him.

He ignored her, tearing down the stairs towards his studio. She followed him with her hands outstretched, hoping to calm him down. She understood that this was upsetting, but knew that his rage would do nothing to help. Standing in the doorway, she watched as he flung open the doors of the tall storage cupboard where handheld lights, portable heaters, fans and background screens were folded and neatly stacked away. Pulling out a dark-grey metal box, he hauled it on to the floor and lifted the top, letting it fall open on its hinges.

'What are you doing?' she asked, half afraid and half exasperated.

'I've had enough.' He dashed her a look as he grabbed a hammer and pushed past her.

'What on earth . . . ? Lockie? Calm down!'

Her pleas fell on deaf ears. As is often the case with anyone who is enraged, the request for calm had the opposite effect.

She followed as he sprinted the first staircase and continued on up, past the kitchen and up towards the bedrooms on the second floor.

Without knocking, he opened Lexi's bedroom door. Freya stood and stared, not knowing how to comment on her child's activity, horrified to discover her sitting with her feet planted under her bed and performing rhythmic sit-ups with her arms folded across her chest. She watched as Lexi shrank back against the wall, discovered, exposed, as Lockie stormed over to the window.

'Dad, what are you doing?' she shrieked.

'I'm fighting back, Lex!'

He placed a few nails between his lips and took one in his hand, then drove it with the hammer through the base of the sash window, straight through the window frame, down into the windowsill. Plucking another nail from his mouth, he did the same a little further along, continuing until there was only one nail left in his mouth.

'Please don't, Dad!' Lexi cried loudly. 'I'm sorry!'

Freya felt torn: she wanted to comfort her child, but also knew that they had to take a stand or she would continue to find new and more ingenious ways to deceive them.

'Please, Dad!' Lexi yelled. 'I'm sorry! I won't do it again!' Her voice was now desperate, shrill.

Lockie ignored her.

'What's going on? Why are you nailing her window shut?' Charlotte enquired from the hallway.

It was all the distraction it took; Lockie pulled back his arm and in a split second of misjudgement he brought the hammer down, catching the flat head at such an angle on the brittle Edwardian glass that it shattered into tiny fragments, falling in shards across Lexi's desk and over the carpet where she sat, coiled and terrified.

Charlotte screamed and Lexi placed her hands over her ears, as if she could undo the deafening crack or the sound of the wind that now whistled through the fist-sized hole in the window. The remainder of the glass then fell away in jagged sheets, falling to the courtyard below.

Freya stared in disbelief at the chaotic scene in front of her. Her tears fell unbidden.

Lockie turned, the glass crunching under his feet.

'You can sleep on the sofa in Mum's study tonight,' he spat. 'There are new rules, Lexi, and they are non-negotiable. You will finish your food before you leave the table – I don't care if we sit there for an hour, two hours, three, so you'd better dig in. You are not to play with the food, anything that touches your fork has to immediately go into your mouth. You will not slouch or wear your hood up at the table. You will never, ever close any bedroom or bathroom door that you are in. Never. If you take a bath, either Mum or your sister will have to come and sit with you; if you need the loo, one of us will be outside. Do you understand?'

Lexi stared, wide-eyed at this unfamiliar version of her dad. Her eyes darted to her mum, who cried quietly and looked at the window, avoiding both of their eyelines.

'Do you understand?' he boomed.

Lexi jumped and nodded.

'Good.' He stared at his wife, daring her to undermine him.

'I can't have a bath,' Lexi whispered.

'What? I can't hear you!' he shouted. His fingers flexed in anger and frustration.

'I can't have a bath anymore.' She was trying to speak loudly, but fear and weakness meant her voice was still barely more than a whisper.

'Is that right? No baths? Well, that's a new one. Did you hear that, Freya? No bathing! Why not?' he spat, shaking his head at his wife.

Lexi looked up at him, her large eyes staring from inside her lollipop head. 'The bones in my bottom feel like they are cutting through my skin if I sit in a bath; it hurts me,' she managed.

And just like that, the anger dissipated and the Braithwaite family were awash with sorrow at this simple truth, shared by their sick child.

Lockie let the hammer fall to the floor, as if the strength had left his hand. Charlotte leant on the wall and cried to herself, and Lexi laid her head with its thin covering of patchy hair on her raised enormous knees, as if trying to block out the world.

There was the sudden sound of pitter-patter as the heavens opened and rain fell, finding its way into the room, as if their sorrow had summoned it and pulled it into the space where they stood.

'I'll go and call Brewster in,' Charlotte offered, seemingly relieved to be escaping the room her family occupied, each feeling like they might suffocate.

Four hours, thirty minutes . . .

Charlotte crept into the study.

'Hey, Mum, just wanted to let you know that Toby has just dropped this off. I messaged him.'

Charlotte spoke as she entered the study, placing the folded piece of paper on the edge of the desk and taking a seat on the sofa.

Freya turned to look at her daughter. 'How are you feeling?'

'Oh . . . you know.'

Reaching out, Freya took the note in her fingers and opened it. Toby had a neat, professorial hand, just as she might have predicted.

'Shall I read it out?'

Charlotte nodded again, pulling the soft mohair blanket up over her shoulder, inhaling the scent of those in her family who had taken comfort from it in recent times.

Freya coughed and read aloud:

> You are my only friend, Alexia. You have never laughed
> at me. You are the kindest person I have ever met. You

told me that everyone has their time and that my time wasn't while I was at school, but not to be sad, as my time would come later when I discovered something great in maths or used it to change the world. I never thought I could change the world, but I know if you think that, Alexia, then it might be true.

And I love you.

Toby.

Charlotte sobbed and fell forward from the sofa on to the floor. 'Mum!' she managed. 'Oh, Mum!' She gasped for air.

'It's okay, darling, it's okay.'

Freya left the chair to hold her girl tightly, glancing over her shoulder at the beautiful words she held in her hand, written by the boy she had thought so little of.

ELEVEN

'Can I go out with Fennella on Saturday?' Lexi asked, quite out of the blue and with an air of brightness that was rare of late. She forked the last piece of broccoli into her mouth and chewed. It was the first time she had shown any interest in seeing or being seen by her friends in a long time.

'What's brought this on? You usually don't want to see anyone.' Lockie cut to the chase.

Lexi nodded. 'I know, but I thought they wouldn't want to see me. I'm so weird, and because I'm not at school I don't really know what's going on, but Fennella WhatsApp'd me and said that she would really like to see me, and it felt nice to know that they kind of missed me.'

'I don't see why not, if you feel up to it.' Freya raised her eyebrows at Lockie, delighted by the development, the display of normality. 'And you are not "weird", darling. Just poorly.'

Lexi ignored her.

'As long as you stay close to home,' Lockie added. 'Maybe get Nutella to come here and go for a walk or whatever, but don't stray too far, I think that might be best. We promise to give you space and privacy, but you're not quite fighting fit yet, Lex.'

'And you have to promise not to call her Nutella!' Lexi sighed.

'I promise!' Lockie held up three fingers in a salute reminiscent of the Boy Scouts. 'Fennella Fenackerpants.' He laughed loudly.

'Da-ad!'

Lexi shoved him, and in that second Freya was reminded of the family life she used to enjoy, the humorous exchanges that were their glue, the relaxed atmosphere that meant to sit around the family table at mealtimes was the only place they wanted to be. This was a very good sign.

It broke Freya's heart to watch Lexi brushing her long hair that was now so thin and lank. The blusher she then applied sat on her sharpened cheekbones, strikingly incongruous against her grey pallor. The smudge of dark eyeshadow on her swollen lids mirrored the blue-black stain of fatigue and stress that lived permanently beneath her sunken eyes. Far from prettifying her elfin face, the addition, the artifice, had quite the opposite effect, making her look comic, almost grotesque.

'How do I look?' Lexi smiled in her direction, pulling the hem of her hoodie down over the flattened bottom of her super-skinny jeans. Her Doc Martens hung on the end of her spindly legs.

'You look lovely,' Freya lied, rewarded by her daughter's grin as she stacked the dishwasher. The scent of Lexi's perfume, liberally applied, filled the kitchen.

'You'll be pleased to hear that I haven't made any cakes and Dad has been given strict instructions not to be himself. I promise we will be very well behaved.' She smiled.

Lexi sighed. 'Even you saying that makes me feel nervous, like you're not going to be yourselves.'

'I thought you didn't want us to be ourselves!' Freya was genuinely a little confused.

'I don't! Well, I do . . . I want you to be the nice bits of yourself, but not the loony bits. You can be nice and friendly, but no singing or mucking about or talking to the cat – and absolutely no kissing Dad!'

'Yuck!' Freya pulled a face in mock horror. 'As if!'

She caught the minty tones of mouthwash when Lexi spoke, only just discernible above her heady perfume.

Lexi continued, undeterred. 'I'd like you to be more like Fennella's parents, just for today.'

Freya pictured the dour, sober, tweed-skirt-wearing woman and her joyless husband who had once managed to hold them captive at a barbecue for nearly two hours with their detailed recollection of a weekend spent on a narrow boat near Solihull and the various locks they had encountered en route.

'I'll do my very best.' She nodded.

Lexi's face broke into a smile. This was obviously important to her.

'You do look lovely, by the way.'

'I don't.' Lexi kicked her Doc Marten against the wooden floor. 'I wish I was pretty, like Charlotte.'

'Lexi?' Freya walked over to her and looked her daughter in the eye. 'You are so beautiful! Don't ever doubt that. You are the kindest, sweetest person and that lights you up from within. You have no idea how very beautiful you are, inside and out.'

Lexi sat, preoccupied by her phone, reading, scrolling and texting with lightning speed.

'Bit nervous, Lex?' Lockie asked, as he clicked the kettle to boil, still none the wiser when it came to operating the coffee machine.

She nodded. 'A bit.'

'If you want me to come and pick you up in the car, just shout, even if it's after five minutes. Only you know how you feel. I'm doing nothing other than sitting here, reading and waiting for your call, whilst making out not to be waiting for your call. Okay?'

She nodded.

'Is your phone fully charged?' he asked.

'Dad! I used to go out all the time! I thought Fennella might have forgotten about me, but she hasn't. She asked me out and so I'm going. I'm fine and if I need you, I'll call you. I promise.' She rolled her eyes. Her reprimand and irritation were so gloriously normal and teenage-like, Lockie looked close to tears.

'I can't help it, Lex. You will always be my little girl. And no matter how old you get . . .' He swallowed. 'I will worry about you just the same.'

Lexi stared at his tear-filled eyes. It was a second before she spoke. 'If you dare cry in front of Fennella or say anything that mushy, I will actually kill you!' She sighed again.

Lockie's roar of laughter filled the kitchen, as Freya reached for the basket full of clean laundry waiting to be folded. She too laughed, happy to be part of the joke.

'Our daughter has just put me firmly in my place,' he announced.

'That's my girl!' Freya winked.

The doorbell rang.

'I'll get it!' Charlotte called from the TV room downstairs, where she was ensconced on the sofa with Milly and Tara watching *Game of Thrones* from under duvets, shovelling popcorn and giggling though the sex scenes.

Fennella appeared in the kitchen in all her glossy, blonde, breath-less glory. Freya couldn't help but stare at the natural bloom to her rounded cheeks, her thick, healthy hair, her white, white teeth in their pink gums, her sparkling eyes and full bust, the perfect symmetry to her high, pert bottom. She felt a twinge of envy for this girl's parents, wondering how things had turned out so very different for Lexi.

'Lovely to see you, Fennella.' She smiled.

'Oh my God! Lex! You look amazing!' The girl enthusiastically embraced her friend before standing back to get a better look at her. 'Seriously, Lex, you look brilliant.' She shook her head.

Freya was confused at first, wondering if Fennella had been instructed to be kind and was simply overplaying her part. She was more than a little concerned with the way Fennella viewed Lexi's emaciated frame with something close to admiration, as though being this skinny were in itself an achievement.

She tried to catch Lockie's eye, nervous of the girl's reaction.

'I don't think so.' Lexi looked at the floor.

'But you do!' Fennella emphasised, linking her arm through her friend's.

'How's Mum and Dad?' Lockie asked, seemingly unaffected.

'Good, thank you.' Her voice was saccharine sweet with practised manners. 'They are on a boating holiday. My nan is looking after me.'

'Oh, where have they gone? Somewhere nice? Solihull?' Lockie avoided his wife's knowing look.

'Solihull? No, they're in Northampton.' Fennella looked confused.

'Oh, smashing. Northampton.' He beamed at his wife.

'Come on, Lex. We've got *so* much to talk about.' She pulled Lexi towards the door.

'Have fun!' Freya called after them, listening to the sweet sound of their girlish babble, interspersed with giggles, floating up the stairs. It would have been hard to explain to anyone not in this situation just how incredible it was to be experiencing this normality. It was like any other Saturday, the thousands they had spent before anorexia pecked at their child, pulling her into its clutches. Freya decided not to dilute the happy atmosphere with her concerns.

'This is a good day.' She smiled at her husband, who nodded in agreement.

'It really is.'

Freya eyed the clock. The girls had been gone for an hour, and she had started to relax. Pulling out her laptop, she constructed an email to Marcia.

> **Hey Boss, good news and bad news. Good news: I think we have turned a corner, which means I am back in work mode. Bad news: I shall be badgering you for an assignment. Speak Monday? Much love, F x**

'What are you looking so smug about?' Lockie walked up behind her and lifted her hair; he kissed the nape of her neck.

'I don't know.' She let her head hang forward, enjoying the touch of his lips against her skin. 'I guess I'm just happy!'

'Well, amen to that.' He smiled. 'How long do you think we've got before Lexi gets back?' He ran his hands down the sides of her waist as she lifted her arms, running her fingers through his thick hair.

'I'm not sure,' she whispered. 'But Charlotte and her mates are downstairs,' she reminded him.

'It's not like they're going to move from the sofa anytime soon. They have popcorn, duvets and men fighting naked from the chest up – they're all set. Why don't we take advantage of this lull in proceedings and nip upstairs?' He kissed her once again.

Freya turned in her seat and returned his kiss on the mouth, their ardour building.

'I suppose we could . . .' She giggled.

'Come on! We need to strike while the iron is hot, as they say!' He nodded his head towards the stairs.

Freya placed her finger on her lips, as if deep in concentration. 'Just give me a second. I'm trying to think what Fennella's parents would do in this situation. After all, we do need to be more like them.'

'They would definitely go upstairs and have quick but satisfying sex.' He pulled a very innocent face.

'I'm not so sure . . .' She flicked her hair.

'Hang on a minute!' Lockie ran over to the fruit bowl and picked up a banana, holding it to his ear.

'Oh, hello, Mr Fenackerpants . . . What's that? . . . You heartily recommend making the most of this short window of time alone with my beautiful wife? Okay, then!'

He put the banana back in the bowl and grabbed the hand of his giggling spouse.

It was with exquisite timing that as she stood, Lockie's phone rang.

'If it's anyone other than Lexi I'm ignoring it,' he stated, grabbing at the phone. He closed his eyes and pursed his lips, as he swiped the screen.

'Yes, darling?'

His expression changed instantly to one of concern. Highly agitated, he stood tall, placing his hand on his hip.

Freya felt the joy drain from their day.

'Okay! Just calm down, Lex, calm down, darling. I'm on my way. Where are you exactly?'

He turned his head to the side and cupped his hand over his ear.

'I can hardly hear you, Lex . . . Don't cry, darling, please don't cry! I am on my way. Just tell me where you are.'

Freya's pulse quickened. She grabbed the car keys and stood inches from him, waiting to see where they were headed and desperate to know what had happened.

'Right . . . Don't move, Lex! Stay right where you are! We'll be there in a couple of minutes.'

He ended the call and stared at Freya. She felt her stomach knot.

'What's happened?' She hardly dared to ask.

'I'm not really sure.' He shook his head. 'She's outside Costa near the clock tower, she's very upset. I couldn't really make out what she was saying. I don't know if I'll be able to park . . .' He pondered the practicalities.

'That's okay. Get as close as you can, I'll jump out and get her. Is she hurt or just upset?' She tried to figure out the problem, still concerned with so little to go on and running instantly into rescue mode.

'I don't know!' Lockie repeated.

'Mum?' Charlotte called from the ground floor.

Freya thundered down the stairs behind Lockie. 'Not now, darling, we're off to grab Lexi, she's just called Dad and is a bit upset.' She nodded towards the door of the TV room, not wanting to give the limited details she had in front of Milly and Tara.

'Will you *listen* to me?' she shouted. Freya turned to face her, embarrassed to be having this altercation in front of Charlotte's friends.

'I just wanted to show you this!' Charlotte handed her mum an unfamiliar phone. 'Tara just got a Facebook alert. She's in a group because Fennella's brother is her friend and this just came through.'

Freya stared at the image, unable to make it out instantly. Pulling the screen away from her face, she saw that it was the back of Lexi's legs, the picture taken as her daughter bent over. It clearly showed the flattened panel where her bottom used to live, and the wide gap between the top of her fleshless thighs. It shared the screen with another image: the back of a starved donkey, whose emaciated flank showed the bones and whose skinny legs hung down with flies nestling on the matted fur. Someone had written the caption:

Skinny donkey butt! Thigh gap!

There were then a number of comments and emojis growing beneath.

Gross.

LOL!

PMSL. Donkey butt eeeeaauw eeeeaauw !!

Who ate all the pies – not her!

Still the phone continued to ping and the comments grew.

#Thinspiration

Disgusting!

Get some meat on her bones. Who her
family?

#NOTNICESHEDAMSKINNY!

'What on earth . . . ?' Freya looked at Charlotte, whose expression was nothing short of horrified.

Charlotte took the phone from her. It continued to ping with updates, more shares, more likes, more people seeing and commenting on the vile post.

'There are other pictures, Mum. Worse than that.'

'Sweet Jesus!' Lockie commented, then threw open the front door and ran to the car.

Freya had to sprint to keep up.

'Come on! Come on!' He impatiently smacked the steering wheel at every red light, revving the tired engine and leaning forward, as if this might give them the edge of speed.

'When I find out who did this . . .' He let his words hang in the air.

'I can't believe it would be one of her friends.'

She shook her head: that idea was simply too awful to contemplate.

The traffic thinned and Lockie broke all speed limits, caring little for the consequences, intent only on getting to his daughter in the quickest possible time.

'There she is! Outside Zizzi's!' Freya shouted, pointing to the busy cobbled pavement on this Saturday afternoon.

He slowed the car, indicating and braking at the same time, slowing enough for Freya to jump out as he whacked on the hazards on the double yellow line and waited.

Freya ran across the road and into the crowd with her arms outstretched, calling her little girl's name as she ran.

'Lexi! It's okay! Lexi! It's okay now!'

As she drew nearer, her daughter turned her head in the direction of her mum. She had been crying. Her carefully applied make-up was smeared across her face. She closed her eyes in slow blinks and stumbled into her mum's arms.

With her arm across her shoulder, Freya pulled her child towards her, ignoring the stares they drew as she shepherded her across the road and into the safety of the back of the car, where they sat closely together.

'Are you okay?' Lockie asked.

'She's fine,' Freya answered sharply on their daughter's behalf.

Lexi sat in silence, staring out of the window.

Lockie drove home carefully, all urgency now gone, stealing glances at his daughter in the rear-view mirror. Freya twisted her body and stared at the face of her child. Lexi's expression was almost blank, her eyes dead and lifeless, bottomless pools of despair that were as haunting as they were haunted.

'We'll soon have you home, Lex. A nice hot drink and a snuggle under the duvet and you'll feel right as rain.' She smiled broadly, hoping this gesture might be infectious.

Lockie visibly bristled, not only at his apparent exclusion from events, but also at the tone Freya used, belittling the event and suggesting that, like she'd merely been caught in a storm, a hot drink and a warm blanket would see her restored.

Lexi barely seemed to register her mum's comments or her expression. It was as if she had withdrawn further, and even the thought of this sent a renewed quiver of fear through Freya's bones.

Charlotte and her two friends provided the welcome committee around the kitchen table.

'Are you okay?' Charlotte asked her sister as they trod the stairs.

'She's fine – aren't you, love?' Freya rubbed the top of Lexi's arms and answered for her.

'She's not fine.' Lockie kept his tone low. Freya shot him a look.

'That Fennella is a bitch. Everyone knows it.' Milly offered the insight good-naturedly.

'I can't believe it would have been Fennella,' Freya began. 'She—'

'It *was* Fennella.' Lexi spoke, cutting her mum short and giving confirmation.

'But . . .' Freya found herself lost for words of explanation or justification; because there were none.

Lexi looked at the assembled group, as if committing them to memory. Turning slowly, she made her way from the kitchen to the bottom of the stairs.

'I don't know why you are all so surprised,' she said. 'This is a horrible world, full of horrible people, and horrible people do horrible things.' She offered this without emotion as she trod the stairs to her room.

Freya gave Lexi a chance to settle and waited until Charlotte, Milly and Tara had left for the cinema. It saddened her, waving off the three girls for a night out. Pizza and a movie: nothing too outrageous, and yet both were so out of reach for Lexi. Freya could never have imagined that the highest aspiration she could have for her children was to be averagely normal, but this was exactly what she prayed for. It didn't feel like too much to ask for – a child who ate and was able to leave the house on a Saturday night – but just at that point in time it was.

Finding the room in darkness, she switched on the lamp on Lexi's bedside table. The window was still boarded up, waiting to be reglazed. It felt like a job of gargantuan proportions. Lexi sat propped up on the stack of pillows that supported her delicate frame, with two duvets heaped on top of her.

'Will you eat something for me . . . even if it's just a shake . . . something?' Freya sat on the side of the bed.

Lexi shook her head, her face still expressionless. 'No.'

There was something in her tone that told Freya this resistance was not going to be easy to break. She decided to try a less direct tack.

'I thought Fennella's behaviour today was shocking. Not nice at all.'

Lexi's lids flickered. 'We're not really that close anymore, not since I haven't been going to school. It doesn't matter. It was a stupid dare from her new gang. I don't care.'

'That's no justification, darling. That is not how you treat a friend.' Freya decided to keep her stronger opinions to herself.

'She's not my friend. Toby is my friend.'

'Toby?' She pictured the pale boy with his weird ways.

'Yes. I miss him.'

'You must ask him over,' she cooed.

'Dad said he was banned,' her daughter reminded her, looking up at her with desperate eyes.

'I know. Because he was angry, and because we didn't understand.'

Freya no longer cared about the right or wrong of the situation; she would do anything to try to give Lexi a moment of happiness. She would have to talk Lockie round. With events twisting and unfolding with each new day, it was all Freya could do not to fall over with dizziness. Right now, it was all about trying to lift her from the shell into which she had retreated and getting food into her.

'I need you to eat something. A shake? Crackers?' Freya pushed.

Lexi began to cry.

It was hard to explain the bitter joy she felt at the sight of her daughter's tears; a happiness, at least, that she was showing some emotion. It made her seem human.

Lexi took a deep breath. 'Sometimes, Mum, I feel like I'm on the planet, but not part of it.'

'In what way?' Freya leant forward from the edge of the bed, tucking the two thick duvets over Lexi's legs.

She shrugged. 'It's hard to explain, but it's like all the things that fill up everyone else's head don't bother me, not even a little bit. And the things that fill up my head feel too big to ever sort out. It's like I'd be better off not being here. I think it would be simpler, less tiring.'

'Don't you *ever* think that.' Freya swallowed her terror at Lexi's revelation, suppressing her first reaction to shout and allow her fear to manifest itself as anger; it took all her concentration to keep her voice level. 'Don't ever think you are not valued or valid, because you are! And your life will get easier, and you will come out of this dark time, Lexi, and you will be stronger because of it. I want you to believe that.'

'But I don't believe that,' Lexi admitted. Her voice was clear and calm. 'And the idea of not being here . . . it doesn't frighten me, Mum. Not at all.'

Freya felt the knock of fear in her chest. It took all her remaining strength not to go hysterical. The idea, the very thought, of her baby girl wanting to give up on life was unbearable. She opened her mouth to speak, but the ball of fear blocking her throat made speech impossible.

Four hours . . .

'It must be time for more tea?' Charlotte sniffed, disengaging herself from her mum's embrace.

'Definitely.' Freya nodded, retaking her place at the desk as Charlotte slipped from the room.

She coughed to clear her head and continued writing.

> *I think about something you said to me once, Lexi. You said that the idea of not being here anymore didn't frighten you. I didn't say anything at the time. Frankly I was shocked and wary of my reaction. It felt like an axe blow to my heart. I am your mother! And to have held you in my arms and watched you grow, knowing at that moment that you had lost interest in the life I gave you? It's hard to put into words the wave of grief that threatened to pull me under.*

I went away and drew up a list of all the things you wouldn't have to suffer if you weren't here anymore. It was something like this:

1. *No more illness, no more struggling to be healthy. No struggling – period.*
2. *No loss: you would never have to grieve the passing of another.*
3. *Heartbreak! How lovely not to have to wake in the morning with a heart full of fragments and eyes full of grit.*
4. *No ageing – here's a universal truth: the older you get, the more life loses its sparkle, loses a little of the magic. The endless, wonderful possibilities of youth where everything and anything feel possible – that fades . . .*

But then I considered all the things you would not experience:

1. *Falling hopelessly in love.*
2. *Your wedding day.*
3. *Knowing the blessing of a child.*
4. *Seeing the sunset in places far and wide.*
5. *Earning the right in old age to become eccentric, even cantankerous.*
6. *Getting properly drunk on champagne.*
7. *Sleeping in a meadow, by a brook.*
8. *Decorating a room.*
9. *Waking wrapped in the arms of the one you love.*
10. *Fresh caught lobster, eaten on a dock.*
11. *Being old enough to know better, but still laughing so hard at nothing much that you feel dizzy with happiness.*

Oh, my darling, this list is endless, it stretches on for infinity . . .

And then I thought about what it might feel like from my perspective not to have you here anymore, and I got so mad at the waste of it all that I shredded that list and balled my fists and vowed that no matter what anorexia threw at me, I would fight, fight, fight to keep you with me.

I had been lying: there was no good trade-off; the idea of losing you – well, it was quite simply more than I could even bear to contemplate.

Then and now.

TWELVE

Lexi had refused food for two days.

This single fact spun around inside Freya's head like a frantic spider weaving a web from the idea that covered every other thought and action. She still sipped water, almost continually, but anything more substantial had been rebuffed in the strongest terms.

The conversation between her and Lockie was one she would never forget: stumbling from Lexi's room and having to repeat the fact that their child wanted to give up on life, saw death as a kind of relief, was horrific. He had clung to her, crying and asking over and over again, *Why does she want to leave us? We love her so much! Our baby girl!* And in the dim light of the early hours, she had, as now, no answer to give. Instead, she stroked his hair and cooed empty words of comfort, their purpose purely designed to help him hang on until the dawn with the hope that the rising sun might bring some clarity.

Iris spoke to Lexi on the phone, explaining, as agreed with Freya and Lockie, that a persistent refusal to eat would result in hospitalisation, where forced feeding would be the only option. Her stern words had made Lexi cry.

'Don't you get it, Iris?' she stuttered through her tears. 'I can't! I just can't!'

'I think what you don't get, Lexi, is that you have to! You just have to! Because if you don't, things are going to get a lot worse very quickly and you will lose all control over the situation. Do you think the team in hospital will let you pick and choose what you eat, and when, and run up the stairs with different-flavoured shakes or a different type of cracker? They won't. It will be a nasal tube feeding you with calories pumped directly into your stomach. I shall leave it with you and will be checking in with your parents later. If we are in the same situation, then make no mistake that I will make that call, Lexi.'

Freya had been slightly horrified and at the same time delighted by Iris's very direct message, delivered with an undercurrent of irritation, as if to say *Enough is enough*: words she was not yet brave enough to deliver herself. The woman was sufficiently removed emotionally for this to be possible. Easy to picture the troubled girl she was dealing with, and not the crochet-wrapped baby who had lain in her mother's arms.

'I hate Iris! I hate her! I won't talk to her again and I don't want to see her!' Lexi yelled.

Half an hour after the phone call, after Lexi had screamed and cried, her actions best described as a tantrum, she appeared in the kitchen and requested a slice of toast with a thin layer of honey, no butter.

Freya could never have imagined taking such joy from the sound of bread popping in the toaster, as she stood eagerly by the countertop, waiting with knife and honey primed, wanting to serve it quickly, lest her daughter change her mind.

Lexi sat at the table and nibbled the toast, taking minute bites, and chewing, and chewing some more, as if trying to delay the inevitable.

'It tastes super sweet and horrible.'

Freya kept her eyes averted, listening, as her child struggled to swallow. After she managed a whole slice, Freya decided to push her luck and took a leaf from Iris's book.

'Anything else?' she suggested. 'What about some yoghurt or an apple?'

Lexi shook her head. 'I can't, Mum, but I will have something later.'

'Okay, deal – *if* you have at least one of your shakes now.'

To her surprise, Lexi nodded, without offering a single word of protest. Good to her word, she managed a few sips and then stood slowly on creaky knees, placing the remainder in the fridge for later.

Freya watched as her child, who had not so long ago loved the sourcing and handling of ingredients, now eyed the butter dish, wax-wrapped cheese, streaky bacon, eggs and milk on the shelves with a look of total disgust. It was her default setting to pull this particular face when she came into close contact with food. Freya had seen similar looks when others discussed human waste or decay, something so offensive that noses wrinkled and eyes closed and the mouth produced saliva to wash away the vomit that threatened. This was how Lexi reacted when standing only inches away from the beautiful produce she used to thrive on.

Freya arranged the freesias in the bowl on the table. She wanted the house to look as welcoming as possible. Lockie came up from the studio.

'Any chance of a posh coffee?'

'Every chance.' She smiled and proceeded to push the buttons that always left him mystified.

'He'll be here any minute.' She gave a nervous shrug.

'Don't worry. I have been fully briefed.' He sighed. Their conversation about allowing Toby back into the house had been fraught, but even Lockie had yielded at the simple fact that Lexi needed someone.

'We just need to remember. This isn't about what we want, but about what will make Lexi happy,' she reminded him.

'Uh-huh.'

His muted response told her he was simply toeing the line; whether he agreed with it or not was another thing entirely.

Freya handed him his coffee as the doorbell rang. She gave him a parting look as she went to answer the door.

'Toby's here!' she called to her husband, as if his arrival were a complete surprise.

Lockie strolled over with his hand outstretched towards the boy whose hair had grown in length since they last saw him. He looked a little lankier; his skin was just as pale and greasy, and his trousers now sat on his ankle bone, 'half-masters', as her dad would have called them.

'Hello, Toby, good to see you.' Lockie pumped the boy's hand, making his arm wiggle up and down like spaghetti.

'Hello, Mr Braithwaite. I would like to apologise for what happened the last time I was here.'

He instantly brought to the fore the very topic she was hoping they might avoid, might gloss over in a soap-opera fashion. But no: Toby was not practised in artifice – unlike Freya herself, who had spent the last few months presenting a particular face to Lexi, another to Charlotte, and a very different one to Lockie and the rest of the world. None of which truly represented what churned inside her.

'Please, don't mention it!' Lockie raised his palm, as if hoping the boy would take the instruction literally.

'I would like to tell you that I would never do or suggest anything that would bring Alexia harm. Never.' He stared at Lockie, unblinking, steadfast and sincere.

Freya smiled. He might be a funny old fish, but he was no Fickle-Fennella.

'That means no looking at those sites, not encouraging any behaviour that you know we would disapprove of. Is that clear?' Lockie kept a steady tone.

The boy nodded.

'Come up, Toby!' Lexi called from the upstairs landing. He gave a brief nod and made his way up the stairs.

The fact that she sounded so bright and glad of his visit, Freya found heartening.

'What do you think they are talking about?' Lockie asked casually, after a while.

'I have no idea.' She swiped her iPad, pausing *Eastenders*, which she was watching on catch-up. 'But whatever it is, I'm just glad that she seems to have a bit more life in her, more energy. I keep picturing her face on Saturday, she looked . . .' Freya shook her head, afraid to voice the fear that Lexi's cold, blank stare had filled her with.

'I know.' Lockie squeezed her hand. He too was still reeling from the revelation.

'And if Toby is the means to give her an interest in life . . .'

'I suppose so,' Lockie conceded reluctantly. 'I'm off to B&Q. Going to get the glass to fit the window. About time I got that replaced. The girl needs a view.' He smiled.

'She does indeed.'

When Toby hovered by the doorway a couple of hours later, Freya sat up straight and smiled at him. 'Are you off, Toby?'

'Yes.' He stared at her, unsmiling.

'Thank you so much for coming to visit Lexi. I know she will feel much better for seeing a friendly face. Please come anytime, don't wait for an invite, just pop in whenever!' She gave a single clap, trying not to sound too desperate for her child to have company.

He nodded at her, turning as if to leave, before looking back at her and Lockie, who, fresh back from his trip empty-handed, unable to source the glass he needed, stood grinning falsely.

'I . . . I think . . .' Toby shook his head, thinking better of it; he closed his mouth tightly to prevent the words from escaping. 'It doesn't matter.'

'What were you going to say?' she pressed him, wary of his leaving without imparting whatever sliver of wisdom he might have gleaned. 'I remember you told us that you don't believe in lying through omission.' She paused. 'What did you want to say, Toby? It's fine,' she pushed. 'Whatever it is.'

Toby faced her, as if wondering how much to disclose. 'I don't think Alexia is quite as well as I might have hoped.' He looked at the ground and flicked his head to move the long fringe from his eyes.

'In what way?' Lockie sounded curious as to what this fresh pair of eyes had seen.

Freya held her breath. Until the boy began to speak.

'She doesn't look very bright. A bit grey . . . but she used to look rosy, and she used to talk a lot about what she would like to do when she got better. But today she says she doesn't know if she *will* get better. And that has made me feel quite worried.'

The fact that someone as aloof as Toby had made this observation sent a new ripple of fear through Freya's bones.

'Thank you for being so forthright, Toby. It helps us. Sometimes, when you are very close to someone or a situation, you can't see the wood for the trees,' Lockie offered the insight to the boy who had the courage to talk so openly.

'Yes. I understand.' He nodded. 'I told her it is her sadness talking and that once she has overcome that, her sunniness will return.'

'That was a good thing to tell her, thank you. She's had a tricky few days.' Freya spoke freely, fighting her tears. It was one thing to privately fear for Lexi's mental decline, but quite another to have it confirmed by Toby.

'Fennella and her little gaggle are garbage,' he spat. 'They have zero concern for anyone, they hurt people and have brains the size of peas.' His nostrils flared, his eyes blazed, suggesting that he too might have been on the receiving end of that hurt.

'My dad used to say to me, "If you have one friend, consider yourself lucky, because one good one is all you need."' Lockie spoke calmly. 'I always think that people who are capable of being nasty in that way must have a kernel of something dark inside them, something that makes them deeply unhappy, and I feel sorry for them, because that must be a terrible way to live. Who wants that going on inside?' Lockie looked at the boy. 'And for what it's worth, I think Lexi is very lucky to have a friend like you.'

'I suppose that's us burying the hatchet.' Toby gave his tight-lipped smile before treading the stairs in his soft-soled shoes to let himself out.

Lockie smiled at his wife. 'I suppose it is.'

Her friend's visit seemed to have sparked something in Lexi, which lifted the whole house. Lockie whistled as he poured his cereal into the bowl.

'You sound very chirpy this morning – not that I am complaining.' Freya laughed, wiping her hands dry on the thighs of her jeans. 'It makes a change from the old grump I usually have to face over the breakfast table,' she teased.

'I *am* chirpy.' He beamed. 'I told Lexi she needs to get some fresh air and she agreed, just like that! Hurrah for the Toby effect!' He carried his breakfast to the table. 'I think a walk around the block might be good: a bit of fresh air, inhale the real world for a while . . .'

'Well, clever old you. I'll take her out this morning. Where are you working today?'

'London. An agency portrait shoot for an article. Seven women of different ages who have all experienced grief. A moody sepia tone should do the trick. I've worked there before; the lighting is great. Won't be too late either – home by four, tops.'

'Can you drop me at school, Dad?'

Charlotte rushed into the kitchen, heading straight for the cupboard. She grabbed a box of crackers and the butter and cheese from the fridge. Rather than waste time in transporting her breakfast, she stood at the counter and loaded the crackers one by one with what looked to be equal amounts of butter and cheese and popped them into her mouth while she prepared the next.

Freya was tempted to suggest it wasn't the most elegant way to eat, or the most mess-free, as Charlotte sprinkled the area and floor with crumbs, but the fact that she ate so keenly, without prompting, was good enough.

'I got an email this morning inviting me to go on the Geneva trip with the orchestra. We are visiting with three other schools and staying with host families, and then we are going to, like, jam for four days and put on an informal concert on the fifth.'

She paused to shove another cracker into her mouth.

'That sounds great!' Freya enthused. 'When is it?'

'Leaving in two weeks,' she managed, holding her hand over her mouth as a crumb-guard.

'Two weeks? That's not much notice!' Freya was thinking of logistics and money.

'I wasn't supposed to be going . . . They offered it to the pupils in the year below me because it's our exam year, but Harriet's got glandular fever and had to drop out, so they're cello-less unless I can make it. School will pay half, and I need to pay one hundred and sixty-four pounds by tomorrow – if I *can* go?' She looked at them with a downturned expression, as if she expected to be told she couldn't.

Lockie smiled. 'Sounds like an adventure . . . and if you are sure it won't impact your exams, of course you should go. And I must admit, I love your use of the word "jam". I'm thinking "musical symposium" might be more appropriate; "jam" in my mind conjures a dingy basement with a couple of guitars, a honky-tonk piano and bearded men taking drugs of a non-medicinal nature.'

'Lockie!' Freya tutted. 'Ignore him, Charlotte.'

'I usually do.' She smiled at her dad, clearly relieved and happy that this trip was happening.

'Charming!' Lockie finished up his cereal and popped the bowl in the sink. 'I shall write you a cheque, darling. Just let me know who to make it out to.'

Freya narrowed her eyes at him affectionately; they would find the money somehow.

'All set?' Freya turned to Lexi as they headed out of the front door.

'Yep.' She smiled.

She tried not to stare at her child's discoloured teeth, which looked huge inside her petite mouth, now that her face was so thin. In the bright light of day she had to admit the unpalatable truth that Lexi had lost some of her 'pretty'. She looked haggard. The dilemma was how to keep this fact from her already delicate self-esteem.

'We can just take it slowly, a quick once-around-the-block. Who knows, we could even stop at the corner shop if there was anything you fancied – like a magazine?'

'Thanks, Mum, but they now have this thing called the "internet", which means I have all the magazines I want at the touch of a button.'

'The "internet", you say? Sounds intriguing.' She pulled back her hand to tap her daughter's bottom lightly, in jest, but stopped when she remembered her words: *The bones in my bottom feel like they are cutting through my skin if I sit in a bath; it hurts . . .*

'Are you okay, Mum?' Lexi had noted the collapse of her face.

'Yes! Goodness, yes! I'm fine, really looking forward to our stroll.'

Looping her arm through Lexi's, they stepped out on to the pavement.

'Was it nice to see Toby?' Freya asked as they walked, happy to feel the sun on her face and be in the fresh air with her daughter.

'Yes. He's smart. I know he's a bit odd, but he just says it how it is and I quite like that.'

'I agree. Friends like that are the best kind. Marcia has never sugar-coated anything, not sure she knows how. I know when she says "This is not good enough, go back to the drawing board" or "God, look at the state of you, have you gained weight?" I need to take notice.'

Freya had been lulled into a false state of security by their activity, forgotten that the subject of weight was taboo, and in truth it had felt like sweet relief to be able to talk without censorship. She stiffened and decided not to pause, but to change the topic, trying to gloss over the fact as if it had not happened.

'I think Charlotte will have a lovely time in Switzerland, don't you? It's quite a thing, isn't it? I always think it's amazing how kids get to go on these lovely trips with school. The world must feel much smaller to you guys than it ever did for me.'

'I think the world feels massive.'

Freya could only imagine that this must be the case when your world consisted of the four walls of your bedroom and the odd trip to the kitchen.

'Well, when you are feeling better, you will rediscover your lust for travel and exploration and you can go anywhere! Gosh, Lexi, it was hard holding you back when you were little. You were the one who wanted to jump feet first, quite literally, into whatever came your way. Daddy used to say your motto should be "Leap before you look!" as that's what you did most of the time.'

'That feels like a different person.' She looked up, taking a deep lungful of fresh air.

'She's still in there, Lex. Maybe she's hibernating? Waiting to burst into action. And when she does? Oh boy – watch out, world! You were scarily fearless!'

'Now I'm just scared.' She gave a small smile as they navigated the narrowing path, Freya treading slightly ahead.

'That won't always be the case, darling. I promise.' She patted the bony fingers that gripped her forearm, resisting the urge to wrap her arms around her daughter and hold her tight.

'Good morning!'

Freya looked up and into the face of Mr Rendleton, who was coming in the opposite direction, pulling a shopping cart behind him.

'Morning, Mr Rendleton, how are you today?' She smiled.

'Good, enjoying the break in the weather.' He turned his face to the sun like a recumbent daisy.

'Mrs Rendleton not with you today?' It felt odd, seeing him without her.

'No, getting her hair done. She does like to look her best.'

'She always looks lovely.' Freya spoke the truth.

He turned to Lexi. 'And goodness me, Lexi! Look at you!' He took a deep breath, as if seeing her properly for the first time. 'You *have* lost weight!' He narrowed his gaze. 'I expect it's the fashion nowadays, but you could do a lot worse than popping by for a slice of Mrs Rendleton's fruit cake. Looks like you want feeding up, to me!'

Freya felt at a loss for words, struck by how casually he felt able to comment on Lexi's size and shape, as if they were still discussing the weather.

He smiled, and continued to offer the words that must have gone through her thin skin like knives, lodging in the brittle ribs and bones that hovered so dangerously close to the surface.

'Looks like it would only take one big puff of wind to carry you off over the abbey!' He chortled.

Freya felt her daughter shrink by her side, convinced that if she could have jumped under her coat and hidden, she would have.

'I . . . I want to go home,' Lexi whispered. 'I want to go home now!' A little louder now, her eyes fixed downwards.

Freya patted her hand. 'Okay, let's turn you around.'

She avoided Mr Rendleton's gaze, worried about saying the wrong thing, reminding herself that he was old and didn't mean any offence. This mantra was easy to repeat, but Freya still had to concentrate on keeping a lid on the torrent of anger and upset that cued up on her tongue, knowing that it would only be to vent her frustration, serving no purpose other than upsetting their old neighbour, whom she knew meant no malice, and further upsetting Lexi.

'I hope I haven't said the wrong thing?'

Mr Rendleton stood on the pavement, watching as they swapped sides on the pavement, Lexi's arm still linked through her mother's.

Freya lifted her hand in a wave of goodbye and whispered soft words of reassurance to her child as they carefully trod the fifty yards back to the safety of their front door. She tried to blot out the numerous times she had commented on the skinniness of someone – new mums who had lost baby weight, women who had got in shape. To point out someone's fatness was taboo, frowned upon, but if you were thin, it was fair game, almost as if, in some warped way, it was a compliment, a measure of success.

Immediately after arriving home, Lexi went back to bed.

Freya, exhausted by the effort of their stroll and interaction with Mr Rendleton, lay on the sofa in her study and let her eyes close. She wished, just for an hour or so, to be able to run away, thinking as she often did of her brother, Hugh, and envying the fact he had that wide, long Florida beach at his disposal. What wouldn't she give now for half an hour alone to lie on that sand and watch the water?

'Here you are!'

She opened her eyes to find Lockie kneeling on the thin Persian rug by her side.

'I was looking all over for you, thought you'd run away with a sailor!' He kissed her nose.

'I don't know any sailors.' She smiled. 'Apart from Hugh, and I don't want to run away with him – lived with him for a big chunk of my life already and he has some gross habits. Funny actually, I was just thinking about the beach in Naples.'

'Ah, bliss, but I'm afraid Hugh's flashy gin palace doesn't count. That's not proper sailing.' He kissed her again. 'Did you see the lovely letter he sent? We email, of course, but for him to sit down and hand-write . . . That meant a lot. He suggested we send Lexi to go and stay with him and Melissa.'

'I know. It was kind,' she acknowledged. 'He's a good man.'

'But we don't want her on the other side of the Atlantic, do we?' He smiled.

'No, we don't. I love you, Lockie.'

She sat up, resting her head on his shoulder while he held her. Her tears flowed steadily.

'Hey! What's this all about?' He pulled her away and ran his thumb over her cheek, scooting the tears away.

'Lexi fancied a walk, as you know,' she whispered, wary that her little girl was only across the hallway. 'We bumped into Mr Rendleton and he was only being sweet and unaware, but he told her how thin she looked, said she needed some cake.' She closed her eyes briefly. 'Lexi folded, couldn't wait to get home. I felt terrible, but I've been lying here feeling a bit cheated, fed up with how it feels to live in a house with anorexia inside it. I hate the way it has taken over our lives . . . We can't even go for a walk! It's like being battered by waves against rocks, and just when you think you have found your footing, the next one rolls in and you are knocked down again, and I'm sick of it, Lockie. I do feel like running away sometimes. And that makes me feel like a bad person. She's my daughter!'

Lockie shook his head and cupped the side of her face. 'My beautiful Freya, it doesn't make you a bad person, it makes you a human one. No one would choose to live like this, and in a sense you are grieving for the life you used to have. I know I do. I long for the easy chats, the laughter, the holidays, even going out for supper; food was one of the things we looked forward to the most. But now? It's like something rotten that stinks and we all make out we can't smell it, yet we breathe it in, day and night.'

She nodded. He was right; that was exactly what it was like.

'And for the record . . .' He sighed. 'I feel like running away more than sometimes.'

As she opened her mouth to tell him how much that thought scared her, and that without him the situation would be unbearable, the front doorbell rang.

'I'll go.' He kissed her lightly and trod the stairs.

Freya stretched from the sofa and shook off the mohair blanket that had found its way from Lexi's room back to her study.

She heard male voices, and after checking her blotchy face in the mirror, she made her way down to the kitchen.

Lockie was filling the kettle and Mr and Mrs Rendleton were taking seats at the table.

'Oh, how lovely! Hello!' She smiled. 'Your hair looks lovely, Mrs Rendleton.'

The woman beamed at her, nodding silently, as if happy to be introduced to the pretty lady.

'Freya, I've been worried all afternoon about saying the wrong thing,' her husband said. 'I would not want to upset Lexi for the world!'

Freya took a seat opposite him. 'I know that, and you aren't to worry. She is very sensitive about her weight, but certainly nothing you have said or done will change that.' She smiled.

'Tea or coffee?' Lockie asked, as he reached into the cupboard for mugs.

'Ooh, tea for us both, Earl Grey if you have it, and no milk.' He patted his wife's hand.

Lockie reached for the Earl Grey teabags. 'Oh, well, that's easy.'

'Do you know, we love our house—' Mr Rendleton began.

'How long have you lived there?' She was curious, interrupting him.

'It will be sixty years this Christmas . . .'

'Goodness me! A long time.' She nodded.

'Yes, a long time, and the best times for us have been in the last twenty years, having you and the girls living behind us. It's been wonderful. This house used to be quite soulless, quiet, we never heard or saw a peep. And then you moved in, with a bang! The noise, the shouts, the cat! The light that streams over our garden!'

She looked at Lockie and held her breath, wondering if he was complaining subtly about the chaos and energy they had brought into the street. What came next calmed her.

'We weren't blessed with children, or of course grandchildren, but we have been listening and watching the girls since they were babies. Their laughter, tears, tantrums, we've heard it all!' He smiled. 'They brought a new dimension to our lives. Like, whenever we got snow . . .' He shook his head and chuckled. 'They'd be out there in the back garden, morning, noon and night! Packing little snowballs in their hands until their skin was red and numb, but they didn't care . . . They have always had such joy of life, and that in turn gave us such joy. It's been a privilege to be part of their lives in this way. A little part, but a part nonetheless, and when I saw Lexi today, looking so very frail . . . well, I don't mind telling you that it quite upset me. Is there anything we can do?' He looked from Lockie to Freya earnestly. Both stared at him, transfixed by his beautiful words of recollection.

Freya turned to look at Lockie, wondering if he too felt the full force of despair at hearing how their child was viewed: *so very frail* . . .

The irony was not lost on her that the words came from a robust man in his mid-eighties.

The kitchen door creaked open and Lexi walked in.

Freya wondered how long she had been standing there listening. She walked over and took the seat next to her mum, opposite their guests.

'I like living backing on to you too.' Lexi smiled. 'I have always thought that if we needed anything, like in an emergency, we could call out the window and you'd come and help us.'

'And indeed we would!' He nodded, happy, smiling at his wife as if this were quite a thing. Lexi nodded, as if happy too that this was the arrangement. She continued.

'And I love the smell of the lilac that grows over the back of your house. When I start to smell it, I know that winter is over and summer is on the way, and that means good things – a new season, a new start.'

'Me too!' Mrs Rendleton called out.

The neighbours let out a slow chuckle of delight as her husband held her hand. The room was calm and quiet.

'I have anorexia, Mr Rendleton.'

Freya stared at her child. This was the first time she had heard her own it in this way and use this phrase out loud.

'Oh, Lexi!' He paused. 'I have to confess, much to my shame, that I don't really know what it is . . . I know it's about dieting, isn't it?'

Her response, when it came, was considered. 'It was a bit about dieting in the beginning, but not anymore.'

She tried to explain. With her index finger tapping out a rhythm on the tabletop, she stared at it and began to speak.

'It's horrible. It has taken my sunniness and it controls every part of my life. Even being here right now in the kitchen, I am worried that there might be calories from food in the air and that I might be breathing them in, and I know that's nuts, but it still scares me. I have a headache all the time. I live with it and try to ignore it. It's worse when

I wake up in the middle of the night and it's the first thing I remember, that I have this horrible headache.' She touched her temple, as if feeling the pain right there and then. 'I can feel my heartbeats here, and here' – she touched her fingertips to her sternum and the side of her neck – 'and they feel odd a lot of the time and that makes me feel scared. I feel like I'm not really here, like I'm floating, like my body and my mind aren't properly connected anymore. But nothing, *nothing*, matters to me more than keeping control of the food that goes into my system. I am frightened that if I eat, if I put on weight, bad things will happen and I will fall apart, even more than I'm falling apart now. I'm trapped.'

Freya, Lockie and their guests were transfixed and fascinated by her brutal admission. Freya resisted the temptation to wrap her in her arms, wary of halting her flow and wanting her to continue talking, which she did.

'I'm so aware of food, all food, that if someone unwraps a salad pot or a sandwich I can smell it. I can smell it across the room, I can smell it on the back of the bus and I can smell it through the floorboards.' She shuddered. 'Everywhere I look – in magazines, on car journeys, TV programmes, newspapers – I see the pictures of food over and above everything else. They could be talking about anything, showing anything, but all I see is the hot dog or the ice cream, and even the idea of putting that stuff in my body makes me feel so sick, so afraid, that I nearly pass out. It has got worse; I used to be able to cook, and I enjoyed giving it to other people, and it made me feel normal, touching food. And I feel I can tell you this, Mr Rendleton, because you know me – but you *don't* know me; you have always listened more than you talked, and Toby says I need to tell people – he said that sometimes saying things out loud helps you make sense of it a bit, and so I decided to tell you.'

Lexi looked up as Freya's sob filled the air. She covered her mouth, embarrassed.

'And even though I am starving, and I know I am starving, I would rather that than put food inside my body. I would rather die.' She dashed the tears that trickled slowly down her cheeks. 'I can only think about being thin and getting thinner, smaller, and I know that if I get small enough I will disappear, and that's kind of like winning.'

Lockie made his way to the table and placed one hand on Lexi's shoulder and the other on his wife's back. He didn't seem to know what to say. Freya was silent, numbed, saddened, and feeling quite useless, still processing her daughter's eloquent explanation, whilst reeling from the fact that Lexi had expressed how she herself often felt, overly obsessed with food.

Mrs Rendleton placed her palms on the table and pushed herself up into a standing position. With her slow walk, she made her way to the other side of the table and stopped by Lexi. Lockie stood back as she tilted the girl's face up towards her own. With her gnarled, liver-spotted hands either side of Lexi's pale face, she smiled, speaking clearly. Hers was the voice of someone who was coherent and present.

'Summer is on the way!' She smiled into Lexi's eyes, her message one of hope.

Three hours, thirty minutes . . .

'I'll be off now.' Lockie took a deep breath and cleared his throat.

Freya stood and held him tightly. 'Oh God, Lockie!'

'It's okay. It's just paperwork – that's how I'm looking at it: a couple of signatures, that's all. You stay here and carry on. I'll be back before you know it.'

She kissed his cheek and watched him leave the study.

Charlotte heard the front door close. She grabbed a pen from the pen pot on her desk and opened her notepad; she rested it on her raised knees and started to write.

> *There's something I wanted to say, something I've been thinking about.*

> *It wasn't only Toby's weirdness that bothered me, the fact that he was a bit odd. It was how he looked at you, so in love, so besotted, and I now know I was jealous of that, Lex.*

No one had ever looked at me that way. But not only that, and it sounds ridiculous, but I didn't want anyone to love you the way I do. You are my little sister and I don't want anyone else to muscle in on that.

I'm sorry for the things I said about Toby. You are lucky to have a friend like him and he is very lucky to have a friend like you.

That's it.

I'm going to take this to Mum now. X

THIRTEEN

Freya noticed a change in Lockie. It seemed to coincide with Lexi's outpouring to the Rendletons. He was angry, frustrated by her apparent lack of progress, as if it made all that they had gone through as a family feel like a waste of time.

She could see it in his every gesture: the heavy-handed bang of a mug on the table, the aggressive head shaking, and short, hard tut in response to anything he read in the newspaper; his agitated, fast pacing of the room when repeating how work was slow coming in and money was getting tight; his thin-lipped, half-hearted welcome of Iris into the house, and lack of enthusiasm when discussing a visit to Hilary – both of which he had deemed 'completely bloody pointless'. Before storming off to the pub.

She knew his behaviour was born of love, his desire to fix his baby girl, and the futility of every suggestion, rebuffed, was a bitter pill to swallow.

Like the yin to his yang, Freya tried doubly hard to present a positive spin, smiling while crying on the inside and humming clichéd messages of positivity to drown out his monologues of doom, hoping some of it might stick.

Lexi had taken a mental tumble – unsurprising in the face of Fennella's harsh betrayal and her further physical decline. Freya alternated between soothing her with words of encouragement and urging her to look to the future, offering glimpses of a sunny time ahead: 'When you are better, we can . . .'

The looks of mistrust Lexi fired in her direction did little to bolster her confidence.

Freya was ignoring Marcia's requests for an article on diet trends and how they affected health, the great 'fat versus carbs' debate, 'Atkins or Paleo?', 'fasting or juicing?' . . . The choices were endless and confusing, and to be frank, she felt they were all rather redundant in the face of what was happening under her own roof. The thought of someone wrangling with the choice of whether to go fat-free, vegan or raw, when she battled daily to get Lexi to consume a slice of toast, was frankly irritating. She felt a new wave of responsibility for every food-related article she cast out into the ether, aware in a way she never had been before of how her words could influence.

Instead of getting down to work, Freya spent hours, days, negotiating with Lexi over food. Her new authoritative stance seemed to be having little impact, which took its toll, and when she wasn't in direct negotiations, she was building up the courage for the next bout – ding-ding!

'Right, Lexi, half a sandwich or a piece of cheese?' she offered, followed quickly by shouting, 'Did you not hear what Iris said? If you do not eat, this will be taken out of our control, they will hospitalise you, Lex, and they will feed you with a tube! A tube!'

Lexi shook her head, tucking in her lips and folding her arms across her chest, apparently afraid now to talk in case her mother took advantage of the opportunity and shoved some food in her open mouth. The last time Freya had seen her daughter look this way, she was sitting on the other side of a plastic tray, attached to a high chair, being encouraged to try broccoli: *Look! It's a baby tree!*

The memory caused Freya's tears to pool. Awash with tiredness, she cried. Miraculously, her tears seemed to do the trick.

'Okay, Mummy, I'll do it, but not cheese or milk.' She gagged at the thought. 'I'll . . . I'll have some tuna . . . plain tuna, no mayonnaise or anything with it, and only in brine, not oil.' Again she gagged and swallowed. 'And I can only take tiny spoonfuls . . . but I'll do it. I will, Mum.'

'Oh, Lexi!' Freya grinned, dashing away her tears with the back of her hand. 'That is the best thing I've heard all day! Tuna it is! I'll be right back!' She kissed her daughter hard on the forehead and skipped to the kitchen cupboards. Moving packets and tins this way and that, she searched, but the ready supply of tuna she kept in the corner of the cupboard had gone.

'Where's the tuna?' she shouted, angrily, slamming the cupboard door so forcefully that it sprang open again.

She instantly regretted shouting; it was no big deal if Charlotte or Lockie had made the odd sandwich for lunch, and she knew it.

Grabbing the front door keys, she ran from the house, jogging along the pavement to the shop half a mile away, which doubled as a post office and social hub, where dog walkers, teens with bikes on a quest for sweets, and dads and mums pushing strollers, all loitered to chat in the bumpy car park.

Freya scanned the shelves while catching her breath. 'Tuna, tuna, tuna . . .' she muttered, until she spied a tin and her heart leapt with relief. Her happiness quickly turned to angst when she saw it was tuna in olive oil. She looked either side of the stack of tins, hoping there might be some in brine, but knowing that if there were, they would be right there.

She queued, bouncing on the spot, as the lady in front told the smiley girl behind the counter that her daughter lived in Australia, but might, fingers crossed, be coming home for Christmas with the grand-son she had only seen on the 'Skype thingy'. It felt like an age until the woman loaded her bread and box of shortbread biscuits into her woven jute shopping bag that advertised a much bigger store, and left.

Freya was aware of her lack of neighbourly banter, but simply didn't have the time. 'Do you have any tuna in brine, or just this?' she launched without greeting. She held the tin aloft.

'Let's have a look.' The girl smiled, going at her usual unhurried pace. She took the tin into her hand and read the label aloud. 'This is in olive oil.'

She handed it back to Freya, who was biting her cheek to stop from shouting out.

'Yes . . .' She coughed. 'But do you have any that *isn't* in olive oil?'

'Was there none on the shelf?' The girl looked over her shoulder, as if she could magically see through the different varieties of crisps and two-litre bottles of cider that blocked her view.

'No,' Freya managed. 'It's just that my daughter won't eat it if it's in oil.'

The girl gave a partial snort. 'You'll have to do what I do, love: tell her it's that or nothing. Sometimes I think mine think they live in a hotel!' She laughed.

Freya held the tin out to be scanned so she could pay and leave as quickly as possible.

She made it back to the house, noting that she had been gone for twenty-six minutes, desperately hoping Lexi hadn't changed her mind. Her heart raced as she tipped the tuna into a sieve and watched the oil drip through the wire mesh. With the excess gone, she then tipped it on to folded sheets of paper towel, patting the remnants of oil as best she could. Flaking it into a bowl, she ferried it up the stairs to Lexi's room.

'Here we go!' She smiled.

Lexi sat up. 'I thought you'd forgotten.'

'Course not.'

Freya handed her the teaspoon and the bowl. She watched as Lexi dipped the edge of the teaspoon into the fish and withdrew a small amount. She placed a fleck or two on her lip and tasted.

'It's oily.' She screwed her face up.

'It isn't. Not really. I removed the oil, so it's fine now.' She smiled again.

Lexi shook her head. 'It's not fine, Mum! I can see the oil. I can't eat it. I'll be really sick. It's disgusting.' She spoke with a rising panic.

'Just have one mouthful for me,' she pressed. 'Just one.'

Lexi started to retch and Freya knew there was a very real danger of her daughter vomiting the remains of the protein shake she had taken earlier. The thought of her losing that sustenance upset and concerned her.

'Okay, okay . . .' She took the bowl from Lexi's hand and sloped out of the room.

'I'm sorry, Mummy,' Lexi called after her.

Freya felt the stab of irritation in her gut: aware that she had jogged and queued, pandering to Lexi's delectation, knowing that she would travel anywhere and do anything to get this child to eat. She began to realise that for all her words and intentions, taking a tough stance was difficult, and she wasn't sure she was cut out for it. The fact that Lexi had chosen not to eat felt nothing short of punishment. And it was wearing.

'There you are, I've looked all over the house,' Lockie snapped, freshly emerged from his studio and looking for company. It punctuated what had been a very solitary day.

'I just had to nip to the shop for tuna.' She raised the bowl before letting it clatter on the drainer.

'Oh, right.' He nodded.

'Lexi said she'd eat some, but not this kind.' She stirred the spoon, listening to the sucking stickiness of oil-coated fish flakes against the china bowl.

'Can you hear yourself?' He paused. 'It's preposterous. The wrong kind of tuna?'

'I know how it sounds, but you know how she is, this illness—'

'Just stop!' he interrupted her. 'I honestly cannot listen to any more justification or reasoning. Not today.'

Lockie made his way back down to his studio, seemingly deciding against company after all.

Freya stood by the window and looked towards the sky. A bruise of purple cloud rolled over the garden.

'Perfect,' she whispered.

It felt as if she could do nothing right. Everyone was angry, everyone was hurting and she was the one at which they spat their venom.

One week later, a little before bedtime at the end of a busy day when her energy had been focused on getting Charlotte packed and prepared for her trip to Geneva, Freya placed a freshly filled water bottle on her younger daughter's bedside table and tucked the patchwork quilt over her duvets. She was walking backwards out of the room when a small voice drifted from under the pile of down, whispered into the darkness.

'I'm scared, Mum.'

'Oh, darling! Would you like me to leave the light on or sit with you?'

'I'd like you to sit with me,' she whispered.

'What are you scared of?' Freya probed, hoping Lexi was taking Toby's advice and voicing the fears that haunted her.

'I . . .' Lexi struggled to begin. 'I feel like I'm in a dark place. I can't see any light at the end of the tunnel and I don't think I am ever going to feel better because the thinner I get, the uglier I feel, and if I eat more, I will *hate* myself and the uglier I will feel. I feel like I am closing down and I can't win. I know that I am never going to win.'

'Don't say that! This is just a blip.' Freya suppressed her panic and shook off the mental image of her leaving the office after her chat with Miss Burke, ignoring the terrified voice in her head that screamed: *Why didn't you act sooner, why didn't you listen! You could lose her!*

'You are going to win, Lexi. You are going to get stronger and you will feel better, and this time next year we will look back and think: "Phew, we made it! We came out the other side." We will keep seeing Hilary, and Dr Morris is great, and Iris . . . there's a whole team of people all working to get you better, and they will!'

Please let this be true! Please! she offered up the silent mantra.

'I love you, Mum.' Lexi turned slowly on to her side, until she was facing the wall.

Freya sat stroking her thin back beneath the bulky covers until her breathing was regular and her body still. She closed the door behind her, unable and unwilling to further process this desire of Lexi's to quit, fearing that if she did, she just might scream.

'Can I get you a drink before bed?' Lockie asked, as he heaped Ovaltine into a mug.

'Nothing for me, thanks.' She shook her head and set the dishwasher whirring.

'What's the matter?' he asked, able to sense her mood, but his tone indicating a reluctance to have this conversation again.

Both already knew what the matter was, and to ask was merely going through the motions. There were only so many variants with which you could discuss the same topic; eventually the monotony, without ever reaching a solution, was wearing. The fact that the majority of their interactions were now pre-empted by a similar shrug or sigh set the spiral of decline in motion before they had uttered a word.

Freya stood and placed one hand on her hip. 'Lexi just nodded off, but she more or less told me that she feels like giving up.' She heard the quaver to her voice; this new level of fear was very real.

He stared at her. 'Well, that's bullshit! The consequence of her giving up is death. Is that what she wants?' he spat, abandoning the spoon in the mug. He began to pace.

'Please don't shout at me, Lockie. I am only telling you what she said.'

'But why is she talking like that?' he continued, seemingly keener to get back on point than apologise. 'Isn't it bad enough that we have to spend every second of every day trying to make her eat? Her hair's falling out, her bones are brittle, her teeth are loose in her gums, her heart is weak – for Christ's sake! Her *heart*!'

'I know, Lockie! Do you think I don't? Shouting at me won't change a thing and it's unfair!' The facts he emphasised rattled around her mind continually; she didn't need or welcome his pointed reminders.

'How much more broken does she want to get?'

Freya stared at him, feeling that she was merely an observer to this monologue; she could offer nothing that would help. 'I don't know what to say to you.'

'No. No one knows what to say anymore, no one knows what to *do* anymore, and I am sick of it! I'm not about to sit back and let her make those choices. I won't.'

He stormed from the room, up the stairs, to where Lexi lay very still. The beginnings of sleep peeled from her at the murmur of the row that rose up between the Edwardian flooring and swam around her room.

Freya followed, arriving a second behind Lockie as he switched on the main light and told Lexi to sit up.

'You need to listen!' he barked.

She watched as her daughter's thin, pointy arm reached over the top of the duvet mountain and anchored her as she twisted into a sitting position. Her eyes blinked, trying to adjust to the sudden, harsh light. Her every move was now deliberate, considered and slow. With no fuel in her system and no layer of fat and very little muscle, her bones ground against each other, pushing against skin that had to be at the very least uncomfortable, if not excruciating.

Lexi propped herself up on her pillows and stared with her big sunken eyes as Lockie stood in the middle of her bedroom, clearing his throat and changing his stance, working up the steam to begin.

'Enough, Lexi! This is what I have come to tell you. I have listened to your mum and all the advice from the professionals. I've driven myself nuts reading views and information from parents in similar positions, and all the time I've been ignoring that little voice on my shoulder, my gut instinct.' He tapped his chest.

Lexi looked at her mum and back to her dad, her expression one of concern, in case she was caught not giving him her full attention, and also fear of what might come next. Freya avoided her eyes; part of her wanted this intervention, because if Lockie was taking control it meant she had time to draw breath, not only giving her time to reload, but more crucially, with him at the helm, it was no longer her fault.

'You are going to start eating. You will take on food. And that's that.' He let his hands fall to his sides.

Lexi began to cry.

'Tears won't make a difference. Not this time. I will not let you give up! You are fifteen years of age! Fifteen! You are a child. You have so much life ahead of you, and yet you spend your days shivering in this room . . .' He shook his head. 'You were always the wild card, Lexi. The way you ran at life scared me. I used to wake with a jolt, trying to picture you at fifteen, thinking if she is this crazy, this gung-ho, at eight, nine, ten, what's she going to be like as a teenager? I imagined you jumping on trains and calling up from Istanbul. I saw the rowdy parties, the mayhem, the sleepless nights . . .' He paused, and looked at her face with tears slipping down her loose, sallow skin.

Freya pushed her fingers into her jeans – anything to fight the desire to swoop forward and cuddle her, knowing this would not only distract from Lockie's message but would yet again set her role as the protector. She felt torn.

'But I never in my wildest dreams could have imagined you like this, and I've got to tell you that how you live now scares me more than I ever thought possible, more than any rowdy party. I am beyond scared. I am petrified. I love you, Lexi. I'm your dad and that is why I need to take control, I need to tell you enough is enough, because I will not lose you. Do you understand?' His last words coasted from a throat tight with emotion, his voice reed thin.

She nodded, gulping the salty sobs that filled her throat.

'Good.' He sniffed, and made for the door. 'Now we do it my way.'

This sounded very much like a fait accompli. Freya watched as he walked past her with barely a glance. It was the first time she felt like he didn't see her, didn't want to see her, and her gut churned as she saw what others would see: a couple who were set apart, splintered.

'Morning, darling! Up you get!'

Freya woke to the sound of clapping and the command shouted from the hallway, not directed at her, but at Lexi, as Lockie stretched on the landing, sounding part holiday-camp entertainment officer and part army PT officer.

Their bed had felt very small as they spent the night, with muscles coiled, lying on opposite sides of the mattress, both feigning then praying for sleep, their deceit given away by the loud swallows that they tried to suppress.

'Two minutes!' he bellowed. 'And I shall meet you in the kitchen.'

Freya sat up, and mixed with the desire to intervene, concern at his over-exuberance and volume that might unnerve their girl, was the slight flicker of relief that for now, at least, someone else seemed to be shouldering the responsibility, being the bad guy. She felt she could take her foot off the gas for the first time in forever.

She took her time showering and slipping into her jeans and favourite long-sleeved red-and-white raglan T-shirt, then made her way down the stairs, kissing the newly risen Charlotte on the landing, who ambled from the loo back to her bedroom.

Downstairs, Lexi sat at the head of the table, her hands clamped between her bony knees, sitting inside striped pyjamas that hung from her frame.

'Good morning!' Lockie beamed from the stove. 'Take a seat and let me serve you.'

'Have I woken up in an alternate universe?' She smiled at her daughter, trying to smooth the morning, keeping things, as ever, as bright as possible, painting a picture for the kids, aware that this was what she did, but not knowing how to change without adding another layer of tension to an already almost intolerable situation.

'Nope.' Lockie ran to the fridge and back to the stove. She noticed he was wearing her *Masterchef* apron, a freebie she had received after writing about the series. It made her laugh.

'I know you are laughing at my apron, but I think it's nervous laughter. You don't want me to steal your cooking crown.' He cracked an egg into the sizzling skillet and splashed in some milk and a knob of butter.

'Lockie, if it means you cooking all the meals, shopping for them, doing the dishes, and running up to the shop when we run out of milk, be my guest!' She pulled a face at Lexi, who managed a half-smile.

'Your coffee, madam!' Lockie placed the little glass demitasse in front of her. He looked rather pleased with himself.

'That coffee machine is easy once you get the hang of it. I will not be beaten by technology.' He smiled, with his hands on his hips, a wooden spoon in one.

'Toast is burning.' She calmly nodded her head towards the wisp of smoke that curled from the toaster.

'Argh!' He dashed over and pinched his fingers on the blackened bread, touching it for the shortest possible time and flinging it on to the draining board.

'It's okay, Dad. I didn't want toast anyway,' Lexi confirmed.

'Yes, but this is not about what you want, Lex, it's about what you need!' He smiled at her, his manner excited.

Freya sipped her coffee, keeping her head down rather than make eye contact with Lexi, knowing to do so might inadvertently ally her with the negativity she could sense her daughter wanted to express.

'Here we go. One very tiny plain omelette, cooked without oil. One slice of bacon, crisped under the grill to perfection. And one grilled tomato, lightly sprinkled with black pepper. Enjoy!' He placed the small plate in front of her and twirled the dishcloth around with flourish.

And then in an instant they were back in the familiar grip of anxiety, where no amount of glitter or bluster could detract from the fact that she and Lockie waited with breath held to see if Lexi would eat. It was like watching an injured marathon runner crawling towards the finish line, no one knowing if they would make it or simply give up and face-plant on to the tarmac.

It was with a mixture of nervous anticipation and frustration that Freya's jaw clenched, watching Lexi slowly, slowly, pick up the cutlery and methodically saw the strip of bacon into morsels before using the side of the fork to break down the omelette. She then let her wrist rest on the edge of the table, with the fork poised, and looked up at her mum.

Freya knew a hungry Charlotte or a hurried Lockie would have eaten the food on the plate in the time it took for Lexi to prepare it to her liking for eating.

'How is it?' Lockie called from the sink.

'Lovely,' Lexi replied, and Freya knew that to an unknowing ear, this might sound like she had tasted it. Lexi let her eyes sweep her mother's face, as if testing the water to see if she would rat on her.

It was in that split second that Freya realised Lexi viewed her without threat, as someone who would not make a stand, as an enabler – and her heart flipped.

Very slowly, Freya rose from the table and went to stand behind Lockie, all the time, silently willing, *Go on! Eat it, Lex! Please!*

Lexi watched her mum's retreat as she touched the outer tine of the fork to a single speck of crispy bacon. It stuck. She brought it up to her mouth, slow in the transfer; she brought it to her nose, smelling it first, then poked out her tongue.

Freya watched as Lexi closed her eyes and, with her body rigid and her eyes screwed tightly shut, she touched the fork to her tongue, transferring the tiny dot of protein.

Freya looked again into her coffee cup, swirling the reduced contents; anything other than witness the tortured struggle of her child trying to eat. She placed her free hand on Lockie's shoulder. In response, he patted her fingers.

Freya jolted when, without warning, the loud noise filled the room. Her coffee splashed from her mug as Lexi slammed her wrists against the table, her palms splayed, throwing the cutlery on to the china plate, as she pushed her chair back with force, scooting backwards while simultaneously spitting profusely. Long gobs of saliva fell from her mouth, over her chin and down her chest. Eventually she wiped her tongue repeatedly on the sleeve of her pyjama top, trying to rid her mouth of all traces. She was shaking her head.

'Lexi!' Lockie shouted. He sounded angry rather than concerned.

Her response, which Freya would never forget, was explosive.

Jumping up from the chair with an energy that had been absent of late, Lexi swiped the plate from the table with force. It landed on the floor, shattering and scattering the measly breakfast over the stripped wood, to lie among the china.

'I won't eat it! I won't! And you can't make me! I hate you! I fucking hate you! Both of you!' She pointed from one parent to the other.

For a second, Freya was paralysed, completely taken aback by the severity of her language and outburst. Gripping the countertop, she looked from Lexi to the floor and then her husband, whose expression was equally shocked, as he stood with mouth agape.

Charlotte appeared at the door, standing behind her sister. 'What's all the racket?'

Lexi rounded on her, eyes blazing, mouth set in a teeth-bearing sneer. 'I don't care what you want or what you say. You can't make me do anything! You are trying to make me fat!'

She turned her attention back to Lockie, her head darting, face muscles twitching. 'You are not human. You are the devil! I can see it! I can see your fire! You are the devil!' She pointed at her dad with a trembling finger and, without removing her eyes from his face, her expression blazing, she backed slowly out of the room and darted up the stairs.

'Are you guys okay?' Charlotte held one hand to her chest as she peered into the room, wary, unnerved.

Freya nodded, not only shocked by Lexi's outburst, but stunned by her choice of words. *I hate you! Both of you!* It was her worst fears come true.

'We're okay.' She caught her breath. 'That wasn't her, Lockie. You know that, don't you? That wasn't her.' Her words were as much a reminder for herself.

He looked at her. 'I don't know . . .' he began.

'Don't know what?' she prompted, waiting to hear the end of his sentence, guessing at *what happened, how to make her eat, what to do next . . .*

'I don't know . . .' He paused. 'How much more I can take.'

His words sent a bolt of terror through her body. She wanted to stay and calm him, but her desire to check on Lexi was stronger. Once again, she felt like she was being pulled in two different directions.

'I'm going to check she's okay. She'll need me.' She spoke quickly, firmly, indicating that going to comfort her daughter was non-negotiable.

Charlotte cried, quietly, as Lockie stared at his wife and she left the room without further comment.

Freya cracked open Lexi's bedroom door, finding it quite hard to accept the level of fear she felt at having to converse with her little girl. It was a situation she could never have imagined.

'Can I come in?' she whispered to her child, who now sat on the corner of her mattress, coiled against her wall with her right wrist resting on her left hand. Her eyes were bloodshot and red from sobbing.

'Mummy?' Her voice was unusually babyish, the other end of the spectrum to the vile, shrill outburst of earlier.

'What is it, Lex?' She took a step closer, her actions hesitant, nervous in case it was a ruse, in case she lost her temper again.

'I think I've hurt myself!' She lifted her right arm, supported by her other hand, and unfurled her legs on the mattress.

Freya rushed forward and took one look at the limp, swollen limb. She was in little doubt that it was broken.

'Oh God!' she cried, pulling herself together. This was no time for tears. 'We need to get you to the hospital.'

'No, Mummy, please!' she screamed. 'Not hospital!'

'I'm sorry, Lexi, we have no choice.' Her tone was one she had rarely used – assertive, unyielding – and it seemed to do the trick.

Freya threw her zip-up fleece over Lexi's shoulders and bundled her down the stairs, ignoring her shouts and the way she struggled to free herself from her mother's grip. Lockie rushed forward. Freya knew the sight of his child in need sent all thoughts of what had occurred and been said from his mind; at that point he was only concerned.

'What's the matter?'

'I think her arm's broken.' Freya's anguish was written on her face.

'Get her into the car.' He grabbed the keys and shepherded his wife and child down the stairs. 'Charlotte!' he called out. 'Lexi has hurt her arm; we'll be back as soon as we can!'

'It's fractured,' the doctor confirmed, looking at an X-ray. 'You can see here . . .' He pointed to a hairline fracture. 'We'll pop you in a cast, Lexi, and that will do the job.'

'Thank you.' She nodded, looking more than a little ashamed and embarrassed at how her injury had occurred.

'No problem.' He smiled. 'The nurse will take you off to get your cast applied and I am just going to have a word with Mum and Dad, if that's okay.'

'Sure.' She stared at her parents, as if imploring them to keep her secrets; clearly regretting her outburst and her words of hate. Freya watched as Lexi's frail, trembling body shuffled towards the door.

The bearded young doctor closed the door behind Lexi and the nurse, and sat back down. 'I am worried about Lexi's general health.'

'I know, we are too.' Freya thought it easier to cut to the chase.

'I'm sure. We know her heart is suffering and hand in hand with that is an electrolyte imbalance, but it's the bone loss that's worrying me. She should be accruing bone at this stage of her development but she's actually losing it.'

'Osteoporosis.' Freya had read up. Her gut churned; it was one thing to read about the symptoms on a page, quite another to hear it applied to her little girl.

He nodded. 'Her deprivation can also affect her brain function; she is at risk of seizures, hallucination, disordered thinking.'

Freya and Lockie exchanged a glance.

'And we need to keep an eye on her liver.'

Freya placed her hand over her mouth. It was as if they were talking about someone else: bone loss, liver trouble . . . this was her baby girl's body!

'Good Lord!' Lockie spoke aloud, clasping his fists under his chin, as if in prayer.

'I can only imagine how hard this is to hear.' The doctor spoke with a warm sense of understanding.

'She . . .' Freya began. 'She had a kind of episode earlier, when she broke her wrist. It must have happened when she hit the table and thumped her plate on to the floor.' She swallowed; this wasn't easy to recall, and even less so to share with a stranger. She avoided Lockie's gaze, feeling at some level that if he hadn't pushed Lexi this would never have happened. The sound of his chirpy instruction, his clapping, to wake their child from the landing, played in her head on a loop. 'It was like it wasn't her. She was spitting and called us the devil. She swore and said she could see our fire.' Her voice broke. 'It was horrible. Our little girl! To see her like that!'

Lockie reached for her hand and held it fast on his lap. It was an almost instinctive reaction; this was what they did: held hands, united. Today, however, her hand sat limply inside his, as she fought the feeling of resentment that swirled in her mind.

'We weighed her as well . . .' The doctor paused. 'And she registered a weight a shade under seventy-three pounds.'

'She can't be!' Freya shook her head. This was the hardest thing to hear.

'She is,' he repeated softly, looking to Lockie, as if seeking support.

They sat in silence. Freya pictured the number of times she had urged her to eat, pictured the arguments, the sleepless nights, the trudging up and down the stairs, the constant, wearying battle, all for nothing . . .

Eventually Lockie spoke up for the two of them: 'What do we do now? How do we make her better?'

Freya knew he was unaware of just how hard he gripped her fingers. She removed her hand from his.

The doctor took a deep breath. 'I know you have tried hard at home, and I can see that Lexi's illness is taking its toll, not only on her health but yours as well. It's a very stressful, difficult thing to live with, for you all. Do you have other children?'

'Yes.' Freya nodded. 'Charlotte, Lexi's older sister.'

'It can't be easy for her,' he observed.

Freya nodded at the unpalatable truth.

'I think it's best for Lexi if we get her admitted as an in-patient to a facility that can treat her,' continued the doctor. 'Larchcombe House. They will work on getting her weight up and getting her out of immediate danger.'

Freya sat forward. 'She's in danger right now, isn't she?' Her words squeaked.

'Yes, she is.' He confirmed what she already knew, but that didn't make it any easier to hear.

'You have to do what is necessary.' Lockie picked up the reins.

'Oh, Lockie!' she breathed. 'Are we sure it's the best thing for her? Lexi doesn't want to go away, we know that . . .' She was aware that her words, distorted through her tears, sounded like begging. But whilst it was a necessary step, a small part of her wanted Lexi to know that she had fought her corner, no matter how destructive the path. *I'm on your side, Lex, always!*

Lockie's tone was resolute and angry. 'This is no longer about what Lexi wants. This is exactly what we discussed last night. It is all about what she needs, and she needs to be where they can feed her – without quibbling, or refusing the wrong kind of tuna!' He sounded exasperated. 'And it's no longer about what you want or what I want.'

Freya put her face in her hands and wept.

Three hours . . .

Brewster miaowed and climbed up into the warmth of her lap.

Freya looked at the clock above the fireplace. One hundred and eighty minutes to go: that was all.

She shivered and stood; holding Brewster, she reached for the mohair blanket and placed it around her shoulders as a shawl. Lexi's lingering scent brought instant comfort.

'You snuggle down and go to sleep, Brewster. That's a good boy.' She ran her palm over the length of his soft back and smiled.

'Mum, I wrote this.'

Charlotte walked in and placed the sheet on the desk, smoothing Brewster's head before leaving the room.

'Thanks, darling.' She let her eyes rove over the sweet words written from one sister to another and she smiled.

Freya picked up the pen:

> *There have been times in your life, Lexi, when I have done things that I bitterly regret.*

Freya paused and closed her eyes, breathing in and out slowly, trying to calm her flustered pulse before resuming.

When you were little, you decided to play on my computer; what happened was my fault entirely, for not properly saving my work before nipping to the loo. I then became distracted by laundry and was gone for a good ten minutes.

By the time I came back into the kitchen, Dad and Charlotte were watching TV and you were sat in the chair I had vacated, tip-tapping into the keyboard, wearing my glasses askew on your tiny nose, your little fingers hitting the keys randomly, and you were nodding your head, as if deep in thought.

I laughed, and you turned around, informing me that you were working.

I remembered the four hours of work that I had left unattended. We never did find them, to this day — those words, ideas, sentences, wrung from me with thought and deliberation. I have no idea how you managed to make them disappear! Trouble was, you had no idea how you did it either, and so the chances of recovering them were very slim.

Oh, Lexi! I shouted at you.

I watched as in the wake of my rant, your little face crumpled, the glasses fell off and your bottom lip stuck out. You dropped your chin to your chest and you howled! I'm sitting here crying as I write this. I shouted because I was tired and I shouldn't have. It was all my fault and I am sorry.

I think I will always be able to picture your face on that day. I wish I couldn't.

Freya put the pen down and reached for a tissue; blowing her nose and blotting her tears, she sat back in the chair.

The front doorbell rang.

Please, please just go away . . .

FOURTEEN

They had driven home in silence.

And now, in the dark house, where shards of china sat on the floor, swept into the corner by a kind, helpful Charlotte, they observed the no-speaking rule, passing each other in the hallway, removing coats and filling glasses with water to soothe their throats, which were parched and sore from crying. The silence suggested Charlotte had gone out. Freya didn't blame her; if she had a choice, she would be elsewhere too.

It felt like they had been away for days and not merely the seven hours since they had slammed the front door shut.

Freya would never forget how it felt, standing outside the heavy, locked internal door of the facility, where nothing she had learnt in all her years as a parent could possibly have prepared her for what lay ahead. It was unbearable to consider, and she suspected it always would be.

'I don't like being here when she is having to sleep in that place!'

She spoke through gritted teeth. The words were meant as an affirmation, not a conversation starter. The last thing she wanted was to chat to her husband, chat to anyone. She wanted to rage against the unfairness of it all. Why Lexi? Why did this cruel disease have to pick her? She took her frustration out on Lockie, knowing it was unfair: he had made the tough decisions, the right decisions – but that didn't make it any more palatable.

The image of Lexi, with her skinny arm covered in its blond down, bent over in the bed, her thin hair covering her face as she tried to leave the mattress – by falling out, if necessary. And the nurses – one male, one female – restraining her, holding her down so they could sedate her before inserting the nasal gastric tube to feed her.

'It's okay, darling! It's all going to be okay, Lexi, you just need to lie still, my darling!' She had tried to calm her baby girl, hoping her words might somehow permeate. Her sobbing and her own desire to faint, however, actually did very little to help the situation.

'I hate you! I hate you!' Lexi's shrill, hoarse screams would haunt her dreams.

'Don't hurt her!' she called to the nurses who had dealt with a hundred Lexis on a hundred different days, but that didn't matter to Freya.

'Lie down, Lexi!' The male nurse did nothing to soften the instruction.

'Mummy!' her daughter called. 'Mummy, please, help me! Mummy!'

Lockie left the room, crying so hard she saw him reach twice for the handle, as if his vision were fogged. And then Lexi seemed to go floppy. Her emaciated form slumped back on the mattress as the sedation did its job.

What came next was horrific, and was an image that now played on a loop in Freya's mind. The little baby girl she brought into the world was held down while the male nurse tipped her head back and measured a length of tube, stretching it from her nose along her ear and then down to her stomach, before cutting it to size. He then placed it down her nose, pushing down her throat and into her stomach.

Lexi used the last of her strength to resist; under the fog of drowsiness she managed to turn her head slowly from side to side, until this too became too difficult.

The noise she made when not gagging reminded Freya of an injured fox she had once happened upon on Diana's driveway. It had lain broken, making a sound that was part whimper, part scream, but beneath both, it sounded to her like a prayer for sweet release from its pain. It was while she was considering what to do for the best that the little thing went quiet, its prayer finally answered.

Lexi held her gaze and continued to stare at her, wide-eyed, but now thankfully silent.

Freya crept towards her and reached over, smoothing the hair from her forehead, careful not to snag the end of the tube that was now taped across her cheek, its little cap closed and digging into her cheekbone.

The female nurse came close with a filled syringe between her fingers.

'This will make you feel better, Lexi.'

'Please . . .' Lexi slurred, still gagging, her wizened hand lifting slightly on the mattress, reaching out towards her.

'You have to let them make you better,' Freya managed to say before being escorted from the room.

'You can go straight back in the morning.' Lockie stood by the dresser, pulling her back to the present, responding to a statement she had forgotten.

Freya stared at him, feeling an unfamiliar flash of hatred for the man.

'I expect you are happy, aren't you? You didn't even try to find an alternative!' Her fingers balled into fists. 'How do we know Larchcombe is the best place for her?'

'What alternative? That's what they offered us, Freya! And I am running short on alternatives and Lexi is running out of time! How can you say that? As if I could be happy! I am so sad I can barely function!' he admitted. 'She broke her little wrist.' He shook his head. 'Her bone so frail, it snapped. It's too horrific to think about. I know that she needs more help than we can give her. She needs to be somewhere where there

Amanda Prowse

is no room for emotion or sentiment.' He struggled to find the words. 'It's as if we love her too much to do the right thing. We don't want to hurt her, it feels cruel, and so we give in to her, but that is not going to get her better.'

'She hates me.' Freya sobbed. 'Oh, Lockie, she hates me!'

Lockie wrapped his arms around her and rocked her gently. 'No, she doesn't, she loves you! When she says those things, it's just her illness talking, it's not her, remember? And sometimes we need to do what's right, even if that means putting a chasm between her and us. It's not easy, I know, but if she thinks she hates us and gets better, does it matter? It's no longer about being liked. We are way past that.'

'I wish I could go to sleep and wake up when it's all over. I just want my little girl back!' she howled.

'I know, I know.' He rubbed her back as he held her.

'Hey.' Charlotte's voice surprised them. They turned to face their eldest, who stood with red-rimmed eyes and blotchy skin, her arms folded around her trunk. Her hair was pulled messily into a ponytail.

'Charlotte, we didn't know you were in.' Lockie straightened, trying to find a semblance of normality for his daughter's benefit.

'Oh, darling! Have you been crying too?' Freya freed herself from her husband's grip.

'A bit,' Charlotte admitted, looking at the floor. They had called from Larchcombe and left a stilted message explaining the situation.

'Don't be too upset. Dad is right; she is in a place that will help her. They'll get her to eat and then she can come home and we can start over.'

She desperately wanted to believe this.

Charlotte took a deep breath and folded her arms. 'It's partly that, but also . . .' Freya watched her trying not to cry again, waving a hand in front of her face as if that might make a difference.

'What is it, love?' Lockie asked gently.

'I didn't get your message until this afternoon, and I didn't know what was happening. There was no one to take me to the coach with my luggage. I didn't know where everyone was, I tried calling . . .'

'I left my phone here!' Freya realised in that instant and felt quite sick at how she had let Charlotte down. Again.

'Mine ran out of battery,' Lockie confirmed. He balled his fingers into fists.

'I was supposed to leave for my trip today. I thought about getting a taxi, but then I figured it must be an emergency for everyone to just disappear like that. I mean, I know it was only good old Charlotte and her crappy trip, nothing important, but still . . .' She took a breath. 'I couldn't get hold of anyone and I was really worried. I even called Gran, but she didn't know what to do. It's not her fault, though.'

No, it's mine . . . Freya swallowed. 'Charlotte, I don't know what to say, other than I am so sorry!' *I forgot you, my own daughter. What kind of mother does that?* She stood and, with arms wide, went to hold her child. Charlotte stepped backwards out of reach; to be held by her mother was the last thing she wanted.

'I called Mr Gordon and dropped out at the last minute. He was really mad, but it doesn't matter.' Charlotte shook her head as her tears fell, confirming to Freya what she knew already: that it actually mattered a lot.

'I am so sorry. I feel sick.' Lockie sighed.

'Charlotte, we will make it up to you. I am sorry.' Freya held out her hands to her daughter, who ignored the gesture.

'Sure you will,' she snapped. 'I'm going to bed.' She turned and left them alone in the kitchen.

Lockie slumped down on to a dining chair. 'I can't believe it. I completely forgot; her trip went clean out of my head.'

'I'm going to bed,' Freya whispered, wanting to put as much distance between her and this terrible day as possible.

Both silently noted the distinction between 'bed' and 'sleep', knowing that whilst they might lie in their bedroom through the night-time hours, there would be very little rest for either of them that night.

Freya jolted on the mattress, the remnants of a dream lurking around the edges of her subconscious; she had been falling. A quick glance at the clock told her it was a little before 5 a.m. This was her hour of reckoning.

It had always been this way; when preoccupied with worry, or struggling with a problem, this was the time the universe called her to action. No matter how long it was until daylight broke, or that the alarm wasn't set, come 5 a.m. she was wide, wide awake.

Freya crept from the bathroom and across the landing. She placed her fingers on Lexi's door handle, but decided against entering, preferring instead to imagine her sleeping in her bed on the other side. Her tears fell; clearly the pretence wasn't working. Her footfall was light, deliberate; the last thing she wanted at that time of day was for Lockie to jump up and join her. Knowing she would have to live in the tension-filled environment all day, she wanted this brief window of respite before he rose.

She looked at Charlotte's door and pictured her sweet eldest girl crying herself to sleep. Beautiful Charlotte, who was rightly angry and disappointed, her world crumbling because anorexia had knocked on the door of their house and left its mark.

While the coffee machine warmed up, Freya wandered to the window in the den and looked down into the Rendletons' kitchen. A lamp had been left on, presumably in case Mrs Rendleton strayed in the night, or in case of emergency. It made the place look homey, inviting, even at this, the stillest time of the day.

Two mugs sat side by side on their table, and two piles of laundry, neatly folded and ready to be taken up and put away. Her eyes roamed up the side of their house, coming to rest on their bedroom window. She pictured them under a candlewick bedspread, spooning gently in their nightwear, him keeping her safe and her holding his arm, liking to feel him close in such bewildering times.

Freya felt the stirring of something in her stomach; it felt like hunger, but was sharper, sour. She gasped when she recognised it as envy. For the briefest beat of time, she had wondered what it might feel like to have no children, to not have the worry, the desperate fretting that had accompanied every waking moment since walking from Mrs Janosik's office.

I'm sorry! I didn't mean to think that!

She closed her eyes, offering the silent prayer as she pictured her daughters, her beautiful girls, who had been her greatest gift and had brought her more joy than she had ever known possible.

As she watched the dark-brown liquid flow into the little glass mug, she wondered what time she would be able to visit Lexi, wondered if she was asleep. She simultaneously tried to think of how to make things up to Charlotte, and tried *not* to think of the hundred and sixty-four quid that they might as well have shredded and used as confetti.

Freya sat at the head of the table and opened her laptop. An email popped up from Marcia:

Hello,

Remember me? I'm the one who needs you to give me words that I can sell, so that you can eat and keep Lockie in crayons.

Topics like FOOD? HEALTH?

Any of this sounding familiar? Blink once for yes.

M x

P.S. I love you

P.P.S. I'm only half joking (about the article, not the love thing) x

Freya flexed her fingers and took a sip of her coffee. She wrote, typing furiously, without pause, venting her anger, thoughts and frustrations, bashing the keys without mercy, each stroke hard and aggressive, as she transferred her anger on to the screen, watching as her words formed an uncomfortable tapestry.

'The Food of Love'

I live on a strange planet where half of the inhabitants don't have enough to eat and the other half have so much that they discard millions of tons of the stuff. How can that be right? I have been reminded that back in the day, eating was to provide fuel for work, a necessity of life as mundane as bathing or sleeping. Pleasurable, sure, but when did it become such an obsession?

We are bombarded daily with adverts, images, ideas and offers, all urging us to eat more, eat better, eat different, eat cheaply, and then ironically the list of diets available to us to help balance the overconsumption are so varied and many that they are too numerous to list.

Here's an exercise: try to name six members of the current cabinet. Most people struggle after three. Now try naming me six diets. Easy, huh?

As a food lover and writer, I can say that the eating, preparation and sourcing of food has been a lifelong pleasure. I believe that one of the greatest expressions of love is to cook for someone.

For the last year, however, I have found myself hating not only food, but also the word itself.

I live in a house where it has become taboo.

I live in a house where anorexia has swept all of the joy associated with eating out of the door and in its place left an awkward dust that lingers on surfaces, tainting our everyday actions and yes, even tainting the food we place in our mouths.

Freya paused, glancing at the fragments of china that sat in a heap by the counter in the corner.

Anorexia has distorted my daughter's perception. Her negative mental images have invaded every aspect of her life. Her constant analysis of fat content and calories, and her quest to deceive and starve, affect us all.

It is as if we live in a hidden bunker, removed from all that we used to consider routine, normal. No days out, no friends, no shopping trips, no casual lunches, no movie nights, no laughter, no unity, no happiness.

Anorexia is the enemy of all the above and I hate it with a passion.

Her struggle has become our struggle.

We are a family shattered, trying every day to hold together what is left.

The physical effects are too horrible and too personal for me to recount; they haunt me and they always will. It is as if my little girl, with the body and face of an old, frail woman, is drowning in a sea of self-abuse. Every time I think I have a grip of her wrists, bracing myself to haul her up and into my arms, she is sucked under again and I lose her to something stronger and more powerful than me, stronger even than my love for her. I stand helpless, reaching out, as she is ripped from my grasp to float alone in the abyss.

It must be lonely for her.

It's lonely for me, watching her sail off into the distance.

Food is her sickness and food is her cure.

And until someone can tell me how to break the conundrum I fear that this living hell is where we will remain.

The sun is rising as I write – a brand-new day, and another when I will look at my life, the cycle we are trapped in, wondering how food went from being the demonstration of love that bound us and became the enemy. And another when I can't help but wonder where it might end.

Freya pressed 'Send' and slammed her laptop shut.

'You're up early.'

She turned to face Lockie. He looked dreadful. His dark stubble seemed to accentuate the unhealthy pallor to his skin. Two dark crescents sat beneath his puffy eyes, the telltale of the insomniac.

'Did you get much sleep?' he asked; they were both similarly obsessed by their mutual fatigue.

'Not really.' She coughed, her voice croaky and underused at this time of day.

'What time can we go and see her?' he asked.

'Ten o'clock, they said, but I can call after eight to see how she is.'

'I wish I could wind the clock back to this time yesterday.' He sighed.

She let a ripple of laughter escape her lips. 'I wish I could turn the clock back to before this started, to whatever the catalyst was that wired her in this way.'

'But we don't know what or why.'

'No, that's right, Lockie, we don't. Was it trying to keep her occupied by giving her a glossy magazine to look at on a plane, stuffed with pictures of stick-thin models? Was it poking her rounded tum in her little swimming costume, telling her she was adorable, like a fat puppy, whilst joking that she'd have to travel home in the hold of the plane? Was it me, monitoring my size, pinching an inch? God, I wish I knew. It is everywhere, Lockie, the messages, the pressure, the imagery, and I am as guilty as the next person for getting sucked into the whole horrible superficial carnival!' She rubbed her eyes, instantly regretting her snipe, but she was in no mood to hear the obvious so casually stated, as if it was news. 'I'm sorry.' She took a deep breath. 'I am not having a good day.'

'It's not yet six in the morning, I have to say this doesn't bode well.' He gave a small smile. 'I have been thinking similar thoughts, the times

I've teased them both about eating sweets, told them they were too heavy to lift up – jokes, I thought. But now I'm not so sure.' He sighed. 'Another coffee?'

'Yes, please.'

She opened her laptop and as she did so, a ding alerted her to a new email. She saw Marcia's reply in the inbox.

Freya, I am on my way.

'Oh God! Marcia is coming over.' She looked at Lockie, 'I don't want to see anyone and I don't want to be sitting here waiting for her. I need to be with Lexi by ten!' The idea of not being there on the dot, of missing a second of visiting time, filled her with panic.

'Text Marcia, tell her that, she'll understand.'

She did as he suggested, only to receive a rather curt reply informing her that she was twenty minutes away.

'I'd better go and grab a quick shower.'

'Okay, coffee can wait.' He nodded.

Freya towel-dried her hair as she sat on the bed. Brewster was curled illegally on the duvet. If Lockie discovered him, it would mean instant dismissal. She nodded in response to the knowing look he gave her, as if they were co-conspirators.

The front doorbell rang. Freya glimpsed her reflection in the mirror; she looked pale and flat – not that it mattered, not in the grand scheme of things.

'Freya, the witch is here!' Lockie called up the stairs, trying to lighten the mood and at least give the illusion of normal.

She walked down the stairs to see her dear friend and agent standing behind her husband.

'A witch who might cast a spell and turn you into a toad!'

Marcia prodded Lockie in the shoulder with her long red-painted fingernail, a colour that clashed quite dramatically with her spiky marmalade-coloured hair.

'Oh, could you summon me a new fifty-two-inch curved-screen TV first?'

'That's right, Lockie, if we could have one wish right now, it would definitely be for a new TV.'

He ignored Freya's barb.

She pulled a face and slipped off the bottom step, into her friend's waiting arms.

'Freya, my girl, what are we going to do with you?' Marcia spoke over her shoulder. Lockie trod the stairs to the studio, giving them privacy.

'What can I get you? Coffee? Herbal tea?' Freya perused the cupboard.

'Herbal tea? Do I look like a hippie?' Marcia scoffed.

'I don't think I've ever seen you this early in the day,' she noted as she made coffee.

'Yes, you have: when we were in Nice for that hotel opening and we stayed up all night mixing with the great and good, swigging champagne and watching the sun rise over Saint-Jean-Cap-Ferrat. That was some party.'

'I'd forgotten that. Yes, it was.' She felt instantly guilty to be smiling at the memory, while Lexi was . . . Her face crumpled and her tears flowed.

'Sorry, Marcia, I can't help it.'

'Don't apologise. I get it. You are having a really shit time. I wish you had told me sooner.'

Freya was grateful for the lack of padding on her friend's summary.

'Do you know what? Having you only half aware has meant that one aspect of my life wasn't dominated by Lexi's illness. It was an escape of sorts.' Freya also knew that at some level, she hadn't wanted to shatter the illusion that her lovely life with her two beautiful girls was not what it seemed.

'How's Charlotte doing?'

Freya ran her hand over her face. 'Poor old Charlotte, she's having to fend for herself pretty much. I know how unfair that is, but it's like the ship is sinking and my hands are busy bailing; everything else takes second priority. I keep telling myself I will make it up to her, but I'm sure that's scant comfort to her right now.'

She thought of how excited her daughter had been about her trip to Geneva and felt the spike of guilt go straight through her once again.

'Your article was . . .' Marcia paused.

'You didn't like it? That's okay. I can't even remember what I wrote; it just flowed.'

'No, I did like it. I liked it very much, but it's so raw, I wonder, if you want it published, it's such a very personal statement of affairs . . . I thought maybe Lexi should approve it? I wondered whether it was more like a self-soothing therapy session. We both know that sometimes it's good to get stuff down on paper, shift it from inside your head.'

'You're right.'

'Shall I sit on it? Let you think, let you be? I'll wait until you say you want me to push the button, *if* you want me to push the button, otherwise it can be between you and me. It's a beautiful account, moving, thought-provoking, and I think one of the most honest pieces you have ever written.'

'Goodness me, Marcia, are you sure you don't want herbal tea? You certainly sound like a hippie.' She laughed mockingly, the only way to dilute the pain of her friend's words and to halt the next bout of tears that hovered close to the surface.

'So what can I do?' Marcia banged the tabletop.

'Nothing, sadly, but I really do appreciate you asking.'

'I feel helpless and useless and I'm not used to it and I don't like it. There's usually a solution that I can throw at things.' Marcia sighed.

Freya recognised her own frustration in her friend's words. 'I know and if it was a case of us *doing* something, she'd be fine, she'd be fixed by now. But we can't do any more than we have,' she acknowledged. 'We have had to hand her over to people who know better than us, even if they don't know Lexi better than us. And it's not easy for me to admit that, Marcia. It hurts. And leaving her there last night was one of the hardest things I have ever done.'

It was the first time she had said it aloud, and once the words had been exorcised, her body slumped a little, as if beaten.

'I can only picture her as a little girl who needs her mum, and so when I'm not with her, it's like I've abandoned her. I see her face constantly. We lost her once in the market – only for a minute, she had wandered off and I couldn't see her behind a clothes rack. I remember feeling this blind panic, a surge of fear that I'd not experienced before, and suddenly there she was, standing in front of me, smiling. I don't think she'd been afraid until she saw my face, and then she cried. I held on to her so tightly.' She coughed and placed the mugs on the countertop. 'But that blind panic, that adrenaline-fuelled surge of fear, that's how I feel all the time. It's like I'm waiting for her to stand in front of me again, smiling, and until she does . . .'

'She's lucky to have you. Both of you,' Marcia whispered. 'With you guys in her corner, I'd say she has every chance of beating this horrible thing.'

'It feels like a war. And every time you think you are advancing, winning, the enemy comes at you from directions you haven't got covered, with weapons that outweigh whatever you have. It's exhausting.'

'But this place she's in, they'll take away some of that burden, won't they?'

'Larchcombe House, yes, they will, I guess. They are . . .' She paused and pictured the moment they put the tube into her nose. 'They are giving her nutrition.'

'It sounds like this might crack it.'

Freya nodded. 'I hope so. Otherwise what we are putting her through would be pointless. Truth is, Marcia, she's my little girl! I don't want her to go away, to be in a hospital with people like that.' Her tears again pooled.

'But what if it's the only way she can get better? What if she *is* people like that?'

Freya opened her mouth to reply, to rebuff, but there were no words, not this time.

Two hours, thirty minutes . . .

Freya listened but there were no shouts from the front door. Charlotte was clearly dealing with it, probably another delivery or unwanted package. She remembered the three books she had ordered an age ago.

Reaching down, she pulled the drawer open and there they were, pristine and unmarked: *My Journey In and Out of Love with Food*; *Starvation and Me: A Tale of Anorexia*; *Ten Steps to Recovery from Self-Loathing to Self-Love*. She once again let the books fall open at various pages and let her eyes rove over the painful accounts. She felt a spike of sadness pierce her core at the photographs of emaciated bodies and words that leapt from the page: 'disgust', 'purge', 'decay'.

Closing the pages, Freya remembered quietly putting the books in the bottom drawer of her desk, deciding it might be a mistake to read these very graphic accounts, written by women who seemed to be suffering to a far greater degree than Lexi. Now, however, the images were no more shocking than the sights she had seen every day in her own home, the declarations and descriptions no worse than anything she had regularly dealt with.

This marker of Lexi's decline brought a whole new level of sadness. How naïve she had been. How different her family life . . .

'Mum?' Charlotte crept around the door.

'Yes, love?' She wiped away her tears and tried out a smile. 'What is it?'

'Daddy's back, he'd forgotten his key . . .'

FIFTEEN

They sat in the car park at Larchcombe House from 9.30, making sure they could go in on the dot of ten o'clock.

As they entered, a harrowing wail of distress floated towards them. It was the sound of a girl crying; her distress, most extreme, made the hairs on the back of Freya's neck stand up. When Mikey, the male nurse, spoke without mentioning it, Freya wondered if she had imagined it.

'Beds are at a premium here. For every place available, we have at least five patients needing care, waiting, and I've seen that number double at times and so it's a fairly intensive routine. It has to be. We need to get results in the quickest possible timescale and we need absolute compliance, otherwise patients, no matter what their condition, will be discharged.' Mikey spoke openly as they trotted behind him, navigating the soulless, silent white corridor to Lexi's room.

'If they fail here, the only other option locally is Morningside Hospital, and that place makes Larchcombe seem like two weeks on the Riviera.' There was something in his tone that suggested it might be a warning, and the idea of somewhere worse than this place was unthinkable.

'Is Lexi being compliant?'

She hardly dared ask, hating the use of the word when talking about the child she had always encouraged to be a free thinker.

Mikey stopped and turned to face them, his manner that of a man who was weary of fighting against the odds. It was the first time Freya considered how hard it must be to be dealing with such a foul disease and simultaneously battling a patient who did not want to get better.

Freya knew the statistics, could see that much of what he did was futile, and that not all of his patients would make it out alive. The thought that Lexi might end up as one of those they were unable to save was terrifying.

'She removed her feeding tube.' He delivered the words neutrally.

'Oh, dear God!' Lockie placed his hand over his mouth.

Freya stared straight ahead, unable to imagine how that must have felt and what kind of emotional state her daughter must have been in to do such a thing.

'We reinserted it this morning and she has been given her second syringe already. And we have sedated her further, just until things calm down a little.'

He continued to walk, leaving the Braithwaites to follow in his wake, trying to take in the new, devastating piece of information.

'What's to stop her pulling it out again?' Freya asked, wary of the response.

Mikey spoke over his shoulder. 'It won't happen. She's being monitored twenty-four seven. For now.'

The wall gave way to a communal area on the right-hand side. It was a large sunny space with a laminated wood floor, well lit, with an assortment of tables, chairs and small sofas positioned in front of a television and others next to bookshelves, the contents of which looked a little sparse. More shelves held board games. Freya spied all the usual suspects: Monopoly, Uno, Trivial Pursuit. The sight of the games that were so familiar in their house, the ones they argued over at Christmas, while they laughed and nibbled on leftovers, caused a lump to form in her throat.

Freya reached for Lockie's hand as they strolled past patients. Nearly all were female and young. All in similar attire of baggy joggers and long-sleeved sweatshirts or hoodies, Lexi's uniform of choice. And all with the skeletal frame and haunted eyes that similarly marked her daughter. Having spent time on Pro Ana sites and having spoken to Lexi at length, she knew that the pairs of eyes that now followed her progress along the dust-free floor would be taking in her toned flank, her pert bottom, her full bust, and they would be doing so with disgust. She felt horribly self-conscious, gripping Lockie's hand even tighter and looking to the left, peering at closed doors, wondering what lurked behind them – anything other than meet the stares that scorched her skin.

Her eyes were drawn to a laminated notice, stuck to a door with tape. It read:

> These toilets will be locked at all times. For entry please approach a member of staff who will be happy to escort you. Other toilets are available near the main desk and the kitchen, where members of staff are on hand at all times. Thank you.

The words were followed with the little floral Larchcombe House logo, as if the addition of a petal or two might make the message more palatable.

It didn't.

Even though she was impatient to see her baby girl, Freya felt her stomach lurch as they approached Lexi's room. Mikey turned the handle and nodded to the tall nurse who sat in the corner.

Lockie inadequately stifled a sob that filled the room.

Mikey laid his hand on his shoulder. 'I'll be back in a bit.'

The female nurse stood and wiped the creases from her pale-green tunic. 'I'll give you folks some privacy. Be back in a minute, Lexi. I'll just be outside.' She whispered the last bit to Freya, who nodded absently, her full attention given to her daughter.

There was a smear of blood at the corner of Lexi's nostril, whether from the insertion or removal of a tube she wasn't sure – not that it mattered; both ideas were equally distressing.

Freya took a step closer to her child, who lay flat on the mattress; a thin pillow had been placed under her head, which listed to the left. Her eyes stared in their general direction, but looked past them towards the wall with an impossibly slow blink, coming from eyes that looked empty.

'Hello, darling.' She tried her best to keep her voice level. 'I missed you very much.'

Lexi didn't move, didn't react at all.

'Charlotte sends you all her love.'

As her tears pooled, she turned to Lockie, whose colour had drained from his face. She managed to suppress the words of regret and sorrow that she wanted to hurl at him, at everyone!

Tentatively Freya reached out and stroked her daughter's narrow forearm with her finger. Still she didn't react.

'She's out of it, Lockie.'

He was unable to respond, his distress seeming to take up all his reserves and rendering speech impossible.

'I can't leave her here! I can't leave her here on her own like this. I know she needs their help . . . but look at her, Lockie!' she pleaded, a little louder than she had intended.

'It's going to be okay,' he whispered. 'It'll all be okay.' Whether his words were meant for her, Lexi or himself she wasn't sure.

The female nurse came back into the room.

'How are we doing?' she whispered, clearly alerted by her raised voice.

'She hasn't spoken and I'm not sure she's noticed me,' Freya admitted.

'She's been quite heavily sedated.'

'Is it really necessary?' Lockie's voice was still hushed.

'It is,' the nurse asserted.

Freya shook her head. 'But only yesterday we were in A & E, waiting for her to see someone about her arm, and we chatted about stuff like' – she wiped her nose – 'like music and schoolwork, and just one day later I come and find her like this!'

She let her palm hover over her child's head. Lockie stood by her side.

'I understand, but yesterday her heart rate was dangerously slow. It is vital we get nutrition into her system. I know this must be traumatic for you to see, but we only care about getting food into her. To remove a feeding tube you have to be pretty determined, but it's that determination that can mean the difference between success and failure. We need to be *more* determined than Lexi; we need to take measures, like these' – she pointed at the bed – 'to get her to eat. That's it. It's that simple.'

The nurse made it sound that simple; no one could fault her logic or question the strategy, and were they discussing any other patient, Freya could see that this was the right thing to do. But no one could account for the pull of her heartstrings linking her to the fifteen-year-old girl who lay on the bed. The child who was so frail she looked to be at risk of floating away.

Stay with me Lexi . . . Stay here . . .

'How was she?' Charlotte asked, as she lay on the sofa in the den, her long legs crossed at the ankle, resting on the arm of the sofa, and her mood thankfully lifted from the previous night.

'She was great! Doing really well. Sends you all her love.' Freya beamed, but her fake smile and false demeanour was getting harder to enact. Lockie threw his keys into the bowl on the sideboard.

Despite the fraught nature of their relationship at that moment, both were in agreement that they would do whatever necessary to keep things as positive as possible for Charlotte, whose exams were looming.

'How long will she have to stay in?' Charlotte asked.

'Not sure, love. But they are doing all they can, she's in a good place.' Lockie's smile of reassurance was fleeting. He headed for the kettle.

'I want to go and see her, take her in some magazines and stuff.' Charlotte turned her head back to her textbook.

'She would love that!' Freya smiled. 'When she's a bit better. In the meantime you need to study.'

'What do you think I've been doing all day?' She waved her book in the air.

Freya swallowed the bile of guilt. She was such a good girl, sitting alone studying all day despite the disappointment of her trip. She made a new vow to make it up to her, somehow, when all this was over . . .

'I feel terrible, you know, Charlotte, about Geneva. I really do. We will make it up to you.'

'Mum's right, we will,' Lockie echoed as he put the teabags into the mugs.

Charlotte jumped up and rushed towards her mum. 'Don't. Right now I can honestly say that I'm glad I'm not there.'

'Well, you've changed your tune!' Lockie sounded glad of the slight upturn in the atmosphere.

'Tara's having a house party.' She hugged herself.

'Do her parents know?' he asked.

'Um, the answer is the one that means you don't try and stop me going.'

'I think that answers it perfectly. I must say I have to question the sanity of any parent willingly giving over their home to a bunch of teenagers.' He tutted. 'Just be careful. Don't go nuts.'

'Dad. I play the cello. I read French textbooks in my spare time. I have never had a boyfriend and I only hang around with Milly and Tara. I'm hardly a party animal.'

'Is Daniel going?' Freya tried to keep the enquiry casual.

'Who is this Daniel you speak of?' Lockie asked sternly.

'Fear not, Dad, he is uber cool and way out of my league.' She sighed.

The glint in her eye told them both that whilst that might be the case, she was not averse to trying her luck. Freya gave Lockie a knowing smile; Charlotte's anticipation was almost palpable.

'What do you want for supper?' Freya asked, again feeling the flash of relief at being able to mention food and cook without worrying about Lexi's reaction, followed almost immediately by an equally strong feeling of guilt.

'Nothing for me, thanks.'

'Don't be ridiculous, Charlotte!' Freya was loud. 'You have to eat something! You really do!'

'Mum! For God's sake calm down! I've already eaten,' she explained. 'I got a pizza.'

'Oh.' She looked at the contents of the fridge, picturing the small clot of blood on the edge of Lexi's nose. 'I'm sorry, darling.'

'It's okay, Mum. I get it.' She sounded exasperated. 'I'm going to straighten my hair.'

Freya nodded, keeping her face hidden inside the fridge door.

Lockie walked behind her and ran his hand down her back.

'It's all right.'

She shook her head. 'Is it? I don't care what they said. I'm going back in tonight to go and sit with her, but I didn't want to say that to Charlotte, didn't want to worry her. Can you drop her at the party?'

'Sure. Marshalswick, isn't it?'

'Yep,' she confirmed where Tara lived.

'Do you want me to come with you?' he offered. 'I could swoop by after drop-off?'

'No, it's okay. You make sure Charlotte is happy. I just know I won't sleep if I don't see Lexi a little bit more settled.'

'I get it.' His knuckle gently grazed her cheek with something close to regret.

She twisted her face away.

'Do you want supper, Lockie?'

'No.' He shook his head. 'I can't eat.'

'Me neither.' She closed the fridge door.

Freya kissed Charlotte goodbye. She had obviously taken great care in her appearance and looked beautiful in her sheer floral shirt, with a vest underneath and her hair curled in loose waves by her deft hand on the hair-straighteners.

'You look gorgeous! You really do. Have a lovely time.'

'Thanks, Mum.' Charlotte smiled.

Lockie grabbed the car keys.

'See you in a bit,' he chirped with a hesitant smile.

Freya pressed the buzzer to gain entry. A different nurse met her at the front door. She was pale with her hair pulled back into a severe bun.

'Hello, my daughter, Lexi, she—'

'Yes, Mrs Braithwaite, we saw you on the CCTV, my colleague recognised you. Were you not informed about visiting hours yesterday?'

Freya found it hard not to be put off by the woman's cool demeanour.

'Yes, but I just wanted to come and sit with her for a little bit; she wasn't quite with it earlier and I must admit it's upset me.'

Don't cry, Freya! Keep it together.

'We don't have a drop-in policy in the evening. During the day it's fine, but at night-time we find that routine is very important. It's not really appropriate for you to just pop in as and when you feel like it.'

The woman stood loftily in the gap between the door and the frame, blocking her entry. Freya peered over her shoulder, into the building where her little girl lay.

'I . . . I appreciate that, but all I am asking for is five minutes with my child.' Her voice quavered. 'That's all. Just five minutes to wish her goodnight and that will help us both sleep, I'm sure. Please.'

The nurse hesitated, looking her up and down, making a judgement call. 'Five minutes.'

Freya nodded, beyond grateful as she stepped over the threshold and into the corridor. She keenly felt the absence of Lockie by her side as they approached Lexi's room. The common room was eerily empty.

A new nurse sat on the chair in the corner of Lexi's room, busy with forms, writing under lamplight with a ballpoint in her hand and her head close to the desk.

Freya walked in. 'Hello. I'm Lexi's mum.'

The nurse waved. She looked kind; this was a massive relief to Freya.

'Hello there, I'm Jenny. We've been chatting this afternoon; well, more of a one-sided chat, but we're getting there.' Her face crinkled into a smile.

Freya tiptoed towards the bed. It was becoming an almost automatic response: as soon as she set eyes on her little girl, her tears fell.

She didn't look as if she had moved, lying in the same position. The differences were subtle: her eyes were not so still, instead they darted at each new sound, and her muscles looked coiled despite her recumbence. Her body was rigid with fear.

'Hello, darling, hello, my baby girl.'

Freya found it impossible not to stare at the little blue cap on the feeding tube, or the tape affixing it to her cheek.

Freya would have found it hard to describe to a stranger the relief she felt at the sight of her child's tears. Anything, *anything*, was better than the muted, hazy reaction of earlier; that person was merely the shell of her daughter, and that had been unbearable to watch.

'Don't cry, Lexi, please don't cry. It's all going to be okay. They are going to make you better and then you'll come home and you will be back to your old self before you know it.' She nodded, smiling through her own tears as she mopped at her child's wet cheek with her sleeve.

Lexi whispered, her words indiscernible, a mumble.

'What's that, darling? Say it again.'

Freya tucked her long hair behind her ears and bent low, her face close to Lexi's. She could feel her breath on her cheek; it had a new, slightly chemical tang to it.

She heard her swallow, as if speaking was painful or uncomfortable at the least. With her eyes narrowed, she listened to her little girl, whose words she heard loud and clear.

'Don't . . . don't leave me here, Mummy. I promise. I will eat. Please, Mummy . . .' she managed, as her tears fell again.

'Oh, Lexi, Lexi . . .' She held her small hand and placed it against her mouth, kissing the fragile skin of the arm without a cast. 'I can't take you home, darling. I can't. But you know that I am not far away from you. I am around the corner, minutes really, and if you need me, I'll come in straight away and I'll be back tomorrow and the day after that and every day until you come home. I promise.' Her voice broke away in sobs. 'I'm sorry. I am so sorry.'

'I'm afraid it's time for you to go now, Mrs Braithwaite.' The pale nurse had come to collect her.

Freya felt panic rise in her throat. 'Just five more minutes, please!'

'I'm sorry.' She shook her head and gestured towards the door.

'Mummy!' Lexi called, her voice a little stronger now. 'Mummy!' She screamed this time. 'Please, Mummy, I promise! I promise, Mum, please!'

Jenny rushed forward to try and comfort Lexi as the nurse ushered her outside and closed the door.

Freya could hear her child calling out for her on the other side of the door. She placed her hand on it, feeling her whole body cave in distress, not knowing how she would walk away.

'I was afraid this might happen.'

Freya turned to the woman, about to spit venom, but instead the nurse placed her arm around Freya's shoulder and spoke gently as she pulled her away from the door and down the corridor.

'I cannot imagine how hard this must be for you, seeing Lexi like this, but I give you my word that we know what we are doing and we know what works. As cruel as it seems, as difficult as it is to witness, this programme is all about getting her to take on food. That's it. We are trying to save her life.'

'I didn't want to unsettle her, I wanted to say goodnight and tuck her in, that's all!'

'I understand.' And it seemed that, despite her cool manner, she really did. 'But sometimes you have to let us do our job.'

Freya wondered if letting her in, and the inevitable result, was a way of teaching her a lesson. She leant into her, allowing the woman to take her weight, until they reached the car park.

'Can I call someone for you?'

'No.' Freya shook her head. 'I'll call my husband,' she managed, the rhythm of her breathing fractured.

'No doubt we'll see you tomorrow. I'll go and check on her now, and I guarantee that she is so tired, she will be asleep.' She gave a brief smile and Freya knew she was lying. It was the same smile she had given Charlotte earlier: *She sends you all her love!* It wasn't as easy to pretend when you were on the receiving end.

Switching on her phone, she called Lockie.

'Come and get me,' she managed, falling back on to the low wall where she would sit and wait.

Freya flopped down on the sofa and kicked off her shoes before folding her legs underneath her.

'Do you have any brandy?' she asked, knowing it was going to be the only way to get through the night, the only way to rid her mind of the images that played every time she closed her lids.

'In my studio. I'll go and grab it.' Lockie sounded as low as she felt.

He came back minutes later, with the brandy bottle and two glasses from the shelf. He poured her a generous slug that she knocked back, letting the alcohol warm the back of her throat. She held the glass out for a refill.

After half an hour, the booze was doing its job.

'I thought I knew what was best. I figured if I could have five minutes with her, it would calm her, but it was the opposite. I wound her up, disturbed her. I felt the atmosphere change the moment she saw me. She begged me to bring her home, Lockie, and I wanted to, I wanted to so . . . so badly!' She hiccupped through her tears.

'I know.' He placed his arm around her shoulders. 'I feel torn,' he admitted. 'I want her home, here where she belongs, but I want her better.'

'I used to think I could make her better all on my own,' Freya whispered, sipping again at her drink.

Lockie shook his head. 'I thought that, but it's bigger than us. I shan't ever forget the sight of her in that room. But this thing she brought into our house, it's upset the balance. It's the first thing we think about when we wake up and the first thing we see when we walk into a room. It's not fair, on her or us! It's hijacked our lives. I never could have imagined anything, *anything*, causing tension or disagreement between us, you and me, Freya!' He paused at the devastating truth. 'And as much as I love her . . .' His voice broke then; he cleared his throat. 'And I do. I liked how it used to be, that simpler life when we worried about money and the kids' exam results. I miss that life. This one is exhausting.'

He cried then, the loud, gulping tears of a man on the edge. Freya had neither the guile nor the courage to challenge his words.

'I know.' Reaching across the sofa, she held his hand, trying to repair some of the broken ground that lay between them, but his touch felt different.

Gone was the relaxed palm-to-palm, from which they both drew comfort in the familiar. This was a *grip*, tense muscles and stiff fingers, holding on tightly, fearful of what might happen when they let go.

An hour later, the brandy bottle was much depleted and the two slumped on the cushions, waiting for the welcoming cloak of oblivion.

Freya suddenly sat up straight.

'I can't be here without her, Lockie!' she howled.

'Where do you want to go?' he asked, as if she might have a plan.

'Right now?' She laughed. 'I want to go anywhere – the other side of space!'

She laughed before falling down into her husband's arms.

Lockie reached for his coat, discarded on the floor, and threw it over them both, and there they lay, until the tendrils of dawn snaked over them, shaking them gently awake to face another day.

Freya sat up and stretched. Her headache was the first thing she noticed; the second was an insatiable thirst.

'Oh God!' Lockie sat forward and placed his head in his hands. 'I think we should go to bed, get a few more hours' sleep.' He stood, twisting his back with his hands on his hips until it cracked. Lockie trod the stairs while she went to get a drink of water. It was as she stood at the sink that she heard the key in the front door.

Charlotte jumped at the sight of her mum.

'What are you doing? Surely you're not waiting up for me?' she gasped.

'No. Just getting a glass of water. I thought you were already home and in bed.' She placed her palm on her forehead. 'I think I've got a hangover or I might still be a bit sloshed, I'm not sure. How was your party?'

'Bit rubbish, really.' Charlotte looked at her feet.

'How did you get home? You are very late.'

'Daniel dropped me off.'

'Oh, Daniel! Any developments on that front?' She feigned interest for the sake of her girl.

'Nope.' Charlotte shook her head. 'None at all.'

'Oh, well, that's a shame.'

'Not really.' Charlotte stared at her mum. 'Can I have a hug?'

Freya felt her face break into a smile, recalling how she had shrugged her off earlier. 'You never have to ask. Of those, I have a limitless supply.'

Freya held her child close and inhaled the scent of her hair. 'You smell like a party, all boozy and horrible.' She smiled.

'That's funny, I was thinking the exact same thing about you.'

They held each other close, as the sun streamed in through the window.

'I love you, Charlotte Belle.' Freya closed her eyes.

'I love you too.'

It was a rare, golden moment.

Two hours . . .

'Oh!' Her hand flew to her chest. 'He's back?'

'Yes.' Charlotte nodded. 'He's in the kitchen.'

Freya scrambled from the desk, her foot slipping in haste, and her knee banged the chair as she fled the room, jumping the stairs two at a time, racing, running to get to the kitchen where her Lockie stood.

She almost jumped, crashing into him, flinging her arms around his neck and holding him tightly to her, as they fought for breath.

'Lockie!' she cried. 'Lockie!' she yelled again.

'I've got you,' he cried. 'I've got you.'

This was how they stood, with precious minutes ticking by as they held each other, each gaining strength from the other, each processing what was happening today.

He placed his hands either side of her face and kissed her lightly on the mouth.

'Is it done?'

'Yes. We're all ready. Charlotte and I . . . we've been writing notes, letters, stories. You still need to do one.'

'Okay.' He nodded. 'What should I write?'

'Anything you'd want Lexi to hear.' She smiled sadly.

'Will you sit next to me?' he asked.

She nodded, taking a seat at the kitchen table; she placed her hand on his leg and waited.

SIXTEEN

Freya thought that Lexi being admitted as an in-patient and the struggle they had faced since she first stopped eating were the worst things they, as a family, would have to face. What they hadn't considered was that things could possibly get any tougher.

Diana pointed out on a visit that Charlotte seemed a little withdrawn, devoid of her usual spark. She had greeted her gran with a near-silent hug and retreated to her room.

Lockie noted Freya's fallen expression and decided to handle this one. 'She's preoccupied with studying. It's a horrible time of year, but I do think it's tough on her, Mum. We have taken her up to visit her sister a couple of times and it hit her hard. She hasn't wanted to go again, which I completely understand. And we are both up with Lexi at Larchcombe every day, and to be honest, it's quite a depressing place. When you get back, being jolly is the last thing you feel like. We try, but I suspect Charlotte isn't getting the best of us at the moment.'

Freya didn't comment on his understatement, knowing that it was hard to give your best when you were falling apart; and that was what it felt like. Larchcombe House was not only depressing, it was soul destroying.

'But Charlotte's going to need a lot more support during her exams, isn't she?' Diana asked.

Freya bit her lip, reminding herself to be patient and that it was her own stress and fatigue that made her want to scream.

It wasn't Diana's fault.

'We know she will,' she managed. 'We really are doing all we can to keep both girls in a good place, but it's tough, Diana, we are emotionally and physically spent.'

'Well, shall I come and stay? Help out, I mean? I'm no Freya in the kitchen, but I can keep an eye on Charlotte . . .'

Only someone who knew Freya as well as Lockie did would have noticed the almost imperceptible clench of her jaw, as if she felt she were being judged in some way, the suggestion being that she couldn't cope.

'That's really kind, Mum, but we'll manage. Please try not to worry about us. And if we need you here, we promise to shout.' He smiled.

'How are you working if you are both at the hospital, or whatever that place is, every day?' Again she pushed; it was like she had been briefed on the worst possible topics of conversation.

'We're not. Not really.' Lockie sighed.

'Well, how are you earning money?' Diana stared at her son, quite perplexed.

'Again, the simple answer is we are not. We are living off our credit cards, which I worry about between three and three-fifteen in the morning, and only because the other twenty-three hours and forty-five minutes are spent thinking about Lexi, Charlotte and Freya, and not always in that order.' He forced a laugh.

'Why didn't you say something? I might not be able to help in other ways, but I can ease your financial burden. It's all yours anyway – there's not a lot of cash, everything is tied up in the house, but it makes no odds to me when you have it. Would it help if I transferred some money over to you now?'

Lockie placed his hand over his eyes, trying to hide his tears. 'It . . . it would help a lot,' he managed.

'Well, that's that, then! I'll do it first thing in the morning.'

Diana smiled at her and Freya smiled back, mouthing *Thank you* to the kind woman who was her family.

Diana's concern over Charlotte filled Freya's mind; it was just before bedtime that Freya knocked on her girl's bedroom door.

'Am I disturbing you?' she asked as she popped her head around the door frame.

'Nope.'

Charlotte sat up on her bed and placed her notebook face down on top of her duvet.

'It was nice to see Gran, wasn't it?'

'Yes.' Charlotte nodded.

Freya tested the water. 'She said she thought you were a little quiet.'

Charlotte shrugged. 'I guess. I'm worried about my exams and when I'm not talking I'm revising in my head.'

'My clever girl.' She smiled. 'I know we're neglecting you a bit. It feels like all our focus has to be on Lex because she's poorly and you are so capable and kind. You never complain, but I'm worried I've been taking advantage of that nice nature, worried that you feel you can't say if anything is bothering you, like you can't speak out.'

'I'm fine, Mum, don't worry.' She avoided her mother's eyeline.

'Ah, but I do worry, that's the biggest part of my job.'

'I heard what Dad said to Gran about me visiting Lexi, how horrible it was in there.'

Freya nodded. There was no denying it.

'I know I should go and visit her more, but . . .'

'But what, love?' Freya wanted her to open up.

'I feel horrible saying it, Mum.'

'You can say anything to me,' she urged, bracing herself for whatever verbal arrows were about to be fired.

Charlotte opened her mouth to speak, but it was a while before she found the courage. 'I quite like it here without Lexi. It's more peaceful and I can pretend things are just like they used to be. I know that makes me sound horrible. But that's the truth.'

Freya indeed felt the sharp bite of her daughter's words, knowing that in her expression lay a kernel of unpalatable truth for them all.

'And also, Mum, I'm scared to go and visit her.' Charlotte picked at a loose thread on her duvet.

'Why, darling?'

'I always think . . .'

'Always think what?' Freya pushed.

'That it might be the last time I see her, and I worry that I might lose it and tell her that, or go nuts or something.'

Freya sat on the mattress and wrapped her arms around her girl, feeling the solidity of her beneath her palms: her muscle, her comfortable contours, the thin layers of fat on her beautiful body. She held her in silence, not wanting to admit to often feeling the same.

Call it instinct, but as Lockie parked the car outside Larchcombe and Freya climbed from the passenger seat, she had a feeling in her gut that something had happened. Pressing the doorbell with a sense of urgency, she bit her bottom lip.

'You okay?' Lockie bent his head to look into her eyes.

'I don't know. I feel . . .' She scanned her racing thoughts to find the words.

The door opened before she had a chance to speak.

'Good morning, Braithwaites!' Jenny smiled at them. Her friendly demeanour went some way to calming Freya's nerves, who figured that anything bad would have warranted a more sober greeting.

'Someone is very keen to see you today.' Jenny smiled again as they followed her along that darned corridor.

Stopping at the common area, Jenny indicated Lexi, a lone figure at the table. She had brushed her thin hair and had fastened it with a loose plait. Her skin looked a little less ashen, and there were the beginnings of a smile on her lips. The changes were subtle, but to Freya they represented the many miles travelled over the last few weeks here in the facility.

'Hey, Lexi!' Lockie called as they approached.

She lifted her head, her back straight, her hand steady.

'How are you today?' Freya issued her standard greeting that was usually met with a shrug, a sneer or, on better days, a whispered ''Kay'.

'I'm coming home.'

Her face broke into a smile, revealing her once beautiful teeth that were now dull and grotty. Not that it mattered; nothing did as much as getting her home where she belonged and to continue her journey back to a normal life.

'Oh, Lex!' Freya's tears bloomed. 'When?' She reached out and gripped her hand.

'Soon. But proper soon, Mum, later this week, not your soon.' She smiled again.

Lockie was quite overcome. 'That is' – he beamed – 'the best news in the whole wide world!'

'You have done so well, Lex, we are incredibly proud of you.'

Lexi nodded with a slight blush to her cheek, indicating that for the first time in as long as Freya could recall, Lexi seemed to be a little proud of herself.

With the window fixed and a promise from Lockie not to put a hammer through the new pane of glass, fresh flowers on her dressing table, and crisp bed linen, Lexi's bedroom was ready for her homecoming.

Freya took a moment, as she stood in the kitchen and looked into the fridge, suppressing the anxiety that leapt in her throat. She would never confess to the fear she felt at the prospect of feeding her family with Lexi in the house, or indeed the fear at the thought of having to feed Lexi herself.

Whilst her three-month residence at Larchcombe House had been torturous, it had also, in hindsight, taken the burden from Freya's shoulders. Remembering the struggle and the atmosphere fraught with tension around every mealtime . . . Freya shook her head and took a deep breath, and reminded herself that this was a day of celebration.

The goal had always been to get her home, and that day had arrived. Larchcombe House had given them a lifeline, but no amount of fresh white paint, bright Ikea furnishing and potted plants could hide the human misery that lurked in the air and ran down the walls.

She noticed that the new admissions to the unit, the sicker, skinnier patients, were a new source of misery for the residents, as if their distress added a new layer of wretchedness, but also that the girls who were about to be discharged looked at them with something close to envy, realising, when faced with their former selves, just how much their bodies had changed.

She mentioned this to Nurse Mikey. 'It's so sick!' Freya shook her head.

'Yes, it is,' he reminded her. 'That's why they are here.'

Lexi had put on weight; they were winning the war, but this gain came at a cost. Gone was her sparkle, her laugh and her light.

The girl who had earned common-room privileges and had been able to sit on the sofa by the window, looking at the sky, or could wander in the garden under supervision, feeling snatches of sunlight on her wan face, was the husk of Lexi.

Her eyes were dead, her pupils dull, and her expression never altered. She had been tube fed for six weeks and had in the last four weeks transitioned to solid food.

Freya had daily cooed words of encouragement, but in truth there were only so many variants of how she could say *You're doing great! Keep going, Lexi, nearly there, darling!* until she was as bored of uttering the words as her daughter was of hearing them.

She had a favoured mantra, written on a piece of paper and fixed above Lexi's bed to the wall of the shared room; it read: 'Today is all that matters, not tomorrow or the day after that, just today, because that's all there is . . .'

Freya would tap it when she kissed her goodbye.

'Remember, Lex, we only need to get through today. That's how we are going to do this, one day at a time.'

'Take me home, Mummy, please . . .' she would utter with a mono-tone delivery, to which Freya gave a now standard one-word reply.

'Soon.'

Occasionally Lexi would snap. The worst episodes were when she growled at Freya like a wild animal, repeating how much she hated her and how this was all her fault, and another when she threw her food out of the window in the common room and was threatened with sedation.

At these times, Freya could only plead with her to behave, trying to hint that she was powerless to stop them restraining and sedating her, and banning all visitors.

All this was now behind them: they were travelling home! She kept looking to the backseat, taking in the fact that this journey, which she had done every day for months, was being made for the last time, and her little girl really was coming home.

'I feel a bit nervous, being outside.'

Freya smiled; even this admission felt like a breakthrough. 'I bet, but we'll just take baby steps, no need to rush. We will go at your pace and only when you are ready.'

'What will I eat today?' Lexi asked from the backseat of the car, her question, her preoccupation, quickly wiping away the frisson of joy Freya had felt only seconds earlier.

'I've got your meal plan, so pretty much what you had yesterday. A small amount of protein, some dairy and vegetables. I won't change a thing or add a thing, not until you are ready, okay?'

'Okay.' Lexi seemed to relax a little.

'We're home!' Lockie shouted, as they made their way up to the kitchen.

Charlotte was ready and waiting with arms wide open. She hugged her sister to her chest. 'It's been very quiet without you – bliss in fact!'

Lexi tutted.

Freya was grateful for the normality; their joking helped to mask the very real grain of truth in Charlotte's words, as well as the nerves that all four of them felt.

'Look what arrived for you.'

Charlotte indicated a stunning bouquet of flowers, white lilies in full bloom, two-tone roses of pink and cream and a healthy bunch of variegated leaves. It was beautiful, and the first bouquet Lexi had ever received.

'Is there a note?' Lexi peered at the arrangement that Charlotte had placed in a glass vase.

'No . . .' Charlotte began.

'In that case, I will confess they are from me!' Lockie boomed. 'All thanks and gratitude to be cast in my direction!'

Charlotte ignored him. 'Toby dropped them off and sends you his very best wishes.'

'Ahh.' Freya was touched. 'That was so kind of him. Daddy and I did put a little bunch of flowers in your room to welcome you home, but nothing like this!' She laughed.

Lockie picked up a banana from the fruit bowl. 'Hello? Toby? Please stop showing me up in this fashion!' He placed it back in the bowl.

The girls groaned.

'It's good to have my baby girl back.' Freya liked this warm, happy feeling.

'I'm glad to be back.' She smiled, looking a lot like her old self.

'And I want to show you something!' Charlotte took her sister's hand, freshly revealed from the cast that had been removed a couple of weeks before, and walked her slowly up the stairs; for all the joy of her return and the bloom to her cheeks, Lexi was still weak.

Freya followed them.

'What is it?' Lexi was curious.

'You'll see!' Charlotte walked ahead. She opened Lexi's bedroom door and stood back. 'Ta-dah!'

She held out her arm to reveal the 'Hello Kitty' poster that her gran had given her for Christmas. Charlotte had popped it inside a large Ikea frame and hung it on the wall.

'Told you it would look cool and retro.' She folded her arms, pleased with her efforts.

'Ahh, thank you, Charlotte!'

''S'okay.' She kissed her sister.

'Did you miss me really?' Lexi whispered.

'I did.' She kept her eyes downcast. 'I've been really scared for you.'

It was an admission that moved Freya, as any display of affection between her kids always had done.

'Me too,' Lexi admitted, in barely more than a whisper.

When Iris arrived the next day, Freya admired her attire, which was as unconventional as ever. She looked a picture in navy culottes, a navy-and-mustard-striped tank top over a floral shirt, and her now famous yellow shoes.

The two women sipped coffee and chatted. Freya had a notepad open and at the ready, hoping for pearls of wisdom on advice on what to do next. Such were her nerves, her lack of confidence that she could fix things with enough love and soup, that she preferred to be instructed than have to rely on trial and error, knowing the margin for success was still small.

'It feels like I have been passed the gauntlet.'

'You have, in a way.' Iris smiled. 'And there's no denying that the first few weeks, transitioning from an in-patient facility to home life, can be some of the hardest. She is still very frail and not out of the woods yet – you know that, don't you?'

Freya nodded. Yes, she knew that.

'Lexi will be happy to be home, but also it's quite normal for her to feel a bit fearful of the freedom she now has.'

'She said as much,' Freya confirmed.

'Well, the fact that she can talk about how she's feeling is not to be underestimated, that's good. I would, however, pay particular attention to any habits that were banned at Larchcombe that she may have been considering. We need to break those habits here too; she needs to know it's not okay to do certain things just because she is home.'

'Habits like . . . ?' Freya was a little confused.

'You know the kind of thing: over-exercising, purging after food, using laxatives.' Iris, as ever, spoke with ease about topics that conjured the most horrible images. Freya knew she was suggesting that the threat of Lexi indulging in all three was very real. They were in danger. Even this thought sent a rush of fear through her veins. She and Lockie had over the last weeks reclaimed much of the closeness that they had temporarily lost, Charlotte was more settled and, of course, Lexi was home. The idea that this was only transitory was one she couldn't entertain. She kept her expression blank, nodding at Iris. The woman might be an expert in her field, but Freya was an expert on her family, and she knew things were getting better. She could feel it.

'Okay.'

Iris spoke slowly. 'You look a little worried.'

'Not worried, no.'

'Okay, because I don't want to scare you. Our mission hasn't changed: we need to learn what Lexi needs right now to thrive, and help put it in place. If you keep her eating then you can keep her home, it's as simple as that.'

Tiptoeing into the TV room, she watched the girls sitting side by side on the sofa, laughing at *The Big Bang Theory*. It felt good to see them so relaxed.

'Supper in five minutes!'

'Can we eat it on our laps?' Lexi looked up hopefully.

'No, darling, all around the table please. It's nice to all sit together, as a family. Plus I don't want food spilled in here.'

Lexi curled her lip. Freya was glad she didn't push further, each of them knowing the real reason: that she needed to be supervised during mealtimes and immediately afterwards.

No one commented on how small Lexi cut her food. The strip of chicken, strand of broccoli, and her single roast potato were reduced to pea-sized lumps, easy to swallow and hard to taste. They also failed to mention the never-empty glass of water that was always within reach, helping her wash the food down into a stomach no longer so averse to nutrition.

She and Lockie worked hard to keep the conversation flowing, averting their eyes, distracting with tales of the mundane, informing how the tubs were coming along in the courtyard and the fact that they hadn't seen the Rendletons for a while. Anything other than sit and stare at each mouthful that passed Lexi's lips. Willing her to keep going and hoping that she kept it down.

Over the next few weeks, Charlotte's exams got under way, and Lexi even mentioned going into school. She and Lockie seemed to be on the same page, and the house had a glorious air of normality about it. The money that Diana had gifted them nestled in an account, which meant that, for the first time in an age, she and Lockie slept without worrying where their next commission was coming from. She had to admit it was a wonderful feeling. Not that they had ever suffered; bills had always been met, eventually, and Christmas and birthdays were celebrated in certain style, but this was the first time in their lives that they had what they termed 'spare cash'. Not a huge amount, but enough that they could relax a little.

Lockie pulled back the duvet and patted the mattress.

'I was thinking . . .' he started.

'Oh no, you know that never ends well.' She laughed as she hopped into bed.

'Ha, ha!' He feigned offence. 'How about we go crazy and book up to go and see Hugh and Melissa?

'In Florida?'

'No, Freya, didn't you hear, they've moved to Margate!'

'Well, aren't you on fire tonight!' She jabbed his ribs, making him yelp.

Lockie pulled her towards him and anchored her against his chest.

'I just think we've had the most horrible year, and what better way to put it all behind us than to go and sit on that glorious beach and watch that incredible sunset with people we love.'

Freya closed her eyes. 'That does sound good.'

'Shall we? When else are we going to have the money or the time? Charlotte will be off to uni, Lexi working to catch up what she's missed at school. It feels like now is the perfect opportunity.'

'They'd love it, wouldn't they, the girls? Do you remember going out on Hugh's boat, eating ice cream, just strolling in the sun and his beautiful house . . . ?' She let her mind drift in memory.

'I think we should do it!' He crushed her to him in a hug.

'Okay!' She giggled. 'But let's agree not to tell them until after Charlotte's exams and when Lexi is a bit stronger. I think we need to take things slowly, no undue excitement.'

'Can't guarantee that, I'm afraid. I am already excited!' He kicked his heels against the mattress, before bending his head to kiss his wife. It had been a while since the two had shared a moment of intimacy like this, and both welcomed it, lying skin to skin; it was an exquisite sign of how they were all healing.

Freya slept well that night. She woke, as ever, at 5 a.m., but now with a smile on her face and feeling rested, a state that she had almost forgotten.

As Charlotte was on study leave, Freya did her best to move quietly, knowing she would have worked until late into the night. She tiptoed across the landing towards the stairs and was drawn by a squeaking sound coming from Lexi's room. An image of the bags lined up in the bottom of Lexi's bed flashed in her head, replaced instantly with a memo of self-recrimination; Lexi was doing great and deserved credit. More likely it was only Brewster, trying to get out.

Twisting the handle gently, she eased the door open, looking at the floor, expecting to see Brewster's upturned nose, giving her his usual look of disdain. Instead, her eyes flew to the floor of the bedroom, where Lexi sat with her feet in thick socks, hooked under the bed, pumping up and down in vigorous sit-ups.

'Lexi!' she breathed.

Her daughter turned to her, her eyes flashing anger at being interrupted and shame at the discovery. She tried to speak, but couldn't; with her body bent forward she fought for breath.

'Oh my God . . . Lexi!'

Freya rushed forward and placed her hand on her back. It felt strangely padded. She then realised that her daughter was wearing two hooded sweatshirts, leggings and jogging bottoms, and there was a scarf wrapped around her neck, all designed to make her sweat whilst partaking in the vigorous exercise. Her face was ashen, her mouth slack, and her eyes seemed to have sunk back into her head.

'Why?' Freya cried. 'Why, Lex? You are doing so well!'

She sat on the floor, staring at her child, who was slowly recovering enough to talk.

'I . . . I have to,' she breathed.

'You don't have to! You don't!' Freya shouted. Her distress sat like a sharp thing below her breastbone. 'Do you want to go back to Larchcombe, to tube feeding? Because that's what will happen! It will! I can't believe this.' She sat back against the bed.

'You are wrong, Freya.' Lockie's voice floated from the landing. They both looked up at him.

'It's not what will happen, it's what is happening. She's going back, the moment they have a place.' He gritted his teeth in anger.

'No . . .' Lexi shook her head. 'It was just . . . just one night,' she managed.

'I don't believe you!' he shouted. 'You are clearly not able to be here, Lexi.'

'She's doing really well, Lockie, this is just a blip!' Freya took sides, trying, as ever to protect her little girl.

Lockie's eyes flashed a look of hurt. In that second Freya realised that the cracks that had formed under their feet were far from filled: they had merely been papered over during the distraction of happiness, and now once again they were standing on the edge of the ravine.

'Just a blip? Do you know how many times you have used that excuse? Face it, Freya, we are failing! Good God, if this is where we are today then the whole of the last few months has been pointless!'

'What's all the shouting about?' Charlotte squinted from her door. 'I have an exam today! An A level! And you are all up at the crack of dawn, shouting? Don't I count? This is one of the most important days of my life so far! This is so unfair!' She slammed her door shut.

Lockie looked at his wife. 'She's right. It is unfair; it's unfair on all of us. I'll call Larchcombe as soon as I can.'

'No!' Lexi screamed. 'Please don't, Dad!'

'Yes, Lexi!' he countered. 'Look at you! What is the point? What is the point of everyone running around and trying to make you better when the first chance you get you undo all that work? It's like banging your head against a wall. Eventually you figure out that it hurts a lot less if you stop. And this is where we stop!'

He raced down the room, away from Lexi's sobbing. Freya put her to bed and tried to calm her. 'It's okay, darling, please don't cry. I will go and talk to Daddy. He's right, though, Lexi, we can't go on like this. But try not to worry, sleep now . . .'

Freya closed the kitchen door behind her. She and Lockie stood either side of the table.

And then it happened: the stopper that had kept their true feelings at bay popped. And all the things that they had wanted to say over the last few tumultuous months bubbled from them like the champagne froth with which they celebrated so many family occasions, only unlike the bubbles, the words would not evaporate so quickly, but would live in Freya's memory always.

'I'd rather you didn't contact Larchcombe immediately.' She sighed.

'I can and I will.' He paced around the table, fury and disbelief firing his movement.

'You're right; if we are back to square one we need to find alternatives. But Larchcombe obviously didn't work. We nearly lost her in there, Lockie!'

'We are losing her here!' he cut in, shouting now. 'How many times do you want to go back to square one? It's like a never-ending game of snakes and ladders, and you can't see it. You think that by wrapping her in a duvet and pandering to her every outburst you can make everything okay, but you can't!'

'Sometimes that makes everything feel better. Sometimes I can comfort her and that makes her feel stronger so that she can cope!'

'Oh God! Listen to yourself! That's like giving an alcoholic a drink – yes, it might make them feel better for a while, but it doesn't help! It is the opposite of helping.'

'I am not to blame here!'

'You want to talk about blame? You want to talk about exclusion and division?'

'What are you talking about?' She shook her head.

'I am talking about how you shut me out from day one, her very first doctor's appointment. I sat at home, on the sidelines, excluded, because Freya knew best! And that is how it's been during this whole nightmare – you leading the dance and me left wondering if I am keeping time.'

'Well, is that any wonder? Good God, Lockie, you thought she might be making the whole thing up, asked if we were just *indulging* her. "Is it really a thing?" Remember saying that? And for your information, the reason I have led, taken the burden, was to make things easier for her and for you. I just wanted to protect her, to look after her!'

He laughed as he paced back and forth. 'That's bullshit, Freya. It wasn't about relieving my burden; it was about control!'

'Is that what you think?'

'Yes,' he spat. 'You shy away from making the hard decisions and doing the right thing because you are way more concerned with being the good guy!'

There was a second or two of silence while both mentally reloaded. Freya felt a surge of sadness laced with anger, knowing that there was more than a grain of truth in his words, but also overwhelmed by the fact that her husband did not understand why. When she next spoke, her words were more calmly delivered.

'I'm her mum.' She swallowed. 'I carried her inside my body for nine months, I fed her, she lived on nothing but my milk for the first six months of her life. I puréed her food, built her up, and watched her grow. It's my job to feed my child and make her better! My job!'

He shook his head, enraged by her assertion. 'And what about *my* job? I'm her dad, does that not count?'

'It's different!' she fired back, wiping her nose on the back of her hand.

Lockie was quite taken aback. 'What a thing to say to me. I'm her dad, how is it different?'

'It just is,' she almost whispered.

'No, Freya, you don't get to make a statement like that and justify it with "It just is". You are attacking my fundamental rights and role as her father, making me the outsider and the bad guy rolled into one!' He banged the tabletop.

She stared at the floor with her shoulders rounded, trying to make herself small, trying to keep everything in.

'Come on, Freya, explain it to me, because I am struggling here!'

'*You're* struggling?' she screamed, shouting louder and with more force than she knew she possessed. 'Don't you get it, Lockie? *I* need to fix it! *I* need to make her better because it's my fault! It's all my fault. I'm her mum and I went into that school nearly a year ago and you're right, I thought I knew best but I didn't, why didn't I do something then? Why didn't I listen? I was so confident, arrogant, and now I'm paying the price. I could have got to it sooner, could have acted, intervened. And we might lose her and it's all my fault.' She felt her body cave as she leant forward, her hands resting on her thighs.

'So why didn't you?'

'Because I couldn't believe that anything so awful could possibly be part of my little girl's life. That was not how I planned it!'

Lockie stared at her. His words when they came shook them both. 'I'm not saying you are to blame for her illness, not at all. I think it's more complicated and multilayered than any of us can grasp, but . . .' He paused, as if aiming the verbal arrows he was about to fire. 'I think in many ways her lack of progress and even her deterioration at times has been because you have found it too difficult to take the hard line.

I think a more robust, tough regimen in the beginning might have stopped things advancing in the way they have, and I think you could have done better.'

'I . . .' She tried to speak, but her throat closed and her words faltered. Her shaking body folded and she slipped down into a dining chair. They were both quiet while the air around them settled.

It was Lockie who broke the silence.

'I'm going to go and stay at my mum's for a bit.'

'Don't be ridiculous! You can't run out on us!'

'I'm not running out on you.' He sighed. 'I'm giving you the space you need to get your head straight. Mine too.'

'But . . . but we need you!'

Lockie laughed. 'Well, that'll be a first.'

'Don't be so selfish, Lockie! You can't just run out when things get tough!'

'Things aren't getting tough, Freya: things have been tough for a very long time. I said living with her illness was like walking barefoot surrounded by broken glass, but it's not!' He shook his head. 'It's like walking barefoot surrounded by broken glass, while juggling with sharpened razors and the building is on fire and I'm shouting that we have to jump while you close up all the windows and arrange the curtains!' He threw his hands in the air. 'It's impossible for us to do this and come out unscathed.'

'We have no choice!' she screamed.

Lockie held his wife's gaze and waited for a moment of calm before speaking. 'We have plenty of choices, it's just a case of whether you are open to making them and whether you are going to let me help. If Lexi was choking you'd do anything, cut her throat, break her bones, anything to stop her dying. But with this . . .' He shook his head. 'It might be called anorexia, Freya, but make no mistake, she is slowly choking, and if it was left solely to me I would be breaking her bones and cutting her throat to remove the obstruction, I'd do anything.'

'And I will do anything! Of course!' she cried.

'I'm not sure that's true. I'm not sure you can.' He dripped the words like poison and her reaction was to cry even harder.

'How dare you! Of course I will do anything – but it's you who's forgotten that she's still a little girl, that's all she is, a little girl!'

'A little girl with a mental illness,' he reminded her.

'God, Lockie, I don't know what to say to you, but I have to keep battling *and* defending her. I don't expect you to understand.'

'And that, Freya, is why I am going to my mum's.'

One hour, thirty minutes . . .

Lockie sat in his favourite chair at the long kitchen table, with Freya by his side and her hand resting gently on his leg.

Charlotte placed the pen and pad in front of him. She flipped it open to a crisp blank page and nodded at him.

Lockie coughed and picked up the pen, rolling it between his fingers. He sniffed up his tears and looked up towards the ceiling, before pulling his glasses from the top of his head and starting.

> *Well, Lexi, it's your dad here.*
>
> *Haven't thought exactly about what to write, so am just going to see what flows. I love you, that's the most important thing to tell you.*

Lockie paused and swiped the tears from his cheeks and coughed again before resuming.

I love you and I always have. My baby girl. I can't think of you over the last year. If I picture you, which I do a lot, I see your smiling face, laughing at the most ridiculous things. Like any time I order poppadums and call them 'ploppadums' and it sends you into fits of giggles. I don't think anyone laughs at my rubbish jokes quite as much as you.

I have a note that you wrote for me when you were little. I carry it with me in my camera case. It's quite short, poignant, and makes me smile every time I see it. It says 'Bring me back a comic'. At least that's what it's supposed to say, but it's in Lexi speak, so it's written back to front and upside down and a little muddled, but I love it nonetheless. It reminds me of a simpler time when that was all it took to make you happy: a comic and a cuddle from your dad.

Lockie paused again and smiled at his wife before continuing.

I think I let you down, Lexi, and for that I am really, truly sorry.

I'm not good when I'm out of sync with your mum, never have been. She's always been the anchor, keeping this rocky old ship steady.

Lockie stopped again as the next bout of tears came.

I am, Lexi, really, truly sorry . . .

SEVENTEEN

Charlotte had cornered her on the landing as she headed for the shower. 'Where's Dad?' she asked casually, looking over her mum's shoulder and down the stairs, as if expecting him to pop up.

'He's gone to stay at Gran's.' Her chin wobbled in an effort to contain her sadness; speaking the fact aloud made it no more palatable.

'Why?' Her nose wrinkled quizzically.

'He's gone to cool off, I guess.'

'When's he coming back?'

'I don't know, Charlotte!' Her tone was a little sharper than she had intended and once again her eldest daughter was on the receiving end of an emotion that should have been directed elsewhere.

Charlotte turned on her heel and slammed the bathroom door behind her. Freya hid her face in her hands and stood behind it, speaking to the glossy wood. 'I'm sorry. I shouldn't have snapped at you. I'm sorry, love.' Her apology sounded hollow, even to her own ears.

'Mum?' Lexi called, alerted by their exchange. Freya wandered across the hallway to once again inhale the stale air of sickness. 'Where's Dad gone?' She levered herself up on to creaky elbows.

Freya felt the pulse of a lively headache behind her eyes; she rubbed at her temples to no avail. 'He's gone to stay at Gran's.'

'Were you fighting because of me?' Her tears came quickly, and Freya silently cursed, fearful that even tears might take valuable sustenance from Lexi's body.

'Not really . . .' She considered. 'It's complicated. It's not your fault.' She tried out a conciliatory smile.

'Will he come back soon?'

'I don't know, Lex.' Her delivery was soft and calm.

Lexi shrank back against her pillows, clearly unsettled by the discord.

As she left the room, she pictured Charlotte, no doubt crying in the shower, and her heart sank.

Freya wandered the house, touching her fingers to handles and listening at doors, in the vain hope that Lockie might have snuck back in to take refuge on a sofa or behind his desk. She wanted to talk to him. His abandoned coffee cup sat in the sink, his discarded laundry in a small pile in the corner of the bathroom, and his cameras were on the table, but he was not there. This was so out of character for him, but then their whole lives were out of character, as if they were living someone else's life, and one they could not have imagined only a year ago. She felt swamped by loneliness, admitting that a Lockie with whom she was quarrelling was better than no Lockie at all.

She wandered into the den. Her eyes felt sore, as if full of grit, and her headache was taking hold. She stared at the lamp shining brightly in the Rendletons' window and swallowed the tears that slipped down the back of her throat.

Marcia came as soon as she phoned, turning up bright and early, offering support and words of encouragement in her own inimitable way. Fatigue and shredded nerves gave Freya's rant an air of hysteria.

Still in her pyjamas, she held the photograph and strolled across the kitchen to the den.

'Look at her face! Look at her! This is what we need to return to! This is what I was trying to explain to him!'

Marcia took the small framed black-and-white print into her hands and stared at the child with her head tipped back, caught mid-giggle, her eyes half-closed, her nose wrinkled and her long fringe falling in fine wisps over her high forehead.

'This is the child I raised, full of laughter! She always had a special light that shone from her, a joy of life. Hard to imagine when you see her now, I know.'

She and Marcia had, only minutes before, trodden the stairs after gently closing the door on Lexi's room. It was the first time Freya could recall seeing Marcia so emotional. She had coughed, as if to clear her tear-lined throat, and buried her face in her handkerchief.

'Are you okay?'

Marcia had only been able to nod vigorously, trying to keep her upper lip stiff.

'This is a lovely picture,' she managed now. 'Is it one of Lockie's?'

Freya nodded.

'Are you going to call him?' Marcia tapped her painted talons on the tabletop.

Freya shrugged. 'Why should I? He's hiding – that's what he's doing, burying his head in the sand and hoping that by the time he looks up, everything will be back to normal.' She gave a small laugh. 'Normal! Whatever that is – not sure I remember anymore. His instant reaction is to send her back to Larchcombe and that didn't exactly work before.' She shook her head. 'I can't make him see, Marcia, just how careful we have to be of not pushing her over the edge. My instinct has always been to wrap her up, but I conceded a long time ago that I can't do it alone, and I think intense therapy is the answer. And I was thinking that maybe I should stop work for a bit, properly concentrate on Lexi. In the meantime, I'm going to monitor her more closely, feed her more regularly . . .'

Her friend gave a less than sanguine smile, shifting in her seat. 'Sounds like you have a plan.'

'I do, and I feel happier for it, knowing what needs to be done.'

'But isn't that what you tried before and it didn't work?'

Freya held Marcia's gaze; the last thing she wanted to do was fall out with her best friend as well. She chose her words carefully. 'I look at it this way: we have learnt a lot since then, and I admit I need to do it differently. I just want her better. I'll have her friend Toby drop in more – he's a good lad, offering old-fashioned words of encouragement that she seems to listen to. He's an important link to life outside of this building.'

'Sounds like you've got it all figured out.' Marcia's statement carried an edge that made Freya feel a little uncomfortable. She had hoped for unconditional support. 'But do remember, Freya . . . Lockie's not a bad man.'

'No, just a bit of a stubborn one.'

Marcia raised her eyebrows. 'Perhaps, but he's also kind, and totally devoted to you and the girls.'

'Yes, as is evident by his wonderful support at this very difficult time – oh no, wait a minute, he's run off to his mum's, silly me!' She tapped her forehead.

'I know you are upset.'

'You think?'

'And I can only imagine how rubbish it must be,' Marcia continued. 'But I know you and I know Lockie, and he must be going through some tough stuff if he feels the only way to cope is to run away.'

'Since when did you become such a Lockie fan? And how lovely to have the option of running away! Can you imagine if we both felt like that? Things would be a little tricky right now for Lexi and Charlotte.' She shook her head, aware of a certain defensiveness in her tone.

They were quiet for a second before Marcia spoke.

'He can only fall apart because he knows the girls can rely on you. It's always been that way, but maybe he's gone to try and get you to look at things in a different way; maybe things need to change?'

Freya heard his words of accusation loud and clear: *I think in many ways her lack of progress and even her deterioration at times has been because you have found it too hard to take the hard line.*

'Have you been talking to Lockie? You sound just like him.' She sniffed.

'No, but I love Lockie; you know that. Mainly I love him because you work, as a couple, like peaches and cream. You are better with him. He makes you happy.' She shrugged; there it was, this simple truth, honestly delivered.

'Don't forget, Marcia, it was *him* that walked, not me.' She tried to remember the last time she had felt truly happy. 'Why does everyone think I am in the wrong here?' She gave a short, angry snort of laughter.

'I don't think you are in the wrong. I just think that sometimes it's hard to see clearly when you are in so deep.'

Freya ignored her. With trembling hands, she popped a pan on the stove to heat with a knob of butter in it and picked up the spatula, deciding to make pancakes for breakfast; anything to try to get some fat into Lexi. Facing the stove, she found it easier to talk to her friend with her back to her. 'She's so fragile, Marcia. So very fragile, a very delicate thing. Sending her away would be like putting fine china in a box and shipping it off without any packaging. I think it's better to hold it to my chest here, keeping it intact.'

'I don't know if that's right, Freya. I think it might be too insular. Lexi is not fine china, she's a young woman who you can't pop on a shelf; she needs a life, a future.'

Freya closed her eyes and took a deep breath before turning around to face her friend. 'I'm aware of that, but I need to protect the life she has right now. One wrong move and she could break and I am not going to let that happen.'

I don't know if I can do it, Marcia. I don't know if I can hand her over like that. No one loves her like I do or knows her like I do . . .

'But what if the one wrong move is denying her expertise outside of your care? What if that's the thing that breaks her? How do you come back from that?'

Freya tossed the spatula on to the counter. 'I wish people would have a little bit more faith that with proper nurturing I can get her weight up and do it in a way that doesn't shock or hurt her!' She had expected different from Marcia, almost preferring it when she nodded her agreement and allied herself with her, no matter what.

'Just to clarify: by "people" you mean me?' Marcia questioned.

'Yes, I mean you! God, as if things aren't hard enough!'

Marcia bristled. 'Maybe she *needs* a bit of shock or hurt to make her realise how high the stakes are.'

'With all due respect, that's exactly the kind of phrase I'd expect from someone who is not a mother.'

Marcia visibly flinched. For a second, her veil of bluster and brazenness lifted and her eyes flashed genuine hurt.

As soon as the words had leapt unfiltered from her mouth Freya was instantly sick with regret – but also frustration and panic at not being able to convince her husband nor her good friend that she knew best.

'I'm sorry. I am.' She pinched the bridge of her nose. 'But I truly believe that my way will work, we just need time.'

Marcia gave her friend a searching look, her eyes questioning, as she reached for her handbag that nestled on the floor. 'But, Freya . . . what if you are running out of time?'

Freya watched her stand, still trying to think of the right response, while Marcia gathered up her bag and made for the stairs.

Freya felt as if she were hanging by a thread, having spent the last two days in a cocoon of her own making. She had never felt so alone, without the reassuring presence of Lockie, and too nervous now to pick up the phone to Marcia. Her smile, fixed in place for all and every interaction with her girls, was pulled thin; all her reserves were running low.

She knocked gingerly on Charlotte's door.

'Come in,' she called.

'Last exam today, darling.' Freya pointed out the obvious, as though Charlotte did not have a highlighted chart on the pinboard above her desk with the days crossed through in red, ending with today, which had been ringed with a pink heart and three tiny balloons.

'I'm a bit nervous,' Charlotte admitted, nibbling her toast and peanut butter.

'Do you want me to run you in? I'm very happy to.'

Charlotte shook her head. 'No, Tara's coming here and we're going to get the bus together and she can test me on my French.'

'I didn't know Tara spoke French.' This was news to Freya.

'She doesn't.' Charlotte swallowed. 'But I talk at her and she listens.'

'So how does she know if you make any mistakes?'

'She doesn't! She gives me an A star every time!' She laughed.

'I see.' Freya stared out of the window.

Charlotte replaced the toast on the plate and sighed.

'Try not to worry about your exam. You can do this. You have worked hard and French is your thing. It'll be a doddle.'

'Are you okay, Mum?'

'Of course! I'm fine.' Freya nodded a little too enthusiastically.

'I wish Dad was here. I liked knowing he was around even when he wasn't in the room.' Her statement came out of the blue.

'I know, me too.'

'He said we should go out for ice cream to celebrate the end of my exams. But if you'd rather I didn't?'

Freya felt a stab of sadness at the fact that her daughter already felt the need to pick sides, or at least offer to, especially on a day when her focus should be solely on her exam. 'No! Of course not. I'm happy for you to see him, of course, just because we are having a bit of a wobble, it shouldn't make a jot of difference to your relationship with him or his with you. He adores you, you know that. Everything is okay.'

'Well . . .' Charlotte slapped her thighs, as if in conclusion. 'As long as everything is okay . . .'

Freya noted her daughter's sarcastic tone, but did not have the energy to get into another fight; even the idea was more than she could stand. Instead, she dug deep to find a smile for her girl on this important day, hiding the fact that even the mention of Lockie's name sent a swirl of angst into her gut. She missed him, of that there was no doubt, but was still struggling to mentally absorb his hurtful words, analysing and re-analysing how much was spoken in anger and how much in truth.

'I wish I could see him before my exam.' Charlotte bit her nail.

'Why don't you call him?'

'I will.'

With Charlotte duly dispatched for school with a good-luck kiss, Freya trod the stairs to Lexi's room.

She knocked and walked in. 'Morning, sleepyhead.' Freya drew the curtains and opened the window a little. 'It's a beautiful day. Look, Lexi: lovely blue sky!'

Lexi slowly wriggled into a sitting position. Each and every day, the sight of her daughter's huge jaw, large teeth and sunken cheekbones startled her a little.

'I don't feel too good,' Lexi whined.

'In what way?' Freya sat on the edge of the bed and ran her hand over her daughter's bony forehead.

'My tummy hurts,' she managed.

'Let's get you to Dr Morris. I was going to call her anyway, but we'll get you in to see her.' Freya spoke reassuringly.

Lexi shook her head no.

Freya stood and paced the room a couple of times. 'You can't keep saying no to everything. You can't! If you are feeling poorly, you need to see the doctor. End of discussion.'

What if you are running out of time? Marcia's question played in her head on a loop.

'I don't want to.' Even crying seemed to take the greatest effort, as her face crumpled and she bared her teeth, her face ugly and contorted.

Freya placed her hands on her head and closed her eyes. 'Lexi, please listen to me. You are poorly, so poorly, and now your tummy hurts. You need to see the doctor, and if you won't let me take you to her, then I shall call an ambulance and they will take you to the hospital; this is not up for debate.'

Lockie was wrong – she *could* assert her authority, even while her heart twisted in agony at her daughter's plight.

'I can't do that, Mum!' Lexi cried.

'I'll give you ten minutes to yourself and then I'm coming up to help you get ready. I'll call ahead and make you an appointment.'

With that she swept from the room, ignoring Lexi's pleas and trying to hide her own trembling hands.

It took minutes of reasoning and explaining before she was given a late-afternoon appointment, reserved for emergencies. When she used the word 'critical', the receptionist suggested Freya try the accident and emergency department. She bit the inside of her cheek, giving only the briefest of outlines as to why her daughter was afraid of this option, only just managing to keep her cool and knowing that despite this irritating gatekeeper, Dr Morris would see her.

As she replaced the receiver the front doorbell rang. She raced down the stairs, pulling her long hair free from where it had caught in the neck of her T-shirt. Expecting the postman, she was surprised to see Lockie on the doorstep. Her natural reaction was to smile at the man she loved, before instantly remembering the impasse they had reached. His hair looked dishevelled and he needed a shave; he too looked like a man who had forgone a few good nights' sleep.

'You've got a key!' she snapped.

'I know, but I wasn't sure if I should use it.' He looked at her sheepishly.

'Oh, Lockie, don't be ridiculous, we are hardly estranged.' She hated the feel of the word in her mouth. She looked to see if he had his overnight bag with him and was saddened to see that he didn't. 'Just come in. I'm glad you're here. I'm worried about Lex, she has a tummy ache. I've called the doctor; we've got an appointment this afternoon. I've told Lexi that if she refuses to go, then I'll take her to the hospital,' she asserted as she walked back up the stairs.

'What's brought that on?' he asked when they reached the kitchen.

'I'm not sure, but she's not right.'

He took off his glasses and rubbed his eyes. She recognised his expression; knew what it felt like to hope each day for an improvement and be greeted with the exact opposite.

'I'll stay here today. If that's okay? I don't want to be away if she isn't feeling great.'

'Of course. This is your home, Lockie, you don't have to ask if you can stay.' She decided against detailing just how very lonely it had been to lie in their bed without him.

Brewster twisted around Lockie's legs and miaowed. He reached down and lifted the puss to his chin. It tugged at her heartstrings that even the cat missed having Dad around.

'I'll go up and see Lexi?' he asked, lowering Brewster to the floor.

'Yes, do.' She disliked the way he felt the need to ask; this, on top of not using his key, made him feel like a stranger.

She busied herself with the breakfast dishes, turning her back on him.

Lockie reappeared twenty minutes later.

'She's a bit sleepy, but I got the odd grunt and the occasional word. She says her tummy feels a bit better.'

'That's good.' She felt her pulse calm a little.

'She looks terrible, Freya,' he whispered, the verbal equivalent of raising his palms, letting her know he came in peace.

She nodded calmly. Her desire and energy to mentally joust with him was now non-existent.

'I know. Do you think she looks worse than when you saw her last?' She bit her cheek, waiting for his reply.

'I would say so, yes. What's she eaten?' he asked calmly.

Freya shook her head. 'Very little.' It felt like an admission of failure and her cheeks flamed.

Lockie let out a deep breath. 'I'll come with you to the doctor.'

The words of their row came flooding back to her: . . . *You shut me out from day one, her very first doctor's appointment. I sat at home, on the sidelines, excluded, because Freya knew best!*

'They may suggest she goes into hospital,' he warned.

'It'll be good to get her out in the sunshine today, even if it's only for a minute from the car to the surgery.'

He placed his hands on his hips, his stance quite confrontational, as if gearing up for a fight, but then clearly thought better of it. 'Yes.'

Neither mentioned the fact that only days ago they were planning a family trip to Florida to sit in the sun. Neither could have guessed on that happy night just how far they would have fallen and how quickly. Diana's money would now be put towards the kids' future and not frittered away on anything as frivolous as a holiday.

'I'm hoping that with Dr Morris's help, we can turn this corner quickly,' Freya enthused. 'I have a plan that involves bribery, Toby, and a strict regimen of therapy and feeding.'

'Another blip, Freya?'

She recoiled at his words and felt her tears threaten. 'I always thought anorexia, anxiety, bulimia – that was stuff that happened to other families, families who weren't close to their kids who didn't communicate, or kids who for some reason sought attention. I thought we were exempt.'

'Me too,' he confessed.

'I'm hollowed out, Lockie, a shell. I've got nothing left. I'm exhausted, confused, upset, but as long as she needs me I will keep on going. I won't give up on her, ever. I tried to explain that to Marcia, how hard it is!'

'I know and I don't want us to give up on her either, but I do think she needs to be somewhere, restrained if necessary, sedated even, anything to get food into her system!' He raised his voice.

'This is not a physical illness where you can give her a pill or stick a part of her in a plaster cast and, hey presto, she'll be fixed. It's so much more than that!'

'You think I don't know this? But you've just said yourself, it's all about getting her weight up,' he retorted. 'I feel like we have the same bloody conversation over and over. This isn't about you! It's about what's best for Lexi, and I shouldn't have to remind you of that, not now,' he railed.

'I don't need reminding! I know it's not about me and I resent you suggesting otherwise! But I do know that to get her healthy is going to take more than forcefully shoving a tube down her neck – we tried that, remember! We have made good progress in the past and we can again.'

'This is a mental illness! Our daughter is mentally ill.' Lockie matched her stare. Even to hear him use the words and to see the expression on his face was enough to make her tears pool.

'Anorexia is not going to kill her,' she whispered. 'I won't let it.'

Lockie put his hands in his pockets. 'You're right, Freya, no one dies of anorexia. They die of starvation, of organ failure and other horrible ailments brought on by starvation. And that's why we need help.'

An unwanted image of Lexi, struggling for breath, along with the words that had heralded her decline, filled her head: *My heart feels funny . . .*

Freya crept into Lexi's room, lest she should be sleeping. She was awake, but slumped on her pillows.

'Hey, I brought you a shake.' She rattled the carton in her daughter's direction.

Lexi spoke faintly. 'Shaking it doesn't make it any more appealing.' She gave a lopsided smile.

Freya placed the carton on the bedside table, in the hope that she might manage a few sips. She noticed that her skin had taken on a worrying greyish hue.

'I don't feel too good, Mum. I can't go out.' Lexi's speech was laboured. She appeared further weakened.

Freya managed to stop the scream that hovered in her throat as she went off to consult with Lockie. She found him sitting at the breakfast bar.

'I don't think we should haul her out of the house and down to the surgery. She doesn't look well enough.' She bit her thumbnail.

'Is this just another way to keep her at home?'

His words offended and angered her in equal measure.

'Is that what you think? Go and look at her! Her skin is grey! I don't think it's a good idea to drag her out of the house.' She cursed the warble to her tone and the glint of tears that she couldn't contain.

'Okay.' He touched his fingers into a pyramid and held them against his chin, as if deep in thought. 'I'm sorry. Call them. The doctor will come here, I'm sure, if you explain.'

Freya nodded and made the call.

It was late afternoon, after her surgery finished, when Dr Morris made a house visit.

Lexi sat up in the bed with her shoulders hunched and her translucent skin stretched thin over her suddenly aged bones. Freya caught Dr Morris's expression: it was one of horror.

The doctor had not once in their year of dealing with her let her professional mask slip. Freya had never found her to be anything other than calm, professional and positive, and it made a huge difference to them.

She remembered Mrs Janosik's words: *Some are brilliant, sympathetic and aware, others not so much – it's pretty much the luck of the draw.* They had certainly struck lucky.

But today, the doctor's first flash of uncontrolled emotion made Freya's stomach bunch and her bowels turn to ice.

'Good to see you, Lexi,' she offered brightly. 'Mum says you have a tummy ache?'

Lexi nodded, running her hand over her abdomen. 'It was worse earlier, but not so bad now . . . It's like a stabbing pain.'

'Okay. Well, you know what I'm going to say: we need to get you checked out in the hospital. It could be nothing, just a bug, but it could be something more significant, something nasty, and we need to get it seen.'

Lexi shook her head. 'I think it's just a bug. I can't go to the hospital,' she whispered.

'Well, I'm going to give you a quick check-over and then we can decide what to do for the best.' She smiled at them all and grabbed her stethoscope. Freya decided not to comment on the scale that poked from the doctor's bag.

With Lexi settled, Freya and Lockie walked Dr Morris to the floor below, where they stood in the kitchen.

'I wanted to talk to you both in private,' she began.

'Yes.' Freya nodded, willing her to get to the point. Her heart rate increased and her palms were peppered with sweat.

'Lexi is in very bad shape.'

'I know,' she whispered, closing her eyes, as if this might make the conversation easier to have. She felt Lockie take her hand, then coiled her fingers around his.

The doctor sighed. 'Her stomach pains are because of poor circulation. I suspect her arteries are closing from pressure inside her body, as there's no fat to cushion them. It's complicated, but more common than you might think in starvation.'

Freya stared at her; each word she spoke was like a punch to the gut. She glanced at Lockie. He looked like he might collapse.

'We need to get her into hospital as soon as possible,' Dr Morris continued, 'and then we need to consider our options. I can push for Larchcombe, but my fear is that we would find ourselves back here in a few months, if she hung on that long.'

Freya felt her blood turn to ice. *Don't say that! Please don't say that! She will hang on! She has to! We just need more time!*

The doctor took a deep breath. 'We do have the option of having her sectioned and sent to a psychiatric facility, Morningside, but it has a far tougher regimen than Larchcombe . . .'

Sweet Jesus, help me! Freya closed her eyes.

'Yes, we know it.' Lockie's voice was reedy.

'Or we could stick to the Larchcombe option; but personally, I think that feels risky, given her previous failure with the programme.'

'How bad is she?' Freya whispered, knowing the likely response but needing to hear it.

'She's giving a weight of a little under sixty-two pounds. That's the weight of an average nine-year-old child.'

'Oh my God!' Freya cried. This was her lowest weight yet. 'Lexi!'

Lockie made a sound as if winded. She looked at his stricken face and could see that the air, along with any flicker of optimism, had left his body.

'And that, in my view' – the doctor's voice slowed and her tone dipped – 'is something that is very hard to come back from. Some consider it the point of no return.'

It felt to Freya as if there were an echo to her words that reverberated, ricocheting around her head, trying to find a spot to settle on that might make comprehension possible.

'Are you saying that she is dying?' Lockie was breathing very quickly, as if the doctor's words were only just permeating.

Dr Morris looked at the floor. There was a pause that told them all they needed to know; the gap could have easily been filled with denials and words of reassurance.

'I think,' the doctor began, regaining her composure, 'that is a possibility that you need to prepare yourself for.'

Freya bent her head suddenly and lunged forward, racing towards the counter, until her mouth was over the sink – just. She vomited; her stomach lurched again, as Lockie walked over and palmed circles on her back. Eventually she straightened, wiping her mouth on her arm.

'Are you okay?' Dr Morris sounded concerned.

Freya felt another surge of nausea and for a second thought she might suffocate; she placed her hand on her chest and concentrated on trying to take a breath. A picture loomed in her mind of her holding her newborn: her damp, pink face, her shock of hair, her tiny, grasping fingers, grabbing at the air. *My baby girl . . .*

She recalled the hopes and dreams she held for that child: a wonderful, wonderful life, a full life – a long life! Turning to Lockie, she searched his face for the answers. As she studied the tears that slid down his cheeks, she felt the sledgehammer of realisation, shattering her conviction that she knew best. *She could die. Lexi might die. The point of no return . . .*

'We need to save her! We . . . we need to do everything we can. We're her parents, it's our job!' She sobbed, her face contorted with tears. For the first time, she realised that there was no room for soft sentiment. It was time to take the hard line.

'Okay.' Dr Morris nodded.

'Yes, do it! Call the hospital, call them now! Tell them it's urgent; tell them that she's only fifteen and that she will be very, very scared. She's like china! She's . . . she's very fragile.' Getting her words out was a struggle.

Lockie placed his arm around her waist, pulling her close. Freya welcomed his touch, grateful that he was there to lean on. She turned her head towards him. He nodded through his tears, his expression one of pure relief.

Dr Morris sighed, interrupting the moment. 'I know this is hard. But I believe that you are giving Lexi the best chance of survival.' She pulled out her mobile phone and punched some digits, talking to the couple while she waited for a response. 'We'll get her admitted and we can take things from there.' She spoke softly. She held up her finger, indicating that the call had been answered.

'Yes, hello, it's Dr Rosemary Morris. I need an ambulance.'

◆ ◆ ◆

Freya thanked the doctor as Lockie opened the front door.

'They will fix her, won't they?' she whispered.

Dr Morris paused. 'They will do their best, but I should also tell you, Mrs Braithwaite, that there are no guarantees. Lexi is very poorly.'

Freya placed her palm over the back of her husband's hand as they closed the door and stood facing each other. She stared at Lockie, hoping that she might wake up now from this horrible nightmare.

'Lockie!' She fell against him.

'I've got you!' he cried into her hair.

'Lockie! Help me! Help me!'

'I've got you,' he repeated, holding her tight.

'I can't . . . I can't fix her, can I? I can't do it, Lockie! Not on my own.' She buried her face in his shoulder.

'No, my love. Not this time.'

'I don't want her to hate me!' she sobbed. 'I've let her down. I can't keep her with me, and I've let her down!'

'No. No, you haven't! You've fought for her and she will love you for it.' His words were of scant comfort.

'My Lockie.' She closed her eyes against the fabric of his shirt.

A moment later they straightened and Lockie held her by the top of her arms.

'We need to be strong, Freya. Remember that she will take her lead from you. We are going to keep calm.'

She nodded. 'Can I be the one to tell her she's being admitted, Lockie, please?'

'Of course.' He nodded. 'You're her mum.' He kissed her forehead.

The sound of a key in the door heralded Charlotte's arrival.

Freya dug deep to find a smile for her daughter's big day. 'Hey! How did it go?'

'Really great.' Charlotte nodded, happy, but looking wary at seeing her parents with tear-stained faces standing so close together behind the front door. 'What's going on?'

Freya wrapped her in a hug and kissed her scalp, reminding herself not to cry.

'Lexi's not so good, darling,' she began.

Lockie stepped forward and interrupted, addressing his child while holding his wife's eyeline. 'The doctor has just left and the fact is, it's a little more than "not so good", Charlotte.'

Freya acknowledged his almost imperceptible nod, and she understood. This was the time for honesty, for the truth without the false smile that no longer fooled anyone.

'Dad's right. Lexi has to go into hospital. There's an ambulance on its way.'

'Oh no! How bad is she? And please don't try to protect me. She's my sister and I want to know.' Charlotte twisted her sleeves around her fingers, agitated.

Freya met her child's eyes, now moist with tears. 'She's very sick, darling.'

'Do you think . . .' She sniffed. 'Do you think she might die, Mummy?' Her choice of words saw her revert to a little girl in need of reassurance.

Lockie whimpered at the question.

Freya breathed in and stood tall. 'Things are about as bad as they can get, that's true. But we need to focus on doing everything we can to help her fight this horrible disease, okay?'

She pulled her child to her chest and held her tight while she cried, aware that her answer had been the hardest thing to hear. She thought about her warning not to let this illness shade her life. Today, however, it seemed to be blocking out all of the light.

'Go and say hi to Lexi, then why don't you help Dad pack her overnight bag? Can you do that for me?' She tilted Charlotte's chin towards her. Her daughter nodded, earnestly. Lockie gave her the briefest smile. 'I'll go and find a bag.'

◆　◆　◆

'Hey, Lex.' Charlotte looked at her mum, trying with eye gestures alone to let her know that Lexi did not look too good, and following instructions to try to keep her sister calm.

Freya ignored her, concentrating on opening the window wide. She was well aware of how Lexi looked. Charlotte's perfume lingered in the air; she looked fresh and bright. The contrast between her girls was, as ever, jarring.

'Well done on your exams. I will get you a congratulations card the next time I am out,' Lexi managed.

Charlotte nodded. 'Thanks, Lex, I'm just glad they're over.'

Lexi sat forward slightly and reached under the duvet. 'I made you these.'

With great effort on her part, she reached into the pocket of her hoodie and pulled out two finely woven plaited friendship bracelets.

Freya could only imagine how hard it must have been to weave the fine thread with inflexible, numb fingers.

Charlotte took them, swallowing the emotion that threatened. 'This means we are friends, best friends.'

Lexi beamed. 'You can be anything you want to be, you know, Charlotte.'

Lexi and her big sister exchanged a lingering look.

Charlotte nodded and walked forward, crouching low; she took Lexi into her arms, and held her gently, as if afraid of her withered trunk and brittle bones.

'I love you.' She cried, unable to stem the tears that broke their banks.

'I love you too,' Lexi managed.

Freya looked away, unable to witness the moment of tenderness.

Aware of the seconds ticking by, Freya entered a kind of twilight where everything had a dreamlike quality. Her vision was a little more hazy than usual, softening all that her eyes fell upon. Her words echoed, and she felt as if she were falling. The idea of landing, however, did not frighten her; quite the opposite in fact.

She sat on the side of Lexi's bed.

The trees bowed and rustled in the warm whisper of the wind.

There was a beat of silence while Freya decided how to begin, knowing she had to tell Lexi what was going to happen, and soon.

'Do you believe in God, Mum?'

Lexi's words threw her off track. She gave a truthful reply. 'I'm not sure. I want to.'

It was the best she could offer, rather than confess that her faith had been shaken by what she had witnessed, struggling to reconcile her idea of God with an omnipotent being that would allow her little girl to live in this way.

'Why aren't you sure?' Lexi pushed, her breathing laboured.

Freya swallowed the emotions that threatened to burst from her. 'I would like to believe . . . I'd like to think that it wasn't just this little life, but I don't know anymore.'

'Sounds like you are . . . hedging your bets!' She struggled to get her words out.

'I think you might be right.'

'I like to think that you get to see the people you've lost again,' Lexi whispered. 'But they are all better, cured.'

'That *would* be nice, darling.' She closed her eyes and concentrated on breathing, fighting the desire to scream out and beat her breast in sadness.

Freya imagined she heard the wail of the ambulance several times, only for it to be false alarms, her mind playing tricks.

'I can see the stars,' Lexi wheezed, looking up, out of the open window.

Her breath came in an irregular pattern, her chest heaved and a large vein on the side of her neck seemed to pulse. Freya stared up at the beautiful sky of the summer evening, trying to see what Lexi saw, remembering that deep inky blue of the night sky, punctuated by a million stars and a big, big moon that hung tantalisingly close, that great adventure in the middle of the night, all those years ago.

'Look at all those stars, Lexi, so far away.' She touched her finger to her daughter's cheek.

Lexi slowly raised her fingers, as if reaching out.

'That's it, darling, you can put one in your pocket.'

'I'm cold.'

Freya reached for the soft mohair blanket that had been folded on to the chair. She wrapped it around her daughter, lifting her to make her comfortable. She was insubstantial, feather-light. It was like holding nothing.

Freya closed her eyes, sniffing up her tears, rubbing them away with the back of her hand. Lexi flexed her fingers and Freya feared they might break. She looked down at her daughter's hand: her bones were now brittle, exposed, bent and barely able to support the thin, stretched skin that covered them.

Lexi sighed. 'You said you would always help me get to wherever I wanted to go, and I am asking you to let me go. I want to go to sleep.'

Freya felt a wave of panic rise in her chest. She began to cry, loudly. She couldn't control it. 'No, no! I don't want you to talk like that!' She slid to the floor and knelt by the side of her bed. 'This is just how you are feeling right now! But it will pass. It will.'

'No, Mum.' Lexi shook her head from side to side. 'It's how I have always felt. Always.'

'Listen to me, Lexi.' Freya sat up straight, her face inches from her little girl's. 'Look at me! I am on my knees and I am begging you to help me get through this! You cannot give up!' She cried, huge sobs that shook her frame. 'Just one night, Lex, that's all! Because you are running out of time!' The words slid from her mouth like broken glass, painful and damaging. 'That's the truth! You are running out of time!'

'I can't.' Her voice was weak, her breathing shallow.

'You have to, Lexi,' she managed through her tears. 'Please don't leave me!'

Lexi reached out the stiff, whitened bones where nimble fingers used to live and rested her hand on her mum's arm. Freya leant in, her face inches from her daughter's skeletal face, where the skin hung in lined pouches around her jawline and beneath her eyes. She looked a hundred years old.

'Please, Mummy, . . .' Lexi said, her lips grey and cracked. 'I want to go . . . to the other side of space.' Her wide eyes that had sunk back in their sockets pleaded.

Freya felt a jolt of fear in her gut.

'No, no no, *no*, Lexi, no! You need to stay and fight this! You need to stay here with me!' Her voice was little more than a reedy whisper, her voice box stripped bare with grief. 'We had a good chat with Dr Morris.' She remembered her promise of keeping impassive, and shook her head, exhaling, as she reached for her daughter's hand.

'It's okay, Mum.'

'What's okay?' She blinked at her daughter.

'I already know,' she whispered.

'Already know what?' Freya whispered back.

'How ill I am.'

Freya let her head fall forward towards her chest, struggling to find the words, understanding at that moment that, without the mask of pretence and the illusion of strength, she felt quite lost.

'Please don't be sad, Mum.' She lifted her hand and let her fingers trail Freya's cheekbone. 'I can't stop and I can't change things, not now.' Lexi swallowed. 'And it's okay. I'm happy here. I just want to stay here with you and Dad and Charlotte until . . .'

Freya felt a surge of anger.

'No, Lexi, it is *not* okay!' Distress made her words harder to discern. 'I want you to fight! Fight hard!' She balled her fingers into a fist.

'I'm so tired of fighting,' Lexi whispered.

'I love you, Lexi.'

'I love you too. I love you so much because you're my mum and I know that you are the best mum in the world and I'm going to miss you.'

'Do not talk like that!' she snapped. 'You are not going to miss me because you are not going anywhere. I won't let you. I won't!'

Lexi sat forward a little, struggling for breath, her body folded, as if the pain in her gut had kicked in again.

'What is it, darling?' Freya sniffed up her tears and ran her hand over Lexi's face.

'I don't . . . I don't feel too good.' She grimaced, her eyes screwed tightly shut.

'Is it getting worse?' She felt her own heart rate increase; the flames of fear licked all her thoughts.

Lexi nodded, her eyes half-closed.

Freya jumped up and ran into the hallway.

'Lockie!' she called out to him, closing the door behind her.

'What is it? Is she okay?' He stood with the overnight bag in his hand, breathing quickly; his nerves were palpable.

'Where is that bloody ambulance? She's . . . she's giving up, Lockie! Oh God, she's giving up, and I don't know what to do! I can't lose her!'

He took a step closer, until he could talk softly and still be heard. 'You *do* know what to do. You do.'

'Yes.' Freya swallowed, fighting for composure, closing her eyes and trying to erase the sound of Mikey the nurse, whose voice loomed loud in her ears: *That place makes Larchcombe seem like two weeks on the Riviera.* 'I'm going to go and call Dr Morris and tell her that we need to get her into Morningside and we need to do it now! That's right, isn't it?'

'Yes, my love.' He closed his eyes briefly. 'I'll go and sit with her while you make the call.' He squeezed her hand, then slipped into Lexi's room.

Freya had set the wheels in motion.

And now she had to go and tell Lexi.

Time was quite distorted; it had been less than half an hour since Dr Morris had left, but felt like a lot longer. 'Hurry up, please!' she spoke her thoughts aloud, as she trod the stairs with anger, grief and fear washing over her in waves. *She's running out of time. My girl is running out of time . . .*

As if in response to her demand, the sound of a siren grew louder and louder. Lockie and Charlotte appeared on the landing and ran down the stairs, calling out that they would shepherd them into the correct house and up the stairs.

Lexi seemed to hover in and out of sleep. Freya sat by her side and stroked her arm.

'I'm scared, Mummy.'

'It's okay, baby girl. I've got you,' she whispered, knowing that this was the time to be brave.

She spoke quietly, calmly drawing strength and composure from a hitherto untapped source. She would have found it hard to explain how she was imbued with a rush of energy and what could only be described as clarity.

'Never forget that I'm your mum and I'll always be here for you. Always. Never forget how much you are loved.' Freya took a deep breath. Her stomach muscles tightened in angst.

The sound of boots hammered up the stairs.

Lexi sat up and looked at her mum. There was a second of understanding exchanged between the two.

And then two burly male paramedics rushed into the room.

'No! Mum! No!' Lexi shot her a look as she shrank back against the wall.

With a surge of strength, Lexi's arms flailed. She pulled off her hat to reveal her thin hair and threw off the quilts that had cushioned her. Her sticklike arms beat the pillows, her foot lunging out, narrowly missing her mum, who jumped up and stood with her mouth open, not entirely sure what to do next.

Lexi's voice was not one Freya recognised: it sounded low, gravelly and desperate, and her words were venomous.

'Why are you doing this to me! You promised! You promised me!' Lexi's eyes were wild and her mouth contorted, with flecks of foam at the side of her lips.

Freya felt her stomach shrink with fear. She was certain that if her daughter had had the strength, she would have tried to hit her.

A paramedic tried to lower her gently against her pillows.

'You need to stay calm, Lex,' Freya tried to remind her. 'Your heart!' Her words, however, fell on deaf ears as Lexi called upon every reserve of energy she had to make a stand. Throwing her body forward, she screamed out, 'Why are you letting them do this to me?'

Lockie reached for his wife, pulling her to stand beside him at the window, with Charlotte on his other side. Freya watched as her daughter was pinned flat on the mattress. It was the most distressing thing to watch and it took all her strength not to intervene and demand they get their hands off her little girl.

Lexi continued to thrash.

'Don't touch me! Stay away!' she screamed. 'Don't you fucking touch me!' Saliva fell from her mouth in long gobs and tears streaked her face. She was hysterical.

Lockie took Charlotte into his arms and they both sobbed. Freya wrapped her arms around them both, calling out to Lexi, trying to tend her whole family.

'You need to calm down, Lex, you need to try to stay calm!' she managed, uncertain where her daughter was finding the strength to fuel her rage, but knowing she didn't have it to spare.

Her child responded with loud, guttural yells that sounded to her like an animal in distress.

Lexi was struggling for breath; her words coasted from a mouth twisted with anger. 'I will . . . I will never forgive you! Never!'

Freya closed her eyes briefly, catching every word as if they were tiny knives that lodged in her heart and mind.

'Lexi! I'm sorry!' she cried. 'I love you, but you are running out of time!'

The paramedics worked quickly, unzipping bags and removing syringes as they tended to her child. Still Lexi strained against them, trying to sit, trying to bite, snarling and growling.

Restrained now, Lexi lifted her head and banged it against the wall. She held her mother's gaze as the oxygen mask was lifted towards her face; her last words, before the sedative took its toll, were loud and clear:

'I hate you! You are killing me! I hate you! I will never forgive you.'

Freya turned her head towards the garden; her limbs shook, but her resolve was strong.

You need help, help from experts, outside of my care. This is your one chance, my Lexi . . .

The hour is now . . .

The clock on the stove ticked loudly.

Freya and Lockie sat at the table, holding hands in quiet reflection. The still of the hour could not erase the echo of their child's distress on the day before. It clung to the walls and would forever be part of the fabric of the building.

Freya's thoughts continually returned to the sight of Lexi's face, fighting until the end.

'I think peace is above all what we all seek, a life free from struggle, don't you?' Lockie spoke slowly.

Freya nodded. 'I do.'

'You need to go and change out of your pyjamas,' he prompted.

She looked down, as if this hadn't occurred to her.

'Yes, yes of course.'

She left the table and trod the stairs.

Charlotte took a deep breath and walked from the sofa in the den to the table where Lockie sat writing.

'How you doing, Dad?' she asked sweetly.

He nodded and put three *X*s on the page before laying the pen on the table. 'The last pen I held was to sign the forms at the hospital.' He rubbed his face, trying to erase the memory; the weight of his action was one he would carry on his shoulders for a lifetime.

Charlotte bent to kiss him on the cheek.

Freya walked in, changed now into her jeans and Lockie's checked shirt. Having Lexi sectioned was the hardest thing they had ever had to do. It was also the bravest.

She would never forget those initial moments in the hospital, Lexi's expression one of fury and fear. Held back by two nurses, she continued, despite her frailty, to flail and scream, snarling at them both, 'I don't want to see you ever again! Just go! Go away!' shrieking until her voice was hoarse and the exertion left her spent.

Freya's own heart had hammered so hard in her chest she thought it might stop. Lockie had held her hand. 'It's not her, remember? It's her illness talking,' he offered as he glanced her cheek with a kiss.

Now dressed and a little more composed, Freya gathered the pages into her hands.

'What are we going to do with these notes? The stories?' Charlotte asked.

'Well . . .' Freya took a breath. 'We have to get them to Lexi. I made her a promise a long time ago, when she was little.'

She heard the words, burbled from Lexi's seven-year-old mouth: *If you went away, Mum, I would write you a note or one of my stories, like I do for Daddy to take with him on his trips, and you could read it and you wouldn't feel so sad. And if I went away, you could write me a note or a story to take with me, and I would read it and I wouldn't feel so sad.*

'These stories are important. They are how she finds her way back to us, a big part of her journey, reminders of how much we love her, her memories. They will help her find her way out of the fog. These are the truth, and they will help bring her home. I'm sure of it.' She smiled; a genuine smile.

Charlotte tried to stifle her tears as Lockie clung to her.

'There are no guarantees, Freya, you heard what Dr Morris said.' He spoke kindly to his wife, as if trying to soften the blow of what might occur.

'I know.' Freya swallowed and steadied herself on the table. 'But I have to keep going. I have to keep thinking it's possible. I have to. I'm her mum.'

The three stood in silence for a second, each considering her words.

Charlotte's sob cracked the atmosphere. 'I can't bear the idea of my little sister being in there with no visitors for weeks, locked up like she's done something wrong!'

Freya closed her eyes; the parting image of her child was forever behind her eyelids.

'The thing is, we love her too much to help her ourselves, Charlotte; this is how we save her, by sending her to Morningside. To let people help her who do this every day, all day, people who can make good decisions for her, hard decisions.'

Lockie nodded at his wife and she knew she spoke the truth.

'They *will* make her better, won't they, Mum?'

'They will certainly try.' She nodded at her lovely girl. It was the best she could offer.

'I'm scared about seeing it,' Charlotte admitted. 'About going inside.'

Freya pictured the harsh sterility of Larchcombe, the locked doors, the lack of privacy, the forced feeding, the wails of distress and the atmosphere of desperation, and she knew that Morningside would be worse. Much worse.

'Me too.' She smiled at her child as Lockie gripped her hand. 'It's time.' Freya stood tall and placed her hand on the back of the chair for support.

The three stepped out into the street, and climbed into their car. Lockie drove.

She spoke to Lexi in her mind, thinking about her happy days of childhood.

Remember, Lexi, that mothers and daughters are made from the same batch of stardust, and when you are sad, I'm sad, and when you are happy, my heart sings!

Freya climbed out into the bright, sunny day, vaguely aware of the fact that they had arrived. She chose to look at the full trees that edged the lawn rather than the imposing secure facility hewed from grey stone.

She smiled briefly at her husband as she took his arm, holding Charlotte's hand on the other side. The trio walked up the steps where they would enter and sign some more forms and learn of the routine, meet with the surgical team and be given a telephone number to call twice a week. They would not, however, be able to see Lexi, not for a while. These were the rules. This was the process and she had to trust it.

'We can get through this,' Lockie urged from his own trembling mouth. 'We can get through anything if we do it together.'

'Yes.' She nodded. 'One day at a time . . .'

EPILOGUE

Lockie threaded his arm through his wife's and let it snake along her back. She turned and kissed the side of his face.

'I love you, you know.'

'I had noticed.' She smiled, leaning into him.

Having walked across the sand for half an hour, they were happy to find the perfect deserted spot, on an incline set a little way back from the water's edge in front of a dense row of scarlet flowering hibiscus.

Melissa, Freya's sister-in-law, placed the beach chairs in a semicircle, facing out to sea, while Hugh wiggled the firepit into the sand until it was stable and loaded it up with charcoal, firelighters and a couple of large logs.

'You have the honour, sir.' Hugh passed the box of matches to Lockie, who knelt down and pushed his long hair from his eyes, before striking away from the box and angling the match to see the orange flame lick up the wood. He then bent low, picked a gap and placed it against a firelighter. It sizzled and after twenty minutes the thriving fire warranted a round of polite applause.

'More champagne, Diana?' Melissa poured another generous glass.

'I'm already a little tipsy,' Diana confessed. 'But go on, then.'

'Don't worry, Gran, I can always carry you home,' Charlotte offered, as she twisted the precious friendship bracelets that never left her wrist.

Freya smiled at her sweet girl, who in two weeks would be off to start her second year at Durham University, where she was studying history of art.

Lexi shared a knowing look with her sister, both aware that their gran was not averse to getting a little tipsy. Their friendship had bloomed, with love and compassion as the glue.

'How you doing?' Charlotte asked, as Lexi took a chair by the fireside.

'Good.' She beamed.

As the huge red sun started to sink into the ocean, they gathered around the roaring firepit. Freya slipped into a cardigan, taking the chill off her sun-kissed shoulders, and Charlotte pulled up the hood on her sister's favourite Jack Wills sweatshirt that she liked to wear.

Pelicans in shadow stretched their magnificent wings and landed on poles sticking up from the seabed, looming like prehistoric time travellers as they too faced the sinking sun.

It was hard not to think about their first trip, all those years ago, when life had been pretty perfect and no one had any idea of how things might unravel.

'Anorexia' had been a word without meaning, and not one in their vocabulary, yet now it was a word that filtered their every memory and their every thought.

Freya felt confident that she had done the right thing earlier: with her family's support, she sent a message to her dear friend Marcia:

Press the button. Publish the article. It's too important. People need to know . . .

Lockie tapped the side of his beer bottle with his wedding ring; a hush came over the group.

'This is a very special day for a very special girl: Alexia Valentine Braithwaite. I shall now hand over to her mum, my beautiful Freya!' He smiled.

Making his way back to his seat, he stopped where Lexi sat and kissed her on the cheek.

Freya slid from the chair and took a seat on the sand, her face illuminated by the glow from the fire.

She very carefully lifted the little bundle of paper from her rucksack and opened the sheets of paper one by one. She smiled as her eyes danced upon words put down on paper by those who loved Lexi – memories, stories and notes, even a declaration of love from dear, dear Toby, whose studies were going brilliantly at Imperial: all had been written when emotions were raw.

'It feels very fitting that today we are here as a family and with Lexi's stories so beautifully written by those who love her. We are all so very proud of you, Lexi.' She smiled at her daughter before continuing. 'Our journey is one we have taken as a family, and it's not one I would wish anyone else to travel, but good has come out of it. We know that no matter what life throws at us, we will never stop fighting. We will never give up on you. The fact that you carry these words around with you means you don't give up on us; a reminder, if you like, of all that is worth fighting for.'

'It's true.' Lexi smiled, looking at the sheets in her mum's hand.

All were transfixed; the fire began to take hold, the smoke rising up towards the burnished sky.

'What's that?' Diana queried of the pressed flower that Freya lifted in the firelight.

'It's lilac from our neighbours' garden. Lexi loves it.'

'I really do.' She spoke quietly. 'It always reminds me of the Rendletons.'

Lexi sipped at her glass of champagne, for tonight they were celebrating a year of recovery, a year of fighting in a battle that continued, and maybe always would. But at least now she could see a future, and that alone was enough to make it look bright.

Freya inhaled the sprig of lilac where the faintest trace of its intoxicating scent still lingered. She hugged her knees to her chest and smiled at her beautiful, brilliant little girl whose words spoken at the height of her illness seemed to drift towards her on the salt-tinged breeze: *When I smell it, I know that summer is on the way, and that means good things – a new season, a new start . . .*

Lexi rose from her chair and peeled off her sweatshirt; she held her arms across her trunk, still conscious of showing off her very slim body that bore the invisible scars of anorexia.

There she stood in front of her mum, smiling.

'Where are you off to, darling?' Lockie asked.

'I fancy a swim!' She quickened her pace towards the shoreline.

'In the dark?' Diana queried.

'Why not?' Lexi smiled.

'Be careful, there's sharks in these waters, you know!' Hugh teased.

Lexi turned and smiled at her family, sat in a semicircle.

'That's okay.' She grinned. 'If anything dangerous or life-threatening comes my way, I'll just punch it on the nose!'

Freya watched as her girl ran, without breaking her stride, without looking back and without hesitation; her brave girl leapt high, landing in the water with a splash, diving into the unknown.

BOOK CLUB QUESTIONS

1. Did Lexi's story alter your view of anorexia? If so, how?
2. Which member of the Braithwaite family did you most sympathise with, and why?
3. Has *The Food of Love* changed you or broadened your perspective? If so, how?
4. What for you was the book's main message?
5. In a movie, who would play which parts?
6. There were a number of moral and ethical choices that Freya and Lockie made. What did you think of those choices? Did you agree/disagree?
7. Did any parts of the book make you feel uncomfortable? If so, which parts and why?
8. What will be the overriding memory from *The Food of Love*, the one incident or paragraph that will stay with you?

ACKNOWLEDGEMENTS

'An author is only ever as good as their editor': never has this been truer than in the case of *The Food of Love*.

To this end I owe a BIG thank you to the wonderful Tiffany Yates Martin.

Thank you, Tiffania Teaseblossom, for patiently adding the fairy dust!

Thank you to the lovely gang at Lake Union, and Sammia and Emilie for their leap of faith.

And as ever a huge thank you to my lovely family, who fend for themselves, order pizza and let me live in my own little world while I write.

Especially you, Simeon, my support network. My love.

I love you all.

ABOUT THE AUTHOR

Photo © Paul Smith of Paul Smith Photography at www.paulsmithphotography.info

Amanda Prowse likens her own life story to those she writes about in her books. After self-publishing her debut novel, *Poppy Day*, in 2011, she has gone on to author twelve novels and six novellas. Her books have been translated into a dozen languages and she regularly tops bestseller charts all over the world.

Remaining true to her ethos, Amanda writes stories of ordinary women and their families who find their strength, courage and love tested in ways they never imagined. The most prolific female contemporary fiction writer in the UK, with a legion of loyal readers, she goes from strength to strength. Being crowned 'queen of domestic drama' by the *Daily Mail* was one of her finest moments.

Amanda is a regular contributor on TV and radio, but her first love is and will always be writing.

You can find her online at www.amandaprowse.com, on Twitter @MrsAmandaProwse, and on Facebook at www.facebook.com/amandaprowsenogreaterlove.